A KISS FOR LUCK

The Oklahoma Land Run race was about to begin. The moment Chelsea had waited for her entire twenty-eight years was only a heartbeat away. She should be using this time to do a last minute check on her saddle cinch. And that was exactly what she would have done had she been able to tear her gaze away from the man on the black horse, right next to her. As she watched, Mitch moved his horse closer. . . .

His breath washed raggedly over her face. Hot, branding, and sweet. She felt the warmth of his lips before they actually touched hers, and the feeling shot all the way down to her toes.

"For luck," he whispered hoarsely against her mouth before his lips pressed down on hers.

Without his arm around her waist, Chelsea would never have been able to stay in the saddle.

"The Run is getting ready to start, sweetheart," he murmured against her lips. "Better get a grip." He nodded to the reins she'd dropped when he'd kissed her.

"My grip," she muttered, her voice husky and raw, "is none of your concern." Her words were drowned out by the echoing reports of gunfire, the thundering of hooves, and the jubilant cheer of the crowd.

Whether she was ready for it or not, the race had begun.

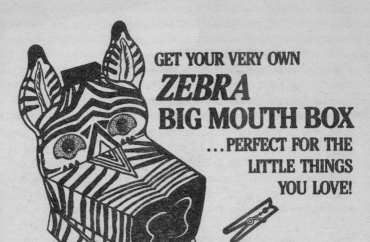

PRAIRIE ANGEL
Rebecca Sinclair

ZEBRA BOOKS
KENSINGTON PUBLISHING CORP.

To
Colleen Culver and Judy French
and
Pat Coughlin, JoAnn Ferguson, and Nancy Bulk
Special ladies, all!

ZEBRA BOOKS

are published by

Kensington Publishing Corp.
475 Park Avenue South
New York, NY 10016

Copyright © 1990 by Rebecca Sinclair

First printing: November, 1990

Printed in the United States of America

Chapter One

Oklahoma Border—April 21, 1889

"When I get my hands on that girl. Oh, when I get my hands on her!" Chelsea Hogan's fingers clenched and un- clenched at her sides. In her mind, it was her sister's en- viably long neck she felt beneath her palms, not the cool, empty night air. "Where on earth did she go?!"

Gritting her teeth, she plunked down on the grass and sucked in a calming breath. She released it through her teeth, slowly, but it didn't make her feel better.

For two hours she'd been searching for Emilee, her wayward sister. The girl was nowhere to be found. Chel- sea's frustration grew with each moonswept inch of Okla- homa prairie she searched. It stood to reason Emmy had to be here *somewhere*. But where? That was the question. The other question—the one that kept gnawing at the back of her mind—tempting . . . tempting . . . was when would she finally be able to get some much needed sleep?

Sleep. How long had it been since she'd rested her head on something soft? How long since she'd given herself over to vague, floating dreams? Hours? Days? No, it was more like a week.

The last good rest she could remember had been when she and Emmy had crossed that godforsaken place known as the Cherokee Strip. A more barren, desolate chunk of land Chelsea had never seen. She only prayed the Oklahoma District would be more appealing. From what she'd seen of it so far, though, she couldn't say the outlook was promising. No, not promising at all.

Chelsea wrinkled her nose, her amber gaze sweeping the moonlit prairie. The land was flat, desolate, endless. The only movement to be had was that of the knee-high bluestem swaying like a silver blanket over the ground, the light that of a high, full moon and the soft orange glow of so many dwindling campfires it was impossible to count their numbers.

It was rumored that fifty thousand people had rushed to Old Oklahoma, the Oklahoma District, Oklahoma Country, the Unassigned Lands . . . whatever the papers were calling this place today. The only fact the papers did agree upon was that this was Indian Territory, plain and simple. Tomorrow at high noon, in accordance with President Harrison's proclamation of one month ago, "Harrison's Hoss Race" — the frantic dash for thousands of free one hundred and sixty acre homesteads — would commence.

Whether she found Emilee or not, Chelsea Hogan planned to be counted in that number.

"Come on, Emmy, where *are* you?!"

After a quick, tasteless supper, Chelsea had sent her sister to the river to draw a bucket of fresh water. A simple request. Or so she'd thought. She should have known better!

That had been four hours ago. Emmy hadn't returned. After two long hours, Chelsea had stopped waiting and had set out to find her sister. In truth, Emmy's disappearance had come as no surprise. Her younger sister was a rebel of the worst order. Since birth, the girl had seemed set to disobey every order given to her. This wasn't the first time Emmy had wandered off. Since their father's death three years ago, hunting down Emmy had become a constant chore. One Chelsea was bone-weary of.

Her open palm slapped the prickly bed of grass a second before she pushed to her feet. Her legs, weary from riding half the day and walking half the night, ached in protest. Swiping the copper curls back from her brow, Chelsea stood statue still, giving her throbbing feet time to adjust. She was just about to move, determined to push on, determined to find Emmy while there was still enough darkness left in the night to snatch a quick nap, when she heard the grass behind her crunch.

"Emmy?" The name left her in a breathless rush, no louder than the whisper of a cool spring breeze rustling the grass around her ankles. Her spine stiffened, her breath clogged in her lungs. Instinct told Chelsea it wasn't her sister standing behind her. So did the copper wisps at her nape, the ones that prickled as she perked her ears, listening. . . .

"See, Jase? Didn't I tell ya he wouldn't be here? Didn't I tell ya?" The voice was gritty, and as rough as the bark of an oak tree. It was also, thankfully, distant.

"Hush up, fool. I know what you told me, and I know Mitch Bryant. He'll be here. Give him time." The second voice was smoother, richer, but just as menacing to a panicked Chelsea.

"I could give the fella a year, won't matter none. He ain't comin'."

"He's coming."

"He ain't."

"Oh no? Then who the hell's that?"

If ever Chelsea wished she could disappear, it was now. Though her back was to the two intruders, she knew the second their curious gazes shifted her way. Their eyes drilled holes into her rigidly held back. A shiver of dread scratched down her spine. It increased to visible tremors when the voices and crunching footsteps started her way.

Run! her mind screamed. It seemed like the best plan. Too bad her boots felt as though they were encased in lead. Her legs refused to obey even the simplest command. In truth, she didn't think her quivering knees would support her even if she'd had the presence of mind to try.

"Shoot, that ain't Bryant," the first, grittier voice exclaimed. His chuckle was as short and as crass as Chelsea imagined the man who made it to be. "Brother, ya'd better lay off that rotgut. Startin' to eat yer mind right fierce. Can't ya see the skirt? That's a gal over there. And from the looks a' her, she's a perty one."

The second voice lowered, his words edged hard. "Is that a fact? And what makes you so sure she's pretty, Whip? All you can see is her back."

"I got a sixth sense 'bout these things, Jase. The gal's perty all right. Yup, dang perty. Look at the way all that red hair just sparkles in the moonlight like a fire without the kindling. Bet ya her skin's all creamy and soft, too."

"I'll bet *you* she don't let you close enough to find out."

"Oh, yeah? Well, we'll just see 'bout that."

The crunching footsteps—so close she thought she felt their hot, slimy breaths on her neck—brought Chelsea back to her senses. Snapping out of her trance of fear, she blinked hard and let her hands stray to the front of her skirt. Her fingers curled inward, fisting the coarse brown homespun. She lifted the hem off the ground ever so slowly.

As soon as the bottom of the skirt had cleared her knees and no longer threatened to trip her, Chelsea was off. The breeze whipped at her hair, pulling more of the copper strands from the braid that bounced at her waist with each running step. Her breaths came hard and ragged, ripping through her burning lungs as she charged across the seemingly endless prairie.

She darted this way and that, not wanting to give them a straight line to follow. The twisting path, coupled with white-hot fear, made her lose direction. Everything looked the same, the glowing silver prairie blending into itself until she couldn't remember which direction she'd come from—or which direction she should be running in. Nor did she care. She'd find her way back to her campfire just as soon as she was safely away from those two crass-sounding men—and not one second before.

Her heart thundered in her ears, masking the sound of her own running footsteps as well as the clomping ones that gained on her from behind . . . until it was too late.

A strangled yelp tore from her throat when thick fingers coiled like steel bands around her upper arm. Desperately, she tried to shake the hand off, but the grip was too tight.

The man gave a vicious tug, yanking her around. She was in mid-stride, the momentum of still trying to run making it impossible to avoid a collision with his chest. It was a contact Chelsea would have given her life to have been spared.

He was short, he was dirty, and he smelled. But that wasn't the worst of it. His eyes, *they* were the worst of it: permanently squinted slashes set in a tanned, leathery face. The hungry way his gaze raked her made Chelsea's skin crawl.

"Let go of me," she panted, shoving at his shoulder with the heel of her palm. Even that slight but unavoidable contact with his dirty, wrinkled shirt—and the sweaty, too-warm flesh beneath it—made her gag. She stumbled back a step, as much distance as the manacle of his fingers allowed. It was, she reasoned, better than nothing.

"Aw, come on now, gal, be a sport." Her captor flashed her a lecherous grin that looked as though it was missing more teeth than it had retained. What few teeth he had were yellowed and crooked. "My brother and me're just itchin' for a little fun. Nothin' wrong with that, is there?"

"Yes," she hissed, pushing the *s* through her teeth and making the single word sound as reprehensible as the man's hand squeezing her arm felt. "If your *fun* is at my expense, then there's *a lot* wrong with it."

His grin broadened, and his next words blasted over her in a wash of stale, whiskey-sour air. "Don't tell me ya don't like a little rough and rowdy, gal. *All* you skirts like

9

a little rough and rowdy every once'n a while. Even if ya don't admit to it."

As loath as she was to touch him, Chelsea started clawing frantically at his hand, trying to pry his fingers from their painful grip on her arm. When that didn't work, she turned her foot in and kicked him hard in the shin with her heel. That didn't work either. Indeed, she was beginning to wonder if the gruesome man was capable of feeling pain. Her kick had landed solidly, the collision of heel smashing bone vibrating up her leg, but it hadn't brought so much as a grunt from him.

Curling her hand into a claw, she slashed the leathery flesh covering his knuckles with her nails. A wave of shock washed over her when he merely laughed—a cruel, biting sound—and tightened his grip. Her voice rose to a high, hysterical pitch. "I said let me go, you—you—" She couldn't think of words foul enough to describe the beast—at least, none she'd dare repeat.

"You heard her, Whip, let go," the second, smoother voice intervened. And not a second too soon, to Chelsea's way of thinking. In her struggles with this piece of vermin, she'd forgotten about the other man. Now she thanked God he was there.

The one called Whip sent a furious glare over his shoulder. "Uh-uh. I ain't done with her yet. Or did ya forget, I still got me a bet to win."

"Please," Chelsea pleaded, her tone frantic, "make him let go." Her gaze fixed hard on the shadowy figure of the second man. He was taller than the first, broader, not quite so grubby. Only the sandy blond hair hanging in stringy strands down to a point past his shoulders said he was no friend to soap and water.

The second man, Jase, stepped to Chelsea's side. The smell of stale whiskey doubled. She wasn't pleased when he made no attempt to free her from the rabid Whip.

"My brother's a might bullheaded when it comes to women," Jase told her, equal measures of amusement and sarcasm lacing his slurred, drawling tone. "But don't take it personal, sugar. He's like this with all the gals."

"Is that supposed to make me feel better?" she snapped, fear making her bold.

"Hell no. It's supposed to warn you not to mess around with my brother."

"I am *not* 'messing around' with him." Again, she tried to yank her arm free. Again, she got only a burning pain in her shoulder for her efforts. "Please, mister, just tell him to let me go and I promise to forget any of this ever happened. Otherwise," she took a deep, shaky breath and plunged on, "I'll be forced to find the nearest sheriff and—"

"Sheriff!" Whip roared. "Hey, Jase, ain't that a hoot? The gal's gonna call a *sheriff*." The last word slipped past his thin lips like a childish taunt. He held out a leathery hand, forcing the bony fingers to tremble. "Are you shakin' in yer boots yet? I sure as hell am."

"Knock it off, Whip. Show some respect for the law . . . and the lady." Jase's hand came up. The crook of his index finger hooked under Chelsea's jaw, yanking her gaze up to his.

His eyes were a dark emerald-green. That was the first thing she noticed. The second was that she might have mistaken him for handsome—were it not for the prickly stubble on his jaw, his too-lean cheeks, and his stringy blond hair.

"*Lady*, is she?" Whip snorted. "Don't look like one to me."

Chelsea tore her gaze from those devilish green eyes and fixed the smaller man with a lethal glare. Her voice dripped with sarcasm. "How would you know? Have you ever seen one to compare me to?"

"Why ya little—!"

Lightning quick, Whip's free hand came up, the palm drawn back and ready to slap. Chelsea flinched. It took great effort to draw on her father's years of instruction, but she thought he would have been proud of her refusal to cower. Bracing herself for the sting of his open palm

11

meeting her cheek, she prayed silently that the man wouldn't hit her too hard. And prayed that if he did, she would at least stay conscious.

The air around her face was disturbed by the downward arc of Whip's hand. Chelsea's eyes began to close as she planted her feet and mentally prepared to weather the blow.

It didn't come. Whip's palm stopped a mere inch from her flesh, so close she could feel the heat of his hand scorching her cheek. The cause, she realized as she pried her eyes open, was Jase's fingers coiled tightly around his brother's wrist.

"What the hell'd ya do that for?"

Jase's eyes narrowed to dangerous slits. "When I told you to show some respect for the lady, I wasn't chewing my gums!" With an angry snarl, he shoved his brother away.

Surprised, Whip stumbled back a step. He had no choice but to let Chelsea's arm go.

While the brothers exchanged hot, warring glares, Chelsea's gaze slipped low. The urge to run was strong, but it was countered by the twin gunbelts riding each man's hip. She stood a minimal chance of outrunning the men. But four pistols . . . well, she didn't stand a snowball's chance against them!

Afraid to move, afraid to even breathe, she stood there, her gaze flickering uncertainly between the brothers while her heart hammered in her chest. Her arm hurt from where Whip had grabbed her and held on tight. The circulation rushing back felt hot and prickly, but she was afraid to rub the area and hasten the flow lest she draw unnecessary attention to herself.

"Apologize," Jase demanded, his voice low and firm. The single, unexpected word made Chelsea start.

"What!" Whip bellowed. "Have ya gone loco? Just how much a' that rotgut did ya drink, Jase?"

"Enough to drag the words out of you with my fist if you don't spit 'em out shortly."

Whip's jaw set hard. His glare leveled on Chelsea, and she felt it burn straight through her. An icy chill raked down her spine, making her shiver. "No. I ain't apologizin' to no skirt. Beat me to a pulp if'n ya think ya gotta, but I won't do it."

"We'll just see about—" Jase didn't have time to finish his threat as the blast of a gunshot slammed through the night.

"Son of a bitch!" Whip cried.

Chelsea thought the man must be used to bullets whipping past his head, for he dove headfirst into the swaying bed of bluestem before his words were completely out. His body landed with a thump and a roll, his brother's close behind.

She was free! For the first time in her life, Chelsea didn't weigh choices before making a decision; she reacted on gut instinct alone. Hoisting her skirt, she bolted.

Suddenly, the starry Oklahoma night was no longer calm and peaceful. It had become a battleground of terror, one she was half running, half stumbling through for her life. The air cut through her lungs. Her calves, already sore, screamed with each step. Ignoring the pain, she forced her feet on, whispering a prayer beneath her breath that her watery knees would hold her weight long enough to get her away from this place . . . and away from those gruesome men with the guns.

A second shot exploded, the sound deafening as it rolled over the prairie in receding waves. A third was quick to follow.

It was only when Chelsea braced herself to feel the sharp slice of a bullet tearing through flesh that she realized she was running in plain sight of anyone who cared to turn his gun her way and take aim. Her dress was dreary brown, but against a backdrop of flat land and sky, she'd make an easy target.

The fingers fisting her skirt loosened with uncertainty as she wavered between dropping to the ground the way

13

she'd seen the two men do, or keep running and hope she didn't get shot. In the end, the decision was taken from her.

The skirt slipped from her slackened grasp. She bent to retrieve it, and at the same time kept pushing on, but her fingers were trembling too badly. A fourth shot — was this one closer? — cut through the air at the same time the brown homespun tangled around her running legs. The bullet whipped by, close enough for her to hear the whistle of its passing.

Chelsea gave a strangled cry. She was going down, hard, but could do nothing to stop herself. The world tipped. Her hands rose to cushion the blow a split second too late. Her knuckles scraped dirt and grass as she slammed into the ground with enough force to push the air from her lungs with a grunt.

Closing her eyes, Chelsea rolled onto her side and curled her legs, wedging her knees against her heaving chest. She groaned. Every muscle in her body felt as though it were on fire, burning with even the slightest movement. Getting up and running again was inconceivable. But staying where she was didn't seem like a good idea, either.

Gradually, she noted a sound that was out of place against the normal night noises that, in themselves, seemed abnormal compared to the gunshots that had preceded them. The sound was a man's voice, deep and rich. Chelsea judged his distance to be threateningly close, and she judged his vehement curses to mean he was madder than a bull in a bumblebee patch.

Scowling, she listened closely, glad for any distraction — so long as it wasn't more gunfire — that would take her mind off herself. The voice didn't belong to Jase; the tone was too rich, too husky. Nor was it Whip's; the words, although colorful curses the lot of them, were too cultured and refined. But if it wasn't the other two, then who on earth? . . .

"Are they gone?" Chelsea needed no one to tell her

that this disembodied voice was a woman's. The tone was sultry, a silky sort of purr that reminded her of Emmy.

"Yeah, they're gone," the man stopped swearing to growl. His tone was one of leashed fury. Chelsea wondered what had made him so mad. A second later, when she found out, she wished she didn't know. "No thanks to that floozie they had with them. I had a perfect shot. I could have wounded him, and then we'd finally have those bastards. But no! That stupid broad had to run in front of me! Christ, I don't know how I missed her."

"Maybe you didn't, Mitch. Ever think of that?"

"No, Brenda, I—Ah, damn!"

"Come on, I'll help you look."

Chelsea listened to their crunching footsteps and thought of all the terrible things she would do to Emmy once she got her hands on the girl. No doubt about it, her sister deserved death, slow and painful. After all, it was Emmy's fault she was out here being shot at, when all Chelsea really wanted was to be wrapped in her nice warm bedroll beside a crackling campfire.

But no, fool that she was, she'd once again taken on the responsibility of saving Emmy from herself. And what had it gotten her? Not only had she been accosted by those two wretched men, but now she had two more people out searching for her. Was this horrible night never going to end?

Apparently not, Chelsea decided, as bravely, she lifted her head and peeked over the tips of swaying bluestem. Another of what was turning into an endless list of mistakes. It was bad enough knowing that those people and their guns were out there searching for her. It was quite another thing—a slow form of torture, actually—to get a good, long look at one of them.

Her shocked amber gaze fastened on the man, and Chelsea instantly wished it had not. He was close enough for her to make out even the most minute detail, and she was terrified enough to be unable to tear her eyes away.

He was tall; she guessed the top of his head would

stand a good six inches above Jase's straggly blond one. And he was broad. Incredibly, intimidatingly broad. He was facing away from her, so she couldn't get a look at his face. It was just as well. The sight of his blue flannel shirt and the way it strained over the rippling muscles of his back and shoulders was enough to clog the air in her lungs. Permanently.

His hair was pitch-black, glistening with a silver sheen in the pale moonlight. The strands were unruly and un-fashionably long—not that anyone who wore denim trousers so indecently snug would care about fashion, she thought bitterly! The ragged fringe of hair scraped his collar in the back, and when he turned his head, the raven tips brushed a shelf of shoulders so wide it literally defined the word *broad*.

Chelsea was awarded an unobstructed view of his profile when he glanced out over the prairie that spread end-lessly to her left. Her heart skipped a throbbing beat, then thudded to frantic life.

His nose was long and straight, his cheeks high and sharp above an untrimmed mustache and beard black enough to melt into the swept-back hair covering his ears. She couldn't see his jaw for the silky whiskers coat-ing it, but she imagined the line of it to be nicely squared and uncompromisingly hard. Through the downward curl of his moustache, she caught a glimpse of his lips—sensuously thin and firm—and thought she could easily imagine that mouth forming the swears she'd heard ear-lier. No doubt about it, he looked the type.

"Find her yet?" the woman called out, her voice dis-tant.

"No. But she couldn't have gone far."

Chelsea stiffened, then very, very slowly eased herself back to the ground. The tips of the grass poked through her skirt and bodice, prickling at her skin. The cool evening breeze wafted over her exposed legs, making her shiver. But she wasn't entirely sure her instinctive trem-ors were caused by the chilly night air and not by the man who was so terribly close she thought she could actually feel the heat of his body seeping over her.

"Give it up, Mitch. If she's got any common sense at all, she's long gone by now."

"Give up? That woman just ruined what may be the last chance I'll ever have to get Dobbs. I don't care where the hell she went, I'll find her, Brenda. And when I do . . ."

The footsteps crunched, moving closer. Chelsea gritted her teeth and tried her best to melt into the bed of prickly grass. The man was so close now she was surprised the wild throbbing of her heart hadn't alerted him to her presence.

Then, abruptly, the footsteps stopped. The ensuing silence was so loud it was deafening.

Chelsea lay in her cramped position, her eyes squeezed tightly shut, for what felt like a dozen very slow lifetimes. She wondered if she'd been discovered, yet at the same time was too terrified to look around and find out. Did he know where she was? Was he even now towering over her, glaring down at her while contemplating all sorts of hideous ways to end her life?

She sucked in a shaky breath, searching within herself for a courage she wasn't entirely sure she possessed. Not knowing where the dark-haired man was or what he was doing conjured up too many unbearable, grisly images. She had to know. Her presence of mind, such as it was, demanded it.

Swallowing hard, Chelsea pried open her eyes. Her copper lashes hadn't even completed their ascent when she found her breath clogging in her throat, her gaze captured by eyes so incredibly blue they didn't look real.

The gasp that left her throat was audible.

Chapter Two

"Who the hell are you?" Mitch Bryant growled the second the woman's fiery red hair, large amber eyes, and pert little nose registered in his angry mind. His gaze narrowed, his attention dropped. Her skirt had bunched to mid-thigh, revealing long, shapely legs that were an alluring pearly-white in the moonlight.

A sharp breath hissed through his teeth. Mitch barely heard the sound over the blood pumping hotly in his ears, simmering to a near boil as it warmed in his veins. Jesus! The woman was a tiny little thing, but she had enough seductive curves lurking beneath that unflattering brown rag to make his head reel.

The gaze rose in time to see a spark of outrage flash in her large, whiskey-amber eyes. Her small chin lifted proudly. Only the trembling of her full, pouty lower lip gave her nervousness away.

"I could ask you the same thing," she said finally. Her voice was soft and sweet, carefully controlled. The tone, he noted absently, was throatier than he thought it should be.

"But you won't." His left hand lifted and he turned his wrist inward, letting the moonlight glint off the blue-cast barrel of his Colt .45. "See this, lady? This means I'm the one who asks the questions here. You, on the other hand, are relegated to answering them."

"I have nothing to say to you." She pushed herself to a

sit. The grass crunched beneath her nicely shaped bottom as she scooted backward. Whipping the skirt back over her legs looked, to Mitch's appraising eye, like an afterthought. "I mean . . . sweet heavens, I don't even *know* you!"

His grin was fast and merciless. "Yet," he agreed with a sharp nod, "the night's not over."

Chelsea was beginning to wonder if this night would *ever* be over. Without a doubt, these past four hours had to have been the worst ones of her life. And it was steadily getting worse. "Listen, mister," she whispered on a shaky sigh. Her trembling fingers brushed the stray copper wisps from her brow. "I don't know who you are or what you want. If you don't mind, I'd like to keep it that way."

"Yeah, I'll just bet you would. Pity it's too late. You've got information I need, lady. Damned if I won't get it out of you . . . one way or the other." His grin, half hidden by the ragged inward curl of his moustache, broadened.

Chelsea caught a flash of white teeth between the pitch-black beard and moustache before the man hunkered down in the grass by her side. He was close enough for her to feel the heat of his body smoldering through her clothes, close enough to smell the tangy, soapy scent of him on the chilly night air. She was smart enough—or nervous enough—to overlook all of that.

What she couldn't overlook was the bent elbow he cushioned atop a denim-clad thigh that looked as hard and as solid as a rock. She paid scarce attention to the rolled-up sleeve, a bit more attention to the sinewy, sun-bronzed forearm that was pelted with a thin sheet of raven curls, and a great deal of attention to the gun he was so casually swinging between his knees.

His free hand snaked out. Chelsea gasped and did something she'd refused to do before; she closed her eyes and cringed. The sight of thick, powerful fingers so close to her face frightened her in a way the other men could never do.

His skin was as rough as she'd expected it to be, and warm. His calloused fingertips scraped the line of her jaw. The touch wasn't harsh, nor was it gentle. It was merely insistent. He curled his index finger inward and lifted her chin with the crook of his knuckle.

"Open your eyes, lady. I'm not going to kill you, if that's what you're thinking."

The long copper lashes snapped up. Whiskey-amber locked hard with incredible blue.

Against his will, Mitch felt a surge—a tiny, *tiny* surge—of admiration. It was clear she was petrified. Even now her oh, so soft flesh quivered beneath his touch. It was also clear she wasn't going to give in to that fear. How could he not admire that? Mitch knew damn well how intimidating he could be when he tried. And he was trying like hell right now. It took guts to return his gaze the way this woman was doing; guts most of the women he knew did not possess.

"Did you find her yet?" the silky voice Chelsea had heard earlier asked from somewhere close by.

Mitch's gaze never left the tiny redhead, though his words were addressed to the blonde who stopped just behind his back. "Yeah, I found her all right. And it looks like we're in luck, Brenda. The lady was just about to tell us where her friends went. Isn't that right, sweetheart?"

Chelsea's gaze strayed over the man's imposingly broad shoulders and fixed on the woman who stood behind him. She was beautiful in an earthy sort of way, what with her long, curly blond hair and creamy skin. But it was her bluish-grey eyes that shattered the illusion. They were narrow, catlike, predatory.

Can I turn this woman into an ally? Chelsea wondered, then thought she had nothing to lose by trying. The man didn't look as though he was in any frame of mind to listen to reason.

"I don't know what he's talking about," Chelsea said, hoping another female would hear the edge of conviction she threaded into her words. She jerked her chin at the

20

man, glad the movement made his hand drop away. The touch was sizzling, and more disturbing than she cared to admit—heaven only knew why. "I've already told him I can't tell you a thing."

Whether the blond woman believed her or not was difficult to tell. Her expression remained impassive, guarded. Her slitted crystal-blue gaze settled on the top of the man's raven head. "I take it you don't believe her?"

Again, Chelsea caught a white flash of teeth as his lips pulled back in a sneer of disgust. "What do you think?"

"Christ, Mitch, how the hell should I know? You're the one who's always bragging about what a great judge of character you are. Now's the time to prove it. Is she lying or isn't she?"

His gaze darkened, burning hot blue fire as it smoldered over fiery red hair, flushed cheeks, and the full lower lip she nibbled between her teeth. His gaze lingered on the pulse throbbing in the shadowy base of her long, creamy throat.

"Yeah," he said slowly, "I think she's lying. What I can't figure out is why she'd bother. We're going to drag the information out of her sooner or later. She must know that."

"Maybe. Or maybe she knows that no matter what you do to her, she won't be able to tell you anything because *he* didn't tell *her* anything. Ever think of that?"

"Nope. And I'm sure as hell not going to waste my time thinking of it now. Got any ideas on how to make her talk?" His gaze narrowed, settling on her breasts. The generous curves strained against the coarse brown cloth with each ragged breath. "I've got a few."

A chill scurried up Chelsea's spine, and she was alarmed to find that not all of it was the result of fear. Oh, no. There was a good dose of white-hot anticipation slicing through her as well. It was an inexplicable reaction. It was also undeniable. Just the thought of him touching her again made her feel all hot and breathless and nervous. She didn't know why. Sweet heavens, she didn't *want* to know why.

"Go easy on her, Mitch," the woman warned. "She's just a tiny little thing. And you're a goddamn brute."

"Oh, I plan to," he said, his voice a deep, husky promise. "Nice and easy."

His hand was back, wedging her chin between his roughened index finger and thumb, forcing her to return his gaze when she might have looked away. But Chelsea had no intention of looking away. She'd already cowered before him once. She wouldn't do it again.

She was tired, her emotions frazzled; that was why she was no longer thinking straight. What other reason could she have for yanking her chin from his disturbing grasp the way she did? Or for slapping his hand away when he moved to recapture her jaw? Chelsea thought she saw a twinkle of amusement flash in his dark blue eyes, but she could have been mistaken.

"Don't touch me," she hissed. The ground was hard beneath her as she scooted backward another foot. Remembering the way his gaze had scorched her naked legs before, she was careful to keep her skirt in place as she moved. She didn't want to feel that strange, warm, tingling sensation again if she could avoid it. It was too sensuous, her reaction to it too disturbing.

One raven brow cocked high, his voice edged with steely challenge. "Then tell me what I want to know, lady."

"How can I? You haven't told *me* what you want to know." Chelsea sucked in a sharp breath between gritted teeth. "Look, mister . . . whatever your name is, if you have a question, then ask it. If I can answer it, I will. Believe me, I don't want to be here right now any more than you seem to want me here."

He rolled back on his haunches, again pillowing his elbows atop his rock-hard thighs. His gaze was sharp and assessing, raking her from the top of her fiery red head to the booted tips of her toes. "All right," he grumbled, obviously not pleased with this method but willing to give it a try. "Tell me where they went. And I mean I want to know *exactly*."

Chelsea scowled, her head swimming. "Who?"

The man sent a sharp glance over his shoulder. "This isn't going to work, Brenda."

"Play the game, Mitch. Try again."

The blue eyes swept back, their depths dark, dangerous, impatient. "Dobbs," he snapped, as though Chelsea should know immediately who he was talking about.

"Dobbs," she repeated flatly, her eyes widening. Was the name supposed to mean something to her? Lord, she'd never heard it before. The look on the man's sharply chiseled features said he expected an answer. Chelsea shook her head and shrugged weakly. "I don't know anyone named Dobbs."

"Like hell you don't!" In one lithe shove, he was on his feet, towering over her, fists straddling lean hips. The glare he shot down at her was hot and angry. "I was watching from the grass, lady. I saw you with those two guys. . . ."

"Them?" Chelsea blurted out, her fingers fluttering to her throat. Her copper brows shot high, causing her forehead to crease. "Do you mean to tell me all of this nonsense is because of *them?*"

"Who the hell *else* would it be about?"

"That's a very good question," she muttered beneath her breath, her gaze wandering out over the moonswept prairie. "Who else indeed?"

A small part of her had clung to the belief that this entire episode related back to Emmy in some convoluted way. The girl was always getting herself into one scrape or another. But this didn't have anything to do with Emmy, she realized suddenly, then wondered if she should be relieved, or worried sick. Chelsea was used to extricating her sister from self-made disasters, but she had never had to extricate herself from one. She'd had no need.

Until tonight.

"You haven't answered my question, lady," the man growled. "What's the matter? Can't think of a good lie?"

"Actually, I can think of several," she blurted out. "But, since I don't lie"—she paused a second to let *that* information sink in,—"I'll keep them to myself and concentrate on how I can phrase the truth so you'll believe it."

"Keep it simple. You'll stand a better chance."

Chelsea rolled her lips inward to keep an angry retort from slipping off her tongue. The man's arrogance was beginning to wear on her well-past frazzled nerves. So were his demands.

Bending her knees and jerking the hem of her skirt well below her ankles, she cradled her legs close to her chest. The fringe of her thick copper braid scraped the grass as she craned her neck and glanced up at him.

"Try this on for simple, mister: I don't know anyone named Dobbs!" Chelsea held up a silencing hand when he opened his mouth, probably to yell at her again. "You said yourself you were hiding in the grass—God only knows why—watching those men. Fine. Far be it from me to ask why you didn't offer a little help," she sniffed indignantly. "Now, if you were really where you said you were, then you must have noticed I wasn't thrilled to be in those despicable men's company."

"Right," he groused. "Next thing I know you're going to tell me they jumped out at you from nowhere. And that you've never seen them before in your life." He chuckled sarcastically, then shook his head and muttered under his breath, "Then you're going to swoon, I'll bet."

Lifting her chin, she glared him into silence. "I don't swoon."

"You don't lie too good either, sweetheart."

Chelsea planted her fists on her hips, her look shooting hot amber fire. "Are you calling me a liar? *Me?!*" she huffed. Sweet heavens, the thought was almost laughable. Almost. But right now, the very last thing she felt like doing was laughing. Slapping the arrogant grin off his handsome face—ah, well, now *that* was certainly a consideration! If she'd been standing, she might have done just that. Instead, she snapped, "Believe whatever you want. You will anyway. But the fact of the matter is those men *accosted* me." This point was emphasized by the long, thin finger she jabbed at her upper chest—a place to which the man's eyes kept straying much too frequently. "Before you and your lady-friend came along, I was trying to get away from them."

"She did run, Mitch. We saw her. In fact, didn't you ask me why she would—?"

"Shut up, Mennard."

Chelsea felt the heat of two inquisitive gazes boring into her, but she stood her ground. Holding her hands palm up, her slender shoulders rose and fell with a helpless shrug. "That's it. That's all I have to say. I can't tell you any more because I don't *know* any more. As for where those two are now . . ." She snorted in disgust, a shiver trickling visibly down her spine. "I don't know. I don't *care*. My guess is they crawled back under the same slimy rock they were born under."

"Is that a fact?" Mitch's jaw bunched hard beneath the beard. He raked a palm down the bristled length of it, his gaze sharpening on the woman who was staring up at him intently. Her chest—*Christ, she was nicely formed!*—puffed with indignation.

"Yes, it's a fact," she mimicked icily. "But don't take my word for it. After all, I'm nothing but a two-bit liar. Isn't that right? Although, for the life of me, I can't think of one good reason I'd have to lie to you!"

Why indeed? There wasn't a fiber of Mitch's being that wanted to believe a word the woman said. Still, the confident way she spoke, coupled with her red-faced indignation and her pinched expression—so filled with rightful conviction—tossed in the recesses of his normally logical mind. All that, combined with the flash of sincerity in her large, amber-colored eyes, couldn't be overlooked—as much as he'd liked to.

His gut instinct had always been right. It was one of

25

the skills Mitch took immense pride in having honed, one of the few things in his life he could depend on. Unfortunately, the gut instinct he put so much stock in was now telling him something he didn't want to hear . . . that this fiery little redhead was telling the truth. She didn't know where Dobbs was. Her meeting with him and his brother tonight had been as unlucky as it was coincidental.

Either that, he mused, or she was one hell of an actress. God knows she had the looks for it. Large eyes that begged to drown a man's soul while she twisted a knife in his gut; a delicately boned face that made his calloused palms itch to feel the soft, feminine turns beneath them; and—he gulped—those lips! His gaze narrowed and his breathing turned ragged as Mitch forced himself—it didn't take a whole lot of effort—to look at that mouth. Poutily shaped, shell-pink, and moist, her tempting lips were the epitome of innocence . . . and the perfect foil for deception.

Should I believe her? he wondered, and at the same time stifled a husky groan. *Do I dare?*

Mitch shifted uncomfortably, his gaze straying over the moonlit prairie at the woman's back. Dobbs was out there, somewhere, and there was a chance this sexy little redhead knew where. A very small chance, true, but a chance nonetheless. Unfortunately, she wasn't talking; the stubborn set of her jaw told him that.

Damn it! He and Brenda had a lot riding on being able to find Dobbs. A hell of a lot. And if he were to take this woman's word that she *didn't* know the man or where he was camped, then that meant he was right back where he'd started. Of course, if she truly didn't know, he was back there anyway. *If* she really didn't know. But what if she was lying?

Mitch glanced over his shoulder, fixing Brenda with a piercing glare. "What do you think?"

She pursed her lips and shrugged. Crossing her slender arms over her chest, she sent the redhead a curious

26

glance. "For what it's worth, I think she's telling the truth."

Mitch scowled. Damn it! If only he could be positive . . .

But he wasn't. Not by a long shot. And as long as he clung to his suspicions, there wasn't a snowball's chance in hell he'd trust this woman long enough to let her out of his sight. Just his luck, she'd leave and go running straight to Dobbs. That would be *all* he needed!

"Yeah," he lied finally, deciding a change of tactics was definitely in order. "So do I."

The grass crunched beneath his stacked boot heel as he spun around and started to stalk away. Just as quickly, he stopped and turned back again.

"So what do we do now?" he asked the blonde. "It's too late to go after them. We wasted so much time on this one"—his bearded chin jerked at Chelsea—"they've got to be miles away by now. Damn it!"

"We'll do the same as always, Mitch," Brenda said. "We'll wait for another chance. If we're patient enough, we'll get it."

"Yeah, patience," he snapped. "One of my many virtues."

The woman chuckled and shook her head. "Not hardly, pal. Not hardly. In the meantime . . ." Her feline gaze drifted past Mitch's shoulder, settling on the woman who sat huddled in the grass, watching them suspiciously.

Chelsea stiffened. She knew the second the man's incredible blue eyes swept back to her. And even if she hadn't seen it, she would have felt it—narrow and probing, hot and disturbing. Deciding now would not be a good time to let her brave front slip, she sucked in a quick breath and lifted her chin, levelly meeting his gaze. "What about me?"

"You can go anytime."

Her smile was as sarcastic as her voice. "Thanks ever so much. So glad I could be of help."

27

Getting to her feet without letting the two who were staring at her know how badly her knees were shaking proved to be a lesson in coordination. Somehow, Chelsea managed it.

It wasn't until she was standing that she realized just how tall the man was. He stood a few feet away, but even with that distance separating them, she knew the top of her head would barely clear the broad shelf of his shoulders. And sweet heavens, he was wide! The wedge of his chest, coupled with the breadth of those steely biceps outlined beneath his flannel sleeves, suggested a power she'd rarely seen before. And hoped never to see again!

The effect was properly intimidating. Chelsea found the only sane way to deal with all that raw muscle and strength was to turn her back and ignore it . . . if she could.

The grass rustled around her ankles as she hoisted the bulky skirt and began to walk. She had no idea where she was going. Nor did she care. Away from these two would be fine with her! Her legs, she was pleased to find, did her proud. She didn't stumble, didn't stagger, but kept her back rigid, her pace sedate. It wouldn't do for them to know just how badly she wanted to put distance between herself and them.

She'd taken less than two dozen steps and had just begun to contemplate in which direction she should head, when the man's husky voice shot out from behind, stopping her cold.

"Just out of curiosity, lady, what the hell are you doing out here alone?"

"Looking for my sister, as if it's any of *your* business," she snapped over her shoulder, forcing her feet to trudge on. She was more than a little relieved when he didn't call out to her again.

"Oh, but it *is*, sweetheart," Mitch growled under his breath. "I'm making it my business."

Reaching into his shirt pocket, he took out the cigarette he'd rolled hours before but had never had the opportunity to smoke. He stuck the tip between his teeth, then removed a match from the same pocket and struck it on the heel of his boot. He squinted at the bright orange flame, touching it to the end and drawing until the tip glowed red and ribbons of grey smoke curled around his head.

"Uh-oh," Brenda said, clicking her tongue. "I don't like that look. What are you up to now, Mitch Bryant?"

"Up to? Me? Not a goddamn thing." He blew out the match and flicked it to the ground. "Except having a smoke."

"Now, why don't I believe that?"

"I don't know, Brenda. You tell me." His raven brows shot up in mock innocence. But there was nothing innocent in the way his lusty gaze picked out the seductive sway of a certain sexy little redhead's hips. The gentle curve, he noted, was outlined to tempting perfection beneath the swish of her dark skirt. While the material itself was coarse and unappealing—he preferred his women in satin and silks any day—what that ugly brown stuff concealed . . . ah, well, that was appealing as hell.

"Maybe because I know you too well, Mitch." Brenda's gaze raked him assessively. Nothing, from the way he looked startled to hear her voice to the unusual color staining his prominent cheeks, was missed. Her gaze sharpened and she continued. "Maybe because I know you take your job seriously, and that right now finding Dobbs is your job. That's what Thiel's hired you for—and Thiel's doesn't consider you one of their best detectives for nothing. Or maybe, just maybe, it's because I don't think you're totally convinced the girl was telling the truth."

"Well?" Brenda asked when Mitch said nothing. "Am I right? *Are* you up to something?"

"Maybe."

A waft of breeze sent a stray wisp of hair tossing over his brow. Brenda reached up and smoothed it back. "No maybes about it. I've been your partner for two and a half years now, Bryant. I know when you're up to something, and that look in your eye leaves no question in my mind. I want to know what it is."

His penetrating blue gaze shifted to the redhead, who was moving steadily away from them. His eyes widened imperceptibly when he noted the way she'd stopped and turned back to look at them. He couldn't see her gaze, but he could feel it. Boy, could he ever feel it!

Capturing Brenda's wrist in a ring of calloused fingers, he grazed her soft palm over his cheek, then settled her arm back at her side.

Brenda grinned and slipped her hand free. "My husband would shoot you for that."

Mitch returned her grin, adding a wink for good measure. "Clancy's working on another case. Last time I heard he was in . . . Montana?"

"Dakota," she corrected, "hunting down cattle rustlers. Not that it matters. I'm a happily married woman. Always have been, always will be. And don't you forget it." She nodded to the girl in the distance. "Now stop trying to change the subject and tell me what you're up to."

Mitch shrugged and, deciding Brenda wasn't going to let up until he told her, said, "Insurance. *That's* what I'm up to. I want to make sure our little redheaded friend didn't lie to us."

Her blond brow furrowed. "And how do you propose to do that . . . as if I have to ask?"

"Follow her. How else?" Rolling the cigarette to the other corner of his mouth with his tongue, he shrugged. "Go on back to camp, Mennard. And don't wait up. This could take a while."

"All right." After sending him a penetrating glance, she sighed and turned reluctantly away. She'd learned long ago not to argue with Mitch. When he got something in his head, it very rarely shook itself loose until he was ready to let it. And the feisty little redhead had definitely worked her way into Mitch's head. Brenda wondered how long it would take him to shake *her* loose. The thought made her grin.

"The Land Run starts at noon tomorrow. Looks like we no longer have a choice . . . we'll be participating." She didn't look back as she added the perfunctory warning she'd long ago perfected. "In other words, don't do anything stupid, Bryant."

"Have you ever known me to do anything stupid, Mennard?"

"You really want me to answer that?"

"Hell no!"

Her soft laughter rang out even after she'd melted into the late night shadows.

Mitch took a long drag off the cigarette and turned his attention out over the silver-lit prairie. The redhead had covered a good deal of ground; he could barely make her out now. But he could see her hair. All fiery red, too bright a color to blend smoothly into the night. He had a feeling that even in a pitch-black room, that hair would stand out. Lord knows, he'd welcome the chance to find out.

Snatching the cigarette from his mouth, he flicked it to the grass, watching as the glowing tip made a long downward arch. He ground what was left of it under his heel as he picked his way through the calf-high grass.

Chapter Three

Nervous, anxious, and very, very excited. That was how Chelsea felt as she lined up next to the countless thousands of others ready to make the Run into Oklahoma land.

Tension laced the air, as quick and as hot as the bright April sun scorching the prairie. It could be heard in the hushed whispers of those who'd gathered; in the way the men hustled to add still more grease to already slickened wagon wheel axles; in the way they rushed to check and retighten saddle cinches. Even the horses seemed impatient — snorting and shifting, anxiously awaiting the blast of cannon that would signal the start of this, the country's most publicized event.

Harrison's Hoss Race. History in the making. Everyone present — man, woman, and beast — seemed to know the significance of what they were about to do. They wore the honor with pride, all painfully aware that not everyone who participated in the grueling Run for free one hundred and sixty acre homesteads, or the smaller townsites, would be successful.

Chelsea inhaled deeply and adjusted herself atop the saddle. The smell of man and beast, leather and sweat, sweltering under the late morning sun was pungent. It was also unavoidable and, in an odd way, comforting. It proved she was not alone in her obsession to own her own home.

Her gaze wandered over the sea of "boomers," as they were being called. From the looks of it, few women were participating in the Run itself. In fact, the majority of women were grouped at the sidelines of the sea of bodies, watching expectantly.

Due to her gender, Chelsea was part of a vast minority of the boomers. That didn't bother her in the least. Her horse was fast, her seat atop him confident and sure. If anyone were to come out of this frantic day with a homestead to their name, it would be her. To think differently was inconceivable.

The paint pony beneath her gave an agitated toss of its head and stepped to the side as someone from the crowd behind her sidled into a sliver of space to her right.

Bending low over the pony's neck, she rubbed a palm down its silky mane. Its ear flicked as she cooed the familiar words of her father. "The Lord is my shepherd, I shall not want. He leadeth me to lie down in green pastures . . ." Her lips curled into a soft grin. "Pastures, Babylon. Think of pastures. That should calm you." Then, to herself, she added, "Not that we're likely to find many pastures where we're going, pal. From the looks of it, there isn't a one."

The horse didn't understand the words, but he understood the soothing lilt of her voice and the calming strokes of her hand. He quieted.

Straightening in the saddle, she wiped off the sweat dotting her brow on her green cotton sleeve. Her gauntleted fingers tightened and released on the reins as, from the corner of her eye, she caught a glimpse of shiny black coat and sinewy flanks.

She paid little attention. After last night's frightening escapade, she thought better of making eye contact with any of the other boomers. On the surface, most seemed of a friendly enough nature, but what had happened amidst the moonswept prairie left a bitter aftertaste in her mouth — and a reluctance to trust surface appearances again. It would be best to keep to herself.

The horse beside her—a stallion, she judged from a fleeting glance—gave a toss of its head and moved to the left. Chelsea's thigh grazed the rider's. It was a brief contact, but it was searing. The flesh beneath her baggy trousers sizzled as though she'd just been jostled against a crackling campfire.

She sucked in a breath. Tugging on the reins, she moved her mount to the left. An inexplicable coolness washed over her the instant the intruder's leg was removed. It was almost as alarming as the hotness that had preceded it. Her palms—*sweet heavens, she was trembling!*—moistened inside the gauntlets.

"Well, lady, don't keep me in suspense. Did you find your sister or didn't you? I was awake half the night wondering."

The man's voice was deep, husky, and wretchedly familiar. The amused tone sliced down Chelsea's spine like a knife, only to settle in a warm, churning pool in her belly. "Oh no," she whispered, her voice soft and ragged beneath a strangled rush of breath. "No, no, no."

She closed her eyes tightly against the burning glare of sunlight, praying that the man sitting atop the stallion next to her was *not* the man she thought it was. But she felt the heat of his gaze caressing her profile—knew without looking how blue that gaze would be—and smelled the tangy, distinct scent of him on the air. She knew who it was.

She swallowed hard, her eyes widening. Her gloved fingers tightened on the reins as her heart did an annoying little flip flop. If there was a breath of dry air to be had, her abruptly parched throat refused to let it slip past. "Go away," she croaked. "Just go away. I don't want to see you again. Ever."

"Tsk, tsk. Is that any way to greet the man who saved your life?"

"You did *not* save my life. If anything, you—" Her words melted like butter on her tongue the instant her

34

chin snapped up and her gaze swept to the side. Her breath caught. Lord, how she wished it would stop doing that! In the moonlight, she'd thought this man's eyes were incredible. But now, with those dark indigo depths absorbing the sun, reflecting it, they were spectacular.

The man tilted his head to one side, the shadows beneath his wide-brimmed hat obscuring those astonishing eyes for just an instant. It was barely enough time for Chelsea to catch her breath — such as it was.

"I what?" he prompted, the lips beneath the curl of mustache turning up in a rakish half-grin that did terrible things to her haughty self-composure.

"You interfered," she said, wishing her voice sounded stronger, hating the fact that it did not. "And you almost got me killed. Do *not* expect a warm greeting from me!"

Shifting in the saddle, she kept her back straight and fixed her gaze on the close press of bodies ahead. That helped. She could think straight now . . . well, almost. She would be able to think better, she thought, if only his sinewy thigh weren't so close as to be an exceedingly virile threat to her sanity! "Now go away!" she repeated loudly, firmly, if a bit breathlessly.

"Later. After you've answered my question. Did you find her or didn't you?" Mitch watched as a becoming flush stained her high, almost regal cheeks.

"Yes," she hissed. "I found her just fine. Now, if that's all you want . . ."

"Where was she?"

Chelsea's lips puckered. Grinding her teeth, she tilted her chin — contemptuously, she hoped — and refused to answer. What could she tell him? That she'd found her sister snuggled up in a bedroll with a complete stranger? That she and Emmy had argued hotly? That Emmy had done as Emmy always did, reacting defiantly, daring Chelsea to chastise her wayward behavior as their father would definitely have done?

No, she couldn't tell him any of that. First of all, it was none of his business. Secondly, she was having enough trouble acknowledging it herself. It was too hurtful, too humiliating.

Mitch's gaze burned as it settled hard on that beautiful, pouty shell-pink mouth. The one that tightened with angry memories. His tongue darted out, dragging over his own lips, wondering as he had for the better part of the morning how hers would taste. Soft and sweet, he decided. Innocent and, oh, so moist.

Not that he'd get a chance to find out! The sexy little redhead had a priggish streak longer than her braid. And what would she say if she knew it was exactly that vein of straitlaced propriety that Mitch found so goddamn fascinating? It was a challenge finding out if that fiery temper of hers melted into blazing passion under a few skillful kisses and caresses. For all his arrogance, Mitch Bryant had never backed down from a challenge—spoken or otherwise—especially when that challenge was issued from a woman. And he had no intention of backing down from this one.

With the knuckle of his index finger, he reached up and tipped his hat back, cushioning it on his crown. The kiss of the sun warmed his cheeks. "I take it you aren't talking to me now?"

"I have nothing to say to you."

"So you said last night . . . before you talked your pretty little a—head off."

Her gaze narrowed. Shifting in the saddle, Chelsea pierced him with what she hoped was a hot glare. "If you don't mind, I'm trying to forget last night ever happened."

"Can't say I blame you." His comment was generic. Only Mitch knew its meaning. Her encounter with Dobbs, then the one with Brenda and himself, was memorable enough. But the scene he'd witnessed in the early hours of the morning between this woman and her sister . . . ah, well, how could he blame her for wanting to forget about *that?* His ears were still ringing with the sister's angry shouts and this woman's furious, almost sanctimonious accusations.

Something indefinable in his tone made Chelsea's gaze narrow suspiciously. He was referring to more than just her encounter with him. She knew it, although she couldn't put her finger on exactly what it was that made her think that. She decided to let the matter drop . . . decided it would be best not to know what he was talking about. "Are you going to leave, or do I have to call one of those soldiers over and have him remove you?"

Mitch followed her gaze to the group of bluecoated men standing guard over the border of the district as though they were protecting the apple from Eve. His grin was slow and cocky. So was his shrug. "Go ahead. I'd love to see how you plan to convince them getting me away from you is more important than making sure no one slips past the starting line before noon."

His gaze swept back to her, and Chelsea felt her cheeks redden despite her resolve to not let this man see how much he disturbed her. She met the challenge in his eyes, though she was never sure how she managed it. "Don't you think I can?"

His grin broadened. "Oh, yeah, lady. I think you can do any damn thing you like." His eyes narrowed to assessing blue slits. "I think it's got something to do with your—" His gaze slipped down by excruciatingly slow degrees, until it was searing her mouth. "Yeah, it's those lips, all right. So pouty and pink . . . and tempting as all hell. They'd make a man believe just about anything. I'm convinced of it."

Chelsea's jaw hardened. Her lips thinned, but it was a reflexive gesture. Her mouth felt as though it were on fire—all hot and flushed. It didn't help to know it was a simple gaze—not a touch, but a *gaze*—that made her feel so warm and tingly and . . . well, *decadent*. Deliciously decadent.

Her confusion grew the lower her own gaze strayed. Even an untrained eye could see that the stallion beside her, seemingly unperturbed by the many horses around it, was a magnificent piece of horseflesh, all inky black coat and strong, rippling sinew. Its legs were thick, firm, and powerful, made for running—and running hard. Its chest was velvet-smooth and wide, the leather saddle cinched around it hand-tooled and expensive.

In short, it put her sorry little paint pony to shame.

All in all, though, Chelsea had to admit that the stallion, as fine a specimen as it was, was not nearly as magnificent as the man who straddled it. Against her better judgment, her attentions strayed still lower. She gulped.

Hot color flooded her cheeks when she remembered— vividly, searingly—the feel of his thigh grazing hers. Hard, muscular, warm. His legs gripped the stallion's back, and for the first time she noticed the denims of last night had been replaced by a pair of not-so-clinging black trousers. The hem dipped beneath the knee-high cuff of appealingly scuffed leather boots. His hips were lean as they melded with the saddle, the gunbelt strapped around them riding cockily low.

Chelsea tore her gaze from those hips the instant she realized it was there her attention lingered—for far too long to be considered proper. Lifting her eyes, she found, did nothing to help her confusion. Indeed, it only mounted.

A light spring breeze billowed the grey cotton shirt to the firm wedge of his chest. Even beneath the fluttering sleeves, she thought his shoulders looked wider, firmer than they had bathed in moonlight. The skin of his neck, peeking above his unbuttoned collar, had a rich, bronze hue that melted naturally into the ragged line of his untrimmed beard.

"I've decided not to call the soldiers," she said abruptly, wincing when she heard the high, breathless squeak of her voice.

Apparently, he'd noticed the shaky timbre as well, for his grin was quick and broad. "Well, isn't that nice of you."

"I'm not doing it to be nice. Believe me, if I didn't think they had more important things to do, I'd call them in a minute."

"Sure you would, sweetheart. I never doubted it." His tone was thick with a sarcasm Chelsea refused to acknowledge.

In what she hoped was a dismissive gesture, she turned her attention to the soldier who'd stepped out in front of the anxious crowd. His mission must have been important, because Chelsea thought that even a loaded Winchester leveled point-blank at her temple wouldn't have made her step in front of so many excited people and barely constrained horses.

The soldier was addressing the crowd, saying something that the murmur of nervous voices, yapping dogs, squawking chickens, and snorting horses prohibited Chelsea from hearing no matter how much she strained to catch his words.

A trickle of nervous perspiration ribboned down her spine. She squirmed uncomfortably when her attention shifted to the crowd of women and children.

Chelsea tried to pick out her sister's dainty blond head, but with no luck. If Emmy was there, she wasn't to be seen. Her shoulders bowed forward. She'd hoped Emmy would get over her anger . . . hoped the girl would show up and offer Chelsea a smidgen of support. Why she thought Emmy would come through for her at this late date, however, was beyond Chelsea's understanding. More than likely the girl was off pouting somewhere. Chelsea probably wouldn't see her again until she made her trip into Guthrie — the place she and Emmy had arranged to meet in three day's time.

"Your sister?" the annoying man beside her asked.

The saddle creaked as Chelsea sat back and fixed him with an irritated glare. Why wouldn't he *leave?* Couldn't he see she didn't want him here? Hadn't she done everything in her power, beyond outright rudeness, to give him that impression?

39

He repeated the question, loudly, as though she hadn't heard him. They both knew she had. "I said, is that your sister?"

Annoyed, she followed the thick, calloused path of his index finger to a woman standing on the edge of the crowd. She was short, plump, with a shock of frizzy red hair that would have stood out anywhere. Chelsea grinned despite herself. "Hardly."

"No, hmmm?" The raven brows crunched together in a feigned scowl. Of course he'd known that wasn't her sister. He'd seen her sister last night—*all* of her sister. That woman wasn't her. Which brought Mitch to the reason he'd asked. "Guess that means the guy standing beside her isn't your husband, then."

It wasn't a question, though it had been stated in such a way that it demanded an answer. "No, he isn't," Chelsea replied tightly. Her gaze narrowed as a slice of caution knifed down her spine. She'd stake her life she knew what his next question would be. And she was right.

"Then which one *is* your husband, lady? Point him out. I'd like to get a look at any guy who'd marry a woman who—"

"He isn't here," Chelsea cut him short, deciding she didn't want to hear what "type" of woman he thought her to be.

"Then where the hell is he?"

"I just told you. Not here." She felt that incredible blue gaze sharpen on her and knew the second it dropped, searing through the thick gauntlet covering her left hand. Or, more precisely, the bare ring finger of that hand. Fixing her gaze rigidly ahead, she pretended not to notice his rude stare.

"So you're making the Run yourself?"

She chuckled sarcastically. "I'm alone, aren't I?"

"That doesn't answer my question."

Chelsea shrugged. "It'll have to. It's the only answer you're getting from me."

Mitch reached up and yanked his hat low on his brow.

His eyes sparkled from beneath the brim, burning over her haughtily set profile. "You *are* married, aren't you?"

"That's none of your business," she snapped.

"I'm making it my business."

Chelsea's teeth clamped hard. She continued to stare straight ahead. The soldier had moved away, and now another group of bluecoated men was shoving a cannon into position. The black barrel was pointed safely away from man, beast, and vehicle.

"Answer the damn question, lady," the man beside her growled. "Are you married?"

Chelsea sent him a patronizing glare. "They do say until death do us part, do they not?"

"Then you are?"

"Did I say that?"

Mitch opened his mouth, then slammed it closed. His gaze narrowed, dropping again to the gauntlet-encased hand. His fingers itched to tear the glove off. The urge was strong, leashed only by the way he wrapped his fingers around the reins in a white-knuckled grip.

He didn't remember seeing a wedding band last night, but then, he hadn't looked for one. Mitch cursed the oversight. He wasn't sure why the idea of this woman having a husband somewhere should bother him, but it did. A hell of a lot, it bothered him.

The question of her married state had struck him sometime during the night—make that early morning, since it had been dawn by the time he'd found his bedroll. Like an annoying itch, the question refused to leave. It was still there, just below the surface, gnawing at his gut and circling in his mind—perhaps more than it had a right to. That she'd stubbornly refused to ease his curiosity was aggravating as hell.

Chelsea glanced to the side and saw the splash of red deepening the tan on his prominent cheeks. She recognized the color for what it was: annoyance. Biting back a grin, she found herself abnormally pleased to realize at least *something* she'd said had bothered him as much as

41

his mere presence bothered her.

"Is that the only reason you're here?" she asked finally, her tone degrees lighter. "To find out if I'm married?"

His gaze narrowed, but continued to burn into her from beneath the shadows of his hat. "What do you think?"

"When it comes to you, I'm beyond thinking," she stated flatly. It was the truth. She did very little thinking when this man was close—but she made up for the lack by way of sheer feeling. That sense, traitor that it was, intensified to an acute pitch with this man's warm, virile nearness. Wisely, she chose not to analyze the observation.

"I'm not stupid," she said suddenly, feeling a need to say *something*, anything, that would get him to stop looking at her as though he were famished and she were a juicy, trussed-up Christmas goose. "I—I know you didn't just stumble over here by accident. Not in a crowd this size. Why don't you save us both a lot of trouble, mister, and just tell me what you want?"

"Now that you've mentioned it . . ."

The way his voice trailed off made Chelsea's gaze narrow in alarm and shoot to the side. His left arm was bent, the elbow jutting cockily toward her, the palm open and cushioned atop the rock-solid shelf of his thigh. The heel of his other hand rested against the pummel of his saddle. Fisted in those thick fingers was a black silk scarf she hadn't noticed before. The breeze billowed the scrap of cloth, the hem slapping against a black-clad thigh that Chelsea had the good sense not to look at twice.

She watched as the sun-kissed hand clutching the scarf lifted to waist level, recoiling when she saw it inching toward her.

Her eyes snapped up, locking hard with challenging blue.

A sensation—white-hot and sharp—sizzled through her veins when she saw his hands snaking toward her

42

arm. His grip was arrogantly sure, his fingers thick and capable. Her cambric sleeve was a poor barrier to separate the branding heat of his touch from her — *dear Lord, she was trembling again!* — flesh.

"For luck," he explained, and began to wrap the inky black scarf around her suddenly too-limp arm. The husky timbre of his voice bolted down her spine like a slice of summer lightning, scalding away any of the resistance Chelsea knew she should have felt and didn't.

She sucked in an uneven breath. It was tinged with the smell of leather and a tangy, spicy scent that was mysteriously male. Her gaze dropped to where his skillful fingers were tying the scarf in a secure knot around her arm. Could he feel the quivers racing through her? And did she want to know?

The sight of his hand, so large it dwarfed her arm until she looked delicate and frail by comparison, was enough to make her heart race. The feel of his breath, warm and sweet against her cheek, did nothing to help calm her suddenly frazzled nerves.

"There," he said, giving the scarf one last tug. The saddle squeaked as he sat back and surveyed his handiwork. With his chin down, the wide brim of his hat hid the upper portion of his face from view and cast the lower portion in enticingly vague shadows. It did not, however, hide the tug of beard and mustache that suggested an arrogantly rakish grin.

"T—take it off. I don't want your scarf, Mr. . . ." Chelsea's words trailed off as she tried to remember his name. Her voice sounded high and unnatural to her ears, but she barely noticed. She was too busy focusing on the way her arm felt oddly cold and prickly without the heat of his fingers to warm it.

"Bryant. Mitch Bryant." His chin lifted. Sunshine peeped beneath the wide brim of his hat. The golden light was caught and held prisoner by those incredible blue irises. He seemed to be waiting for her to say something, but for the life of her, Chelsea couldn't guess what it was.

"Mrs . . . ?" His head inclined to the side, the ragged fringe of hair scraping his collar as his gaze pierced her to the quivering core.

A vague, tickling sensation surged through Chelsea's blood as she lost herself in his eyes. She felt as though she were drowning in a sea of vivid blue, and Chelsea wasn't at all sure she would want to be rescued if help should offer itself.

"Mrs?" she echoed stupidly. *Sweet heavens,* she thought, *what's wrong with me?* And where was all that good, healthy anger she'd felt coursing through her blood only a few short minutes ago? Gone, she realized suddenly. Scattered like so much dust under the confusing, searing heat of Mitch Bryant's touch.

"Your name," he prompted when she continued to stare at him.

Her tongue answered before her cautious mind could stop it. "Oh . . . Ch—Chelsea Hogan."

"Ch—Chelsea Hogan," he mimicked, his tone light and teasing. The way he rolled each syllable over his tongue, tasting and testing, made her shiver. His smile broadened appreciatively, a flash of pearly white against coarse black. His eyes darkened when they drifted to her lips. Pink and full, pouty and softly parted. His gaze was hot, her reaction to it disturbing and alarmingly reflexive.

"Different," he said finally. "But nice."

Was he talking about her name or her lips? Chelsea didn't know, but she did know better than to ask. Her lips smoldered under his lusty gaze, making it impossible for her to utter a word. It was just as well. She wasn't entirely sure she was capable of talking right now. Her throat had gone dry and tight, her breaths shallow to the point of being almost nonexistent. Her head felt light and dizzy. It was a feeling that, if she were a liar, she would have attributed to the sun beating down on her bare head or the excitement of the Run that would

44

be starting at any minute.

Chelsea was no liar. She knew what was making her feel as though she was about to do something she *never* did: swoon. It was this man. His warm, virile nearness. His musky male scent. His hot breath caressing her cheeks and the memory of his even hotter fingers grazing her arm. It was the look in his deep, incredible blue eyes that made her feel like a lump of butter left out to melt in the hot summer sun. Nothing else.

His gaze lifted, capturing hers once more. His eyes flashed with understanding, darkened with desire, and glinted with raw challenge. "Okay, Ch—Chelsea Hogan, now that I've given you a little something for good luck, what are going to give me?"

The scarf tied around her arm, while not tight, felt glaringly apparent. She couldn't tear it off and slap it back in his face—even if she could figure out to untie the complicated knot—without offending him. But why she should care if she offended him or not was beyond her understanding.

"I didn't ask for your scarf, Mr. Bryant," she said finally, surprised as how calm and firm her voice sounded. It shouldn't. Not when her heart felt as though it were clamoring frantically beneath her rib cage, begging to burst free.

"But I gave it to you, *Miss* Hogan," he countered, his tone smooth and deceptively light. Deceptive, she thought, because there was nothing at all light about the gaze that held hers ensnared. "I only want, oh, just a little something in return."

Her chin lifted. "I don't have, 'oh, just a little something' to give. Even if I did, I wouldn't give it to *you*."

A snicker from a man near her left scratched up Chelsea's spine just as the penetrating blue gaze settled on her lips. He seemed to be fascinated with her mouth, she thought. This had to be the hundredth time she'd caught his eyes feasting there.

The look on Mitch Bryant's face left no doubt what

the "oh, just a little something" he had in mind was. A kiss. *Dear Lord, he's going to kiss me!* Chelsea felt her heart stutter beneath her breasts. Her palms moistened inside the gloves, and she felt herself start to tremble—from the inside out. The thought of that mouth, temptingly hidden beneath the curl of pitch-black mustache, touching her own tender lips sent her mind spiraling.

"Don't you dare," she gasped when he leaned threateningly forward. Her chest puffed with indignation as she, in turn, leaned back. "I didn't ask for your scarf," she repeated tightly, "and if what I think you want is what you *do* want in return for it, you can take the damn thing back right now."

Oh my, now he has me swearing. Me!

He gave her no time to think on it as his mouth continued its tantalizing descent. "I don't want it back."

His breath was hot and sweet against her face. It was searing, more so than the sun warming her head or the thigh that was an ever constant threat to her sanity. Her trembling increased.

Chelsea began to fumble with the impossibly tied knot of the scarf. His voice, deep, low, and resonantly intense, made her gloved fingers freeze. It didn't matter, since she had precious little chance of ever untying the complicated knot in the first place. But she would have liked the opportunity to try.

"I said I don't want it back, sweetheart."

His hand closed over hers, pinching at the fingers of her gloves and drawing them slowly off. The material slipping over her knuckles was coarse, but not nearly as jarring as the feel of his calloused flesh doing much the same thing. When he was done, he leaned forward and tucked the gauntlets beneath her thigh. She tried not to notice the hot, throbbing sensation that action evoked— tried not to, but did.

Her eyes lifted in confusion, then widened to see his reckless, heart-stopping grin.

"Lady, when you touch me I want to feel skin . . . not

some padded bit of cloth."

"I have no intention of"—her tongue stammered over the word, the thought—"t—touching you at all, Mr. Bryant. Heaven's no," she gasped. The idea was enough to make her head spin, and make her traitorous body go all liquid and light. As though to reinforce her weakly uttered words, her trembling fingers immediately went back to work on the tight black knot. Without the gloves, she could feel the first layer peel loose.

That was as far as Mitch Bryant allowed her to get.

His hand reached out and cupped her jaw, tilting her chin upward. The contact of calloused flesh brushing flawless velvet skin was jarring. Chelsea was pleased to see that she wasn't the only one shaken to the core by it. Mitch Bryant's eyes flashed with momentary confusion before the telltale emotion was quickly doused behind an expression too impassive to be believable.

An excited murmur rippled through the crowd. Chelsea barely heard it over the expectant, erratic pounding of her heart—although a part of her mind did recognize the sound's importance.

Harrison's Hoss Race was about to begin. The moment she'd been waiting for her entire twenty-eight years was only a heartbeat away. She should be using this time to do a last minute check on her saddle cinch. It would be her only chance to make sure everything was ready for the grueling Run. And that was exactly what she would have done had she been able to tear her gaze away from the sensuous descent of Mitch Bryant's mouth.

His breath washed raggedly over her face. Hot, branding, and sweet. She felt the warmth of his lips before they actually touched hers, and the feeling shot all the way to her toes, making them curl like shells within her boots.

"For luck," he whispered hoarsely against her mouth before his lips crashed down on hers.

The kiss was as hard and demanding as the man who

initiated it. Dark and probing. Deliciously thorough. Like the lump of butter Chelsea had likened herself to before, she melted. It was a warm, tingly, liquid feeling. It was also sinfully erotic.

His lips were sensuously thin, his kiss overwhelmingly skillful. He sipped at her full lower lip, nibbling greedily, tasting each satin-moist inch like a starving man prolonging his first solid meal.

She quivered, too stunned to respond, too breathless to refuse his warm, demanding mouth. His tongue darted from between the silky hairs that tickled at her flesh and set a fire burning deep in her blood. The velvety tip stroked, coaxed, devoured until she couldn't stop herself from opening beneath him. A shudder raced through her stomach, seeping rapidly lower. Anticipation of the delights still ahead fired in her blood.

The hands she'd raised with the intent of stopping him were pillowed atop his broad, rippling chest. She could feel the heat of his body, hot and searing, beneath the cloth of his shirt. The sensations such raw masculinity evoked were dizzying to her innocent mind and alarmingly sharp.

Her fingers curled into the pliant cloth. Tight, trembling fists unconsciously tugged him closer. His heart drummed beneath the heel of her hands. The wild, reckless tempo was spiraling and matched that of her own to vivid perfection.

One calloused hand snaked about her waist, drawing her up hard against his rock-solid side. His chest smoldered against her straining breasts as their horses stepped together. Thighs brushed. The contact was electric, charged to a sizzling pitch by the kiss that deepened as his tongue plunged past her lips.

Her soft gasp of surprise, confusion, amazement, was easily swallowed. His husky groan of desire was not.

He tasted of tobacco and coffee. A masculine combination. The sting of it on her tongue as he swirled the moist shaft around the tip of hers was jarring. His strokes were light, as though testing her, coaxing her tongue to come out and play. The temptation was too great to resist. Hesitantly, she met his thrusts and parries. His investigation grew bolder, drawing a response that was torn from a place buried deep in her soul.

Chelsea didn't give her hands permission to travel up the muscular wedge of his chest. Nor did she give her palms permission to worship the appealing broadness of his shoulders, or to test the strength of his neck between her palms, or to entwine her quivering fingers in the pitch-black hair at his nape. They did so of their own accord.

Wispy raven curls tickled her fingertips in tingly waves, matched by the ones his beard and mustache created against her lips. Each strand was soft and baby-fine, making her feel as though she'd buried her fingers in a rich bolt of expensive satin. The dark curls slipped beneath her fingertips. The ragged ends scraped against her sensitive wrists, tickling the pulsebeat that throbbed frantically in the creamy hollow.

A low, husky moan rumbled from deep in his chest as he eased back—just slightly—and dragged his tongue across her parted lips. He tasted the top one first, sucking it into his mouth, nibbling and teasing, then devoured the bottom one until her surrender liquified in a long, airy sigh.

Then, as instantaneously as the kiss had begun, it ended.

Without his arm searing her waist, Chelsea would never have been able to stay in her saddle. Her body felt weak, drained by the sheer power of a kiss that, in reflection, was much too brief. Her knees gripped the pony's sides tightly enough for the horse to toss its head in protest, but not tightly enough to stem the warm, throbbing flood of sensation that had spiraled downward from where their lips had joined. Expectation, hot and sharp, gathered in a simmering pool in her stomach.

As though awakening from a deep, drug-induced

sleep, Chelsea's lashes flickered up. She was captured by a gaze that was deep and intense, shimmering a dark indigo-blue as it burned into her from beneath the shadows of his hat.

Before she realized what he was about and long before she could have stopped him, she felt her left hand seized in his demanding grip. He tugged her limp, trembling fingers beneath his nose and inspected her glaringly naked ring finger.

"If the kiss didn't prove it, this certainly does." The gaze that ensnared hers glistened with triumph. "Lady, you are definitely *not* married."

Chelsea sucked in an uneven breath and yanked her hand from his warm, calloused grasp. She wrapped her quivering fingers around the saddle horn to keep from melting out of her saddle. She should have sent him an appropriately hot retort and would have . . . if only she trusted her voice to speak. She didn't.

"The Run is getting ready to start, sweetheart. Better get a grip." He nodded to the reins she'd dropped when he'd kissed her, but his eyes conveyed a meaning much deeper, much hotter, and much more sensuous.

"My grip," she muttered, her voice husky and raw, "is none of your concern."

He shrugged, adjusting the hat on his head as his gaze swept the anxious crowd. "Wrong again. Everything about you is my concern." The blue eyes fixed her with a penetrating stare that made her go both hot and cold at the same time. His gaze slipped down, smoldering on breasts that heaved erratically with the few ragged breaths she was able to draw into her burning lungs. "You got that, sweetheart? *Everything.*"

Chelsea's mouth went dry as she opened it to speak, to give this man the dressing-down he deserved. She would never know if her voice would have betrayed the passion this man had kindled within her, or the anger, for before she could utter a word, the cannon blasted. The sound roared through the hushed, expectant air and was quickly swallowed up by echoing reports of gunfire, the thundering of hooves, and the jubilant cheer of the crowd.

Whether she was ready for it or not, Harrison's Hoss Race had begun.

Chapter Four

Belatedly, Chelsea realized her position for the start of the Run was not as good as it could have been. She wasn't in the front of the wildly shouting pack, nor was she in the rear. She was somewhere in between and at a disadvantage that had nothing to do with her supposedly weaker feminine gender.

A few rows ahead, beside a carriage decked out in brass, were two men riding bicycles. Their oversized wheels caught in the ruts made by the charging wagon wheels ahead of them and the burrows of horses hooves hidden by the tall bluestem grass. The men kept slipping, unable to get their wobbling bicycle wheels to hold to the land. Therefore, no one in their wake could proceed. But that hadn't stopped excited people behind from charging forward. The result was a dangerous tangle of horses, wagons, and quite a few screaming people.

Babylon, sensing the anxious press from behind, took a nervous sidestep. Chelsea's knees tightened around the horse's side as she drew the reins up hard. Dust was everywhere, like a gritty fog hovering at ground level. Already she'd swallowed what felt like mouthfuls of it as she squinted and tried to find a way out of the mess she was caught in.

There was none. At least, none that she could see.

Her heart slammed against her rib cage. Her fingers chafed from the reins biting into her tender palms. Her gauntlets had disappeared, and she wasted no time trying to find them. A few lacerations on her hands would be a small price to pay for the land that had yet to be claimed. Land she would never see if she couldn't find her way out of this mess!

"Run the idiots over," a booming voice called. "Trample them!" another shouted. The sentiment was shared by raucous cheers. The words could barely be heard over the repeating shots of gunfire and the thunder of trampling hooves ahead.

Normally, Chelsea would have been appalled by the suggestion. But, upon seeing her dreams being dashed by the two men on wavering bicycles, her own thoughts strayed in the same murderous direction. She'd hate herself for it come morning, no doubt, but for right now all she could think of was the tract of land she would never be able to claim if she couldn't break free.

Glancing desperately to the side, Chelsea squinted against the sand that stung her eyes and clogged her nostrils. She was in time to see the back of a jostling wagon disappear into a clouded opening—the only available route.

Chelsea's heart soared. Pulling back on the reins, she turned the pony toward where she'd seen the wagon disappear. She never knew what made her glance back a second before she would have sunk her heels into Babylon's flanks.

Though he was scarcely two yards away, she could barely distinguish the outline of Mitch Bryant's rugged form through the cloying layer of dust. Dust that was thickening at an alarming rate. All she could see was the brim of his hat and a flash of grey shirt. He was clinging to a horse that had finally caught the scent of excitement and wasn't pleased by it.

The stallion reared, snorting and flailing. Only the expert control of its owner saved the wagon bed in front of it from being smashed by those mighty hooves. The stallion snorted, its hooves coming down and smashing the earth. Its head tossed in agitation when a tug on its reins guided it to the side.

It was, in Chelsea's estimation, the wrong way for Mitch Bryant to turn. To the right, the surge from the rear only worsened. The wagon on her left had been the only one to find a way out, and its driver had wisely taken it. But for how long would the opening stay clear?

Clamping her jaw hard, Chelsea jerked her mount to the side she'd just come from. She knew she would regret doing this—with every fiber of her being, she'd regret it—but her conscience forbade her from doing otherwise. Someday in the near future she would curse her father for instilling such a rigid sense of fairness in her. Right now, she had only enough time to react.

When her horse had pulled up close enough for her thigh to graze Mitch Bryant's, she leaned close and made a grab for his reins. The leather was harsh and biting, with no give as he made to snatch it from her grasp.

"Don't be a fool," she yelled. Her voice was swallowed up by the commotion raging around them. "I can get us out of here. Let go!"

Her gaze rose.

His lowered.

Brilliant blue clashed hard with whiskey-amber. It seemed like a lifetime passed, but in reality it took only a brief flash of time for them to size each other up. An understanding born of desperation was forged. Its threads were tenuous at best.

With a curse that echoed over the shouting voices and thunder of hoofbeats, Mitch let go of the reins. Chelsea wasted no time. The second she had the strip of leather secured in her fist, she spun in her saddle, leaned low over the paint pony's back, and sank her heels into its sinewy flanks.

Babylon lurched forward. Chelsea's arm felt as though it had been ripped from its socket before the stallion charged into pace behind her. Her knees were the only thing holding her in the saddle. They gripped the pony surely as, with one hand, she wove her way past horses and buckboards to where she had seen the wagon disappear.

The congestion here thinned . . . at least as far as the cloud of dust would allow her squinting eyes to see, it thinned. She didn't slow her mount, afraid the surge from behind would swiftly catch up to them. Luckily, the stallion made no complaints in keeping to the fast, twisting pace she set.

When they reached the boundaries of the crowd, Chelsea jerked her mount to a stop. She spun in the saddle only long enough to throw the stallion's reins at a stoic Mitch Bryant.

"You're on your own, *sweetheart,*" she snapped over her shoulder. Not looking back, she spurred her mount in the direction everyone else had taken. She could only hope it was the right one. She didn't know where she was going; she'd lost all sense of direction. She didn't care. When she found the spot that was to be hers, she would know it. Until then, she'd rely on gut instinct to be her guide.

Leaning low over the pony's back, she gave the horse his head, careful to stay on the fringes of the rumbling crowd. Everywhere she looked, the wide open prairie was covered with a cloud of kicked-up dirt and moving vehicles of every conceivable sort. They were outnumbered by what appeared to be thousands of riders on horseback. Most of them, she had a feeling, were heading toward the place called Guthrie.

Precious time—time she didn't have to spare—had been wasted in the tangle. More time had been spent saving Mitch Bryant's arrogant hide—something she would never, if she lived to be a thousand, understand why she had done. As a result, she was now farther back from the beginning of the throng than she'd been when the cannon had blasted. If she didn't make up distance now, she might as well kiss her dream of a home goodbye.

The thought made Chelsea's eyes sting with tears that she had neither the time nor the inclination to shed. Now was not the time for weakness. She swiped the telltale moisture away with her fist, consoling herself in a promise to indulge in a very good, very healthy cry later. For now, she intended to find herself a home. She intended to live her dream and see it flourish if it killed her!

Four hours later, Chelsea was kneeling on the bank of a churning river. The water was crisp, sweet to the taste. Using her hands as a cup, she drank in healthy gulps, letting the icy liquid wash away the dirt gritting between her teeth. More was splashed on her sweat-dampened brow. The cool moisture felt like a little bit of heaven as it trickled beneath her collar, pooling in the warm hollow between her breasts.

Satisfied, Chelsea sat back on her thighs and looked around. The cottonwoods grew thick here, the bluestem high and dense. The stalks swayed in the cool spring breeze like rolling waves on a tossing ocean. Wildflowers bordered the sandy riverbed, their flowery aroma scenting air that was amazingly sweet and blessedly free of dust.

It had been thirty minutes since she'd seen another person, horse, or wagon; an hour since she'd crossed the Santa Fe Railroad tracks—the landmark that had finally put her back on course. A corner marker had been planted in the ground just beyond the line of trees, designating this as a plot of land open to homesteaders. Since most of the others were no doubt opting for a position nearer to town, she wasn't surprised this lovely place had not yet been taken. It would be, though, just as soon as the towns were filled and the disheartened claim-seekers began searching elsewhere.

Chelsea sighed in contentment. The grin that curled over her lips was heart-stoppingly beautiful, gloriously happy. She had found her spot and she was happy.

56

Oh, it wasn't the wooded hills of Massachusetts or the jutting mountains of California, to be sure. There were no familiar oaks or fragrant pine trees. No hills, no valleys. Beyond the stand of cottonwoods lay nothing but wide open prairie. Beautiful, rolling prairie. Home. At least it would be once she'd sunk her claiming stake into its clay-red soil.

Babylon hadn't needed to be tethered. The second he'd caught scent of water, he'd dragged his tired body over to the banks and dipped his nose into the gurgling liquid. Chelsea had no fear of him running off. Not only was the horse loyally devoted, but his sides were glistening with foam from the long, grueling run. No, Babylon wasn't going anywhere.

And neither was she, Chelsea thought as she approached him.

The claiming stake she had whittled three nights ago was jammed into her saddlebag. She flipped the leather bag open and removed it. The roughened wood bit at her tender palms . . . palms the leather reins had chafed raw. But even the pain was sweet; it was a symbol of the freedom this gruesome run had earned her.

Chelsea's grin broadened with giddy delight as she entered the cottonwood, emerging on the other side. This was the spot where she would build her cabin, she thought as she bent over and plucked a sturdy branch out of the grass. She'd face the front of the cabin so she could look out one window to see the endless stretch of prairie and out the other to see the gurgling river flowing past the rear. She'd situate the house close enough to the trees so the overhanging cottonwood branches would cut the sun in summer and the wind in winter.

Or perhaps she would find another spot that was even better, she thought as she positioned the sharpened tip of the stake in the grass and started driving it into the dirt with the blunt end of the tree branch. After all, one hundred and sixty acres was a lot of land. And she hadn't yet scratched the surface on all that she owned—or would

57

own at the end of five years time.

Chelsea hammered the stake—on which she had proudly carved her name—into the ground as far as her stinging palms would allow. When she was done, she tossed the branch aside and pushed shakily to her feet.

Crossing her arms about her waist she looked down on the small marker that claimed so much and thought she had never felt so proud. Now that it was all over, her knees were beginning to shake—unavoidable repercussions from the long, exhausting ride. Her legs hadn't yet made the adjustment from jostling saddle to unmoving ground. But there was no need to rush. She wasn't budging from this spot until it was time to file her claim at the land office in Guthrie and fetch Emmy.

Until then, she would guard her property with her life. Heaven help the person who tried to take it from her.

With those thoughts in mind, Chelsea began retracing her steps to the riverbed. Her ears perked to the rhythmic sound of hammering, a sound that grew louder the closer she came to the river. The noise was both comforting and alarming. Comforting, in that it meant she was no longer alone. Alarming, in that it meant *she was no longer alone!*

Her pace increased. The hammering continued, then abruptly stopped. Chelsea's heart raced, her breaths quickened. She broke into a run, despite the screams of protest in her burning thighs. The throbbing in her hands had receded at the thought that someone, somewhere, was trying to steal her claim. She'd expected it to happen—a woman alone, who wouldn't try?—but she hadn't been prepared to be challenged so soon!

Chelsea cleared the trees in a burst of what was probably the last of her energy. Her pony had drifted a bit downstream and was now awash to his fetlocks in the crisp, cool water. He was not alone. Adjacent to her mount, on the other side of the river, was a black stallion.

Her eyes widened, fixing on the stallion. She had seen

58

it only once before, and not too long ago at that. Certainly not so long ago that she could forget either the horse or its owner. Her gaze snapped up. Her breath lodged somewhere between her throat and lungs, forming a dry, painful lump that even a hard swallow couldn't clear.

Squinting against the sun, she picked out his rugged form easily — perhaps because she was drawn to it like a magnet.

Mitch Bryant looked like he'd been waiting patiently for her to notice him. He was standing beside a tree, the trunk of which looked as hard and as firm as the broad shoulder resting lazily against it. One leg was bent, one ankle crossed the other. The toe of his dusty leather boot dug into the ground. The stance, flagrantly male, tilted his lean hips at a cocky angle, accentuated by the thumbs he'd hooked in his belt loops.

The shirt that had billowed so nicely in the breeze before was now damp and plastered to his chest. The clinging grey folds drew unnecessary attention to the rippling flesh beneath and the coiled power of his thick biceps. The wetness of his shirt could have been caused by the river. Then again, it could have been caused by spicy male sweat. Chelsea thought she smelled the tangy aroma of the latter clear across the river.

Sucking in a quick breath, she let her stunned gaze drift up. His hat was drawn down low on his brow. The shadows cast by the wide brim concealed his eyes from view. But nothing concealed the arrogant grin tugging at his bearded lips.

She didn't have to know where he was looking. Even at a distance, with not a scrap of proof to confirm it, she could feel the heat of his eyes searing her mouth. Her skin warmed under the intense scrutiny. Her stomach fluttered.

For the second time that day, a blush kissed her cheeks. It wasn't *that* he was looking at her that bothered Chelsea as much as *where* he was looking. She knew the exact moment his gaze settled—and settled hard—on the cloth covering her breasts. The material was moist from where she'd liberally splashed the river water over herself. Clinging. The water-darkened cambric outlined her curves like a glove, leaving no doubt of her reaction to the chilly breeze wafting over her.

"Well, fancy that. Somehow I just knew I'd be seeing you again, Miss Hogan," he said as he pushed away from the tree and took a few steps toward the river. His gait was an unhurried swagger that reeked of masculinity and coiled strength.

Even though he would have had to cross a churning river to get to her, Chelsea took a quick step backward. The gesture was duly noted by his wry grin.

Her attention shifted to his lips, to the way she'd caught brief glimpses of pearly teeth between the black when he spoke. The sight brought the unwelcome memory of his kiss rushing back to her in a warm, tingling flood. Her own lips burned with the memory of his hot, branding kiss, while her jaw smoldered with the memory of his calloused fingertips.

He stopped at the riverbed and looked over it, as though gauging its narrow width and depth. It could be crossed easily, though she didn't think he intended to do that. She was right.

His thumbs were still hooked in his belt loops. One of them was removed so the crook of his index finger could ease the hat back on his head. Sunlight peeked beneath the brim, the golden rays sculpting and enhancing each sun-bronzed angle and hollow. His eyes shimmered a teasing blue as he captured her gaze.

"You took off so fast, I never got the chance to thank you," he said. His broad shoulders rose and fell as he averted his gaze to their peaceful surroundings. But only briefly. All too soon the penetrating blue eyes were boring into her again. "Of course, now that we're going to be neighbors, I guess I'll get plenty of chances to do just that. Won't I?"

Whatever had kept Chelsea mute up to this point evaporated like steam off of a boiling kettle. Her voice returned with surprising force. "Neighbors?" she asked, blinking hard. He couldn't be serious! The quick rise and fall of his raven brows said that, yes, he most definitely was. Dead serious. "Are you trying to tell me you've just — ?"

"Mmm-hmmm." He nodded, jerking his thumb over his shoulder. His gaze never left her face. "I just drove my stake into the ground back there. The land on this half of the river belongs to me now." His grin was quick and sure, much like the rest of him. "And I can tell by the look on your face that you're just pleased as punch to hear it. Isn't that right, Ch — Chelsea Hogan?"

The teasing lilt in his voice, combined with exhaustion, sore muscles, and her stinging palms, made something inside Chelsea snap. The tears that had been steadfastly pushed away hours before came rushing back like a tidal wave bursting through poorly built floodgates. With a groan, she collapsed cross-legged onto the dirt, buried her face in her hands, and released the torrent of sobs that refused to be held back a second longer.

Chelsea cried for what felt like hours. When she was done, her palms stung from her salty tears, her temples throbbed, her lungs hurt, and her back ached from her hunched position. But she felt better.

When she looked up, Mitch Bryant was gone.

Chapter Five

Mitch Bryant had no trouble hunting down the wild chicken. What to do with it now that he'd killed it, however, was another matter. A repulsive one, in his estimation.

Oh, he'd eaten the things before—many times. Who hadn't? But to actually cook one himself . . . well, that was something else again. Had he really been feeling creative enough to try just an hour ago? He sure as hell didn't feel that creative now!

Lifting his hand, he stared in disgust at the dead thing dangling beak-down from his fist. It no longer looked like much of a chicken. Then again, it hadn't when it was alive, either. The scraggly limbs and rumpled feathers looked particularly unappealing, especially when he compared it to the delicious aroma wafting in his nostrils—an aroma that tickled his tastebuds at the same time it taunted his grumbling stomach.

Someone, somewhere, was cooking something that smelled damned good. His mouth watered. Every inhalation of the darkening night air was a malicious form of torture. Of course, that was unavoidable. A man had to breathe, goddamn it!

Mitch knew who was cooking. He even knew *what* she was cooking. In fact, he wouldn't be surprised to learn Ch—Chelsea Hogan had caught this poor-looking excuse for a chicken's brother. But, unlike him, she knew what to do with hers. She'd set it to roasting. Damned if he knew how she'd managed to get hers to smell so good! His looked like it would smell gamy even when plucked and set to cook over an open flame. No amount of basting would enhance this sorry excuse for supper.

Clearing the stand of cottonwoods that led to the riverbank, Mitch tossed the bird in the grass and headed for his saddlebag, his experiment into cookery no longer holding any appeal for him.

He hadn't come *totally* unprepared. Two biscuits left over from breakfast and a can of beans were slipped from the leathery depths. The chunks of bread felt heavy, as hard and unappetizing as rocks as he weighed them in his fist. The beans, he knew without opening, would have a tinny aftertaste.

Damn Ch—Chelsea Hogan to hell and back! He would have been perfectly content to eat the two chunks of bread and cold beans out of the can, were it not for the tempting aroma of that woman's supper. And he might have tried his hand at cooking the ugly chicken, were it not for the smell of her perfectly basted dinner teasing him.

The delicious scent floating across the river was daring him to try and match it. The hell of it was, he knew he couldn't. Now, the two biscuits, the beans, the uncooked chicken . . . well, they just didn't measure up.

He slipped the can of beans back into the saddlebag. The biscuits felt like lead weights as he bounced them in his palms. Heavy and dry. Unappealing. They landed with twin thumps and a rustle of grass when he pitched them toward the line of trees.

Still crouching, he poked around in the leather depths once more. There had to be *something* worth eating in there!

His fingers closed around glass, cool and smooth. Grinning, he pulled a corked bottle free. Ah, now this might not be the most filling meal he'd ever had, but damned if half the bottle wouldn't dull his senses to the empty ache in his gut, the one aggravated by the tempting aroma of Ch—Chelsea Hogan's dinner.

Sitting back on his haunches, Mitch yanked the cork out with his teeth, then spit it onto the grass. He raised the lip of the bottle to his mouth. The fumes made his eyes water even before the potent liquor had a chance to sizzle on his tongue. He took three quick swallows, letting the whiskey cut a nice raw path down his throat. By the time it trickled into the yawning pit of his belly, it had turned into a simmering pool of liquid fire.

The drink alone wasn't filling—he'd been right about that—but it was numbing. He hadn't eaten since breakfast, so odds were he wouldn't have to waste more than a quarter of the bottle getting himself stinking drunk. He looked forward to it.

Turning to the side, Mitch settled on the ground, leaning his back against a solid tree trunk. The bark was harsh as it bit into the sensitive flesh beneath his shirt. Balancing the bottle between his thighs, he reached up and plucked the hat from his head. It was getting dark fast now and he didn't need it. The scrap of wide-brimmed felt was tossed aside, forgotten before it settled atop the thick grass. Plowing his fingers through sweat-dampened hair, he let his gaze drift down the legs he'd crossed lazily at the ankles, past the scuffed toes of his boots, and out over the river.

His groan was audible.

Apparently, Ch—Chelsea Hogan had been a busy little bee since he'd last seen her sitting in the tall, waving bluestem, crying her sexy little heart out. Her camp was set up at the halfway point between the stand of trees and the gurgling river-bank. The inviting glow of her campfire illuminated the crude piece of canvas and tree branches she'd used to build a makeshift tent.

The fire reminded Mitch that he'd yet to build one of his own. The large wild chicken she'd spitted and left to roast over the licking tongues of flame reminded him of how bare his fire would have been had he bothered.

Cursing female efficiency beneath his breath, he snatched up the bottle and tossed back another fiery slug. The whiskey was no longer working the way he'd planned. Instead of dulling his hunger, it magnified it to the point where he actually considered sneaking across the river and stealing the delicious-smelling chicken before she returned.

Easing the bottle back down to his lap, he wiped his mouth on the back of his hand. His gaze fixed hard on the copper-red head that peeked from the folds of stretched canvas. His gut clenched as he watched her step out of the tent and into the ring of firelight.

The cambric shirt he'd seen plastered to breasts his mind had yet to forget had been replaced by the familiar shirtwaist of coarse brown homespun. The trousers were also gone, traded in for a skirt of the same unflattering brown. The full hem rustled around her ankles and cradled her bottom in dark, enticing folds as she bent over the fire to check the progress of her dinner.

Mitch swallowed hard and felt a bolt of something he didn't dare name sizzle through him. He would have liked to blame the hard, instinctive reaction to his gnawing hunger . . . to bleary-eyed exhaustion . . . to the whiskey. Hell, he'd like to blame *anything* for causing the gut-level, primitive surge of sensation that was tearing through his blood right now.

Anything except the truth, that is. Anything except the fact that this sexy little redhead's nicely shaped posterior — outlined to excruciating perfection beneath her skirt — had a disgustingly base effect on his deprived senses.

His blue eyes narrowed when he watched her rip a juicy leg off the chicken. Hungrily, he followed the scrap of food to her mouth. His stomach grumbled.

It also convulsed, but not from hunger this time. A memory, sharp and sweet, sliced through his quickly blurring mind. It was the memory of full, pouty lips and the seductive taste of them dragging beneath his tongue.

It was the memory of silk-soft copper hair tickling his cheek and the feather-light caress of dainty fingers playing timidly with his hair. It was the memory of a gasp — hot as he captured it with his burning mouth — of her total, albeit reluctant, surrender.

Mitch didn't realize he'd shoved himself to his feet until he felt the earth sway beneath him. The whiskey went straight to his head, numbing his normally good sense.

He was starving, he reasoned as he slowly approached the riverbed. Common sense would not fill his empty stomach. But Ch — Chelsea Hogan's dinner would. Quite nicely, too.

The whiskey sloshed in the bottle as he stepped into the water. The hot afternoon sun had evaporated a lot of the depth, until the level had receded with surprising speed. Not that he would have cared. Mitch would have waded across the thing even it were a torrent of churning motion in the middle of a raging thunderstorm. He was hungry, damn it! At least, that was the reason he gave himself for what he was about to do.

The chilly water seeped through his boots, soaking his pants up to mid-thigh. The frigid temperature helped clear his head, but not a lot. And when common sense had the indecency to rear its ugly head at the halfway point across, he held it at bay by tossing back two more fiery slugs of whiskey.

He was feeling quite relaxed, not to mention stubbornly justified, when he stepped from the water onto the opposite bank. The dirt crunched beneath his boots. His steps were squishy and wet as he reached the outer circle of inviting firelight.

The smell of roasted chicken was strong here. The pungent scent wafted in his nostrils, bringing all of his hunger — intense and white-hot — surging to the fore. Not all of it was for food, however.

She hadn't seen him coming, though for the life of him, Mitch couldn't understand why. He'd made no at-

66

tempt to mask his footsteps, and he was sure the splashes he'd made while wading across the river hadn't been overridden by the crackling snaps of her campfire or the sizzling sounds made by drops of meat juice dripping from the chicken into the flames. Still, Mitch thought she looked unpleasantly surprised to see him standing just a few inches out of range of her campfire.

She also looked furious. The chicken leg froze on the way to her suddenly gaping mouth. Her eyes, the same rich shade as the whiskey sloshing in his bottle, widened in alarm. Her entire body froze, the creamy color in her cheeks darkening with a splash of indignant pink. The healthy glow, softened by the glow of firelight, made her delicate features more ravishing than he'd remembered them being when glimpsed beneath a harsh afternoon sun—or a shimmering silver moon, for that matter.

"Good evening, Mr. Bryant. Did you come to fetch your scarf back?" Chelsea asked, the first to recover. Her voice was husky, yet smooth, the tone only slightly biting.

"Nope." Mitch stepped forward, until he was fully bathed in the flickering orange glow.

Chelsea was sitting beside the fire now and felt at a decided disadvantage in her position, since she was forced to glance up the sinewy length of his body to get a glimpse of his face. It was a face sculpted to breathtaking perfection by the play of fire and twisting shadows.

Her heart stopped, then rushed to frantic life. She felt a hot surge of something she didn't want to know about pump through her blood. Her gaze dropped. He was still wearing the black trousers she'd seen on him earlier. Except, unlike this afternoon, the material was dripping wet and plastered to rock-hard thighs and calves. Nothing was left to the imagination, and Chelsea thought that was just as well; she couldn't have imagined so much male perfection if she'd set her mind to it for a year!

Sucking in a deep, uneven breath, her gaze blazed upward. She didn't notice the way the coiled bands of muscles in his legs rippled beneath the wet cloth. Nor did she see the way his lean hips were tilted cockily—and out-lined quite nicely by the clinging cloth. No, she didn't notice any of that. Certainly not! Or so Chelsea would like to have thought. Unfortunately, honest to the end, she knew that her mind was entertaining its own deca-dent thoughts regarding the sun-kissed delights suggested by those coarse, clinging trousers. The unsummoned im-age left her breathless, shaken, and decidedly flushed.

She lifted her chin and met his gaze. His eyes were a crisp, dark blue, their color enhanced by the firelight. He was watching her carefully. Too carefully. "If you didn't come for your scarf, Mr. Bryant, then what exactly did you come for?"

He lifted the bottle that Chelsea hadn't noticed he car-ried. Dark amber liquid sloshed against the glass as he gestured toward his own camp with it. "I was watching you eat." He shrugged, as though this were an everyday occurrence for him. She trembled, knowing it wasn't one for herself. "You looked thirsty."

"Watching me?" Her fingers slackened around the chicken leg. She caught hold of it just as the greasy limb made a plunge for her lap. "Why?"

"I was bored." Again, he shrugged. The casual rise and fall drew unnecessary attention to his broad, broad shoulders. Chelsea would have needed to be dead not to notice the way the grey cloth stretched over the sinewy muscles beneath, then loosened to soft, dusty folds. It was an enticing gesture, since it only magnified a wom-an's desire to explore firsthand the firmness that lay be-neath the cloth.

Did he know that? she wondered. Her gaze narrowed on him. Yes, she had a feeling he did. The same feeling told her Mitch Bryant didn't do a single thing without being motivated by what it would gain him in the end.

"You were bored," she echoed, one copper brow rising in open challenge as she returned his penetrating gaze. "Hmmm . . . I wonder why. I don't suppose you consid-ered building a fire and shelter the way the thousands of us more sensible boomers did? Or you could have spent the time cooking yourself dinner. That would have occupied you until it was time for—" The word clogged in her throat. *Bed*. The mere thought, made in connection with this man, had a devastating effect on her.

To cover her discomfort, she rushed on. "Well, since you're here, why don't you have a—" She was about to say *seat*, but he hadn't waited for the invitation to be extended. In a lithe, effortless motion, he ripped the remaining leg off her dinner and stretched out on the ground beside her. *Closely* beside her, if her smoldering outer thigh had anything to say about it.

"Mind if I join you?" he asked, the chicken leg poised in front of his bearded lips.

Somehow Chelsea didn't think a brisk no would do her much good. "Do I have a choice?"

His grin was reckless and quick. Devastating in its appeal. "Nope. Guess you don't at that."

"You mean you wouldn't go away if I asked you to?"

"What do you think?"

Keeping her expression sternly controlled cost her dearly—especially when her gaze was drawn to his pearly teeth, shimmering against a backdrop of pitch-black, as he bit into the chicken leg. It wasn't difficult to remember the way those dark hairs had felt tickling her lips, or the way his mouth—hard and demanding—had moved over her own. In fact, it would have been impossible to forget. She knew; she'd tried. It hadn't worked.

"What's in the bottle?" she asked finally. Her copper brows rose suspiciously as her gaze fixed on the tapered glass. The bottle in question was leaning against his hip . . . the hip she staunchly refused to look at.

"Whiskey. Want a sip?" His greasy fingers plucked up the bottle and offered it to her as he continued to use the other hand to eat. He grinned around a mouthful of chicken, apparently amused by her horrified expression.

Chelsea recoiled as though struck. "Whiskey! Good heavens, no."

69

"What's the matter, sweetheart? Don't tell me you've never drunk whiskey before?" His tone was half mocking, half amazed. *"Everyone's* had a taste at one time or another."

She sent him a meaningful glare. Then, with a toss of her head, Chelsea turned her attention out over the river, where it was safe. The water no longer churned but meandered in a twisting ribbon that looked like a slash of quicksilver in the moonlight.

"Goda'mighty, you haven't, have you?" he said, as much to himself as to her. The bottle was repropped against his hip.

"You told me not to tell you," she answered, not glancing over her shoulder.

Mitch gave a disgruntled huff and dropped the picked-clean bone onto the grass at his side. His gaze narrowed, sweeping over Ch—Chelsea Hogan's arresting profile.

Caressed by sunlight, it had been beautiful. Enhanced by firelight—and the whiskey that must be turning his brain to mush—it was breathtaking. Peaches and cream complexion. A wide brow and a short, upturned nose that countered high, regal cheekbones. All was softened by the copper-red wisps that refused to stay in the thick braid trailing down her back. The only thing hard about her was her jaw, but that was only because she was gritting her teeth. Everything else was soft and sweet, delicately molded. Perfect.

"Is there another reason you came here tonight, Mr. Bryant?" she asked. Her voice was only slightly high, her cheeks slightly flushed. Both were the residual effects of Mitch Bryant's gaze. "I mean, besides to offer me a sip of your whiskey?"

"What makes you ask?"

"I don't know," she answered honestly. Her brows drew down in a scowl that, judging from the permanent wrinkles etched between the arched copper wings, Mitch assumed was customary with her. "It's just a feeling I have."

"A feeling?" He leaned forward, his gaze dark and

probing. "About me? And what kind of feeling is it, Ch—Chelsea Hogan? Anything I should know about?"

His low, husky tone sizzled down Chelsea's spine. Her abruptly rigid spine. "I don't have *any* feelings about you, Mr. Bryant," she corrected sharply. "Not a one. I'm just suspicious about why you came over here tonight . . . and *nothing* else." Her gaze swept to the side, searing him with its hot amber fire. "Is that clear?"

"Very clear, Miss Hogan. Are you going to eat that?"

"Eat what?"

"Eat *that*. If you don't, I will."

Until she saw him nod to the chicken leg fisted in her greasy palm, she'd forgotten she even held it. She looked down at it with distaste, knowing there was no way the meat, no matter how juicy, would find an easy path down her parched throat.

"Feel free," she replied flatly, holding it out to him.

She overestimated the distance between them.

So did Mitch.

Their fingers grazed. The contact was very brief and very searing. Chelsea snatched her hand back, but not before she noticed how coarse his fingertips felt when they scratched against her much smoother skin.

Her gaze shifted to the chicken that continued to sizzle over the fire. *Anything* to draw her attention away from the way his magnificent blue eyes had darkened with a wicked, teasing light. "Y—you can have the rest as well. I'm not hungry."

"I was hoping you'd say that."

"Of course you were," Chelsea replied, her gaze slowly shifting back to him. Her jaw hardened with realization. "That's why you came over, isn't it? It wasn't to offer me whiskey. That was just an excuse to get into my camp. An excuse to eat my dinner because you're too lazy to cook your own!"

"Not lazy," he corrected between devouring bites of the chicken— *her* chicken, "just not skilled. At least, not when it comes to cooking."

His sly wink, combined with his overtly sensuous tone, shocked Chelsea speechless. Luckily, she didn't need a voice to lift her chin and glare down her nose at him.

"I do brew a pretty mean cup of coffee, though." He raised the half-eaten leg in mock salute. "This is very good, Miss Hogan. Are you sure don't want some whiskey?"

"What I want is for you to get off my land. Now!"

"Can't. I'm not done eating."

Chelsea huffed with disgust and drew her knees up to her chest. In angry, jerking motions, she encircled her shins with her arms, hugging her legs close. "Bring it with you. Please. I won't mind. In fact, I insist."

Mitch sighed, as though he contemplated doing just that, then shook his head. "Nah. Wouldn't be very neighborly of me."

Neighbors. The word shot through Chelsea's mind with all the force of an exploding cannon—as, she had a feeling, was Mitch Bryant's intent. Dear Lord, she was going to be living right next door to this man for at least the next five years! Perhaps longer.

She shivered. The thought didn't bear contemplating.

"Cold?" The single word was taunting, since the tone behind it said the night was too warm and beautiful to be chilled by it.

"No," she snapped through gritted teeth. She glanced over her shoulder, her glare hot and stormy. "Are you done yet?"

"Not hardly." His gaze dropped, raking her hunched form from fiery copper head to bare, curled-in toes. The burning in his eyes left no room for doubt as to what his next words meant, though they were offered innocently enough. "I haven't touched the breast yet, but the legs are damned good."

Chelsea gulped. Her cheeks flamed when her gaze dropped to where his eyes had settled—and settled hard. When she'd drawn her knees up, she'd been too distracted to pay close enough attention to where the hem of her skirt had drifted. It now rested at mid-calf. The exposed skin smoldered under his gaze before she primly jerked the skirt in place.

"You're getting on my nerves, Mr. Bryant," she informed him tightly and as haughtily as her spiraling senses would allow.

"I don't see why, Miss Hogan," he replied. "All I did was compliment your cooking." Mitch lifted the bottle to his lips. Their gazes clashed over the top of the glass. He wasn't sure which was hotter—the whisky that burned a path down his throat or the fire in the sexy redhead's furious amber eyes.

Again, he offered her the bottle. Again, Chelsea shook her head in silent refusal. As tempting as the numbing relief the whiskey offered was, she thought she would do well to keep her senses sharp when near this man.

Mitch shrugged, took another fiery sip, then replaced the bottle at his side. He used the other hand to toss away the chicken bone. "Mind my asking why you've never tasted whiskey?"

Chelsea eyed him carefully. "Did I say that?"

"You didn't have to. Your horrified expression every time you look at my bottle says it for you. You aren't a very good liar, Miss Hogan."

"I don't lie. And, since *you* were the one who said not to tell you I'd never tasted the stuff, I didn't tell you." He grinned, and Chelsea tried to ignore the way her heart flip-flopped beneath her breasts.

"Ah," he said with a knowing nod, "snared by a technicality. I'll try again." His gaze pierced her, his grin abruptly gone. "Have you ever drank whiskey, Miss Hogan?"

"No."

"Why not?"

"I wasn't allowed to." His dark brows rose as he leaned over and removed the spit from the fire. Reluctantly, Chelsea elaborated. "My father was a Baptist preacher. Whiskey wasn't allowed under his roof, nor was anyone who drank it.

"A preacher, huh?" He slipped the chicken from the spit, then tossed the stick aside as though it were a bare bone. He passed the chicken from hand to large, calloused hand as he waited for it to cool. "Whereabouts?"

She shrugged awkwardly. "Everywhere, at one time or another. Papa traveled to wherever he thought souls needed to be salvaged the most. We never stayed in one place very long before moving on."

"To find more souls to salvage?"

"Yes," she replied uncomfortably. The memories he was dredging up were not pleasant ones.

Mitch nibbled on the steamy piece of chicken, his gaze never leaving the woman's face. Her expression had tightened, her shoulders had stiffened. Everything about her small body was coiled and tense. He wondered why. His next question was aimed at getting the answer. "Where is he now, this preacher father of yours? Out salvaging more souls?"

"Something like that," she murmured flatly. There was no hiding the pain in her eyes. She didn't try, though she did turn away so Mitch Bryant wouldn't see it. "My father's dead. Right now his body is buried a few feet under California soil."

The steamy piece of chicken scraped uncomfortably down Mitch's whiskey-raw throat. It wasn't the answers he'd expected. "And your mother?"

Chelsea inhaled sharply, hoping to counter the acute, stabbing pain in her chest. Her hands fisted tightly in the coarse folds of her skirt. "Buried somewhere in Nebraska." She almost stopped the tale there but, feeling a sudden need to lash out, added, "My mother was a week late in delivering my sister when two . . . unsalvageable souls shot her. They were after my father, but their aim was a bit off. It was only by the grace of God that mother lived long enough to give birth. She died before she ever saw Emmy."

Chelsea cleared her throat and looked away. Hiding

74

the pain that sliced through her heart wasn't easy, but she did it. "Are you done eating yet, Mr. Bryant?"

"Yeah," Mitch muttered. "I'm done."

He'd barely started on the chicken breast. Suddenly, he had no taste for it. The last bite had landed in his stomach like a chunk of lead, and Mitch was smart enough to know the reason why.

He harbored no illusions about what had burned away his normally hearty appetite: guilt that he'd caused the pain in Ch—Chelsea Hogan's pretty brown eyes. The emotion, as unusual as it was sharp, twisted in his gut. It was strong enough that, had he been standing, it would have landed him on his knees—but that might have been from the shock of having felt it at all.

"Are you riding into Guthrie tomorrow to file your claim?" he asked, his voice oddly hoarse as he tossed the chicken aside.

"I was planning to. Why?"

"No reason. I just thought that if you were going—and of course I am—that . . ."

"We could go together?" she finished for him. Chelsea glanced over her shoulder, wondering what had put that thread of uncertainty in a voice she never expected to hear it in. There was no reading his face. Hard and chiseled, it guarded his emotions like a thick brick wall. "Do you think that's a good idea?"

"Hell no," he answered quickly. Too quickly. "I was going to suggest I file the claim for you. I'm going in anyway. Might as well save you the trip."

Chelsea's eyes narrowed. "Why would you do that?"

His grin was a quick, disarming flash of white against the blackness of his beard and mustache. "To repay you for supper."

"The same supper you tricked me into providing you with?"

"Yup. That's the one."

"You don't owe me anything, Mr. Bryant. It's not as though you pulled a gun on me and demanded I hand

75

over my chicken."

His grin broadened. "True, but I thought about it."

Chelsea's lips twitched with a smile that she was hard put to suppress. His grin was charming; her reaction to it was frightening. "Then maybe you owe me something after all. But you'll have to think of another way to repay me. I have supplies I need to purchase and a sister to collect."

"No problem. You describe her, I'll find her. As for the supplies . . . write out a list. Yes, Miss Hogan, I *can* read," he added at her skeptical glance. "Besides, it might be a good idea for one of us to stay behind. Keep an eye on things here, just in case someone gets it into his head he deserves these homesteads more than we do."

His logic had its merits. Chelsea was annoyed to realize just how reasonable the suggestion was—especially since it had been offered by a man who didn't have the common sense to fix his own dinner. Or bring someone along who knew how.

"I don't know," she answered hesitantly. "There's no telling what Emmy will do if a strange man comes along to collect her." She would go with him, Chelsea thought. No questions asked—especially if the man were as handsome as this one. That was Emmy. "And the supplies I need are extensive. Enough timber to start work on a cabin, nails, that sort of thing. They won't fit on your horse."

"And they'll fit on yours?"

Chelsea sent him a scathing glare. "I have a wagon to carry them in. My sister's watching it."

His grin came annoyingly easily. "Like I said. No problem."

"You aren't going to take no for an answer, are you, Mr. Bryant?"

His lips, sensuously thin and whiskey-wet, pursed beneath the curl of his enticing raven-black mustache. He shook his head. "And you can call me Mitch. I think we know each other well enough now."

76

His gaze smoldered, leaving no doubt in Chelsea's mind that he was referring to the kiss they'd shared earlier. A kiss that *still*, even in retrospect, disturbed her beyond reason.

Chelsea tore her gaze away and pushed to her feet. She had a sudden need to burn off excess energy. "No," she said abruptly. Then, stronger, "I'll ride into Guthrie myself. If there's a claim to be filed on this land, *I* intend to file it."

She heard, rather than saw him get to his feet. The heat of his body—warm and exciting—melted through the homespun as he materialized at her side. Chelsea turned her head, surprised when her eyes came level with the shelf of his unbelievably broad shoulders. Suddenly, she felt small, daintier than she ever had in her life. It as an uncomfortable feeling.

"What's the matter, Ch—Chelsea Hogan? Don't you trust me?"

His words, while offered innocently enough, had an edge to them. An edge that made her breath catch. The breath, she was dismayed to find, was rich with a mysterious, musky male scent that reeked havoc with her senses.

"You've given me no reason to trust you," she answered cautiously, her gaze lifting. She was captured by his dark, probing eyes. But, she had to admit, even that was better than what she'd been doing, which was staring at his mouth and remembering . . .

Her chin tilted up, her voice sharpened. "Only a fool would trust a complete stranger. And since I don't know you . . ."

"Do you want to know me, sweetheart?" A seductive pause was followed by a low, throaty, "Do you want to know me *well?*"

"Sweet heavens, no," she gasped, and would have taken a sanity-saving step backward if only her feet had been working.

His grin was reckless. It didn't touch his eyes, which

continued to bore into her. "Pity. Could have been fun if you had. Ah, well," he shrugged, and plowed his fingers through his hair, "I guess I'll stop by in the morning to pick you up then."

Chelsea, who had been operating under tense sensations she couldn't even begin to comprehend, did something she rarely did. She lost her temper. "Are you deaf, Mr. Bryant, as well as stubborn?" she screamed. "I said I have a sister to collect and supplies to buy."

Mitch rolled back on his boot heels, hooking his thumbs in his belt loops. His ears were still ringing from her unnaturally loud voice. "I heard you, lady," he growled, "but you obviously didn't hear me. I said I'm riding into Guthrie anyway. If we both have to make the trip, there's no reason we can't make it together. You know what they say about safety in numbers."

No reason? *Safety?* But she didn't feel safe anywhere near this man! And she had not only *one* good reason for not going with him, she had *several:* the way his incredible blue eyes not only looked at her, but through her; the way he sent a tingle coursing down her spine with nothing more than a glance; the disturbing, unremitting thoughts of his kiss and the way her mouth still smoldered with the memory of it; the way—*heaven help her!*—she wanted to feel that sharp, spiraling sensation again.

She couldn't go with him. *She didn't trust herself to be near him!* That realization packed a punch hard enough to make Chelsea's head spin. She staggered back a step, her fingers fluttering at her throat.

Yes, she thought again, if Mitch Bryant arrived to collect Emmy, her sister would go with him. What woman in her right mind wouldn't follow a man like this to the ends of the earth? Me, she thought. *I wouldn't follow him to water if I were a horse dying of thirst.* Her gaze fixed on his lips. *Or would I?*

And then she couldn't think of anything at all, for his hand had come up, cupping her jaw, dragging her unwilling gaze to his.

"Chelsea," he said, his voice deep and husky. His whiskey-laden breath washed hotly over her cheeks. His lips hovered mere inches from her own. All she would have to do to feel them pressing hungrily against her would be to stand on tiptoe and lean forward.

Her breath caught as she stammered, "Y—yes."

His eyes darkened, his gaze devouring her softly parted lips. His whisper was ragged. "What time is breakfast?"

Her stormy glare won her only a deep, pleasant-sounding chuckle. The sound, as nice as it was, scraped against her raw nerves. Chelsea fought an overpowering urge to lash out and kick his arrogant shin. "I think you should leave, Mr. Bryant, while you still have legs to walk on."

"In a minute." His laughter died. Not a trace of it could be had in either his eyes or his expression as his lips made a slow, sensuous descent.

Chelsea, seeing his intent and frightened witless by it, made to step away. His arm snaked out, coiling around her waist. With a breathless gasp, she found herself being yanked against warm, hard river-dampened hips and thighs. Her gaze lifted.

"You looked disappointed," Mitch explained, his voice husky and sharp as he answered the question swimming in her large amber eyes. "And I make it a habit to never, *never* disappoint a lady."

Chelsea opened her mouth. Her reply—which would have been appropriately stinging, she was sure of it—was swallowed up by his warm, moist lips.

Like the last one, this kiss was hard and thorough. He didn't just kiss her lips, his mouth consumed them. His tongue plunged and swirled, demanded and coaxed. And when he won the response he was after—embarrassingly quickly—he ended it.

Chelsea leaned weakly against the firm wedge of his chest, grateful for the steadying strength of it. His heart drummed beneath her cheek, the tempo wild and erratic.

She tried not to notice that its frantic beat was echoed by her own as she attempted to catch her panting breaths. The kiss had been short and masterful, her reaction to it something she would no doubt dwell on long into the warm, lonely night.

"Good night, Ch—Chelsea Hogan," he sighed into her hair. His warm breath kissed her tingling scalp as his lips grazed the crown of her head. She thought she felt him shiver, but she might have been mistaken. "Pleasant dreams."

His hand slipped from where it branded her waist. The chest beneath her melted away. It was only force of will that kept her standing on knees that had the consistency of running water.

Chelsea watched his broad back and the cocky swagger of his hips as he melded into the shadows. He didn't look back. She wasn't surprised.

Collecting her tattered wits about her, she wrapped her arms around her unusually cold, slightly damp waist, then turned toward her makeshift tent. She would douse the fire and bury the rest of dinner later so that animals wouldn't be tempted to investigate. Right now, she needed some time alone to think . . . and to recover.

It was going to be a very long night.

Chapter Six

The air was crisp with the promise of rain. Heavy grey clouds rolled across the sky lazily, as though they hadn't quite decided whether the waves of knee-high bluestem deserved a good dousing.

Chelsea sat atop her paint pony, trying to keep her gaze trained at the prairie stretching endlessly toward the horizon. But it was not an easy chore. Especially when the tantalizing sight of Mitch Bryant, his rugged body swaying atop the massive stallion, kept dragging at her attention time and again.

Yesterday's trousers, she noted, had been traded for a pair of weathered denims. As though God had answered her prayers, these were bone-dry. A blue cotton shirt hugged his shoulders, the fit roomy and loose. At least it appeared to be, until a gust of prairie breeze snapped the enticing folds over the firm wedge of his chest. Over and over she watched the cotton mold over hard muscles that she was still trying to forget the feel of as they glided beneath her open hand.

The silence between them was tense and strained. But then, it had been that way even before they'd mounted up.

Last night's kiss had not faded from Chelsea's mind. Nor had the one before it. Neither had dulled. The memory tainted her every glimpse of him clinging to the saddle, and more than once she'd found herself grateful for the hat riding low on his sun-kissed brow. The shadows beneath spared her the humiliation of being caught in the act of sending him sly, speculative glances—of which there had been far too many.

Mitch was aware of every one. Each time those large amber eyes shifted his way, he knew it. The raven hairs at his nape prickled, his gut tightened, and a peculiar flood of warmth raced down his spine. Her gaze would shift again, and he would be suffused with an unfamiliar emptiness, a sudden coolness that had nothing to do with the sun dipping behind a cloud.

Why the hell had he suggested they ride into Guthrie together? he stormed inwardly. Oh, he knew why. His reasoning just didn't make much sense in the clear light of day.

In his own peculiar way, he'd meant to make restitution for causing her sadness the night before. Of course, there was the added benefit that, should Dobbs make an appearance, he'd be nearby. Damn it, his reasons *had* been sound. But . . .

He should have *followed* her, not ridden *with* her. When he'd made the suggestion, Mitch hadn't counted on the fact it would be a two day ride in and another two back. The four days alone with her were no problem. *I'll just ignore the way her coarse brown trousers hug that tempting little rump. Yup, doesn't bother me a bit!* Not so easily ignored were the two long nights he'd yet to face in the sexy little redhead's company. Ah, now, *that* prospect was disturbing as hell.

The jaw beneath the beard clamped hard. His fingers tightened on the reins as he glanced to the side.

Their eyes locked. Inquisitive amber clashed with taunting blue. The connection was short and blessedly brief. The color that stained soft, feminine cheeks a guilty pink lasted a whole lot longer.

"You never said why you decided to settle in Oklahoma," Chelsea said, thinking that if she had to endure another moment of this tense silence she'd scream.

82

"You never asked," Mitch replied grumpily. The whiskey he'd drunk the night before had left him with a dull, throbbing hangover. The ache in his temples was increased by the warmth of the sun penetrating his hat and the rhythmic jostle of the horse beneath him.

Chelsea bit back an angry remark. This stubborn man was not making conversation very easy. With a toss of her head, she sent him what she hoped was a scathing glare. "I'm asking you now, Mr. Bryant. Why are you settling in Oklahoma?" *And why on the claim next to mine?* she wanted to add, but didn't.

His shrug was casual as he guided the stallion to keep pace with her paint pony. "Why not?"

Her gaze narrowed. "That's hardly an answer."

"Yeah? Well, that's too damn bad, lady, because it's the only one you're getting." With a flick of his wrist, he moved his horse away and in front of her.

Chelsea was left with nothing but his back to glare at—his firm, rigid, muscular back. What *was* the man's problem? She was only trying to be civil. She'd hoped some pleasant small talk would relieve the tension that had been building since they'd left their claims. No matter what he thought, she was *not* trying to pry into his personal life!

She let a little time slip past, then tried again. This time, she changed tactics. "What happened to your lady friend?" She could have bitten her tongue off—especially when he sent that smug look over his shoulder.

"Jealous?"

She groaned and looked away.

Mitch bit back a smile—he didn't feel much like smiling this morning—and eased his mount back until he was riding at her side again. Not close enough for their thighs to touch, but close enough for the searing contact to be a threat.

"My lady friend, as you call her, is probably out filing her own claim right about now," he answered finally, his gaze trained on the horizon. A ghost of a smile he couldn't suppress tugged at the corners of his mouth. "At least, I presume that's what she's doing. I'm not the possessive sort, Miss Hogan. I don't keep constant tabs on her."

"How . . . enlightening." Chelsea's lips thinned and her eyes flashed with irritation. She countered the urge to slap him by telling herself he would no doubt snatch her wrist before she could carry out the gesture. Pity. Her palm itched to wipe that condescending grin off his face.

A toss of her head sent the long, thick copper plait bobbing at her waist. Chelsea turned her attention to the front and refused to so much as look at him. He was teasing her, she knew, but there was a cruel edge to the game he was playing that, even though she couldn't exactly put her finger on it, aggravated her to no end.

Instead of feeling relieved that his teasing had shut off her prying questions, Mitch felt oddly annoyed. He didn't feel like talking, that much was true. His body hurt from tossing on the ground all night, and his head wasn't faring much better. The last thing he wanted was to spend the rest of the afternoon dodging questions he knew damn well he couldn't answer.

Still, he'd be lying if he said he didn't like the way her voice tickled his ears. Something in her husky tone eased the banging in his head—if only by default because it was distracting as hell. And he could, with effort, turn the small talk to his own advantage. He also had to admit to a nagging curiosity about what would prompt two single women to seek out a homestead in the wilds of Oklahoma. The risks were great, the hardships yet to be faced greater. Yet none of that seemed to bother the tiny redhead who was now brooding silently beside him.

Mitch Bryant wanted to know why. And Mitch Bryant was a man used to getting what he wanted.

From the shadows beneath his hat, he sent her a sidelong glance. Her profile was strained and tight, her huge amber gaze focused firmly ahead. Her hair was pulled back in a thick braid that ribboned down her rigid back.

The sun peeked from behind a cloud. The golden rays played over each strand, enhancing and highlighting until the cloud of hair begged him to loosen the fiery coil and drag his fingers through its promised softness.

Mitch cleared his throat. "You never said what brought *you* to these parts, Miss Hogan?"

"Didn't I?" she countered. If he wouldn't tell her anything about himself or his reasons for coming here, she'd be darned if she'd tell him her own. Shrugging, she added, "An oversight on my part, I'm sure. Either that"—her gaze swept to him, her eyes narrowing meaningfully—"or I didn't think it was any of your business."

A gloved hand raised to the brim of his hat. He tipped it ever so slightly, grinning broadly. "Touché Ch—Chelsea Hogan." His grin broadened as he repeated, softer, lower, "Touché."

The subject wasn't brought up again until they'd stopped for the night. A campfire snapped in a bed of rocks as the sun made a flashy exit on the horizon. The rain had yet to start, but Chelsea had a feeling it wouldn't be long now. The crackling, acidy expectancy of it was in the air, she noted as she sat silently beside Mitch Bryant's sinewy form.

And speaking of crackling expectancy . . .

"Best rabbit I've ever eaten, Miss Hogan," Mitch said as he set his plate aside.

"And, as you warned me, you brew a mean cup of coffee. More?" she asked, pushing her own barely touched meal toward him. Behind them, the stallion snorted as it caught a distant rumble of thunder. Their fingers brushed. Chelsea stiffened and tried to ignore the sizzle of alarm that ripped up her spine. She failed miserably.

Mitch took the offered plate with a nod. His gaze raked her suddenly pale face. Her eyes, normally large, looked huge, the hazy orange fingers of dusk playing in their frightened depths. Was it the approaching storm that was bothering her, he wondered, or the touch?

Her stomach knotted, her gaze shifting between Mitch

and the makeshift tent he'd constructed behind them. The tent was small; it would be crowded with one person in it, never mind two.

There was only one tent.

Another rumble of thunder echoed. Shivering, she pulled the sheepskin collar of her coat up high beneath her chin. The thick folds were warm against the night's coolness. Comforting. She was glad she'd thought to bring it.

"Cold?" Mitch asked before popping the last of the meat into his mouth. It had the flavor of chalk for all he tasted of it. His mind was occupied with Ch—Chelsea Hogan's suddenly wary expression and the way she nearly jumped out of her skin at the sound of his voice.

"C—c—cold?" she stammered, before catching herself. "No, of course not. It's a beautiful night."

"Hmmm, beautiful," Mitch murmured, and tore his gaze away from her finely chiseled profile. He scraped the last of his beans off the plate with his fork but didn't scoop them into his mouth. His appetite had disappeared the second he'd seen large amber eyes glancing anxiously toward the tent.

"Where'd you get the coat?" Mitch asked suddenly, thinking the subject of her oddly masculine coat *had* to be better than the one his mind had just settled on. "Not that it's any of my business."

"It was my father's," she answered softly, then startled when another, louder clap of thunder echoed through the air.

What on earth is wrong with me? Chelsea wondered. The swiftly approaching storm was a part of her nervousness—but only a very small part. She was used to the sound of thunder. It usually didn't bother her much. Certainly it had never bothered her to this extent! Whatever the cause, she knew she had to stop shaking and jumping at every little noise. The last thing she wanted was for this man to see how uneasy she was.

Mitch studied her carefully, noting the way the slender

86

shoulders, buried beneath so much padding, were trembling. Her gaze reflected the horizon and the jagged bolt of lightning that cut down from the sky. Her eyes widened, then snapped tightly closed.

"Your father's coat, huh?" he asked, trying to distract her before another clap of thunder could be heard. The storm was getting closer. No doubt about it.

"Didn't I just say that?" Chelsea's heart skipped. Her fingers tightened in thick folds of cloth when her gaze shifted and was met with a flash of white teeth between the beard and mustache. The growing darkness made the sight all the more breathtaking. Another clap of thunder might have reverberated through the air. She was never sure, for it might well have been the sudden racket her heart was making in her chest.

Mitch didn't mean to reach out and drag the back of his knuckles down her pale cheek. When he felt the cool satin-soft skin gliding beneath the heat of his hand, he was damn glad he'd done it. His fingers slipped down, toying with the sheepskin collar. His gaze dropped to her small fingers, and he noted the way they trembled as she clutched at the collar.

"A preacher's coat," he murmured with a wry twist of his lips. His brilliant blue eyes caught the fading light, and they sparkled devilishly. "Does that mean it's sacred?"

Chelsea stiffened and slapped at his hand. It didn't budge. She hadn't thought it would. "What it means, Mr. Bryant, is that it's warm. Are you done eating? If not, I suggest you hurry. I'd like to get the dishes washed and put away before the rain. . . ." Her words drifted off when the storm's first raindrop made its presence know by splashing on the tip of her nose.

"Leave them," Mitch said. His hand dropped back to his lap, but his knuckles still smoldered. Damned if they didn't!

"But—"

"I said leave them," he snapped. "What the rain doesn't

clean, I'll wash in the morning."

"Washing dishes is women's work," she said. Another drop splashed on her cheek. Two plunked atop her head. A few dampened the coat hanging from her shoulders. "Since you shot the—"

"And you cooked the—" His jaw clamped hard, the rest of his words coming from between gritted teeth. "Damn it, lady, as much as I'd like to sit here arguing with you . . . I'm getting wet. Now come on!"

With a litheness that no longer surprised her, he uncurled his rugged frame and towered over her. His calloused hand was extended to help her up. Chelsea ignored it, pushing to her feet and spinning on her heel. The second she saw the tent, she froze. Her resolve channeled into alarm. It burned through her by slow, hot, frightening degrees.

"What's the matter, Ch—Chelsea Hogan?" his taunting voice asked, close enough to her ear for her to feel—and react to—the hot wash of his breath. "You aren't afraid, are you?"

"Afraid?" she squeaked. She was shaking visibly now. Even the folds of her coat, the bulky hem of which grazed mid-calf, couldn't hide it. "No," she added, her voice a bit stronger. "Why should I be?"

His only answer was a husky chuckle that rippled right up her quivering spine.

The rain, now that it had been given freedom to fall, was coming down harder. The drops pattered as they hit the bed of bluestem. The ground would be soaked soon. If they stood there much longer, so would they.

Chelsea gave a toss of her damp head and took a reluctant step toward the canvas shelter. It was crude and quickly built, but it would serve the purpose. If only it were a bit larger!

"Come on," Mitch growled, grabbing her by the upper arm and propelling her toward the tent. "You might not have enough sense to come in out of the rain, but I damn well do."

The gruffness in his tone was born by the image of what would happen if the silly chit *did* get wet. She'd have to take off her damp clothes, of course, or risk coming down with a fever. Her stripping was something Mitch didn't think he could stand to watch—especially in the close confines of that tent!

"I can walk," she argued, but to no avail.

His strides were long, determined. She had to take three to keep pace with each of his own. By the time they reached the tent, Chelsea had only enough air in her panting lungs to yelp in protest as she was shoved roughly through the canvas opening. The ground was warm and dry. It hit her backside with a thump.

Mitch ducked outside, then returned a few seconds later.

"Was that necessary?" Chelsea snapped when he scooted beneath the canvas. His rugged body seemed to take up the entire much-too-small enclosure, leaving her precious little room to move without . . . without . . . well, *touching* him.

"Yeah, it was," he growled. Through the shadows, his blue eyes blazed into her. "I don't know where the hell you come from, lady, but in these parts we don't stand around flapping our gums in the rain when there's a nice warm tent to be had."

A nice warm tent that is only large enough for one person, Chelsea thought, but said, "I've seen rain in every part of the country I've traveled to, Mr. Bryant."

His lips twitched with a wry grin. "Is that a fact? Then maybe you'd care to explain, Miss Hogan, why the hell you were standing there looking at this tent like it was a snake?"

"I . . . er . . . didn't want to leave the dishes dirty." It was only a half truth. They both knew it, but Chelsea would rather die than admit it. She quickly added, "Papa was always very firm that I clean up the supper dishes before I go to—"

Bed. She gulped, unable to say it, unable to even think

it. She thought about it anyway, and her thoughts did not please her.

Her cheeks flamed a warm, vibrant scarlet when her gaze dropped to the bedroll tucked beneath his sinewy arm. She hadn't noticed it. She noticed it now, though, and it reminded her of the one still strapped to her own saddlebag. The one that was probably soaked clean through by now.

One tent. One bedroll. One devilishly handsome man. One woman who was frightened beyond reason. And she thought *last* night had been long!

Thunder rumbled in the distance. The sound was overridden by Chelsea's heart throbbing in her ears.

Slowly, her gaze lifted and locked with probing, brilliant blue. She swallowed hard as the memory of last night's long, sleepless hours skittered through her churning mind. Dear Lord, if she'd lain awake last night, tossing and turning with only *thoughts* of this man to plague her, what could she expect from tonight?

Mitch's gaze narrowed. Some of her hair had worked itself free of the plait. The soft wisps framed her delicate face in damp copper waves. The sight reminded him of the one that had greeted him when he'd woken her up at dawn. She'd looked sweeter than a woman ought to look first thing in the morning, he thought in retrospect. And sexy as all hell.

Chelsea backed as far away from him as the canvas wall would allow. It wasn't very far, and definitely wasn't as far as she would have liked.

Mitch watched her go but didn't trust himself to stop her.

"Are you cold?" he asked again when he saw her shiver. He thought of the way she had looked before he'd woken her up. The way she'd pillowed her cheek with her hands, just like a child.

Chelsea looked at the bedroll he offered to her as though it were a bottle of home-brewed whiskey. Mutely, she shook her head. She thought of the tight black pants that had clung to his thighs the night before and the way the play of firelight had hid nothing from view.

"Coffee?" he asked, his voice oddly husky. The briefest of blinks brought the memory of her expression that morning when he'd offered her the pot he'd brewed at his own camp across the river. *You know how to build a fire!* her amber eyes had teased—before she'd caught herself and frowned.

Chelsea glanced down at the hand he extended to her. His fingers were wrapped around a half-filled cup of steaming coffee, apparently rescued from the rain—something else she hadn't noticed. The smell of the coffee—*the coffee, Chelsea, not the man!*—was strong and pungent and tempting.

She reached for the cup, remembering the way he'd grinned at her that morning when she'd accepted his peculiar peaceoffering. A pot of freshly brewed coffee. *I'm not completely incompetent,* those incredible blue eyes had taunted.

"Thank you," she murmured, lifting the cup to her lips. The taste of the coffee on her tongue was harsh but welcome. He hadn't lied, she thought as the warm liquid trickled down her throat. His coffee was very good.

Her gaze dropped to his shoulders. Even the baggy shirt couldn't hide their broadness, their sinewy male firmness. She bit back a groan. After breakfast he'd bathed in the river. The rustling cloth no longer held any secrets from her.

Her fingers trembled as she passed the cup back to him. "What about the horses?" she asked, and thought her voice sounded oddly high, slightly breathless, and very shaky. Had he noticed?

He had. He noticed everything. Mitch held her gaze over the rim of the cup as he downed a sip. Her eyes; rich pools of deeply expressive amber. His body still smoldered with the feel of those eyes running over his naked chest and back, searing his waist and countering the effects of the cold water he'd splashed over his skin.

"The horses will be fine," he said, lowering the cup to a lap Chelsea was smart enough not to look at. "I built a lean-to for them earlier. It isn't much, but it'll do."

As she nodded, her gaze peeled away the thin layer of his shirt. Skin, tinged bronze from long hours beneath the sun, stretched taut beneath. Firm and rippling. Perfectly formed. She sucked in an uneven breath, remembering the way his skin had gleamed with moisture, the icy river water forming crystal droplets against a backdrop of sun-kissed flesh.

"H—how long before we reach Guthrie?" she asked, snuggling within the folds of her coat. As if a mere coat could protect her from *that* probing gaze!

"Sometime tomorrow, depending on when the rain lets up."

"Oh."

His hair had been appealing tousled, she remembered. Kissed by morning sun, the dark strands glistened. Her palm had itched to reach out and smooth a stray curl from his brow. She'd done no such thing, of course, for that would have meant leaving the protective covering of cottonwoods. But she *had* thought about it.

"And if the rain doesn't let up soon?" she asked hesitantly.

He shrugged. "Better get used to sharing cramped quarters then, lady. We won't be leaving until it stops."

Mitch remembered the exact moment she'd backed away from the cottonwoods and scurried back to camp. It was when he'd started to loosen his belt buckle. She'd run like a frightened rabbit—or an innocent girl. In her haste, she hadn't attempted to cover the sound of leaves crunching beneath her feet, the snap of twigs breaking, the stumbling noise of feet running blindly.

The rain pattered loudly against the canvas. The sound was comforting, yet at the same time confining. It was, after all, the reason Chelsea now found herself alone with this man. "Are—are you planning to stay the entire five years on your claim?" she asked suddenly.

"I expect to. It's not like I have anywhere else to go."

She nodded weakly. "I guess that gives us something in common then. Neither do I."

It was hard to squeeze words out of her suddenly tight throat, but she had to say *something*. She needed a distraction from the memory of his hand reaching for his belt buckle. It wasn't that image alone that stuck with her, though. He'd turned his back on her then, as though he'd known she was standing there watching. It was his back she remembered now, and the scars she'd glimpsed etching his flesh. There were three in all; one beneath his shoulder blade, one hugging the left side of his waist, the third riding the lean hip that dipped beneath the waistband of his trousers. All were healed bullet holes.

Chelsea had wanted to ask him about them but couldn't. To do so would put her in the awkward position of having to explain how she knew they were there. She doubted a man like Mitch Bryant would welcome the news that he had been spied upon while bathing. Wasn't it bad enough she was being eaten alive by acute embarrassment for having done it in the first place?

"You tired yet?" Mitch asked before draining the last of the coffee. The cup was tossed unceremoniously out of the tent. It rattled when it hit the ground. The rain *pinked* off the tin sides. "If the storm lets up, we'll be heading out early in the morning. I suggest we get some sleep."

"Sleep," Chelsea echoed. The idea would have been laughable were he not so serious. Her chin lifted haughtily. She wondered how she accomplished it. Haughty was not how she felt right now. Breathless, nervous, anxious, *that* would have been a better description. "Mr. Bryant, if you think for one minute that I . . . that you and I . . . that *we* . . ."

She swallowed hard and watched him squirm beneath the canvas. The largeness of his body worked against him when he tried to spread the bedroll out over the hard-packed ground. Her stuttering words made him glance up, and his taunting gaze made her shiver in the folds of her coat.

"Mitch," he said, his voice a soft, husky caress. "I told you before, call me Mitch."

"I don't want to call you—" The thunder had stopped. Chelsea only noticed the absence now because she saw a bolt of lightning light up the canvas behind Mitch's back. The flash was followed immediately by a clap of thunder loud enough to make the ground beneath her tremble. Her own trembling was just as real, just as quick, and just as violent.

Mitch's hands snaked out. In an instant he'd wrapped his fingers around her upper arms and dragged her forcibly onto his lap. She felt small against him, fragile. Her entire body quivered, and he instinctively tightened his hold.

Chelsea was enfolded in his strong embrace before she knew what was happening. But even once she did realize it, it never occurred to her to push away the warmth and security he offered. Sucking in a ragged breath, she fisted tight folds of his shirt and pressed her cheek hard against his chest. His heart drummed in her ear. The sound was rhythmic, and as comforting as the strong arms coiled around her.

Another clap of thunder shook the night. Chelsea's whimper was soft and plaintive, gnawing at Mitch's gut. Her copper hair was silky, fragrant. The wayward strands kissed his sensitive cheek like wisps of satin. The scalp beneath was warm, and he thought that even it trembled as he nuzzled into her soothingly.

"Damn it!" he muttered, even as he turned his face and let his lips glide across the top of her head. *Damn it to hell!* The woman was frightened senseless, and he had no experience with hysterical women—except to keep as much distance between himself and them as possible. But there was precious little room to run from her in the close confines of the tent.

The whiskey. The bottle, half gone, was still in his saddlebag. Briefly, Mitch weighed the possibility of going to fetch it. Would it be worth the dousing he was sure to get the second he stepped outside the tent if she wouldn't even take a sip of the stuff? he wondered.

And then he thought of how soft and round her bottom felt pressing into his lap. How hot her ragged breaths felt as they seeped through his shirt. How slender her arms were in his hands, even beneath the padding of the coat sleeves. The feel of her breasts straining against his chest was what finally clinched the decision. It was worth the dousing. She might not drink the whiskey, but damned if he couldn't use a good belt of it right about now!

Mitch lowered his head until his lips grazed her ear. "Chelsea?" he whispered softly, soothingly. "Chelsea, baby, I'm going to leave for a minute, but I'll be right back. Will you be all right?"

Her answer was a breathless sob, as another bolt of lightning lit up the tent, and a tentative nod. Didn't he know that it was more than the thunder and lightning that was making her react this way? It was *him!* She was afraid of the feelings he stirred in her. Deathly afraid . . . because, God help her, she *liked* them.

Mitch let the residual clap of thunder recede before he disentangled himself from the clinging woman and disappeared through the tent flap. He tried not to notice the way his body felt suddenly cold without her small form warming him. But he *did* notice. More than he would have liked, he noticed.

True to his word, he was only gone a minute. As he'd expected, it was enough time for him to get soaked. Slicking his wet hair back from his face, he scanned the tent. Chelsea was at the rear, huddled against the canvas wall.

Her quivering stopped the second her gaze touched the amber liquid sloshing inside the bottle. With more bravado than she actually felt, she tilted her chin up and glared at him. "I don't want any of that, Mr. Bryant."

"You don't have a choice, Miss Hogan." Crouching, Mitch rocked back on his haunches and returned her glare. His blue eyes were bright with a determination that more than one man had seen in the past and flinched from respectfully. "I don't care if I have to wrestle you to the ground and pour this down your stubborn little throat, lady, you *are* going to drink it. I didn't go out there and get this wet for nothing."

Wet. The word made her gaze stray down. The second she saw the shirt plastered to his torso, she regretted the impulse. Her heart raced, her breathing shallowed until it was strangled and almost nonexistent. There was no describing the penetrating warmth that seeped through her. The hot, tingly awareness of this man was overpowering. And nerve-shattering.

Perhaps, just this once, whiskey wasn't such a bad idea. Heaven knows it was a much better idea than this man wrestling her to the ground! Although . . .

"Pass me the bottle, please," Chelsea murmured. Her hand shot out, and she almost recoiled at the feel of cold glass being pressed firmly into her grip. Whiskey. My God, she was actually about to drink whiskey. Were her father alive, he would have shot her on the spot for even considering the idea.

"He isn't here to stop you or to see it," Mitch said, reading the thoughts that were so transparent on her face. "And even if he was, it's for medicinal purposes. You're scared to death. The whiskey will help calm you. Now drink."

Bad storms did make her nervous. While the storm outside wasn't bad yet, it sounded like it was going to be. But the storm inside promised to be worse. Chelsea lifted the bottle to her lips. The fumes alone made her eyes water and her nose crinkle. She hesitated, knowing the stuff would undoubtedly taste worse than it smelled. And it smelled pretty awful.

"Drink!" Mitch ordered. Reaching out, he tipped the bottom of the bottle with the pad of his index finger until

Chelsea had no choice but to obey him.

She had meant to take one tiny sip—just to shut him up. What she got was a mouthful of liquid fire. Her throat was raw long before she'd managed to swallow it all down. Her eyes teared, her cheeks flooded a hot red. She dragged a wheezing breath into her lungs, then coughed and gagged. She tried to catch her breath, at the same time not really wanting to since it only made her lungs hurt more.

"The first sip's always the worst," a husky voice said from somewhere Chelsea couldn't place because she refused to pry open her tightly closed eyelids. "The next one will go down easier."

She opened her mouth to tell the arrogant man that she had no intention of taking a second drink. But she never got the chance. The bottle was pressed to her mouth and she was swallowing down another sip of the god-awful whiskey before she could voice a protest. Then another.

She sat back for a few moments in mute shock. He was right. The second sip did go down easier. And the first one had created an odd sensation in her stomach that she was only now beginning to notice. The feeling was nice, warm, tingly. It started in the sizzling pit of her stomach and seeped in very slow, numbing waves through her blood.

"Did you hear that?" Mitch asked. His voice was close enough for his breath to stir the wisps clinging to his brow.

"Hear what?" she asked, distracted. Resting her head back against the canvas, she opened her eyes and glanced to the side. Her head swam with the quick movement, but the feeling receded when she was captured by a pair of brilliant blue eyes.

He was sitting beside her, she noticed foggily. Closely beside her. His outer thigh grazed her outer thigh. His arm brushed her arm. Funny, she hadn't felt it. She felt it now. Her whole body felt the contact, warming to it.

"The thunder," he elaborated, gently lifting the bottle from her grasp. "It's fading. I think the storm's starting to pass."

"Is it?" she asked. Her voice was steady and calm. She was light-headed, pleasantly so, but not drunk . . . yet. "Funny, I would have sworn the storm was just starting. For us both."

Mitch lifted the bottle to his lips. His gaze never left hers as he tossed down a good, healthy slug. He felt the potency of the whiskey clear down to his toes, and he relished every second of its stinging bite. "Get some sleep, Miss Hogan," he said suddenly. He lowered the bottle, gesturing with it to the bedroll he'd eased over the ground.

"What about you?" she asked, a copper brow sloppily cocked.

"I'll sleep on top of the blanket." He didn't add that he wouldn't trust himself to do anything else. His voice turned low and harsh. "Now get the hell under there and get some sleep before I change my mind."

Chelsea surprised them both by scrambling obediently beneath the bedroll, coat and all. She didn't lie down right away, but propped her weight on one elbow and glanced up at him. He was watching her carefully, his expression tight and guarded.

She didn't realize just how much the whiskey had greased her tongue until she heard herself ask, "Are you going to kiss me again, Mr. Bryant?"

His eyes narrowed to brilliant blue slits. His expression did not change, though the bottle did hesitate on the way to his lips. And were his fingers trembling, or was it the whiskey that made her think so? "Do you want me to kiss you, Miss Hogan?"

Her grin was seductive, born of her first taste of the sin of spirits. It was also appealingly innocent and sweet, missing its mark by a good yard. "Yes," she whispered, softly, huskily, as though she only now realized the answer. "I think I do."

Mitch gulped down that mouthful of whiskey, if only to give himself enough stamina to utter a curt "Go to sleep, woman. If there's any kissing to be done, it'll be done when we both remember it come morning."

"Spoilsport." Chelsea grinned and plopped down on the ground. Perhaps it was the whiskey addling her brain, but she thought Mitch Bryant had looked decidedly uncomfortable with her question. She'd regret having asked it come dawn, no doubt, but for now she found his discomfort intriguing.

So, he wanted to remember having kissed her, did he? Chelsea pillowed her head on the hard ground and closed her eyes. A smile curved over her lips as she began to drift off.

Five minutes. That was her last thought before she let herself go to sleep. Five minutes was all the sleep she'd had the night before, thanks to this man and the tantalizing visions of him that wouldn't let her rest.

Mitch watched her features soften and relax. In sleep, she looked more fragile than she did awake. And that was saying something! *In sleep, she looks every bit the preacher's daughter,* he thought as he wedged the bottle between his thighs and studied her. A sexy little preacher's daughter, true, but a preacher's daughter all the same.

Chapter Seven

"Mitch, are you awake? Please, Mitch, wake up!"

Mitch came out of a dream he had no desire to leave the way he did everything—fast and hard. Unfortunately, though his eyes were open, nothing made any sense to him.

Chelsea was sitting huddled beneath the bedroll to his right, her weight levered on one rigidly straight arm while the other cradled the blanket to her breasts. Her eyes were wide with alarm, and she was staring intently at the tent flap.

Mitch scowled and scratched the jaw beneath his beard. Had he missed something? The last thing he remembered was this woman cuddling sweetly—and perfectly—in his arms the second he'd stretched out atop the bedroll beside her. He could smell the fresh, soapy scent of her in his nostrils, and he remembered her gentle snores in his ear.

But she wasn't snoring now. No, now she was gasping and shoving herself back against the canvas wall.

The gunbelt, heavy with his Colt .45 and a round of fresh ammunition, had been unstrapped from his lean hips seconds before he'd joined Chelsea on the bedroll. It now lay curled atop a bed of trampled bluestem, well within reach. With a whisper of air and an economy of motion, Mitch had the pistol unholstered, the hammer back, and the barrel aimed at the tent flap. The strip of canvas flickered in the early morning breeze. Other than

100

that, he could detect no other movement.

"What the hell am I supposed to be aiming at?" Mitch barked. He turned his head to the side, though his gaze never left the mystery of the tent flap. "What's going on?"

"I heard something out there," Chelsea replied shakily.

"Heard something?" he echoed sarcastically. His customary early morning grumpiness had arrived in force. The bearded jaw clamped hard as he scoured the sleep from his eyes with the heel of his free hand. *"Heard* something? I can't shoot a sound, lady. Can you be a little more specific?"

"It was a—a snap, I think." At his glare, she added more forcefully, "Yes, a definite snap."

Mitch sighed and fought the urge to strangle this woman; getting an answer from her was like yanking teeth. "You want me to shoot a snap? A *particular* 'snap,' or will any one do?"

Chelsea's chin went up. Though her pride stung, she held her ground. "I'm telling you, I heard something out there."

"A snap?"

"Yes, a snap! I think it was a person. Now, are you going to go out there and investigate, or will I?"

"You?" This time Mitch risked taking his eyes off the tent flap. His gaze swept to her, narrowing in disbelief, then widening slightly at her expression. The woman was determined, he had to give her that—even if he couldn't give her credit for a lick of intelligence. "You're kidding me. Right?"

"Wrong." Chelsea gathered the folds of her coat closely about her and made to stand as best she could in such cramped quarters. Even at her diminutive size, her shoulders were hunched so as not to collapse the tent atop them. "If you won't go see what's out there, I will."

Mitch chuckled. It was a cold, sarcastic sound that sliced straight up Chelsea's hunched spine. "Without a gun?"

She glared down her nose at him. Her indignation

101

seemed to have precious little effect. "Of course, without a gun. I won't"—her amber gaze fell to the weapon he brandished so expertly, and a shiver coursed down her spine—"touch one of those things. They kill people."

The lips beneath the mustache twitched, but she never knew if he smiled or sneered, for he turned his back on her then. "Yeah, well, you'd better hope whoever's out there—if anyone *is* out there—feels the same way you do. Most men who carry guns carry them with the intent to use them."

"Even you, Mr. Bryant?" she asked softly, hesitantly. There was something in his tone—hard, cold, uncompromising—that alarmed her. There was something in his next statement that sent an icy chill through her.

"Especially me, Miss Hogan."

Chelsea wanted to ask him what he meant by that. However, she would have needed a voice; and hers had rudely abandoned her. The reason could be easily traced to her suddenly tight throat, together with the image of three puckered scars, lighter than the rest of his sun-kissed back, flashing through her mind. Given the time and circumstances, the memory was less than welcome—and a great deal less than comforting. *"Are* you going out there?"

"Yes, Miss Hogan, I'm going out there," he growled, thrusting himself to a spread-legged squat. "God help me, I am."

Chelsea eased forward two steps, until she was standing directly behind him. The heat of his back seeped through the folds of her trousers, caressing the skin beneath. She ignored that. At least, she tried to.

Her reply was as spontaneous as it was firm. "God only helps those who help themselves, sir."

"Well, if those aren't the words of a true preacher's daughter, I don't know what are," he mumbled under his breath, his tone far from complimentary. "How many other lines like that one have you put to memory, lady?"

"Dozens," Chelsea replied, distracted. Her gaze was focused on the large, calloused hand reaching for the tent flap. Perhaps waking him hadn't been such a good idea, although it had seemed so at the time. What if there *were* men outside, waiting, with — with *guns?* What then?

She didn't want to think that seeing Mitch Bryant gunned down before her very eyes would have any effect on her. She knew better. And not simply because the sight of seeing him die the way her father had would upset her, but because the man doing the dying this time would be Mitch Bryant.

She didn't want him to die. The realization was like a bolt of lightning striking her on the spot. She shivered.

"Mitch?" Chelsea began hesitantly. Her hand came up from her side, the palm poised mere inches from his broad shoulder. The heat he radiated was intense. Her reaction to it was more so. Her hand dropped to her side. "Mitch, maybe you shouldn't go out there. Maybe we should — "

"What?" He sent an annoyed glare over his shoulder. "We should what? Sit here and wait for your 'snap' to come to us?" The ragged fringe of black hair scraped his sleep-wrinkled collar when he shook his head. "Uh-uh. A man doesn't stay alive by sitting and waiting, he stays alive by taking action." His grin was cold, his pause pregnant. "Since I'm still alive to say it . . .that should tell you something."

What it told her was that this man was dangerous. Lethal. That if she had any common sense, she'd get on her horse and ride for Guthrie now — this minute. Leave him behind and never look back. And once she got to Guthrie, she should collect Emmy and buy a ticket on the next train heading out of Oklahoma. Who cared where it was going, just so long it was far away from the confusion that was Mitch Bryant.

She did none of those things. She didn't have time.

Without warning, Mitch ripped the tent flap back and sprang from the opening. Chelsea was awarded a view of virile back, lean hips, and taut legs, all set against a backdrop of bright morning sunshine. It was only a split second flash of sight, for as soon as it was fixed in her vision, he was gone.

Outside she heard the crunch of dirt beneath his heels and . . . yes, she heard a definite snap. It might have been the sound of her patience breaking in two for all the effect it had on her. Propelled into instant motion, she bolted across the tent and burst through the flap.

The morning sun was warm and bright enough to blind her. She felt as though she'd just walked full speed into a hazy yellow wall. Coming to a stand, she commanded her other senses to fill in the gaps where her sight left off. Mitch's musky, easily recognizable scent penetrated her nostrils, mixing with the scent of growing bluestem. Dirt crunched, leaves crinkled, a mockingbird cawed as it flew overhead.

None of these sounds were as loud as that of a rifle being cocked.

Chelsea blinked quickly, striving to clear her vision. Hazy shapes began to form, but she couldn't distinguish a one. All she knew was that the sound had come from somewhere close by.

"Ro — bert! I've got the thieves cornered." The voice was high, shrill, grating. Chelsea felt no great desire for the haze to clear so she could see the woman it emanated from.

"Good work, Erma." Another voice, this one a man's, started at a distance and grew closer. "You're trespassing, stranger. Didn't you see the cornerstone and stake — with *our* name on it? The wife and me own this property now, and we don't cotton to sharing it."

Chelsea began to make out shapes. One was tall and thin as a bean pole; the other was equally as tall but round, in a masculine sort of way. The man?

"Not asking you to share anything, friend," Mitch said. His voice was casual but edged with an emotion Chelsea couldn't put a name to. Nor did she try. Just the comforting sound of his voice was enough to warm her.

"We're not *giving* it to you, either." It was the woman who spoke, and she sounded furious. "You goddamn 'sooners' think you can sneak in here before the official opening and make off with good, honest people's land. *Well!* I won't have it, do you hear? You'll have to shoot us to get this homestead from us—and we don't intend to die easily, *friend.*"

Chelsea rubbed her eyes with her fists, blinked hard, and blessedly saw her vision returning. The thin one, whom she'd originally thought to be the wife, was the husband. He had a bulbous nose and balding salt-and-pepper hair. His scrawny legs and paunchy stomach reminded her of a stuffed pigeon.

The woman had broad shoulders, grey hair tied back in an unflatteringly severe bun, and a rifle pointed directly at Mitch Bryant's heart. It was the rifle that caught and held Chelsea's attention.

"We don't want your property," she blurted out, stepping closer to Mitch's side. He sent her a sideways glance that said she should have stayed in the tent where it was safe. She ignored him, smiling at the peculiar couple instead. "We have land of our own. That's why we're here. We're heading into Guthrie to file a claim."

The woman's eyes narrowed on Chelsea. "Oh really?" she drawled. "And whereabouts is this 'property'?"

"Northwest Quarter Section number 30," Chelsea replied quickly. Then, just to be sure the couple believed her and didn't shoot Mitch, she added, "Our claims border the Sweetwater River."

The woman scowled. "Don't know no homestead that borders the Sweetwater," she mused, but she did lower her rifle.

Chelsea sighed in relief and glanced over at Mitch. The barrel of his pistol hadn't budged. It was still aimed at the plump woman's chest, and his expression was less than trusting.

"Shucks, Erma, you don't know every inch of property around here," the man said just as Chelsea sank her elbow into Mitch's ribs. It was like elbowing a slab of granite. There was no give to him. None at all.

"Maybe not yet," the woman conceded. "But what about the claim Caleb Johnson's staked? Wasn't that—?"

"What'd you do that for?" Mitch hissed in Chelsea's ear, the woman's shrill voice droning on.

"To get your attention. Lower your gun, Mitch, or they'll think you mean to use it."

"Remember what I told you about men who carry guns, lady?"

Chelsea remembered every sarcastically uttered word. She also remembered how expertly the fat woman had wielded her rifle—and where that rifle had been pointed. Didn't Mitch care that she was trying to save his ungrateful hide? "Lower your gun, Mitch," she hissed.

"No."

"Why not? She lowered hers."

"She also pulled hers first."

"That's a very childish way to think of things, Mr. Bryant. Who lifted their gun first. Who lifted theirs second. Do you think it will matter who fired the first shot when both of you are lying on the ground dead?"

His jaw clamped hard. The look he sent her was scathing "You're getting on my nerves, preacher's daughter. Why don't you stop lecturing me and do something useful?"

Her chin lifted indignantly. "Such as?"

"Such as . . . shut your trap and stop trying to salvage my eternally damned soul. And while you're at it, start thinking of a way we can get the hell out of here."

"Yes, yes, Erma, you're right. I forgot about that," the man admitted with a sheepish grin. He rubbed a palm over what little hair coated his scalp, slicking the thin strands back over the bald spot on his crown. "Well, folks what do you say? Sound like a good idea to you?"

"Good idea?" Chelsea gulped. Her gaze shifted between the husband and wife, both of whom looked as though they expected an answer to whatever question they'd broached. Smiling weakly and not wanting to admit she hadn't been listening, Chelsea glanced at Mitch. "Well, I don't know.

106

It's up to—"

"No."

"Are you sure?" Erma asked. She was cradling the rifle to her bulging waist, and looked much less dangerous than Chelsea had originally thought. "It's no trouble."

"I said no," Mitch growled. His thumb eased the hammer of the pistol back in place, though he didn't lower the gun itself. "We're hoping to reach Guthrie by nightfall. Another time."

"Another time," the woman agreed with a nod, then glanced over to her husband. "They said another time."

"I heard 'em."

"So what are you waiting for, you old coot? That stupid cow of yours will be knocking down trees if you don't get to milking her soon. And the chickens need to be fed. And the grass needs to be cut back and burned so that—"

"I know, Erma," the man agreed with a haggard sigh and another passing of his palm over his head. "I know."

Erma, her broad shoulders squared, had already started to walk away. Robert, who followed tiredly in her wake, turned to look back at Chelsea and Mitch. "She can be a little gruff sometimes, but she ain't so bad. Once you get used to her, that is. You two stop on your way back from Guthrie. You're welcome to camp on our land anytime . . . now that we know you're neighbors and all."

Mitch grumbled something under his breath, nodded curtly, and turned away. Chelsea smiled, waited until the couple had disappeared from sight, then spun on her heel and stalked over to Mitch. He was squatting on the ground, shoving the dishes the rain had cleaned and the sun had dried into his saddlebag. The urge to lash out and kick him was strong. Only through the grace of God did she resist it.

Hands on hips, she glared angrily down at him. "Are you always so rude, Mr. Bryant?" she demanded hotly.

He didn't glance up. "Only when I'm looking down the business end of a Winchester, Miss Hogan."

Chelsea's jaw hardened. "The way you treated those

107

people is unforgivable."

This time, he looked up. His blue eyes caught the golden rays of sun, making them shine with unnatural light. His gaze was intense, his expression stormy and hard. "I didn't ask for forgiveness." His rugged frame uncurled and he lithely pushed to his feet. "I don't *want* forgiveness. Yours, or anyone else's."

They were standing toe to toe. Chelsea had to crane her neck to meet his gaze. And when those incredible blue eyes burned into her, she wished she hadn't bothered. The heat of him was smoldering, the smell of him intoxicatingly male. All of this combined to batter down her wall of anger.

"You're a hard man, Mr. Bryant," she said, the snap of fury gone from both her voice and her expression. He was also very confusing. Soft and gentle one minute, ready to shoot complete strangers the next. Would she ever understand what made a man like Mitch Bryant tick? Only a fool would want to.

"Circumstances make the man, lady. Didn't your preacher daddy ever tell you that?" The tip of his index finger traced the delicate line of her jaw. In comparison to his gruff words, the touch was oddly gentle. Enticingly so.

"No." Chelsea couldn't stop the shiver that rippled out from where their flesh touched, like a stone being thrown in a calm lake. "What my father always said was that a man's true colors will always shine through eventually, no matter how hard he tries to hide them."

His eyelids lowered, hooding the expression that darkened his gaze. "Your daddy was wrong."

"I don't think so." She shook her head and sent the sleep-tousled copper braid swinging at her waist. "Another thing he always told me was that a man who lives by a gun dies by a gun."

His grin was cold. It didn't touch the eyes that bored into her. "You're daddy was just a walking fountain of clichés, wasn't he? Must have been a hell of a lot of fun to be around."

His finger gently touched the tip of her chin, then blazed a slow, tantalizing path down her throat, dipping just slightly beneath the collar of her shirt. Hot. Caressing. Inquisitive. He felt her swallow hard and knew she didn't feel as confident as she wanted him to believe. Good. Confident was the last thing he wanted her to feel. Right now he wanted to lash out, to take her down a peg or two. He didn't know why.

"Here's another little saying to add to your list, preacher's daughter," he continued coldly. "Any man who's stupid enough to let himself get involved with another human being to the extent of putting that person's life before his own is a goddamn fool. A guy that dumb deserves to get his back riddled with lead." One dark brow cocked arrogantly high as his gaze raked her. "Feel free to quote me."

The words were uttered so harshly, so savagely, that Chelsea gasped and staggered back a step. The finger that had been caressing her throat turned into a calloused palm caressing the back of her neck. The pressure he exerted was weak, her resistance to it nonexistent.

Her breath caught. The air trapped in her lungs was spicy, hot, undeniably male. The lower front of her body grazed his thighs and firm, lean hips. Her flesh burned with the feel of it. Tingled. Flamed.

Mitch's other hand slipped into the coat and coiled around her waist. He pulled her hard against him. A husky rumble echoed in the back of his throat when his eyes fixed on her lips. Her soft, sweet, gently parted lips. The lower one was firm, fuller than the top one, and temptingly moist. It gave her a pouty look that just begged for a man's kisses. And Mitch Bryant was just the man to see her get them.

Chelsea saw his gaze harden and recognized the intent sparkling in the crystal blue depths of his eyes. Sweet heavens, he was going to kiss her again. Already her mouth smoldered with anticipation, her tongue flickering against the back of her teeth . . . waiting, hoping, already tasting the honeyed promises of his mouth.

His head dipped.

Her chin rose and she went up on tiptoe. She could have pulled away. She *should* have pulled away. She didn't.

"Are you going to kiss me, Mr. Bryant?" she whispered silkily. His lips were poised mere inches from her own. Not close enough to seal the contact, but close enough to threaten it.

Her words were a repeat of last night's, minus the faint slur. To Mitch they were more intoxicating than whiskey. And they were damning as hell, because he knew he couldn't stop himself now if he tried. Mitch Bryant was a strong man, but *no* man was strong enough to resist the temptation of that pouty, so damnably kissable mouth.

"Hell yes, I'm going to kiss you," he growled. His mouth lowered enough for her to feel the tickle of his mustache on her lips. "I'm going to kiss you so damn hard that when I'm done, you won't be able to remember *one* of your father's damn clichés."

The arm around her waist tightened possessively, drawing a startled little breath from her. But he still didn't kiss her, though resisting was far worse than any physical pain he'd ever known. It was also sweet — in a torturous, prolonging, bittersweet sort of way.

His mouth grazed hers. A gentle brushing back and forth motion. His tongue darted out, skated moistly over the line of her quivering lips, teased the place where they parted. Mitch groaned, savoring the sweet, incomparable taste of her.

He sucked, he sipped, he coaxed in feather-light caresses. Against her lips, he murmured, "Damned if you're not going to remember this kiss for the rest of your life, preacher's daughter."

And then his mouth was on hers, ravishing her lips, hard and demanding. His hot palm strayed down, cupping, kneading the soft curve of her bottom. He ground her against his hips in a provocative, sexy onslaught to her innocent senses.

Chelsea's head was flung back, her back arched slightly

110

as he captured her confused whimper with his hot, moist mouth.

Mitch pillowed the upper part of his body against her chest. He could feel the ragged rise and fall of her breasts, crushed beneath him. The feel was hot and searing. Better than anything he had ever known. His tongue dragged across her teeth, then buried itself in the wet velvet of her mouth. His fingers tunneled into the hair above her braid, so silky soft. The airy strands tickled his knuckles. His palms burned to test the weight of the breasts pressed so intimately, so goddamn perfectly, against him.

His hand slipped over her slender shoulder. Even through the coat, she felt small in his hand. Fragile. Her upper arm was willow thin. The wrist that peeked from beneath the cuff was spanned by his thumb and index finger with room to spare. The pulse leaping in the creamy hollow beat wild and erratic, like his own, throbbing like thunder in his ears.

Mitch felt her fingers tremble as he dragged her hand up and pillowed it on his chest. When she tried to snatch it away, he covered the back of it with his own hand, holding it in place. He wanted her to feel the pounding of his heart. He wanted her to know how much she affected him. How she drove him crazy with desire . . . with need . . . with hard, physical want of complete and total possession.

"Put your tongue in my mouth, Chelsea," he gritted hoarsely against her lips. "I want you to taste me. Taste how much I want you."

Chelsea knew how much he wanted her. Her father might have been a Baptist preacher, but he had prepared his daughters for the outside world — one more than the other. She knew what happened to a man when he desired a woman, and she could feel the very real evidence of Mitch's desire straining through the coarse denim, hard and hot, searing her abdomen.

Arching into him, Chelsea obediently slipped her tongue through the barrier of his teeth. The taste of him was tangy and sharp, as thoroughly masculine as the rest

111

of him. His flavor was intoxicating.

Her head swam in a way the whiskey of last night could never have made it do, when he teased the moist, searching tip. He coaxed and, in so doing, taught her the passionate game of thrust and parry, swirl and savor. Encouraged, her strokes grew bolder, deeper, until she found herself hungrily exploring every sweet, wet inch of him.

His hand peeled away, leaving her own trembling fingers trapped between them. It was an exciting feeling, her own curved softness pressing against her knuckles; hard sinew, beneath which was the frantic drumming of his heart, branding her tingling palm. Even their own individual scents entwined until the air around them was bathed in a spicy, flowery fragrance that was headily seductive.

Mitch was vaguely aware of how uncomfortably snug his trousers had become. Vaguely. He was excruciatingly aware of how easily the woman he held in his arms could soothe away that tightness. And how badly he wanted her to do just that.

Dragging his mouth from hers, he locked the fingers of both hands behind her neck and looked down at her. Like a man drowning his troubles in a bottle, he drowned in the soft whiskey-amber of her eyes. They were large, those eyes, and rimmed with long, thick lashes at least two shades darker than her hair. The lids were thick, hooding a gaze that was glassy, confused, and shimmering with newly awoken passion.

"How far do you want me to take this, preacher's daughter?" he rasped. His tongue whisked over his lips. They were moist with the sweet, innocent taste of Chelsea Hogan. It was a taste he savored, one he wanted desperately to sample again and again. "How much of me are you ready for?"

None. All!

Chelsea sucked in an uneven breath. Her heart throbbed, her body felt dizzy and hot. It was a familiar sensation, one she had experienced often in this man's sinewy arms. It was the *other* feelings that mystified and alarmed her. The tightening in her stomach, the keen alertness to all her senses, and the hot, moist, throbbing ache that started in the junction of her thighs and spread like liquid fire throughout the rest of her body.

"I—I don't know," she answered finally, hoarsely. Her voice trembled, but only a little.

If this had been any other woman, Mitch wouldn't have thought twice. He would simply have pressed her down on the grass, crushed her beneath him, and physically coerced her into making up her mind. But she wasn't just another woman. She was Ch—Chelsea Hogan. She was a Baptist preacher's daughter. And, she was as innocent as the day was hot.

When and if he made love to this woman, it would be a mutual thing. He'd be damned if it wasn't. And it would be what she wanted. What *she* asked for. No regrets. No looking back. With a preacher's daughter, it could be no other way.

Damning a sense of honor that held no place in his life, Mitch released her. She staggered back a step, and he had to rein himself in hard to keep from reaching out for more than just her upper arms; to keep from crushing her pouty lips beneath his hungry mouth; to keep from giving into the white-hot demands of his body, straining against coarse, unfulfilling denim.

As soon as she'd righted her precarious balance, he released her again. "Go pack your gear, woman. It's a long ride into Guthrie, and I want to be there by nightfall."

His voice was gritty and sharp. The words had barely receded before he spun on his heel and stalked toward the tent.

Chelsea watched him go. She heard the dirt crunch beneath his boot heels and gave serious thought to obeying his command. But she couldn't. Her knees felt like water, her head was light, and she knew that if she found the power to move, it would be to walk into the steely embrace of Mitch Bryant's arms.

Though her senses were still reeling, she retained enough presence of mind to know just how big a mistake that would be.

Chapter Eight

Chelsea wasn't sure what she'd expected the town of Guthrie to look like. But whatever it was, this wasn't it.

The "Magic City of Guthrie" was splayed out over a flat expanse of prairie that had been virtually uninhabited only a few days ago. It was inhabited now—by what rumor estimated to be no less than ten thousand boomers. Exaggerated accounts boasted over thirty thousand, but that number could be argued.

The only building she could see was an old Santa Fe Railroad depot. Its brown paint was flaking, its boards cracking, and it looked singularly out of place. Looking more "normal" were the hundreds of tents dotting the land in no discernible order—and no discernible color. Flags, blankets, coats, and colorfully decorated streamers were tied to poles, the hems flapping on the ceaseless Oklahoma breeze.

Everywhere, *everywhere,* there were men, women, children, animals, and noise. A *lot* of noise.

Chelsea drew in Babylon on the outskirts of the tent town, giving herself a few much needed minutes to not only soak in the sights, sounds, and pungent smells of so many human beings living in such close quarters, but to also adjust herself to them all. Only a few days ago she had been part of this large gathering. But in the short time she had been away from it, she'd quickly learned to enjoy the gurgle of a river, the shrill call of passing birds, and the taunting timbre of Mitch Bryant's husky voice.

Nothing had prepared her for *this!*

"You ready?" Mitch asked as he drew the stallion up next to her paint pony. "I'd like to get in there, find the land office and your sister, and get the hell out before nightfall if we can." He glanced at her, his gaze hidden by the shadows clinging beneath the wide brim of his hat. "Any objections?"

"None," she agreed readily. "I don't think I could stand to stay in this place any longer than that. Good heavens, will you look at all these people? And the smell!" She gave a gentle shiver and wrinkled her nose.

"There's more than this, sweetheart," he said, nodding his head at the commotion that spread out before them. "Don't forget the settlers who ran for homesteads. For every one of the people living in this town, there's at least another three here just to file a claim." He grinned, his teeth shining white against the black of his beard. "Kinda makes you glad for Northwest Quarter Section number 30, doesn't it?"

Chelsea's back stiffened and she sent him a condescending glare from beneath the floppy brim of her own hat. "Number 31," she corrected stiffly, her fingers tightening on the reins. "*My* claim is number 30. You'd do well not to forget that."

The grin melted. The corners of Mitch's mouth quirked down as he tugged the hat lower on his brow and glanced away. "No need to get touchy, Miss Hogan. It was just a joke."

"An unappreciated one," she snapped. "I worked too hard to get this land to joke about it."

"As did everyone else around you," he snarled, his humor properly doused. "In case you've forgotten, lady, you didn't make that run alone. *You'd* do well not to forget *that*."

Mitch didn't wait for a reply as he nudged the stallion's flanks and began weaving his way through the throngs of people gathered in what would eventually be a street.

Chelsea's lips drew into a thin white line as, glaring at his broad, receding back, she hurried to follow him. Considering the amount of people here, she'd do well not to lose sight of him. If they parted now, chances were they wouldn't see each other again until both arrived back on their claims.

Not that that would be such a bad idea, Chelsea thought as

116

she moved her pony into step beside him. In fact, after this morning's kiss, it was probably a very good idea. A few days away from this man might be just what she needed to restore some form of order to her tattered, still spiralling senses. Then again, it might sharpen them until she wanted a repeat performance even more than she did now.

"I don't know where they put the land office," Mitch said, not glancing her way. His tone had reverted to clipped and curt, the way it had been when they broke up camp that morning. The chilly timbre grated on Chelsea's already frazzled nerves.

"I'm sure it won't be too difficult to find," she murmured, distracted. The thought struck her that if the land office was going to be hard to find—and it was a place where *everyone* needed to go—then how much harder would it be to find Emilee? Looking out at what appeared to be a sea of milling faces, the chore felt heavy, like finding the proverbial needle in a haystack. In short, it looked impossible.

What was she supposed to do? Peer into every tent to see which one her sister was in? Perhaps she could knock on every wagon bed and politely ask, "Excuse me, I hate to bother you, but have you by chance seen Emilee Hogan?" And what if her sister was still angry? Worse, what if she'd never arrived?

Of course, Chelsea thought, Emmy *had* to be here. Her sister had the wagon . . . and the money. But what if? . . .

"That's it," Mitch grumbled, pointing at a long line of people ribboning out from a hastily nailed-together shack.

Chelsea followed his gaze, watched carefully, then stifled her first laugh of the day. "No, I don't think so, Mr. Bryant."

The blue eyes narrowed and turned on her full force. "What do you mean, no? It's a line, isn't it? And a damned long one from the looks of it." She couldn't see his scowl beneath the brim of his hat, but she knew it was there. "What the hell else can it be?"

Fighting a smile, she nodded to the woman who stepped into the first place in line. "Watch the woman in calico," Chelsea instructed. A land office! she thought to herself. Not hardly.

The woman in the faded, ripped calico and tight bun shifted impatiently from foot to foot. Her gaze never strayed from the curtained flap of the shack as she crossed her arms at her waist and tapped her foot, willing the man who'd just disappeared inside to hurry about his business. A few minutes later, the man emerged. He'd barely stepped into the late afternoon sunlight before the woman in calico burst into the shack. Two minutes later she reemerged, her step slower, a relieved expression softening her haggard face. Tossing a coin into the cup the man sitting beside the door held, she readjusted the wrinkled cloth around her legs and strolled away.

"Now *that's* what I call free enterprise," Chelsea quipped, good humor thickening her tone, "Of course, if you don't believe me, feel free to take a place in line. I have plenty of chores to keep me busy — like finding the real land office, ferreting out my sister, buying supplies . . ."

Slowly, Mitch's gaze swept to her. He tried to ignore the way her laughter — soft, delicate, pleasant — tickled his ears and ignited a fire of interest in his gut. He almost succeeded.

"Your idea of a joke?" he asked. His voice was stern, his gaze harsh, but he couldn't help grinning when Chelsea nodded and broke into peals of delighted laughter.

"I wasn't lying," Chelsea said, her tone still light, though most of her laugher had subsided. "I really do have to start searching for Emmy."

Mitch nodded but made no reply. He couldn't. The sight of this woman's mouth curved in a gentle smile was stunning. His gaze was riveted to the sight, refusing to budge. Never before had he wanted to kiss a woman quite so badly as he wanted to kiss this one; here, now, hard.

"Mr. Bryant? Are you all right?" Chelsea asked. Her customary scowl was in place, made visible by the golden rays of late day sun peeking beneath the brim of her hat. The creases between her finely arched brows deepened.

"What?" Mitch whispered hoarsely, dragging his gaze to the large whiskey-amber of her eyes. She was looking at him oddly, but he couldn't for the life of him figure out why.

"I asked if you're all right. Your face is pale . . . and you're grinding your teeth. Was it something I said?"

His gaze dipped back to her lips, like chunks of steel being coaxed by a potent magnet. Swallowing hard, he savored the sight for only a second before dragging his attention away. "I'm fine," he growled, and knew damn well he was anything but.

Sonofabitch! Three kisses he'd shared with this woman. Three lousy—*no, three too-damn-good*—kisses. And still he couldn't keep his eyes off her tempting-as-hell, pouty lips, or the fiery copper satin of her hair, or the seductive curves of her soft, soft body. Hell, he couldn't keep his hands off her, either, if this morning's passionate little interlude were anything to judge by.

How far would he have let things go if she'd said yes? Mitch wondered. His gut churned, his gloved fingers tightened on the reins. How far down the path of debauchery would he have led the sexy little preacher's daughter? It was a question that had haunted him for the better part of the day—mostly because he knew the answer without having to give it a whole lot of thought.

"We're splitting up," he growled suddenly, firmly. "Go find your sister and buy your supplies. I'll find the land office and get the papers started on both our claims."

"But how will we find each other?" she asked, very weakly. Had he thought the same way she had earlier? Was that why he'd made the suggestion? She should be grateful. She wasn't.

Find each other? Mitch thought with a sarcastic glare. *Shit, lady, if you had a brain in your head, you'd never want to see me again.* That wasn't what he said, however. "We'll meet at the train depot at dusk. That shouldn't be too tough."

What he didn't say was that he had no intention of going *near* the train depot. Today or any other day. Not if it meant being close to this woman for another long, sleepless night. A man could only take so much! Wasn't it bad enough he was going to be living a stone's throw away from her for at least the next few weeks? It was a situation that could easily turn hellish — especially if they did what their bodies were begging them to do.

No, Mitch decided. He'd never let passion rule over good sense in the past, and he wouldn't start doing so now. He hadn't lived to the ripe old age of thirty-three without recognizing danger when it smacked him in the face. And this fiery-haired beauty was more lethal than a loaded rifle aimed point-blank at his heart — no matter what his more male parts were telling him.

He would *not*, under any circumstances, be at that train depot come dusk.

Chelsea sighed, thinking the time away from him would be well deserved, probably even pleasurable. His company during the day had been surly at best, aggravating at worst. Cupping a hand beneath her hat and shading her eyes, she scanned the area. So many people! "All right," she murmured, "if that's what you —"

When she turned back, Mitch Bryant was gone. She caught only a faint glimpse of his broad back swaying in the saddle as he melted in with the noisy crowd. It was an impressive back. One that stayed in her mind and heated her blood long after she'd lost sight of him.

Chapter Nine

If it was one thing even strangers agreed upon, it was that Mitch Bryant was as handsome as he was stubborn, arrogant, and reckless. One look at those penetrating blue eyes, prominent cheekbones, and the tight line of his jaw beneath the beard said it all. Only a fool would make the mistake of thinking him a patient man.

Harvey Leeds, while no fool, had just made that mistake.

The young man's gaze drifted past the spectacles perched precariously on the bridge of his nose. His nervous eyes widened when two clenched fists smashed atop the papers cluttering his desk. The blow was hard enough to make the mantel clock on the corner bounce and Harvey jump.

Conversation from the ragged line of people who stood in the sweltering hot, crude little shack waiting to file homesteading claims dulled to a hush. A few of the more curious inched forward, ears perked. From outside, the sound of a hammer pounding a nail into a slab of timber came to a halt, as though the man wielding it had perked his own ears, straining to hear every juicy detail of the coming argument.

From the looks of it, it was going to be a doozy.

The tension radiating from Mitch Bryant was palpable. His fury crackled in the air like the threat of a summer thunderstorm. Harsh and deadly.

Harvey Leeds gulped, sensing the tempest he had unavoidably created in the dark-haired man who leaned threateningly over his desk. His smile was weak, mousy. Pushing the spectacles higher on his nose, he stammered, "Mr. Bryant. Are you b—b—back again?"

"You bet your puny little a—" a woman's gasp from behind made Mitch change paths mid-word—"rump, pal. And this time I'm not leaving until this is fixed . . . to *my* satisfaction."

"Fixed?" the young man squeaked.

"Fixed," Mitch barked, his knuckles cushioned atop the crate that served as a desk. The dusty red cotton shirt scratched against his back as he arched forward. His nose very nearly touched the pointed tip of the clerk's.

"B—b—but there's nothing *to* fix," the man argued very softly and very, very weakly. His gaze dropped to the Colt .45 strapped to Mitch Bryant's hard denim-clad thigh. The dull metal said the pistol wasn't new. The hammer, the top of which was worn down in the shape of a large thumb pad, said the weapon had been fired often.

Harvey swallowed hard and felt what little fight he'd had drain away. "I've already t—told you it isn't up to me. The government says one claim per person. I can't file t—two names on one claim." His gaze lifted, locking with penetrating blue, pleading for mercy. There was none to be had. "I—I just can't."

The jaw beneath the beard clenched hard. Blue eyes narrowed, their depths hard and menacing. "Oh yes you can, Leeds. And you will."

"No, I can't." The man's long, bony fingers trembled as he gestured to the line of people snaking out from behind Mitch. "It w—wouldn't be fair to them. If I did it for you, I'd have to do it for them. F—frankly, Mr. Bryant, there isn't enough land to go around as it is, never mind i—illegally splitting tracts the way you're asking me to do."

"If you split tracts, you'd have more land," Mitch reasoned, his voice cold and biting.

"Yes, but that would make each homestead l—less than the agreed-upon one h—hundred and sixty acres. These people did not suffer through that Run f—for anything less than their due, sir."

When the dark-haired man who wore his holster arrogantly low didn't immediately pull the pistol and shoot Harvey where he sat, the young clerk grew confident. Well, as confident as one could possibly grow when one's face was mere inches from a countenance that was dark with fury. His annoying stammer was exchanged for an equally annoying nasal whine. "Be reasonable, Mr. Bryant. Please. The law is the law."

"I don't give a damn about the law, pal. I want my land, and I want the lady to have hers."

Harvey glanced at his combatant from over the rim of his spectacles. "The lady in question isn't even here to sign the claim form, Mr. Bryant. *You* are." His fingers were still trembling as he shuffled through the sheets of paper he'd set aside two hours before—when he'd thought himself fortunate to have seen the last of Mitch Bryant.

The young clerk cleared his throat. "As I told you earlier, either you put your name on the claim and take the matter up with the courts—when some are organized for the purpose of settling this type of dispute—or you find the young lady and—"

"I tried!" Mitch boomed, to no avail.

The young man continued as though he hadn't been interrupted, "—bring her here to sign the forms instead. The matter can be decided between the two of you, of course, but I have my orders. *One* of you must sign the form. The sooner the better. If a claim isn't filed, someone else could decide to stake it. I needn't tell you what would happen then . . . need I?"

"You do. Pretend I'm stupid, Leeds," Mitch growled, rolling back on his heels. "Tell me."

"Weeell," the clerk whined with a timid shrug, "if no claim is filed, the l—land will be considered vacant and available to be claimed by another family—who *can* sign the form. And once they do, the property will belong to them and—"

"Like hell! I'll shoot anyone who steps foot on my land."

"Y—y—yes, sir . . . well, then, it will *definitely* be a matter for the courts. As it stands now . . ." He sent Mitch a mousy

123

smile. It wasn't returned. "I'm s—sorry I couldn't be of more help, Mr. Bryant, but that's the law. All claims except those allotted for public use—schools and such—must be filed as soon as possible." He cleared his throat and, taking one of the sheets of paper, pushed it toward Mitch. "Now, would you care to sign for the p—p—property in question, sir?"

"But there are *two* pieces of property," Mitch insisted tightly. With an angry growl, he thrust himself to his full, imposing six feet two inches of raw muscle and power. Fists on hips, he glared down his nose at the mousy clerk.

The mousy clerk, encouraged to find himself still alive, looked up from the papers rattling in his hands and glared back. "No, sir, there is only one. The map says the Sweetwater River cuts Northwest Quarter Section number 30 in half. One claim. One owner. *One* signature. Unless, of course, you and the lady are m—married, in which case I'll only need your signature. But you've already denied that. Vehemently, as I recall."

A female giggle fluttered out from behind Mitch. Already irritated, the sound scratched annoyingly down his spine.

Mitch glared down at the rumpled piece of paper. It was the same one he had walked away from, without signing, two hours before. That was when he'd thought Chelsea Hogan wouldn't be too hard to find. Now he knew better. The woman had disappeared to God only knew where; Mitch sure as hell couldn't find her.

He hesitated, eyeing the mousy clerk he would have liked to have strangled—if only because the young man refused to budge his position on the matter.

Damn it! If he signed for the claim, Chelsea Hogan would kill him for stealing her property. If he didn't, there was a chance they'd give the property to someone else and she'd still have nothing. Wouldn't it be better to just sign, then file a dispute? At least that way they'd only be fighting each other for the land. Of course, if he didn't sign, he'd risk drawing in a third party—which the mousy clerk had already suggested would win such a dispute if only because *the person had signed the damn form!*

124

"They're setting up courts for disputed claims?" Mitch asked, still weighing the decision. *She's going to shoot you for signing, Bryant. Damned if she won't.* Then again, it wasn't as though this was the first time someone had wanted him dead. A lot of people did. What was one more? Of course, he'd never had a sexy little preacher's daughter out after his hide before. A wry grin curled his lips. If it was only his *hide* she was after!

Mitch's glare sharpened. "You're sure?"

Harvey Leeds nodded encouragingly. "Oh, yes," he said. "If you think you'll need one." Mentally, he was counting off how many more claims needed to be filed before the desk closed at six o'clock. Too many, judging by the line that continued to grow.

"Oh, I'll need one all right," Mitch growled. Before he could change his mind, he snatched up the pen the clerk had placed on top of the scrap of paper. Taking a deep breath, he scrawled his name at the bottom and tossed the pen aside. "If the lady lets me live long enough to file a dispute, that is."

The clerk took the deed and filed it in another sloppy stack. He said something about Mitch getting it back once his required five years of homesteading had been met.

Mitch barely heard the words. Why bother listening? No matter how tempting the thought of keeping the land was — it would have been a nice place to settle — he knew he'd be signing the deed over to Ch — Chelsea Hogan once his reasons for coming to this place had been settled. Damned if he wouldn't. And damned if that thought didn't bother the hell out of him! He didn't know why — and he knew better than to try and figure out the reason.

"Did you hear me, Mr. Bryant? I s — said —"

"I heard," Mitch snapped. Spinning on his heel, he stalked angrily away. He didn't notice the insistent pounding of the hammer start up again. Nor did he see the appreciative glances that followed his progress down what would eventually be a street but was now rolling prairie dotted with makeshift tents and a few hastily constructed buildings.

He didn't see any of that because he was too busy brooding. An uncomfortable feeling ate at his gut. It was easily traced to the signature he'd left behind with the mousy Harvey Leeds.

Mitch felt as though he'd just signed his own death warrant . . . and once Chelsea Hogan discovered what he'd done, he thought he might as well have.

She wasn't going to be happy when she found out he'd just put his name on a claim she thought she owned. In fact, she was going to be mad as hell. The worst part was, Mitch couldn't blame her. To her self-righteous way of thinking, he'd just stolen the land out from under her nose.

Damn it!

Chelsea knew where her sister was. At least, she knew the name of the woman whose tent Emmy was staying in. Finding the tent was another matter entirely. There were so many!

She wandered down the "streets" of Guthrie for what seemed like days. It was really only two very long hours. During that time she had been luridly propositioned twice and had received three hastily phrased marriage proposals — the last of which had been made on bent knee by the bartender of the tent-saloon she'd unwittingly stumbled into.

Finding the land office had come as a fortunate mistake. One minute she was meandering past a planked building, the next she was standing at the end of a long, weaving line.

Peering through the door to assure herself that she wasn't waiting to use the private facilities, she decided to stay. She knew where Emmy was, but she might not have another opportunity to file her claim. And as long as she was here, she might as well get the paperwork started on Mitch's land as well.

Chelsea chuckled, wondering if Mitch was, even now, standing on the line she'd at first thought herself to be on. Her laughter bubbled forth. It would serve the arrogant know-it-all right if he was! And wouldn't the look on his face be something to see when she proudly told him that *she* had

126

not only found her sister, wagon, and supplies, but she'd also started work on their claims. Oh yes, the sight would be sweet indeed! One to savor.

For an hour she shifted from foot to foot, drank in more sights of the "Magic City" than she ever cared to see, and waited. When her turn finally came, the sun was at the end of its final arch toward the horizon, and the shadows of early dusk were blending over the open prairie in fiery reds and greys.

Chelsea stepped up to the desk. The man behind it looked tired, frazzled, and more than a little relieved when he glanced past her and saw only two other people standing in the flickering glow of his kerosene lamp.

"Number?" he asked, glancing back down at the forms he clutched tiredly in his hands. His spectacles, she noted, had slipped down past the bump on his nose and threatened to fall atop the clutter-scattered desk.

"Northwest Quarter Section number 30," she answered with a smile that went unseen, since the mousy man continued to stare at the papers in his hand.

"Taken." He didn't glance up as he shouted, "Next!"

The man behind Chelsea started to move past her. He was a big man, but her furious glare convinced him to wait just a few moments longer to file his claim. Glaring down at the clerk, she repeated tightly, "Northwest Quarter Section number 30."

"Didn't I just say it was ta—? Oh no, it's *you*."

Very slowly the young man's bespectacled gaze strayed over his desktop and up Chelsea's abruptly rigid body. He made only brief eye contact with her before shifting his nervous attention over her shoulder. She wasn't sure what he saw, but whatever it was, it pleased him greatly.

"I came to file a claim," Chelsea said, drawing his glassy gaze back to her. "This *is* the land office, isn't it?"

The man nodded, and Chelsea scowled when she saw he was fighting a smile. Personally, she could see nothing funny about this. Had he lost the paperwork on her land? Was that why he'd said it was taken? Sweet heavens, she hoped so. If

127

not, the only other explanation she could think of was that a group of "sooners" had squatted on her property and tried to file the claim before she'd arrived. And if they'd succeeded . . .

Chelsea's blood ran cold. "Is there a problem, Mr. . . ?"

"Leeds," he offered, his voice high and nasally thin. "And . . . well . . . yes, I suppose you could say there is a problem, miss. Does the name Mitch Bryant ring a bell with you?"

The young clerk was smiling fully now, and it was all Chelsea could do not to slap the grin off his face. She wasn't a violent person, she reminded herself harshly, repeatedly. Shifting feet, she glared down at the mousy man, waiting, knowing what he was going to say while at the same time not willing to believe the truth of it until she heard it for herself.

"I've heard of him," she replied finally, flatly. Her stomach knotted, her heart throbbed. "Why?"

"Because he's the one who signed the deed to Northwest Quarter Section number 30," the clerk spouted. The eyes behind the spectacles shimmered almost gleefully, as though this were the most fun the young man had had all day.

Chelsea's urge toward violence grew stronger. This time, it was not so easily tempered. "There must be a mistake," she said tightly. "Mr. Bryant has his own claim to file."

The young man chuckled. "That's what he said."

"Of course he did. It's the truth. Our claims border each other, separated by the Sweetwater River."

The mousy smile stayed in place as the young man sighed and began shuffling through papers. "Ah, here it is," he said, pulling free a long, crackling rectangular slip of paper and spreading it out atop all the rest. He looked up at Chelsea, at the same time pointing to a line in the center of the paper that ribboned off the map on both sides. "The Sweetwater River," he announced, tracing his bony finger down the twisting line.

Smaller dotted lines spread out at the place where his finger stopped. Each were neatly numbered. The one marked 30 had no water boundary; the twisting line of the river cut through the center from left to right.

"No." Chelsea shook her head, her teeth firmly clenched.

The man's grin broadened. "Oh yes," he chirped. "As you can see, the land you thought you owned and the land Mr. Bryant thought *he* owned are one and the same." He crossed his thin arms over the map and leaned forward on his elbows. "Tell me something. Didn't either Mr. Bryant or yourself think to check the corner markers on the piece of property? They clearly state the number of each homestead."

"I checked *mine,*" Chelsea snapped, her mind reeling. Damn Mitch Bryant. Damn him to hell and back! Her glare sharpened on the clerk. "He signed for the claim?" she demanded, her voice rising with her growing fury. "And you *let him?!*"

The man sat back hard in his chair. "I—I had no choice. A—all the claims must be filed. It's my job to file them and that is what I do—very well, I might add. It is *not* my job to survey the claims and make sure everyone knows which homestead he should be on. The p—p—proper authorities do that."

Proper authorities, Chelsea thought derisively. A lot of good the *proper authorities* would do her now. Mitch Bryant had already stolen her land!

"Mr. Leeds," Chelsea said, her tone strained. "What would you say if I told you Mr. Bryant has stolen my property?"

The man's grin was back. It fairly beamed from his youthful face. "That I wasn't a bit surprised." The grin faded. "And that there isn't a thing I can do about it. As I told Mr. Bryant, courts are being set up for disputed claims. They should be functioning at week's end. This, I'm sorry to say, is a matter for them, not myself."

Chelsea felt the hot fury of tears stinging her eyes but refused to give in to them. "And there's nothing you can do to help me? Nothing at all?"

He shook his head. "Sorry."

"Not half as sorry as Mitch Bryant will be when I get my hands on him," Chelsea stated, her voice ringing with the threat.

"Yes, I believe he mentioned something along that vein."

Oh yes, Mitch Bryant will be very, very sorry about what he's done! she thought after thanking the man and wandering away from the claim desk. Her feet dragged in the dirt between the tents as she led the paint pony, its hooves clomping behind her.

For the second time that day, she damned herself for not being a violent person. She abhorred firearms, but that didn't mean she didn't know how to shoot one. She did. And right now she'd like nothing more than to put a loaded gun to Mitch Bryant's temple and gleefully pull the trigger. Of course, the day was not over. Her time might yet come.

Her gaze fixed on the Santa Fe Railroad depot, a dark contrast to the squat tents. It was dusk. Was he waiting for her? No. More likely he'd ridden back to the claim *he* now owned. *But not for long,* she thought. *Dead men can't own land.*

What was he doing now? she wondered. Gloating? Uncorking a bottle of his blasted whiskey, celebrating his victory over the stupid preacher's daughter? Oh, it was galling to think how easily she'd been duped!

But I haven't been, Chelsea thought, her feet stomping over grass and dirt. Not by a long shot. The battle had been won, but the war raged on. It would end by her owning her land again, and if it meant taking the slimy Mitch Bryant to court, so be it.

"Damn the arrogant bastard!" she growled aloud, and was surprised to find how natural the curse felt on her tongue. It had fallen from her lips easily — in much the same way it would have fallen from Mitch Bryant's, come to think of it. That worried her . . . but not nearly as much as how she was going to get back her land from that thieving piece of scum.

She stomped onward, no direction in mind, her thoughts never far from Mitch Bryant and the various ways she would torture his ruggedly appealing body when she next saw him.

Perhaps it was her rigid determination to find Emmy and get out of Guthrie just as fast as she could that made the chore even easier. Whatever the reason, the first man she asked not only had heard of Edna Simpson, the woman Emmy was staying with, but was also able to point Chelsea in the direction of the woman's tent.

If possible, the day worsened.

Chelsea was annoyed to discover Edna Simpson's tent was none other than the same blue and yellow striped piece of canvas she had passed at least twenty times that afternoon. That annoyance was minor compared to how she felt when the elderly Mrs. Simpson told her Emilee Hogan had left the day before with "such a nice young man" . . . and their wagonload of supplies.

Chapter Ten

"When I get my hands on that girl . . ." Chelsea muttered under her breath, as leading the horse behind her, she wove her way past a shadowy row of tents and tepee-shaped blankets.

No one took notice of her wanderings through the "streets" of Guthrie, mostly because there was nothing to take notice of. A woman alone at dusk was not uncommon. A woman alone at dusk who looked mad as the devil was also not uncommon. A woman alone at dusk who looked mad as the devil and was muttering foul curses under her breath was a bit more unusual, but most of the boomers were too busy "improving" their claims to pay the furious little redhead much attention.

Chelsea sighed and guided Babylon around a large tent. Male laughter filtered out through the brightly striped canvas, and the snatches of a ribald joke cut through the air. Falsely coy feminine giggles vied with the strains of bad piano music. The tent was obviously another one of the "Magic City's" saloons. It was the third one she'd passed in less than a half hour.

There's whiskey in there, a small voice inside her head taunted as she stalked past the side of the tent. Whiskey. The forbidden fruit — or, in this case, drink. One whose effects she vividly remembered from last night.

So soothing, so *numbing.* What she wouldn't give for just a tiny sip. It would help her relax, help her to forget her troubles with Emilee, with Mitch Bryant, with everything. It would . . . lead to even more trouble than she already had to deal with, that's what a sip of whiskey would do right now. But it was oh, so tempting!

"No," Chelsea hissed into the dusky night air. With a flick of her wrist, she snapped the reins taut and stomped to the end of the tent. She couldn't remember her father's exact words about liquor's numerous vices, but she remembered their meaning. And Chelsea had no reason to doubt Papa. After all, hadn't she asked Mitch Bryant to kiss her last night — after only three sips of the potent stuff? Didn't that *prove* how corruptive drinking could be? Sweet heavens, she blushed just thinking about it!

She reached the back of the tent at the same time the piano music inside faded. The laughter did not, but kept ringing harshly through the warm April air.

Scowling, she scanned her surroundings, surprised at how swiftly one could become lost in a town whose only form of lodging was identical tents. All, that is, except for the Santa Fe Railroad depot, which stood out against the dusky horizon. The murky sky was a masterwork of prairie reds and oranges, masking the peeling brown paint and chipped boards of the building.

Mitch Bryant. The name shot through her mind like a bolt of lightning, stinging her tongue as she squinted at the depot where he was supposed to be waiting for her.

Would he be there? Did she *want* him to be there?

Yes.

No!

Good heavens, I don't know anymore!

She recalled this morning's kiss and her cheeks grew warm. She remembered the kiss that had come before it, and the one before *that*. Her heart stuttered, her breaths grew shallow, the fingers enfolding the reins moistened.

Then, like a bucket of ice water being thrown over a blazing fire, she remembered the land he had stolen from her. She remembered his lies. She remembered how much she really should hate that man and how very much she wanted

133

to get even with him.

Before she could consciously make the decision to meet him, her feet started moving. The train depot loomed larger and larger against the breathtaking sunset. And with each step, her reasons for hating Mitch Bryant echoed prominently in her mind. To hell with his sensuous kisses, the man had stolen her land! He *would* pay for that and pay dearly.

Twenty minutes later, Chelsea was leaning against a slab of clapboard coated with peeling brown paint. Like the rest of Guthrie, this place was not deserted. Trains arrived constantly, carrying new shipments of settlers hoping to strike abandoned or unclaimed homesteads. The ones pulling away from the station carried a considerably lesser amount, mostly those who'd failed in the Run and were turning their sights elsewhere.

Mitch Bryant was nowhere to be seen.

She was only slightly surprised. Why would he come, after all? He'd gotten her land, he had no more need for her. In fact, wouldn't it be to his advantage if something terrible were to happen to her in Guthrie . . . if she were never seen nor heard from again? Then there would be no disputed claim to worry about fighting over. The land would be his, free and clear.

Just the thought made her blood boil.

Damn him! she thought again, her chin sinking wearily, her jaw pillowed atop her collarbone. Leaning back heavily, she sighed. She was tired, her head aching from churning over plans to find Emilee and plans to make Mitch Bryant pay. Her feet were throbbing in protest to all the walking she'd done. All she wanted was a bath, a place to sleep, and some time to plan what to do next, not necessarily in that order. Until she could find Mitch Bryant, she would get none of it.

Where is he?

Back on your claim, girl. Celebrating. Where else?

The sun was a fiery red semicircle on the horizon when Chelsea felt the first nudge against her thigh. With her arms crossed at her waist and her chin sagging, she was almost asleep standing up and didn't at first notice it. The nudge became more insistent. Mumbling something under her breath, she swatted at whatever the annoying thing was.

The ball of her palm struck a bony wrist, but it was the gasp—not her own—that finally made her chin, as well as her gaze, snap up.

Her gaze met and held wide, deceptively innocent brown eyes. It wasn't Mitch, as she'd expected, but a boy who had a crop of dark, scraggly brown hair and a gaunt-looking face. He was tall but thin, and in all couldn't have been older than twelve, though his grin looked far older, far wiser. And he had a hand inside of Chelsea's pocket.

"Ooops," he said. "Guess you're wondering what I . . . er . . ."

"What you're doing with your hand inside my pocket?" she said coldly. Her gaze drifted down to her trouser pocket, to the place where his wrist disappeared inside the coarse folds of cloth. Her smile was less than warm. "Let's say I'd given it some thought."

"I can explain," the boy said in a rush.

"I'm sure you can. And you *will.* Now would be a good time to start." Her attention never left his hand as it slipped free of her pocket, the wrist turning ever so slightly inward as the long, thin fingers tightened into a fist.

Chelsea scowled. She might be a Baptist preacher's daughter, but she was certainly no fool. The pocket in question felt considerably lighter for the coins now warming the young boy's fist. The coins he'd *stolen!* Recrossing her arms over her chest, she tapped a toe impatiently in the dirt and continued to scowl at him. Her lips pursed. "I'm waiting. . . ."

Like a chameleon, the boy's grin melted from sheepish to overpoweringly sincere. Too sincere, she thought. In a movement that was so fast she would only to have blinked to miss it, he slipped the coins into his trouser pocket and extended his long fingered hand in friendship.

"Christopher Claymore," he said, grinning from ear to

ear now. "My friends call me Kit. And yourself, ma'am?"

"Chelsea Hogan," she replied cautiously, placing her hand in his. There was precious little difference in size, she noted as he pumped her arm so enthusiastically her shoulder ached.

"So, tell me, Chels . . . may I call you Chels?" At her single raised eyebrow, he amended, "So tell me, Miss Hogan, what brings you to our bustling city on such a fine evening? Surely not the numerous saloons or tawdry gaming ha—"

"I'll take my money back, Kit," Chelsea cut him off sharply. She'd had a wretched day and was in no mood to be toyed with by a child.

"I beg your pardon, ma'am?" he asked, his eyes all wide and innocent and brown.

"My money," she repeated tightly, her gaze narrowing. "I want it back—all of it—and I want it back now."

The boy's absurdly long lashes batted in mock confusion. He pressed a palm over his narrow breast in a gesture that was too practiced to be sincere—like one of Mitch Bryant's shrugs.

"Oh, ma'am," Kit said, his scratchy voice lowering, "I'd love to help you out, really I would—I mean, you seem like such a nice lady and all—but I haven't a cent to lend you."

Chelsea's jaw clenched hard. Her father had once told her that those who stole from other people did so out of a need that was born of desperation . . . a need that was greater than the need of the person the goods had been stolen from. She tried to remember her father's words as she looked down into the face of the boy who'd just stolen the last of her coins. It wasn't easy. "I'm not asking you for a loan, young man, I'm—"

"Kit," he corrected with a winning smile that Chelsea' s itching palm was tempted to smack off.

"—demanding you return what's mine."

"But I don't have anything of yours, Chels—Miss Hogan. If I did"—his eyes widened in mock offense—"why, that would mean I'd *stolen* it. Surely you don't think I would—"

"What I think, kid, is that I'm going to throw you over my

knee and spank the tar out of you if you don't give me my money back," she snapped. *Sweet heavens, that was a Mitch Bryant threat if ever she'd heard one!* Chelsea tried not to dwell on what *that* meant as she thrust her hand beneath his nose, palm up, and wiggled her fingers expectantly. *"Now!"*

Kit scowled, eyeing the hand as well as the threat. Apparently, the coins in his pocket outweighed the risk, for he took her hand in his, pumped it twice—quick and hard—and grinned devilishly. "Good talking to you, Chels."

Accustomed to threats and fast getaways, the boy flashed a sly smile and spun on his heel. Unfortunately, he hadn't counted on a massive chest blocking his path. With a yelp, Kit collided face first with the solid brick wall that was Mitch Bryant.

Kit's dark brown eyes widened—not with fear or guilt, but with confusion tinged heavily with surprise. It wasn't that he'd never seen a gun before, he had—and many. Some of them had even been pointed at him. But never had he seen one quite so long held in a hand quite so large . . . or a barrel pointed quite so skillfully at his heaving young breast.

"You heard her, brat," a gravelly voice said from above him—*high* above him. "Give the lady her money back. Now." This last word was punctuated by the click of revolving chambers as the hammer was coaxed back by a calloused thumb.

Kit gulped. Reaching the tall man's eyes meant dragging his own widened gaze slowly up raw muscle and power, only slightly concealed beneath a faded red flannel shirt. Even bathed in shadows, Kit thought the sight was impressive. All muscle and coiled strength. But it was the eyes—cold blue and piercing— that sent the first thread of doubt twisting down his spine.

"Money?" Kit gulped. The shrewd smile that was as natural to him as breathing flickered weakly over his lips.

"Money," Mitch growled. "You know . . . coins, greenbacks, that sort of thing."

"Oh, I assure you, mister, I didn't take any of the lady's

coins, greenbacks, or any of that sort of thing. Honestly," he huffed, as though the thought were preposterous, "what sort of kid do you take me for?" He chanced a quick glace at the redhead, who was glowering at him, and gulped again. His attention shifted, checking for a clear escape route, as he said, "And I *am* just a kid."

"You're also a thief!" Chelsea spat, stepping to the boy's side. Though she'd judged him to be only twelve, the top of his dark head reached her shoulders. It wasn't a comforting observation—especially when the detestable Mitch Bryant's shadowy form could be seen hovering behind the boy. Her heart skipped a beat and she forced her gaze back to Kit. "And you're a petty little thief at that. I couldn't have had more than three dollars worth of change in my pocket. Certainly not worth the effort it took you to steal it."

"Is that all?" The lopsided grin melted smoothly over his face as Kit returned her gaze. "Then what's the problem?"

"The problem *is*," Mitch cut in coldly when Chelsea opened her mouth to scream at the boy, "the money wasn't yours to take."

"I never said I took it."

Mitch's fingers tightened around the carved wooden butt of the gun. He wrestled with a strong desire to thrash the boy soundly, then turn him upside down and *shake* Chelsea's money from his pocket. Instead, he said, "What did I see you stuff in your pocket then? Lint?"

The boy's chin went up. It was such a Chelsea Hogan-ish response that Mitch almost laughed. Almost.

"He took my money, Mr. Bryant," Chelsea said. To prove her point, she reached deep in her trouser pocket and turned the linen pocket insideout. It was as empty as they'd all known it would be. The boy, she was pleased to see, had enough decency in him to flush. "All of it. Every last cent I own."

Kit's eyes rounded, sweeping from Chelsea's empty pocket, now flapping on the breeze at her hip, to her large amber eyes. His gut instinct had always been very good— which was one of the reasons he was still alive—and gut instinct was now telling him that the woman spoke the truth. Sonofabitch! For the first time in his life, Kit actually felt a twinge of guilt.

"That's it?" the boy asked skeptically. "Three dollars in change is *all* you own?"

"Yes, that's it!" she shouted. Her gaze strayed to Mitch, who stood silently behind the boy. His eyes were cloaked in shadows, his expression unreadable. Latching onto his gaze, she growled, "Besides the claim I struck yesterday and a wagonful of supplies—*if* I can ever find where my sister took it. It may not be much, but it's a whole lot more than some people have."

"Three dollars in change," Kit muttered under his breath, shaking his wind-tousled head. His gaze shifted between the two adults, who were staring at each other intently. The air fairly crackled with the charged current of their gazes.

His long fingers snaked into his trouser pocket, closing over the coins. They jingled, but the sound was muffled by the threadbare cloth. The boy hesitated only for a second before sighing, mumbling a disgruntled "Sonofabitch," and dragging the scant handful of coins free. Reluctantly, he thrust them at Chelsea, then dropped his attention to the tattered tip of his too-small boot toe.

One dark brow cocked as Mitch silently watched the exchange. He wondered what the preacher's daughter would do next, then thought he was damn glad he wasn't a gambling man because his first guess didn't even come close.

Chelsea dragged her furious gaze from Mitch. Her expression remained guarded as she raked the boy from head to toe. Her amber gaze missed nothing. Not his too large, dirty, worn-to-a-thread clothes, not the ragged cut of his hair, not the gaunt hollows beneath his cheeks, and not his tattered boots. Nothing.

A surge of pity burned through her wall of anger as Papa's words again rang through her mind. The boy made a heart-wrenching sight. One she couldn't ignore.

Sighing in defeat, her gaze drifted back to the closed fist and she shook her head. "Keep them," she said flatly, then turned away and leaned a weary shoulder against the clapboard shingles. With trembling fingers, she swiped the copper wisps from her brow and fixed her sights on the spot on the horizon where the sun was now only a fiery sliver over the land.

"Keep them?" Kit echoed, his small head snapping up. A scowl laced his youthful brow as he sent Chelsea a look of open disbelief. "You mean the coins? You mean all of them?" His gaze swept to Mitch, who was watching them both carefully. "Is she mentally deficient, or is my hearing off?"

Mitch shrugged that careless, practiced shrug and uncocked the pistol, then holstered his weapon. "Yours and mine both," he grumbled as he snapped the strap over the butt, lodging it in place . . . until the next time.

Inwardly Mitch, too, questioned her reasoning. Generosity was wonderful, as far as it went, but letting a young pickpocket steal your last three dollars was a bit excessive. Or so Mitch Bryant—the man who had just stolen this woman's land—was given to believe. Then again, he'd never been known for generosity. Come to think of it, he'd never been known for anything that was good and nice—since his first instinct had been to beat the kid senseless, then snatch Chelsea's money back.

"I said keep it," Chelsea snapped. Her voice sounded loud, oddly husky in the void of silence that stretch taut. Was her reasoning really so bizarre to these two? It made perfect sense to her. "Take it and buy yourself a hat. Your face is sunburned, and your hair is bleaching. You'll get heatstroke in this part of the country without one. And you need a decent meal and a new pair of boots. And a shirt and pants that fit." Without turning toward him, she nodded at his baggy clothes. "Those are much too big."

Kit's scowl deepened. He was quickly regretting having stuck around long enough to meet the person he'd stolen from. In his profession, it was best not to do that . . . not that he'd had a choice, of course. "That's all well and good, ma'am—you won't hear me arguing about the hat and boots—but it's *oooonly* three dollars, after all. I doubt it'll go that far."

"I know, but it's all I have." Her gaze turned to Mitch, waiting for him to offer the boy the rest of the funds he would need. It was the least he could. Wasn't there a code of honor amongst thieves? One swindler aiding another . . . that sort of thing? When he made no such offer, Chelsea realized she should have known better. His black scowl made the idea die a quick and painless death, and her gaze turn to Kit. "Buy what you can."

"Geez, lady," Kit griped, "I can't take your money now." He thrust his small fist at her again, but Chelsea shook her head. "Damn it, Chels—I . . . cr . . . mean, Miss Hogan. Why'd you have to be so *nice?*" The word rolled off his tongue like a cuss. "I can't steal from you after you talked so sweet to me. You should know that."

"What I know is that you need the money a lot more than I do," Chelsea insisted, fixing Mitch Bryant with a level stare that made him do something she never thought she'd see him do: squirm. "At least my clothes aren't falling off my body. And I have food to put in my stomach and"—her fiery amber gaze sharpened on Mitch—"land to build a home on. That's a lot more than you have, Kit."

"Chelsea," Mitch began, knowing deep in his gut that he was about to try to reason with her and knowing just as surely that it would be like reasoning with a stone. Her mind was set. Even a blind man could see it. He tried anyway, mentally damning himself with each word. "Think about what you're saying. Hell, think about who you're saying it *to*. For Christ's sake, lady, the kid stole your money!"

"Because he needed it," Chelsea argued hotly, spinning to face him. Her index finger made a jabbing motion toward the boy's chest. "Look at him! The kid's starving. Three dollars won't get him far, but at least it will buy him a hat and put a warm meal in his stomach."

"And what are you going to do?" he countered, just as hotly. "You've got no money. No—" He almost said *land,* but stopped himself just in time. He didn't want to tell her about that yet. In fact, he didn't want to tell her about it at all. But he'd have to, of course. Eventually.

"No what?" she prodded, chin tilted high, fists straddling hips that Mitch could still remember pressing softly against him during the long, sleepless night.

"No common sense," he growled finally, angrily. *Damn it!* Plowing his fingers through his wind-tousled hair, he returned her glare. Somehow, he doubted his had as much effect on her as hers had on him. She made him feel small, weak . . . *wrong*. It wasn't a feeling Mitch was used to. And it wasn't one he liked.

"*My* common sense is fine, Mr. Bryant," she replied furiously. "It's *yours* I'm questioning."

Chelsea shifted her attention to Kit, who stood openmouthed, watching the angry exchange. Her gaze softened and a sympathetic smile tugged at her lips. She nudged his shoulder and felt its gauntness even through the thin padding of his threadbare shirt. The feel reassured her, told her she was doing the right thing—not that either of these two stubborn males would ever see it that way. Then again, what could she expect from a pair of thieves? *They* wouldn't recognize an act of human kindness if it walked up and introduced itself!

"Take the money, Kit," she repeated firmly. "All I ask is that you spend it wisely." She nodded behind him, indicating the town of Guthrie. The first fragile threads of evening hadn't quieted the town any. "Go on. Get out of here before I change my mind and get the sheriff after you."

Kit Claymore had been living hand to mouth—or, more correctly, other people's pocket change to mouth—for enough years to know an escape route when he saw one. He saw one now, and it was paved with satiny copper and warm liquid amber. He wasn't stupid enough to let the opportunity pass.

Tipping the hat he'd yet to purchase, the boy sent Chelsea a grin that was so sincere it stopped her heart. She wasn't sure, but she thought she saw his brown eyes water. More likely it was a trick of the twisting shadows of dusk, but she would have liked to have thought differently.

"Thank you, ma'am," he whispered hoarsely, his voice cracking. "I won't forget you. Never." Casting a last glance at her, he pocketed the coins, spun on his heel, and ran off into the early evening shadows, a cloud of Oklahoma dust kicking up behind him.

Chelsea watched the small form dart past tents and milling people. All too soon, she lost sight of him. Sighing, she turned to Mitch, only to find him watching her, closely, assessingly. Her entire body hardened. The evening shadows felt suddenly very cold and threatening.

This was it. This was the moment when she would confront him about the land. The moment she had been waiting for, the moment she had been dreading. Now that it was here, now that she was face to face with the man's rugged form and piercing blue eyes, her resolve weakened. Not a lot, but enough for her to feel the penetrating heat of his gaze and to . . .

Sweet, merciful heavens, I'm responding to him again!

"Well?" she asked breathlessly, while bracing herself for the next in what would undoubtedly be many battles between them. "I know you're dying to do it, Mr. Bryant. I know your itching to call me all kinds of a fool. Please, save us both the trouble and just do it and get it over with."

His gaze burned through the clinging shadows. It was sharp, but not condemning. Hot, but not patronizing. It was, in a word, confusing. Why wasn't he gloating? And why wasn't he out getting drunk, celebrating his victory over the stupid little preacher's daughter? In short, why was he *here?*

"Say it," she demanded when he did nothing but stare at her. Her hands balled into fists, her heart throbbed beneath her breasts. She felt as though she were going to explode if he didn't say something — *anything* — soon.

He said nothing.

Chelsea crossed her arms tightly over her waist, her toe tapping nervously on the hard-packed dirt. "Don't you have *anything* to say?"

143

"Yeah, lady, as a matter of fact I do," Mitch said slowly, his gaze raking her from head to toe. "Your pocket's turned inside out, your hair's a mess, and your horse is waiting."

There was a shimmer in his blue, *blue* eyes that she couldn't place. Against her will, it warmed her.

With an insolent smile, Mitch settled the hat atop his coal-black head, dragging the brim low enough to completely shadow his gaze. The hollow between sculpted cheekbones and ragged beard was enhanced by the play of shadows and dim light.

"That's it? That's all you've got to say?" she prodded. Unconsciously, her fingers strayed to the copper strands that had worked themselves free of the braid at her nape and were now being tossed about her face by the breeze. The other hand tucked her pocket back inside the baggy fold of trousers.

"Yup. That's it." He turned, striding down the side of the depot to where he'd tethered the stallion. Over his shoulder, he added, "Unless you'd like to stand here talking and waste even more time, when we could be heading back to"—his hesitation was slight; the self-incriminating tightening of his jaw was not—"the claim. Personally, I'd like to have familiar land under my feet by this time tomorrow."

Chelsea's attention perked. "You mean you found the land office?" she asked, hurrying to catch up with him. This was his chance to tell her. She fell into step beside him, taking two to every one of his long, powerful strides. "You started the paperwork? There weren't any problems filing our claim*s?*

"It's been taken care of," Mitch ground out sharply. "We'll talk about it later."

"But what about the forms? Don't they need my signat—"

"We'll talk about it later!" Stopping, he turned and glared down at her. The unfamiliar tightening in his gut—could it be guilt?—gnawed at him, making him snap, "Christ, lady, you just gave a goddamn kid your last three earthly dollars and now you're questioning *my* word about a stupid slip of paper? Is there no consistency with you?"

144

Chelsea refused to give the quiver that settled in her stomach a name. The quiver that felt like a thousand batting butterfly wings. Later. He wanted to talk about it later. *When* later? When they were alone? When he would have the chance to kill her and ditch her body, and make the claim legally his?

Her gaze narrowed as this thought iced through her blood. Would he kill her? She remembered the way he'd gone for his gun at the first sign of trouble that morning, and she remembered the cold precision of his movements, proving the reaction was not foreign. And she remembered the cold blue resignation she'd glimpsed in his eyes when she'd asked him to lower his gun. The sight had chilled her then. The memory of it still chilled her now.

Yes, she decided. Mitch Bryant could kill; easily, cleanly, guiltlessly. But could he kill *her?*

Chelsea returned his moody stare and thought that, if she were smart, she would back down. She'd think of a way to get away from him while she was still alive to do it. Then she'd look for another claim that wasn't anywhere near Mitch Bryant's.

But I don't want another claim, I want mine. The one I worked so hard to stake. The one this man stole! That was the only claim that would suit her, and if Mitch killed her because of her determination to have it, then so be it. But one thing she swore: She'd go down fighting him!

She lifted her chin, her jaw tight with determination. "I think I have a right to be concerned, Mr. Bryant. It is, after all, *my* land we're talking about here."

"Yeah, it's your land," Mitch growled under his breath. "Damned if it isn't." He stared down at her, taking in the fire in her eyes and the dark flush of anger in her cheeks. She looked suspicious, he thought. Of course, that wasn't possible. He hadn't told her yet, but he would . . . eventually.

No, not eventually. Tonight, Mitch vowed. He'd tell her tonight, probably after he'd gotten them both good and drunk. Ah, now there was the best idea he'd had all day. Drunk.

145

Three sips of whiskey and she asked me to kiss her. An expectant grin tugged at his lips. *And what, preacher's daughter, will you do after four or five?* Mitch had spent the better part of the day wondering about that; tormenting himself about it; and, yes, fantasizing like hell about it, too.

But there was a definite method to his madness that had nothing to do with seduction. Blinded by whiskey, there was a chance she wouldn't take the news too hard. And maybe, just maybe, she'd be soused enough to hear him out, perhaps even understand why he'd done what he had.

No, he reasoned just as quickly. She wouldn't understand and she'd never, never, *never* forgive him. No matter what he said or how he said it, she'd never understand why he'd signed the deed on land that was more precious to her than her own life. As it was, he barely understood his reasons himself, except to know that he'd done what had to be done at the time.

Losing that property would risk six years of hard work — of his own sweat and blood, and of Brenda's above-and-beyond efforts — going straight down the drain. He damn well hadn't come this far only to have that happen now, all on account of one sexy-as-all-hell redhead. Whatever it took to keep that land, Mitch would do. And if it meant hurting this woman in the process . . . well, no one said he had to *like* that part of the job, but it still had to be done. Damned if it didn't!

Releasing a long, slow exhalation, Mitch tore his gaze away and spun on his heel. His boots crunched over the dirt as he stalked down the shadowy side of the train depot, leaving Chelsea to decide whether or not to follow. Personally, he hoped she had the good sense not to, but after the scene he'd witnessed between her and the little pick-pocket, he doubted she had any good sense at all.

After a brief hesitation, he heard her dragging footsteps fall in behind him.

Damn it!

Chapter Eleven

Mitch was stretched out on a bed of crumpled bluestem, his back resting against a weathered boulder. His thoughts volleyed between being grateful the midnight sky showed no hint of rain — unlike last night the strip of black velvet stretching above hadn't a cloud in sight — and hoping against hope that massive thunderheads would roll in and that, by the grace of God, he'd be struck by lightning and thereby saved from having to tell Chelsea Hogan about her land. Make that her *lack* of land.

His gaze slitted, his attention drifting over the crackling campfire and the woman who crouched in front of it. His mouth went cotton-ball dry. Logical thought abandoned him faster than rats swarming off a sinking ship.

Her back was to him. Her thick plait of hair had been rebraided and now swung in a tidy, glistening rope down her back. The fringed end was tied off with a strip of frayed leather. The sight was unsettling only in as much as Mitch's fingers itched to pluck the thong free and unbind those silky strands. The need to feel her hair gliding beneath his fingers was a tangible ache in his gut. His tight, *tight* gut. He almost groaned aloud when he remembered the feel of those soft wisps tickling his cheek the last time he'd kissed her.

The last time he'd kissed her. Christ, had it only been this morning? It felt like a lifetime ago, maybe two. The worst part was the way he remembered — savored — every second of that kiss and the two before it. He replayed them in his mind until his

147

temples throbbed and his teeth clamped so hard his jaw ached. Though he tried, he couldn't forget one detail—not her honeyed taste, not the warm moistness of her mouth, and definitely not the way her tongue had drawn shy, playful circles around the tip of his own. Every torturous fragment was remembered—vividly—but only because those three timid kisses had been the best, most memorable ones of his entire life.

And *that* was what Mitch had spent the better part of the day wracking his brain trying to figure out. *Why* the chaste little kisses of a Baptist preacher's daughter were so damned moving! He'd had better kisses. Damned if he hadn't! More than his share of them—if he was keeping tally, which he wasn't. But none had affected him in the same sweet, seductive way Ch—Chelsea Hogan's fresh-tasting innocence had.

Mitch's gut churned. His gaze lowered. Another groan—this one audible—left him. He quickly sucked it back in through his teeth. His tightly clenched teeth!

Bent over and leaning forward, her enticing little backside was outlined to perfection by the pull of her trousers. He doubted she was aware of it, or she wouldn't be giving him such an enticing view. His gaze traveled hungrily down each delectable side, noticing how the clean line of her waist tapered appealingly in, then even more appealingly flared as the trousers molded themselves around the gentle curve of her hips.

The pants no longer looked baggy to Mitch, and he swore inwardly at the detailed observation. He knew damned well that if the coarse material would just flop around her soft, soft bottom the way it had done most of the day, his gut would not be fisting the way it was now. And he wouldn't be harboring such strong and steady urgings to corrupt this woman's morals by teaching her the *true* meaning of words "sins of the flesh."

But he did feel the urgings—like a bolt of sizzling summer lightning scorching his blood, he felt them!—and they weren't easily ignored. Nor were they close to being forgotten.

Chelsea felt Mitch's gaze warming her. Actually, the feel of those incredible blue eyes roaming over her wasn't warm as much as it was hot. Very, very hot. And . . . tingly. The sensation seeped like liquid fire through her clothes, peeling them away, searing her flesh like the tip of a branding iron. It was an erotic, delicious, melting sensation. It was also a wicked one.

She sent a quick glance over her shoulder. His gaze was fixed exactly where she'd felt it to be . . . on her bottom. The flush that kissed her cheeks did not stem from the fire's heat.

Sweet heavens, he really is staring at my backside! The glint in what little she could see of his eyes was sharp enough to carve through stone. She swallowed hard, her throat abruptly too dry and too tight, as her attention shifted.

His posture was cockily slouched. His long, thick denim-clad legs dipped into the scuffed leather boots that were crossed at the ankles. No gunbelt rode his lean hips, but she remembered how one looked there . . . right at home. The red flannel shirt hung from the broad shelf of his shoulders, the unbuttoned placket parting over his naked chest and puddling in soft folds on the dirt beside his taut, sun-kissed waist. The hairs pelting the sinewy wedge were dark and thick, glistening with the moisture of a recent washing.

The firelight kissed his face in a shadowy orange glow. The twisting light accentuated features that were ruggedly hard, but handsomely so. It danced over the ravens-wing black of his hair and made his straggly beard and mustache look even darker beneath the healthy tan of his sharply carved cheeks. The stub of a very short cigarette was clamped between his lips, its tip glowing a hot, smoldering orange.

He stole your land, girl. Remember that. But it was hard to remember anything with all that sun-bronzed masculinity reclining just a few threatening feet away. Her reaction to him now was the same as it had been the first time she'd seen him—breathless, stirring, intense. Only the hard set of his jaw beneath the beard and the spidery vein throbbing in his temple, its beat unusually quick and erratic, told her he was not as composed as he would have liked her to think he was.

Clearing her throat, she straightened and turned to face him. She didn't exactly tower over him, but it did fill her with a heady sense of confidence to be looking down at him for once.

"Is now a good time?" she asked, surprised at how smooth her voice sounded in her ears.

Mitch rolled the cigarette over his tongue. The opposite corner of his lips pulled up in a wolfish half-grin. A raven brow cocked high. "Now's a great time, sweetheart. What did you have in mind?"

"To talk, Mr. Bryant. You said you'd tell me what happened at the land office 'later.' " Her chin lifted and she glared down the short, pert length of her nose at him. "Is now a good time?"

Mitch's expression hardened. His mood, already bad, turned sour. He dragged the last puff off his cigarette, released the smoke in a slow, steady stream, then flicked the stub into the grass. "Yeah," he grumbled. "As good as any, I expect."

He thought about what he had to say to her, then thought about what her reaction would be once he'd said it. She was going to be mad as hell. Furious. It wouldn't surprise him a bit if she tried to kill him. Mitch's gaze swept to the gunbelt, curled atop the ground at his side. As always, it was within reach . . . if he needed it. His fingers were entwined, pillowed atop the taut expanse of his stomach. They twitched at the familiar sight of the Colt.

Sighing, he closed his eyes and wondered, when the time came, if she *did* try to kill him, would he be able to shoot her? He thought about that in the way he thought about how he would kill anyone. In his mind, he thrust them both into that deadly situation. Mentally, he placed Chelsea a few feet away and shoved a cooking knife into her open palm. The blade was long, sharp, lethal. He wrapped her fingers around the handle and made them tremble. She was a preacher's daughter, he reasoned, and she was mad as hell. She *would* be trembling.

The image sharpened. Her cheeks were flushed. Sweat beaded on her brow, dampening the copper wisps clinging there. Her eyes were wide, shimmering with a mixture of fury and fright. She was scared, shaking. He could feel her terror as though it were a living, breathing part of him. His response

150

to it was unnerving.

She was yelling, but in his head he couldn't hear the words. Her shouts fed her anger. Her cheeks paled when she made her first thrust with the blade toward his heart. Her stroke was awkward, clumsy, easily parried.

He turned and went down hard on one knee, grabbing the pistol and slipping it from the holster. The hammer clicked into place as he squatted and spun to face her. He leveled the barrel at her heart as she made a second lunge at him. His finger twitched on the trigger, not hard enough to fire the gun . . . yet. He braced himself for the pistol's recoil.

"So what happened?" Chelsea demanded, her voice loud enough to jar his wandering thoughts. His eyes had been closed for exactly two seconds, but she didn't dare let him fall asleep. She'd waited long enough. She wanted answers!

Mitch's thick black lashes snapped up. His gaze locked on her. Scowling, he blinked hard, pulling her into focus.

"I need a drink," he growled abruptly, pouncing on the plan he'd made earlier. Rolling to the side, he snatched up his saddlebag and fumbled inside, pulling free a bottle of whiskey he was now damned thankful he'd stopped in one of the Magic City's many saloons to buy. To hell with propriety, thieves, and sexy little preacher's daughters. He needed a goddamn drink. Badly.

"Is that your answer to everything? Getting drunk?"

Mitch knelt in the dirt, uncorking the bottle with his teeth. He spit the cork to the ground and lifted the bottle to his lips, downing three f_ ery slugs as their eyes met and locked over the rounded glass bottom. "Yup," he said, his voice harsh and whiskey-raw. His grin was cold as he wiped the rim of the bottle with his palm and held it out to her. "Isn't it yours?"

Chelsea split a glare between the man and the bottle. Even from where she stood, she could smell the fumes. "You know it isn't."

"Lady, I don't know a goddamn thing anymore," he growled hatefully. "Do you want a drink or don't you?"

Her gaze fixed on the bottle. She remembered the tangy taste of the stuff and the delicious, relaxed feelings that came afterward. Then she remembered the way she had invited Mitch Bryant to kiss her the last time she'd imbibed. "I don't," she said, her tone only a little weak, only a little hesitant.

"Suit yourself, but it'll make the time pass quicker." *And make what I have to say go down a whole lot easier.*

He shrugged and settled back against the rock, wedging the bottle high between his thighs. Only a small portion of his mind acknowledged that the gesture was done purposely and that it had the desired effect. Her whiskey-amber gaze followed his hand and widened. Her cheeks flooded a becoming shade of pink, and her mouth gaped slightly — softly — open.

If possible, he thought she looked even sexier than normal. And that was saying a lot! Resting his head back against the rock, his gaze took its own sweet time traveling up from the tip of her toes to the top of her head. By the time he retraced the path to her eyes, he saw she was trembling. The knowledge pleased him. It was nice to know he wasn't suffering alone.

"Are you going to sit, or am I going to have to keep craning my neck to look up at you?" he asked.

There was very little craning to be done. Even sitting and slouched, he was a tall man. Even standing, spine rigid, she was short. They weren't on eye level, but with a bit of distance separating them, they might as well have been.

The only thing that stopped Chelsea from immediately turning down his offer — gruff as it had been made — was the feel of her knees, weak and watery. The coarse, baggy trousers hid the humiliating quivers from view, but her pants would not hide a fall should her knees decide to buckle. Since they didn't feel as though they would support her for long, she hesitated.

What's wrong with me? she wondered angrily. There was no logical explanation for the annoying shivers that kept icing down her spine. No reason for the rapid pounding of her heart or the cold sweat that was beading on her palms. Unless, of course, her sudden anxiety stemmed from the thought of putting her body anywhere near that rock-solid, denim-clad thigh of his. And what if that muscular upper arm grazed against her?

Yes, girl, what then? a little demon inside her mind asked. Chelsea could have sworn she heard the pixie laugh in delight when her heart skipped a beat.

Mitch's gaze narrowed on her when she didn't respond. Damn it! If he couldn't get her to sit, he'd *never* get her to drink. Deciding he'd waited long enough for an answer, he fished the cork off the ground, plugged it into the bottle, then set it aside. With a lithe shove, he was on his feet. In two steps, he was towering over her.

Close up, he was again struck with how small she was. Her head — *Christ, her hair was gorgeous in the firelight!* — barely grazed the top of his shoulder. It was a shoulder he was surprised to note, that she was staring at with rigid intensity. And had the firelight put that becoming flush in her cheeks? he wondered as he coiled his fingers around her upper arms. Or had something else? Something a little more male.

A shiver raced through the flesh cupped beneath his palm. Mitch would have needed to be dead not to feel it.

His eyes flashed with confusion a split second before the emotion was forcefully doused. Chelsea would have needed to be blind not to see that.

Wisely, neither acknowledged their observations.

"Come on," he said, "let's sit down."

She allowed herself to be guided to the rock, not knowing why she didn't protest. It would have been the smart thing to do. Then again, she hadn't been known for her intelligence lately. Here she was with this remarkably handsome, half-clothed, very dangerous man. That should tell her something.

He pushed her onto the dirt. As if on cue, her knees did what they'd been threatening to do. They buckled.

Stepping over her legs, he eased himself down to her left. The air around her shifted. The cool breeze of his movements wafted over her suddenly too-warm cheeks. Hesitantly, she inhaled and found she'd sucked in a shaky breath that smelled of leather, whiskey, soap . . . and something else — something that was mysterious, unnerving, and flagrantly male.

"Did you file my claim?" she asked, giving in to the urge to

153

hear the sound of her own voice—no matter how weak and shaky.

"What do you think?"

The closeness of his voice, combined with the way his warm breath washed over her cheeks and neck, made Chelsea jump. Her arm did exactly what she'd been afraid it would do: It brushed against his. And, as she'd also been afraid would happen, she wasn't disappointed. Even through both their sleeves, she could feel the raw, coiled power of his arm. Her response was quick and stinging: a shakily indrawn breath, moister palms, and a heart that refused to stop hammering.

A quick corner-glance saw him pulling the cork from the bottle with his teeth again—a flash of white against his dark beard and mustache. He spit the cork into the dirt and, after belting back another slug, held out the bottle.

"The truth is, Mr. Bryant, I don't know *what* to think about you," she answered, her gaze fixed on the bottle. She absolutely forbid her hand to reach for it. "You confuse me."

"*I* confuse *you?*" He chuckled, shook his head, then lowered the bottle back to a lap Chelsea was smart enough not to look at twice. "Hell, lady, you don't know the half of it!"

"Are you talking about Kit?"

"Him . . . and the sister you showed up in Guthrie to find—and left without."

She bristled. "Emilee left town before we arrived. Hardly *my* fault."

"Alone?"

Her lips pinched, her gaze strayed. "No."

"Where'd she go?"

"If I knew that, I wouldn't be sitting here talking to you, would I? No, I'd be out finding her."

"Why? She's a big girl. She doesn't need you chasing after her every time she gets it in her head to—" He stopped short when he remembered the scene he'd witnessed between this woman and her sister. A confrontation *she* didn't know he'd overheard. He thought it would be best to keep it that way. This night was going to be hard enough as it was.

Chelsea watched Mitch seize the bottle in his fist and tip

154

back a healthy swallow of whiskey, then sigh or gasp; she wasn't sure which. Nor did she care. Her traitorous gaze had just fixed on his lips, now visible beneath the curl of his mustache. They were nicely shaped; thin and whiskey-wet.

They were also grinning wickedly. A matching devilish glint could be detected in his eyes. "She do this often, your sister? Take off, I mean?"

"God yes," Chelsea sighed. Her smile was weak and vague as she latched onto any excuse to postpone their inevitable confrontation. "Emmy's been a rebel all her life, Mr. Bryant. It comes with being a preacher's daughter — or so I've been told. The second she found out that promiscuity was enough to anger our father, she made it her lifelong career. Normally, I'd go after her again, but I have land to tend to now." She sent him a sharp glance to catch his reaction. There was none. His expression was impassive. "And a home to build. I can't very well stay on my property for the required five years *and* chase my wayward sister all over the countryside, now, can I?"

Something in the look Mitch sent her made Chelsea's blood go cold. *He isn't going to tell me. Unless forced, he isn't going to tell me.* The bastard! It would serve him right if she shot him through his traitorous heart while he slept, she thought, knowing she'd never do it. Just the thought . . .

"So, what happened to that bottle?" she asked, giving in to the sudden need for a good, stiff drink. At this point, she'd risk crawling over Mitch Bryant's sinewy lap if it meant getting a numbing sip of his liquor — anything to quench this unusual craving for violence, the intensity of which was frightening.

"Thought you didn't drink." Mitch's smile was quick and only a little patronizing. It was also forced.

Her stomach flip-flopped, belying her casual shrug. "I changed my mind," she muttered, accepting the offered bottle.

The glass was cool to the touch, but it felt like a chip of ice compared to the fingers she accidentally brushed. His flesh was hot. Searingly so.

Mitch watched as she took a deep breath, scrunched her face, and lifted the bottle to her lips. She belted down three

155

quick gulps and then his hand snaked out, his fingers coiling around her wrist before she could toss back another fiery swallow.

The wheezing gulps of air Chelsea sucked in hurt. Her eyes watered as she met his gaze and felt the first warmth of the whiskey settle in her stomach.

"Why are you touching me?" she asked. Her tone was husky, her throat raw, as though it had been scraped by a slice of sandpaper. Exactly the way her arm felt, come to think of it, except that part of her body was also hot and very, very aware of the warm roughness of his fingers. Her wrist burned.

"Are you sure you want to do this?" he asked. His voice was also a little husky, and a lot strained. She had a feeling he was talking about more than just drinking whiskey.

"Yes," she answered, scowling. "I think so." And then Chelsea wondered which question she'd just answered.

Mitch glanced at the bottle before his gaze traveled to the wrist he held ensnared. God, she was a tiny thing!

Chelsea tried to draw back. His thumb shifted against her wrist. It wasn't a broad, sweeping stroke, but it might as well have been for all the reaction it stirred. In the back of her mind, the so very different textures of their skin registered. His palm was work-roughened and red. Hers, for all her chores, was degrees softer. And sizes smaller. Both were hot and slightly moist.

"You want more?" He nodded to the bottle.

Mutely, she nodded. Wanted? She *needed* it. More so when her gaze fixed on his lips.

His fingers uncurled from her arm so fast it was all Chelsea could do to right the bottle before it spilled its potent guts onto their laps — which were situated much too closely together, if the tingling in her thigh had anything to say about it.

"Fine. Just don't say I didn't warn you." He shrugged, his hand dropping to a lap she still refused to look at.

The caustic remark she'd planned to utter after her next swallow faded when she lifted the bottle to her lips. Her third swallow went down her throat wrong. The haughty words on her tongue were burned away by the firewater trickling down her throat. Her raw, tight, flaming throat. And she'd thought the whiskey burned when it went down the *right* path!

Her strangled little gasps and wheezes pleased the hell out of Mitch. So much for prim and sanctimonious! Settling back against the hard pillow of rock, he watched as she sat forward, her ragged coughs cutting the night. A grin tugged at his lips as he administered three curt slaps with his open palm between her shoulder blades. His help was not appreciated. Or so said the dark amber glare she shot him from over a slender shoulder. Her look was murderous.

"Are you trying to kill me?" she croaked, her voice whiskey-raw. Her tongue felt large, fuzzy, and very numb. And she didn't even want to think about the sour taste the potent stuff had left in her mouth. How could he drink this stuff? Worse, how could *she* drink it . . . *again?*

His grin broadened. "Hey, lady, I was just trying to help."

"My aching spine says you weren't."

Again his shoulders rose and fell. The red flannel sleeves hugged the rippling male flesh beneath, drawing taut for a split second before reforming into soft bunches. Did he practice doing that when he was alone? Chelsea wondered. He must. The shrug was too smooth, the air it gave him too casual and uncaring to be spontaneous. Bracing herself, she took another sip of the whiskey. This one went down right. So did the next. The last one might as well have been plain river water for all her numbed throat felt of its passing.

Her gaze drifted up. His, which had been studying her fiery hair, drifted down.

Brilliant blue meshed with stormy amber, and in that instant Chelsea knew it would be wise to thrust the bottle back into his hands and seek her bedroll for the night — now, while she still had the presence of mind to do it. To hell with the land. They could talk come morning, in the unforgiving light of day.

With more force than was necessary, she shoved the bottle at him. Unprepared, he didn't reach to take it — until her knuckles came into contact with his chest. The curling black hairs felt as though they had been put there just to tickle and tease her smoldering skin. She could feel his heart drumming and was surprised to find that the tempo skipped as wildly as her own.

Mitch's hand came up. His palm covered her trembling fingers. Ah, they *were* trembling, just as he'd imagined they would be — but for a much different reason. He recognized the response for what it was — desire, white-hot and quick. He doubted the sexy preacher's daughter had figured it out, though.

"I had some trouble at the land office," Mitch said then, though he was never sure why. Probably because he would have seized at any excuse to get this woman mad at him. Because his gaze had just dropped to her lips, and he was fighting the overpowering urge to capture her soft, shallow breaths with his mouth. It was a battle he was losing.

God, he wanted to kiss her. Hell, who was he kidding? He wanted to do a hell of a lot *more* than just kiss her. It was so hard to remember she was a preacher's daughter when she looked at him as though she wanted more from him, too. Damned hard!

"I know," she said, and slipped her hand from beneath his. The night air felt suddenly cool against her too-warm knuckles. Chelsea attributed that to the whiskey, which had formed a nice, warm, numbing pool in the pit of her stomach. The feeling was seeping through the rest of her body with alarming speed, dulling her thoughts, chipping away at her strictly embedded morals.

"Don't you want to know what happened?"

Her gaze dropped to his lips. "No. Yes! I mean . . . Oh my, I think I'm going to be sick."

"Ah, hell." Lightning quick, Mitch was on his knees beside her. She was still sitting, but now she was bent at the waist. Her forehead crushed the thick carpet of bluestem, her braid trailing over the grass like a snake.

"Take slow, deep breaths," he instructed, his palm poised inches from her back. He hesitated for just a second before he touched her, smoothing his hand down her spine, then — *Christ, she was a tiny thing!* — massaged the tense muscles in her neck and shoulders. "I said *slow,*" he growled.

"I" — she sucked in another quick breath — "can't breathe slow" — and another — "when you're touching me like that."

"You'll breathe slow enough when you pass out," he griped. "Which, judging from the way you're breathing, should be in about a minute. Maybe less."

The thought of being unconscious made Chelsea keep her next breath trapped in her lungs until it hurt so bad she thought she would explode. She released it raggedly, then forced the next rush of air to enter her lungs *slowly,* as instructed. She could have slapped Mitch Bryant when she found out he was right, she did feel better. Her nausea subsided and the world, blessedly, stopped spinning.

"You all right?" he asked.

"Hmmm. Fine." But she wasn't fine. How could she be? She'd just realized where his hand had stopped: cushioned on the upper curve of her bottom. She wanted to breathe fast again but resisted the urge.

"You don't look fine."

She glared at his upside-down face. "What do you expect me to look like? I'm drunk, for crying out loud!" And she was. The world had stopped spinning and she wasn't nauseous anymore, but she couldn't have stopped her words from slurring into each other if she'd tried. And she'd forgotten how to try.

"Mr. Bryant?" she began tentatively.

"Yes, Miss Hogan?"

"I think I'm" — she wrinkled her nose and scowled — "stuck. In fact, I think my entire body's melted. I can't move."

Mitch did not laugh. He knew he didn't because his lips hurt from where he had to roll them inward and clamp them between his teeth to stifle the urge. "Want some help?"

"If you wouldn't mind."

Mind? Hell yes, he'd mind! Just the thought of touching her — platonically — did bizarre things to his mind. Wasn't it bad enough his palm felt sizzlingly alive from where it had stopped, cushioned on the rounded curve of her bottom?

Cursing under his breath, he gripped her upper arms and

pulled her back—slowly, so the blood rushing from her head wouldn't make her sick again. He wasn't prepared for her to move so easily. Before he could stop her, Mitch found himself leaning back against the rock, with a very drunk—very sexy—preacher's daughter curled in his embrace.

"Better?" he asked, his voice husky-sharp when he felt her fingers fisting his shirt, her nails biting at the flesh beneath. It wasn't a painful contact. Would that it were!

"Better," she confirmed. Her voice was slurred and almost unrecognizable as she buried her cheek against his nice, warm, spicy-smelling chest. She nodded, and felt the ripple of tense muscle beneath her, felt the arm around her shoulders tightening as his fingers curled inward.

"I think you drank too much too fast," he said, blatantly understating the obvious.

"Hmmm," she murmured against his chest. "I must have. Why else would I feel so good right now?"

"Good?" He chuckled. "I thought you were going to be sick."

"It passed, thank the Lord."

"And me." He turned his head, his cheek stroking the feather-soft top of her head. "What do you mean, you feel good?"

Her shrug was tiny and shy. "I don't know. I feel . . . safe. Secure. I must be drunk." The pounding of his heart was a constant, lulling beat in her ear. Yes, she decided as she snuggled closer to him, it *had* to be the whiskey. "Yup, I'm drunk all right. That's why I feel like I trust you." Sighing, she dragged the tip of her tongue across her lips. They tasted of the pungent tang of whiskey, a taste she would probably always now associate with Mitch Bryant. "Well . . . I mean, I don't trust you exactly," she amended when she felt him stiffen beneath her, "but I feel like I could be persuaded to."

Mitch would have laughed, had he seen anything in her guileless comment to laugh about. He didn't. Her innocent words infuriated him. Did she know what the hell she was saying? And whom she was saying it *to?* No, of course she didn't. She was a preacher's daughter. Trust, turning the other cheek, looking for the best in people; that was what her life was all about. Still, her naiveté did nothing to temper Mitch's anger.

"Lady," he growled, "either you get drunk quicker than anyone I've ever met, or you're just plain stupid." His eyes narrowed to penetrating blue slits, piercing her to the core as he demanded, "Didn't your daddy ever teach you about what happens to nice girls like you who get involved with bad men like me? *They get ruined!*"

"Are you bad?" she asked, scowling sloppily. "Very bad?" She felt rather than saw him nod. "The worst."

"It doesn't matter," she slurred. The whiskey was working in force; warming, numbing, relaxing. Making her forget there was a very good reason she shouldn't trust this man. If only she could remember what it was! "Anyway, I'm not involved with you. Not at all. And why *shouldn't* I trust you? You aren't really as bad as" — she stifled a sloppy yawn with her fist — "all that. A little gruff, maybe. And crass. And you swear far too much. Still, I think you're . . . well, you're . . ."

Say it, Bryant, Tell her the goddamn truth! his mind screamed.

But he couldn't. She shifted then, looking up at him. Her eyes were wide and innocent, and the way the firelight played off their sweet whiskey depths made her gaze almost loving. He was a hard man, true, but it would take a stronger man than himself to destroy the tenderness he saw shimmering in her eyes right now.

Mitch's breath caught. Tenderness. He savored the sight, knowing he'd never seen that expression in a woman's eyes before. His gut wrenched when he realized that, once Ch — Chelsea Hogan's illusions about him were shattered, once she learned the truth and knew he'd lied to her, he would never see that look in her eyes again. Damn, but he'd miss it!

His attention dropped to her lips, and his eyes darkened to devouring blue. He watched as her gaze settled on his mouth. Her lips parted, her chin tilted up, and her long copper lashes flickered shut as she molded into him. The breasts straining into his side rose and fell with breaths that were all soft and shallow and ragged.

"Please, Mitch," she whispered, and he could tell from the scowl flickering over her brow that she didn't have the slightest idea of what she was pleading for. "Please."

He shouldn't. He knew he shouldn't. He also knew he was going to — and that no power on heaven or earth would be able to stop him from leaning down and tasting her, just once more.

"Ah, hell." Mitch shifted, his fingers coiling around her slender upper arms as he dragged her unresisting body across his lap. Her bottom felt warm, soft, perfect as it cradled against him. The way she opened her eyes to stare up at him was all innocent and sexy . . . and tempting as hell.

Mitch's self-restraint splintered around him, aided by the plaintive moan that whispered past lips that were parted in moist anticipation. Soft, pink, pouty lips. Dear God, he was only human! He'd dreamed of her honeyed kisses for days, and for long, restless nights. They filled his waking hours and tortured what little sleep he'd been able to snatch since he'd met her. He couldn't deny his need any longer. Worse, he didn't want to.

With a husky groan, he slipped one hand around her waist, the other around her neck. He crushed her pliable body to his chest. The feel of her breasts — hot and full and ripe — pressing into him, searing him, was his final undoing.

Chelsea gasped in surprise. Not shocked surprise. Not outraged surprise. But pleasant, sensuous, expectant surprise.

The murmur of sound was swallowed up by the hard mouth that crashed down on hers.

Chapter Twelve

The second her moist little tongue slipped into his mouth, Mitch knew what he felt for the sexy preacher's daughter went deeper than physical lust. Oh, the lust was there, pumping quick and hot in his blood, but there was a more powerful need building in him — and the repercussions of that need boggled his mind.

There was the need to touch; he'd felt that need before, but never *this* strong. The need to *be* touched — everywhere, softly, urgently. The need to smell her sweet feminine scent, to surround himself with it, to suck it into his lungs as though it were the last breath he'd ever take. The need to nibble and taste every salty-sweet, creamy inch of her. And the need to hear her gasps of pleasure ringing hot in his ears.

These needs were so strong, so undeniable, that the sheer force of them would have sent Mitch crashing to his knees had he been standing. Each need sluiced through his body, merging, blending into the next until he felt a gnawing, empty void churning in the pit of his stomach. A void that begged to be filled. That begged *her* to fill it with her tender kisses and hesitant, naive little caresses.

Her tongue swirled around the hot, sensitive tip of his. It ran shyly along the even line of his teeth, then behind, searching. The strokes grew longer, bolder, as she tasted him. A growl rumbled in the back of his throat when he tipped his head to the side to facilitate her. His reward was a more thorough exploration. One he wasn't sure he could live through.

The sound of his groan, captured by her lips, melted down the length of Chelsea's spine. She strained closer, her breaths ragged as her hands lifted to wrap around the thick cord of his neck. Raven curls scraped the powerful shelf of his shoulders, tickling her palms and wrists. She shivered, tunneling her fingers deeply in the silky strands. His scalp felt warm when she cupped it in her palms and pulled him closer, deepening the kiss to a frenzied pitch.

She'd swiveled in his arms until she was crushed against the solid wedge of his chest. The whiskey must have heightened her senses, for her breasts felt unnaturally full, the tips straining and sensitive beneath her shirt. There might as well have been no cloth separating them for all the padding it offered. She could feel the rippling muscle and hardness that was Mitch Bryant, could smell his spicy maleness in her nostrils and feel the silky texture of his hair slipping through her fingers. His beard and mustache tickled her searching, hungry lips. It was a sensation comparable to none.

The combination was an assault to her spiraling senses. It was headily disarming. Alarmingly sensual. Her reaction to it was fascinating, for it created an aching need somewhere deep in her stomach; a need that spread through the rest of her body lightning quick; a need that made her want to feel more of him. *All* of him. Now.

"Mitch?" she whispered huskily against his mouth.

The single plaintive word was a warm rush of whiskey-laced air searing his lips. He tingled, aching to draw her back but not daring to just yet. She was scared and confused. He knew it as well as he knew his own lack of experience when it came to corrupting virgins. And he had *no* experience seducing Baptist preacher's daughters to draw on. This was the first one he'd ever *met,* for Christ's sake!

"It's all right, sweetheart," he rasped, while covering the delicate line of her jaw with small but passionate kisses. Her head tipped up and to the side, allowing him better access, which he immediately, unquestionably, took. "Just take it slow. Feel it. Feel it all. There's no rush."

"But, Mitch . . ."

"Shhh." His tongue darted out, moistening, tasting the hollow beneath her chin. The soft, creamy, salty skin. The taste and texture — so sweet, so soft and alluring — drove him insane with the need to taste and feel more. "I won't hurt you, Chelsea," he soothed, his blue eyes dark and blazing. "I'd never hurt you. Know that, sweetheart." He felt the lump in her throat bob against his lips. "Know it and believe it."

"I do," she sighed softly, throatily. She tipped her head back, until her spine arched and her front pressed more firmly against him. Her breasts felt as though they were on fire. The need in her, so alien it was unrecognizable, was building, throbbing, aching for . . . what?

He nuzzled her neck and felt the pulse that leapt wildly in her throat against his tongue. The taste was so heady it was intoxicating. The whiskey was water by comparison.

The hand on her neck slipped lower, cupping her shoulder. His fingers curled around the slender line, squeezing gently as though testing its firmness. It surprised him, for as slender as she was, she was strongly built. No fat, no waste. Her back was not long, he noted as his palm slipped smoothly down its arched length. He felt the fringe of her braid scrape his roughened knuckles. The feel was a tickling sort of burn, one that fueled the fire raging in his blood, almost out of control.

The leather thong was slipped free, her copper hair quickly coaxed from the twined plait and fluffed to frame her face, shoulders, and back in a glistening cloud. As he'd imagined they would be, the strands were baby soft and fine, gliding like satin between his calloused fingertips. Freeing her hair had freed more of her sweet, sweet scent. A waft of the heady feminine aroma enveloped Mitch, drowning him in its fragrant, flowery softness.

Chelsea caught the scent, too, and with a small portion of her mind she noticed the way it entangled itself with the aroma of leather and soap and masculine spices. The two mingled, entwined until it was impossible to tell where one left off and the other began. The backlash of this observation was jarringly intense, white-hot and exciting. The result was a fine keening of her already-sharpened senses.

Her hands left his hair. Her palms pillowed atop his shoulders. Her fingers curled inward, digging into raw sinew and strength, of which there was no give, no softness. His body wasn't pliable, the way hers was, but was wonderfully hard and firm. There was something thrilling about the way his shirt slipped over rippling flesh when she fisted the cloth in her hands, something enthralling and sensual in the way his ragged breaths washed over her neck, wafting beneath her collar, heating the sensitive skin beneath.

"I want you, Ch—Chelsea Hogan," he groaned, between taking tender nips at her neck. He felt her shiver, and he felt his own responsive tremors.

"I—I know," she whispered hoarsely, though deep down she really didn't know. But she wanted to. Heaven help her, she wanted to know the meaning of his words so badly she could cry bittersweet tears from the need of it!

"Do you really?" Mitch pulled back just far enough to look into her passion-thickened gaze. Her amber eyes were dazed, and not only from the whiskey. She returned his gaze, only a little shyly. When she would have looked away, his hand cupped her jaw, forcing her attention back, holding it in place without force.

"Mitch . . ." Chelsea swallowed hard, wishing she knew the words that would make him continue what he'd been doing. It was wrong. It was sinful. The way he was making her ache was too delicious to be proper. But it all felt so good and . . . dear God, she didn't want him to stop!

His eyes were dark, intent, and very, very blue. They seemed to look past her gaze, into the core of her soul. "Lady, do you really know what it means when a man says he 'wants' a woman?" He felt her quake beneath his palms, and Mitch didn't think he'd ever wanted anything as badly as he wanted—needed, *craved*—to wrap his arms around this tiny woman and hold her close. He wanted to wordlessly soothe her fears and at the same time carry this torturously slow seduction to its satisfying end, until they both lay spent and

166

panting on the grass.

He forced himself to continue. "What it means is that I want to peel off all your clothes," he explained throatily, and caught her soft gasp with a brief but smoldering kiss. "It means I want to watch you, to feel you peel off mine. I want you hot and naked beside me . . . against me . . . beneath me. I want to be inside of you, Ch—Chelsea Hogan." Then, so soft she could barely hear him, he groaned and added, "More than I've ever wanted anything in my life, I want to feel what it's like to be inside of you—all warm and tight and soft and wet. Damned if I don't."

"And damned if I do," she whispered softly, her gaze dropping to his lips, a sensuous curve beneath the curl of his mustache. "It's a sin. What you want   what I want . . ."

"Do you want it?" he asked quickly, his hands tightening on her jaw only the barest of degrees. "Do you want me to make love to you? If not, say the word and I'll stop. But say it soon, lady—please, God, say it soon!—because a man gets to the point where he can't stop. No matter what. And I have a sick feeling that, with you, I may already have reached that point."

"I—" She hesitated. Her lips rolled inward, her teeth pressing down as she bit back the words her tongue ached to say.

Making love before marriage was a sin. The worst—aside from murder, of course. Papa had often spouted a list as long as his arm of penance one must serve to make redemption for that sort of promiscuity. Emilee knew the list by heart. And yet . . .

The torment in her whiskey-amber eyes sliced Mitch to the core. His grip relaxed, his gaze softened. The change in him, though slight, seemed to wash away some of her fear. He could feel her relaxing beneath his palms, against his chest, atop his lap. But still, she didn't answer. He was beginning to wonder if she ever would, for every second it took her to speak felt like a torturous lifetime to Mitch.

"Have you ever seen a man naked?" he asked softly, and not at all derisively. "Not a boy, Chelsea. A man."

167

Her eyes were wide, and a spark of curiosity lit their depths to a fiery shade of golden brown. She concealed the inexperienced reaction quickly, but not before Mitch had seen and read it for what it was. Of course, there was no hiding the flush creeping up her neck, pinkening her complexion clear up to her hairline. Mutely, she shook her head.

The fluff of copper hair streamed appealingly around her cheeks and brow. Mitch soothed the strands back with his palm. "Do you want to?"

"No," she whispered huskily. Her gaze darkened. One hand reached up, and her index finger ironed away the wrinkle that creased his brow at her answer. She'd made her decision, probably from the first moment she'd looked into his incredible blue eyes. Now, she had only to speak it out loud. That was proving to be the hard part. "I don't want to see just any man naked," she continued thickly, her fingers traveling to the open placket of his shirt. She fisted the cloth and met his gaze unflinchingly. "It may be a sin, one I'll go straight to hell for even thinking about, let alone acting upon. But . . . I want to see you. All of you. Naked. I want to feel you, to t — touch you. And I want you to t — touch me."

"Are you sure?" he asked softly, raggedly. The words rang in his ears, but he hardly recognized them as his own. Had he — Mitch Bryant — just offered this woman an avenue to escape her inevitable seduction? By God, he had! His voice deepened to a husky, condemning purr. "Lady, if you've got a brain in your head, you'll stop me now — while you still stand a chance of me hearing you. Come on, baby, tell me. Tell me to get on my horse and ride out of here. Tell me to go to hell."

The hand on her jaw tightened, jerking her chin up, forcing her to return his hot, piercing glare.

She gasped. She shivered. She did not pull away. This time, she knew why. And she knew exactly what she wanted. Mitch Bryant. That was what — *who* — she wanted.

In his head, Mitch cursed her for her sudden lack of wisdom. Then he cursed himself for his own bad judgment . . . for still wanting her with every heartbeat that throbbed through his veins. "Tell me to leave you alone, preacher's daughter," he growled. His grip was harsh and biting now. "Tell me. Last chance."

Her hands slipped up his warm, naked chest. Her fingers curled in, until they formed tight, quivering fists. She did not shove him away, though there was a small part of her mind — the part that still retained some sense — begging her to. Swallowing hard, she tipped her chin proudly and said, "I don't want you to leave me alone, Mitch. I want you to make love to me."

Mitch's head came back hard against the rock. His eyelids flickered shut as though in pain. The scowl was back, furrowing his brow. "I was afraid you'd say that."

"And I was afraid you'd say you didn't want me."

The soft admission made his sooty lashes sweep up. Slowly, he drew her closer, until his breath was hot and whiskey-sharp against her face. "Not want you? *Not* — ? Ah, hell."

With a final tug, he sealed their mouths together. The kiss was deep, demanding, passionate. It was also much too brief.

Chelsea put the short time their mouths hungrily explored each other to good use. Her trembling fingers slipped beneath the gaping placket of his shirt. His skin felt smooth and hot gliding beneath her sensitive knuckles. The glossy raven curls there felt soft and tickly. The contrast in skin textures — his and hers — was exciting. Her fingers uncurled, tunneling through the raven pelt until the tips tingled with the silky feel of it. Her breathing grew shallow and rapid, her heartbeat fluttered in her breasts. She strained against him.

The hand fell away from her jaw as he tore his lips from hers, burying his face in the sweet-scented hollow between neck and shoulder. He cupped the side of her neck, angling her head, then pillowed his warm, rough palm on her shoulder. He hesitated for only a second before his palm scorched lower.

Chelsea's breath caught as his fingers hovered over the upper swell of her breast. Passion had burned the whiskey away too quickly, but her desire was stronger, more intoxicating than any liquor could have been. Her senses sharpened, focusing on the fragile cloth covering her. His touch felt hot, even through the shirt, as it seared the barrier away.

Her awareness traced to his other hand—the one that was deftly working free the buttons trailing down from just beneath her chin. The closures sprung free. The baggy tail of the shirt was coaxed from the trouser's waistband. The midnight air felt cool as it snuck beneath the shirt, rushing over her hot flesh. The roughened tips of his fingers stole into the opening, grazing her skin.

Chelsea sucked in a fast, hollow breath and waited, wondering what would come next.

Mitch tensed, then slipped his hand fully inside her shirt. He groaned in tormented delight. Her breast was not large, but it was deliciously firm. The size and shape fit his palm to perfection. The nipple was already pearled, throbbing against his palm, begging for intimate attention . . . attention he couldn't give it without losing hold of his precious self-control.

Chelsea felt as though a branding iron had just closed over her, stamping its imprint on her hot, quivering flesh. The feeling was intense. It was wonderful. Her back arched, and she became aware of something hard, pulsating beneath her thighs.

And then he was gently squeezing, kneading, his hand shifting until his thumbnail was free to flick at her aching nipple. Her concentration focused there with force. Nothing had ever felt so good, so sinful, so provocatively magnificent as Mitch's hand and what it was doing to her breast. She felt the rippling sensations flood like molten fire through her veins, crashing in the junction of her thighs. The feeling was not uncomfortable so much as it was very, very urgent.

Mitch thought his trousers felt abnormally tight and confining. The feminine bottom grinding against him felt warm, soft, inviting. When she twisted to the side, he felt his control slip, felt his desire to bury himself deeply inside of her hone to a fine, torturous pitch. Forcing himself to keep the pace slow was a battle. One he was losing.

Her soft hair against his face felt good. Her heart drumming erratically beneath his calloused fingertips felt good. Her hot breaths washing over his face felt good. *Everything* about her felt good. Too damn good!

Chelsea felt the world shift, and a disappointed sigh whispered through her parted lips when Mitch's hand left her and was replaced by an unsatisfying rush of cool night air.

She murmured no protest when her back came up hard against a bed of prickly bluestem. In fact, she breathed a deep, contented sigh when the coolness of the night was instantly replaced with Mitch's hard, lean body. He was heavy, but she didn't mind the pinning weight as he spread himself on top of her. The hardness of him felt good. Very good.

Their shirts had gaped open. Chest met chest in a straining, sizzling contact. His raven curls scraped against her sensitive nipples, stiffening them until they ached and begged for immediate attention.

At her soft moan, Mitch rose up to see what had caused it. Realization sparked, and a wicked grin turned the lips beneath his mustache as he slowly, *slowly* rubbed against her.

She reached up and grabbed the plackets of his shirt, dragging the flannel sleeves down strong, muscular biceps. He shifted from one side to the other, the only help he gave as she peeled the material off him.

Chelsea watched, marveling at the way his skin glistened a deep bronze in the play of firelight and shadow. Her fingers itched to reach out and touch him, to see if he felt as good as he looked. But shyness prevented her from actually doing it. Was a woman allowed to touch a man when making love? She didn't know, and she was reluctant to shatter the moment by doing something wrong. Not now. Not when she was so close to perfection.

Mitch sensed her hesitation in the same instant his gaze settled on her breasts, revealed by the parted fabric of her shirt. They were small, full, and ripe, the nipples rosy and firm, pertly tipped toward the black velvet sky. He swallowed hard. His tongue was thirsty to taste her, to see if this part of her was as sweet on his tongue as the rest of her, but he held himself back. If he scared her now . . .

"My belt," he rasped as he kept the upper part of his weight positioned rigidly above her. If he moved now, it would be to rip off his clothes and take her hard and swift, the way his body demanded he do. The way he didn't dare to do. Not this time. "Unbuckle my belt."

Her fingers strayed obediently to his belt. The leather was cool and soft, the metal buckle cold and hard. With trembling fingers, she unhooked it, then began to unbutton his trousers without being asked. The denim was coarse against her quivering fingertips, the bulge beneath hard, mystifyingly firm, and long. Her hands brushed the pulsating heat straining beneath only once—just long enough to win a tortured gasp from Mitch.

"Now what?" she asked, her fingers poised over the last button. She wanted to slip her hand inside the gaping denim wedge . . . to satisfy her curiosity . . . to explore. After all, she'd gotten this far, it was too late to be shy. But she hesitated.

"Now you take them off."

"Off?" she echoed, her voice weak and cracking.

"Off," he repeated, his voice strong and firm.

He helped only by moving his hips so the denim could be peeled away. This was accomplished by Chelsea using only one finely honed sense: feel. She'd closed her eyes, afraid to look, yet at the same time infinitely curious to see and touch her first naked male body. Since it was a curiosity only a brazen woman would surrender to—she was promiscuous, true, but certainly *not* brazen!—she fought the temptation.

Somehow, twisting and turning, she managed to get his trousers down to his calves. The denim puddled in coarse folds that refused to clear the thickness of his boots. Thankfully, Mitch took over from there.

Chelsea lay back against the grass, feeling the bluestem prickle beneath her as she listened. The rustle of cloth was loud, the sound of his boots being tossed aside was louder. She heard the crunch of grass and felt the heat of him stretching out by her side.

Mitch propped his head on the hand of his bent arm and

172

let his gaze hungrily rake her body. The flesh that was exposed by her shirt was creamy, orange in the dying firelight, and tinged with slivers of moonbeams. Her hair floated around her, framing and softening her face. Her eyes were so tightly shut that tiny lines shot out from the corners. Her hands were fisted, clamped rigidly at her sides. She looked stiff, like a sacrifice ready to be offered up to the gods.

He grinned. The description was more than apt, except that he was no God. Not even close. He was just one very lusty man who was having a hell of a time holding his passion in check.

"Open your eyes," he said softly, suddenly. The index finger of his free hand traced the line of her jaw. Her delicate tremors vibrated up his arm and tightened like a fist around his heart. "Look at me, lady. I want to feel you looking at me."

Hesitantly, she pried her eyelids open. His face loomed above, his expression stark and serious as he returned her gaze.

His eyes, dark with passion, burned into her. "Lower, Chelsea. Look lower."

Her gaze traveled over the thick cord of his neck, which she was already intimately familiar with, over the broad wedge of his chest, down the strip of curling black hairs that tapered to a narrow ribbon over a taut stomach and settled on . . .

"Mitch?" she whispered, her voice high and frightened. She knew the basics of what happened between a man and a woman. But that was all she knew. For the first time, she felt a stabbing twinge of doubt slice down her spine.

He lowered his head until their lips met. His kiss was soft and bittersweet. Soothing. "Touch me," he whispered raggedly against her moist, trembling mouth. "Don't be afraid. I want to feel you touch me. I *need* to feel it."

Chelsea didn't move. She couldn't. She did, however, respond to his kiss. The warmth of her rekindled passion thawed her fear a bit.

Mitch surprised himself by realizing he would have stopped this madness now — had he not felt her reluctant response. Her back arched off the ground, crushing her breasts to his chest. It was a delicious torment; one that overrode all thoughts of stopping.

His lips coaxed hers as his fingers coiled around her wrist. He rubbed his chest against the rigid tips of her nipples and drew her hand slowly toward the throbbing heat of his need.

She tried to pull away once, but his grip tightened. It was too late to stop. He couldn't leave her like this, in the middle of nothing, with only fear to remember. Not when he knew damned well it was within his power to see she remembered her sensual initiation as pleasurable. He waited until she'd relaxed a bit before prying her fingers from their tight fist and curling each one slowly around him. His hand wrapped over the back of hers and a tortured groan rumbled deep in his throat.

Ah, Christ, she felt good! This was going to be harder than he'd thought. His intentions had been good—slow and easy, don't scare or rush her—but his body was working against him. He was hot and straining, hard and ready for her. Holding himself back was building into a slow form of torture. One he wasn't used to enduring. Restraint was slipping away. The desire to physically possess this woman was riding him hard now, and it couldn't be denied for long. Soon, sensations would be too strong, and he would no longer have any self-control to cling to.

Gritting his teeth and trying to ignore the blistering heat her hand created as it enfolded him, Mitch guided her. Each upward stroke was torture, each tight descent agony in his denial of immediate fulfillment.

She learned quick, he thought. Too damned quick. Soon, she picked up the tempo, until his blood was thundering in his ears and a coat of perspiration beaded his brow, moistening the mustache that curled over the tight line of his lips.

His hand left her wrist, where it wasn't needed any longer, and traveled to the waistband of her trousers. A coil of rope had been used for a belt, and he had a damn hard time peeling it away; his fingers were not cooperating. Eventually, it loosened. The trousers, much too baggy for her lean hips,

174

made unbuttoning them unnecessary. His hand slipped beneath the gaping waistband. Her skin was soft and smooth, warming his palm. He felt a thatch of dense curls beneath his calloused fingertips, felt their warm, damp readiness, and that, combined with what she was doing to his more manly parts, was almost Mitch's undoing.

He froze, took a few long, deep breaths, then very gently peeled the trousers from her hips. In his dreams he'd imagined her bottom to be lean yet soft, her legs to be short yet tapered. His dreams, he was quick to find, did not do her justice.

For all of her petite size, her legs were long and perfectly turned, the skin stretched over them creamy smooth and glistening silver in the moonlight. Her hips were tapered, leaner than most, but femininely curved and inviting. The copper curls nesting between her thighs warranted a fuller, more intimate exploration than merely that of his hungry gaze.

Chelsea unwrapped her fingers from around him and let her palm drift up the rippling, taut expanse of his stomach. Her touch was light and soft as she felt his hand pry her thighs apart, then slip upward. The moisture she felt against his searing, inquisitive fingertips brought an embarrassed stain to her cheeks. Where had it come from? Was this normal? What would he think?

She swallowed hard, her throat dry and tight. "Mitch," she squeaked, her fingers digging into his hard flesh. "It's—"

"—supposed to be," he finished for her. Then, before she could say anything else, he parted the soft velvet flesh and buried his fingers deeply inside of her. He moved, capturing the tip of a rosy, straining nipple in his mouth.

Chelsea gasped, shifting self-consciously. But he was suckling her, exciting her, and his hand was . . . creating a fire that burned out of control now. Self-consciousness melted away under the throbbing sensations his insistent touch evoked.

Her hips arched, matching his sure, steady strokes. He plunged deeper, searching. His teeth gently nibbled her nipple as his free hand, the elbow of which was precariously supporting his trembling weight, paid careful attention to her other breast.

"Now," he rasped hoarsely against her. "I want you now."

She nodded, and when his knee nudged her thighs wider, she let him do it without question.

He rolled on top of her, positioning her arms around his back before supporting his weight on the bent elbows that flanked her sides. His hands slipped beneath her, hooking around her shoulders, holding her steady.

Their gazes met and locked. The only sound was their short, ragged breaths.

Her lashes began to flicker coyly down, but his husky voice snapped them back up again.

"Look at me, preacher's daughter. I want to see your eyes when I'm inside of you."

His hips shifted into position and he arched forward. His first thrust was as it had to be — sure and powerful enough to rip through the fragile membrane that irrevocably separated her from girlhood.

Chelsea felt the slicing pain. She gasped, tensing, her eyes wide open. Tears moistened her eyes, blurring the blue eyes that hovered above her. She wasn't sure, but she thought she saw a stab of regret twist his features.

Mitch froze, feeling her pain as though it were his own. It was unavoidable, he knew, but he would have given anything if only he didn't have to hurt her this first time. The glint of betrayal in her eyes cut him to the core. He moved again, slowly at first. Testing. When no further resistance was met, his strokes grew bolder, deeper, longer.

Chelsea would have liked to have hated this man. He'd lied to her. He'd said he would never hurt her, but he had. Then, slowly, she noticed the pain had fled as quickly as it had come, and the fire inside of her was burning again. Hot enough to consume her.

"Wrap your legs around me," he whispered hoarsely, and buried his face in the fragrant, warm hollow of her neck. "And move your hips. Move with me, sweetheart. Ah . . .

176

that's right."

She felt good, wet and tight as he drove into her. And when her legs wrapped around his hips, when she met his thrusts, when he sank even more deeply into her, she felt better. He groaned in satisfaction, as well as in torment. His release was still an agonizing lifetime away.

"Mitch," Chelsea panted, straining beneath him, straining against him. "I feel . . . funny. Mitch!"

"Go with it, sweetheart." He rose above her, looking down into her eyes. She looked frightened, dazed . . . exactly the way he felt. They were both on the brink of sweet, sweet release. "Just go with it. Let yourself feel it . . . feel *me*."

His thrusts increased, piercing her, making her cry out. He felt the tiny shudders begin around him, wet and hot, tight then loose, enfolding him, rubbing against him, testing his restraint in a way it had never been tested before . . . and he prayed to God it never would be again. A man could only take so much!

Her fingers dug into his back. The short nails sliced into his flesh, causing an odd mix of pleasure/pain to sluice through him.

"Mitch!" she called out in a quick, breathless sigh . . . or a shout . . . or a little of both.

"Go with it!"

Chelsea went with it. She felt the fire between her thighs, felt the burning heat grow hotter with each driving thrust. She whimpered, trying to hold back from . . . what? It was upon her before she could draw another ragged breath into her burning lungs. She couldn't run, couldn't hide. She didn't try. She wanted to know!

She held Mitch's gaze as the first spark, hot and quick, started somewhere in her belly, then spread like an inferno through her blood. Her whole body trembled, tightened, and released, then tightened again. She couldn't breathe, her lungs felt as though they were going to explode. It didn't matter. All that mattered was this sweet, liquid feeling that pumped through in blast after blast of glorious, rapturous sensation.

A moan, low and long, tore from her. She clung to Mitch, burying her cheek against his shoulder. Her jaw clenched hard, her head twisted, and she offered up a silent prayer that this frightening, delicious torment would never, *never* end.

A trickle of perspiration ribboned down Mitch's back, the memory of her eyes melting from passionate amber to amazed, molten honey still burning in his mind. He felt the shuddering vibrations of her climax gripping him, carrying him in her wake.

"Look at me, baby," he said, his breath coming harsh and ragged as he fought to maintain just one last second of control. "Look at me *now*."

She did. Silently, she watched his eyes darken to indigo-blue swirled with steel. She felt his last, powerful thrusts, long and firm, pierce her to the core. His body went rigid beneath her palms. His brow crinkled, the skin over his cheeks drew taut, and his lips pulled back, revealing the tightly clenched teeth between his beard and mustache. He looked as though he was either in excruciating pain or was caught in the grips of the sweetest form of pleasure known to man.

"Oh God," he groaned, his voice raspy and hard. His eyes never left her, even as the spasms of sweet release ripped through him.

The arms that had kept his weight from crushing her felt like liquid. Slowly, he lowered himself on top of her, welcoming the soft, warm bed of feminine curves and valleys. He was panting, but it had little to do with exertion. He was in prime shape, his body taut and firm. Bed activities had never taken much out of him . . . until tonight. He'd never experienced anything like tonight in all his life.

"Mitch, are you all right?" Chelsea asked softly, once her breathing had returned to semi-normal. Well, as normal as it was likely to be with this hard, masculine body atop her, anyway! Sweet heavens, he felt good! Yes, she was going to go to hell for this. No doubt about it. "Are you hurt? Mitch?"

She didn't relax until she felt him shake his head against

her shoulder. Sighing, she closed her eyes and focused her thoughts on her body's lulling tranquillity. She hadn't felt so good, so calm and relaxed, in days . . . weeks . . . months. Oh, who was she kidding? She'd never felt this good in her life!

Mitch stirred atop her. As he gradually came back to himself, he started to wonder how the delectable preacher's daughter had fared with this, her first taste of "sins of the flesh." Had he gone too fast? Had he hurt her? Had he been too rough? Not rough enough? Worse, was she angry? Would her hackles be raised now that it was over and done with? Would she be upset that she hadn't resisted him?

And did he really want the answer to even one of those questions? Hell, no!

Easing the intimacy of their embrace, Mitch rolled to the side. He scooped her close as he went, nestling her snugly against his side. Her silky copper head found a natural pillow atop his shoulder. And that was when Mitch realized the oddness of what he'd just done. Usually, after he'd had a woman, he let her do pretty much what she pleased. In fact, he preferred *not* to cuddle afterward. A small portion of his mind recognized that he hadn't given Chelsea the choice but instead had made it for her.

Another, sharper portion of his mind realized she still hadn't said anything yet. He tensed, waiting for her reaction, at the same time dreading it with every fiber of his thoroughly contented, passion-drained body.

Well, she hadn't hit him, he thought. That was a good sign. And she hadn't made a grab for his pistol. Another good sign. Perhaps she wasn't angry? Perhaps she'd enjoyed their union as much as he had? Her whiskey-amber eyes said she had. They said she'd enjoyed it all very, very much. But that was too much to hope for. She was, after all, a Baptist preacher's daughter. Sexy as hell, but a preacher's daughter nonetheless.

Mitch groaned. When realization hit, it hit unmercifully hard. Good God, he'd just seduced a preacher's daughter! He'd never thought highly of himself, for good reason. God knows he had a lot of sins to answer for once this life was over. But a *preacher's daughter?* Sweet Jesus, what kind of man was he? He couldn't even think of words degrading enough to describe a man who would seduce a woman like the one who now cuddled so softly, so sweetly in his arms. A man like himself.

He felt her stir against him, snuggling closer. His heart rate quickened, his arm tightened. He found himself waiting to catch the open palm that would be sailing for his cheek at any minute. Her warm sigh stirred the hairs on his chest. One leg was thrown over his hips, her hand curled limply atop his breastbone, oblivious to the heart that throbbed beneath it. Her breaths were soft and rhythmic. Satisfied.

"I don't believe it," he mumbled under his breath.

Mitch had lain with enough women to know when one had fallen asleep. And the one tucked in his embrace was dead to the world. No shouts, no recriminations, no curses lavished on his family and friends . . . of which he hadn't a one. And—the oddest part, to his way of thinking—no anger. She was peacefully, contentedly asleep.

Chuckling dryly, he pillowed his bearded chin atop her head. He drank in her scent in long, slow inhalations and closed his eyes. The night was lulling. The fragrant softness curled into him was lulling. His spent passion was lulling most of all.

The fight scenario he'd imagined between them earlier flickered behind his closed eyelids. His finger had been on the trigger, but only now did he realize he hadn't pulled it. He knew why.

Mitch's last thought before he followed Chelsea into the black cavern of a deep, dreamless sleep was that he—stupid, *stupid* man that he was—had fallen in love with a prissy preacher's daughter. Hopelessly, irrevocably in love.

Now, didn't that beat all!

Chapter Thirteen

Chelsea sighed, stretched, and felt languished and content. Beneath her ear echoed the faint, rhythmic throb of a heartbeat. It was a calming sound, one she found pleasant to awaken to.

The bedroll kept her warm. An evening breeze washed over her cheeks and shoulders in cool waves, stirring the copper curls tangled about her. The air didn't feel cold. How could it when she felt as though she were cuddled up next to a deliciously hot brick wall? The pillow of flesh cushioning her cheek felt wonderfully familiar and firm. It breathed.

Breathed?!

Amber eyes snapped opened. She blinked hard, adjusting her sight to the velvet blackness of late night shadows. The fire had died to glowing red embers in its circular bed of stone. The horses whickered in the distance where they'd been tethered to the only tree within miles. Resting on its side, not far from where she lay, was an empty bottle of whiskey.

Whiskey. Her jaw clenched hard, and the movement brought a stab of pain to her aching temples. Memories, hot and fast, came flooding back. Sensuous, exciting memories. Memories of Mitch Bryant's handsome face looming above her . . . of the feel of his hair scraping her flesh . . . of his calloused palms caressing her body . . . of his hot, moist mouth and tongue nibbling and teasing her until she cried out for . . .

A strangled moan left her throat. She'd cried out for more, and she'd gotten it. Her degradation was now complete.

"Sweet heavens, what have I done?" she whispered. Her breath stirred the raven curls that tickled the tip of her nose. They felt silky-soft, smelled fragrant and spicy. It wasn't difficult to recall the satiny texture of each curling strand or how they felt when her fingers tunneled through them. The flesh beneath was hot and firm. She remembered the feel of it vividly.

Oh, who was she trying to fool? It was impossible to *forget* such a wonderful feeling—or her own reckless reaction to it!

Swallowing hard, she noticed that her mouth felt fuzzy, her tongue thick and coated with the unpleasant, bitter aftertaste of mind-numbing liquor. Her thoughts were hazy, disjointed, but sharp enough to know she was now lying naked in the grass. The thick stalks prickled her flesh, while the front of her body molded intimately into Mitch Bryant's hot, rock-solid side. They fit together perfectly, each sculpted hollow enhanced by feminine curves. The observation was at odds with her humiliation.

From the sound of it, he was sleeping soundly. The chest beneath her rose and fell in shallow, even breaths. And he was snoring, ever so slightly. His breath washed over the top of her head, searing her scalp, making her remember their time together whether she wanted to or not. She didn't want to. But she did remember. Vividly.

He was sleeping. Good, Chelsea thought, and gave a mental sigh of relief. She couldn't face him yet. All she needed was to see one glint of victory in those incredible eyes and she would be lost, her tongue hopelessly tied. That wasn't what she wanted. What she wanted was to be calm and reasonable the next time she faced off against him. Right now she felt anything but.

Very slowly, she lifted the large palm cupping her shoulder, linking her to Mitch Bryant's side. His arm was heavy, dead weight as it plopped onto the grass and stretched at full length.

Holding her breath, afraid the sound of her ragged

breathing would awaken him, she eased up on one elbow. That was as far as Chelsea got. She felt a tug of resistance, and traced it back to the thick strand of copper hair that ribboned down the front of her shoulder and disappeared beneath his firm back.

"Damn it!" she swore unconsciously when her trembling fingers wrapped around the soft lock and yanked. The strand pulled taut. Though her scalp stung, her hair didn't budge.

"Try pulling," a voice whispered from behind. The tone was airy, as though the breeze, not a flesh and blood person, had offered the suggestion.

Intent on freeing herself, Chelsea hissed, "I did. It didn't work."

"Then roll him over."

"Be serious, please. The man is twice my size, and every inch of him is—" The words withered on her tongue.

She tensed, her attention whipped over her shoulder. Squinting against the twisting shadows, she forced her whiskey-blurred gaze to focus on the willow-thin boy who stood scarcely a few feet away. He was bent at the waist, his hands pillowed atop lean thighs encased in threadbare, baggy trousers. His gaze, hidden beneath the dark brim of a hat, was trained on the spot where her hair vanished beneath Mitch Bryant's sun-bronzed back.

"Kit?"

"Yes, ma'am?" Even in the shadows, she could see his grin.

"What are you doing here?"

"Looking for you."

"Oh." Then, "Might I ask why?"

The boy straightened. Pillowing small fists on his hips, he glanced down at her. "Well, now, Chels . . . er . . . Miss Hogan, you could say I have a lot of reasons. I would think you'd want me to help work you free before you hear them but, of course, I could be wrong. If you're happy the way you are, I'll just—"

"Roll him over," she snapped, nodding to Mitch. How could he sleep through all this? Then she noticed the whiskey bottle. It had been half full, last she remembered. It was now empty.

"All right, ma'am. Let's get this over with. You push, I'll pull."

Between Kit's gentle tugs on Mitch's shoulder and Chelsea's not-so-gentle nudgings, they managed to untrap her hair.

Clutching the bedroll beneath her chin, Chelsea sat up. She hesitated, a scowl etching her brow when she glanced up at Kit.

"Well?" he asked, shifting from foot to foot. "You're free now. Isn't that what you wanted?"

"Of course," she answered quickly. Too quickly. She winced when her too-loud voice sliced through her aching head, then waited, sure Mitch would awaken. She was surprised when he only muttered something beneath his breath and rolled onto his side.

"Pardon me for asking, Miss Hogan, but if you wanted to be free and you are, then why aren't you getting up?"

Chelsea opened her mouth, then snapped it shut as she plowed back the tousled copper hair framing her face. Her gaze shifted to the glowing embers of what had once been a campfire. The heat it emanated was minimal. Certainly not enough to bring on the flush she now felt warming her cheeks. "I can't," she muttered miserably. "If I take the blanket, Mitch will wake up. And I" — *oh, sweet heavens!* — "I don't have any clothes on."

"In other words, you're naked."

He didn't sound surprised. Chelsea lifted her chin and glared up at the boy, thinking him much too astute for his age.

Kit merely grinned. "If you'd tell me where your clothes are, I'll be glad to get them for you."

The delicate line of her jaw hardened as her gaze swept their surroundings. The knee-high bluestem swayed like moonlit ocean waves that rolled on for as far as the eye could see. What her eye didn't see was her clothes. The last she remembered, Mitch had peeled them off her body, his fingers fast and impatient. She had no idea what he'd done with them.

Chelsea sent Kit a quick, humiliated glance. "I think Mitch has some in his saddlebag," she said finally, shakily. "They'll be too big, but anything will do at this point."

Kit nodded. Pursing his lips, he searched the area, his gaze fixing on the saddlebags. He grinned and walked over to them, wondering why Chels would even suggest he do such a thing. He was, after all, a thief—the one who'd stolen her last three dollars in coins. Yet she not only told him to find the saddlebags, she'd given him permission to rummage through them.

Sighing, he knelt in front of the larger one, unsnapping and lifting the limp flap. As he reached inside the leathery depths, he again marveled at the amount of trust this woman placed in him. As far as Kit was concerned, her trust was unfounded and entirely undeserved. Still, he had to admit it felt nice to be trusted for a change! Different, but nice all the same.

He located a large green and red plaid shirt. There were no trousers to go with it; the only ones he could find were soiled with dirt and grime. He wouldn't give Chelsea Hogan dirty clothes to wear. She deserved better. Shrugging, he took the shirt and carried it back to her. "I suppose you'll want me to turn around now," he grumbled, handing her the shirt.

One copper brow rose accusingly high. "What do you think?"

He grinned again, then spun on his heel. His tattered boots crunched over the grass as he walked to the almost-extinguished fire and plopped down in a cross-legged sit. He kept his back rigid, his gaze trained on one smoldering ash, and tried like hell not to think of what was going on behind him. The soft rustle of cloth was a bittersweet torment . . . one his youthful imagination relished exploring.

The second his back was turned, Chelsea flipped off the bedroll, tugged the shirt over her head, and plowed her arms into the sleeves. The flannel was soft and baggy, the sleeves way too long. She rolled up the cuffs to her elbows and closed

185

the buttons trailing down the center, overlapped by laces. She drew the laces tight but didn't tie them. Her fingers were still too awkward and clumsy . . . whiskey residue.

There. Now that she had some clothes on, scant though they were, she felt better. More human. Not so wanton or decadent. *Decadent.* The word shot through her mind and unwillingly drew her gaze to Mitch Bryant's sleeping form.

He'd turned onto his back while she was donning his shirt, and she now had an unobstructed view of his face. His skin shimmered nicely in the moonlight, smoothing over his wide brow and erasing the weathered cracks shooting out from his eyes. His sooty lashes were long against the curve of his sculpted cheek. The moonlight made his beard and mustache look softer and not as ragged. It was a deceptive sight, for Chelsea could still feel the places on her flesh that tingled with whisker burns.

He looked peaceful, she thought, his features unguarded and boyishly innocent. As though he were simply resting, not passed out from drinking too much whiskey. In sleep, with the moonlight playing softly over his chiseled face, he looked years younger. Not cold and dangerous, the way he appeared when he was awake.

Against her will, her gaze softened. There was no need to hide her enthralled expression, since there was no one around to see it. Kit was staring at the fire and wouldn't turn back unless asked to. Mitch was unconscious. She could look at him as long as she wished, in any way she wished, without fretting about the consequences. And look she did . . . long and hard.

I could trust this face, she thought suddenly, then sighed. Her hand, she realized, had poised in the act of brushing back the tempting curl clinging to his sun-kissed brow. Her fingers trembled, remembering vividly the warm, silky feel of his flesh slipping beneath them . . . remembering, too, the way her own skin felt—hot and alive—when teased by this man's skillful palm.

Drawing in a shaky breath, she dropped her hand to her lap. She took a few seconds to compose her wayward thoughts, condemned herself as all kinds of fools for having entertained them, then forcefully remembered the land this man had stolen only hours before. *Her* land. That gave her the resolve to push to her feet and join Kit beside what was left of the fire.

"I like your hat," Chelsea said as she dropped onto the ground beside him. She reached up and gave a tug on the wide black brim, pulling it down on his brow.

"Hmmm. So do I." Kit grinned and cocked his head to look at her. With the upper portion of his face cloaked in shadows and the hat brim riding arrogantly low, he looked so much like Mitch it unnerved her.

Clearing her throat, she tore her gaze away. It dropped to her legs. Her naked legs. When she was standing, Mitch's shirt reached just above her knees. When she was sitting, it bunched up around her thighs. Gulping, she tugged the shirt down as far as it would go. Unfortunately, it didn't go too far.

"Don't worry about it, Chels — Miss Hogan," Kit said, his young voice rich with strained laughter as his gaze quickly took in what she was doing. "I'm only fourteen. Sights like that don't entice me" — his tone lowered shyly — "much."

"That old?" She glanced up and met his dark velvet-brown gaze. The scowl returned to her brow. "You look younger."

Kit beamed, obviously pleased. "I do try to, ma'am."

Chelsea seized on any excuse to talk and, hopefully, relieve some of the nervousness that felt like it was eating at her from the inside out. "Why would you want to do that?"

"Makes it easier when I get caught . . . if you know what I mean." Her baffled look said she did not know at all what he meant, so he added, "A man's not likely to hang a twelve-year-old for sticking a hand in his pocket, but a fourteen-year-old's supposed to know better."

"You *do* know better, Kit. I know you do."

His narrow shoulders rose and fell in a tight shrug before he glanced away. "Yeah, well . . . you know what they say about desperate times and all."

Her gaze narrowed on him. *Desperate times call for desperate measures.* She remembered the quote well, if only because it had been one of her father's favorites. But she was surprised that *this* boy knew it. "All right, Kit," she said deciding not to ask him where he'd heard such a thing and getting straight to the point. "What are you doing here?"

"Following you." His answer was swift and honest.

Chelsea's gaze widened. "Following me? Why?"

"Because I don't trust him." He nodded to Mitch, who slept peacefully unaware of the conversation buzzing around him, then shifted his attention back to the woman at his side. His eyes blazed with youthful intensity. "Good thing, too. You're real lucky, you know. It might not have been me who came here tonight. What if it was someone else whose intentions weren't so good? I hate to say it, Chels, but that man of yours is passed-out drunk. He couldn't have protected himself, let alone you."

"He's not *my* man," Chelsea replied hotly, her cheeks coloring for what felt like the umpteenth time today. "Sweet heavens, no!"

Kit's brows lifted in youthful challenge. His gaze raked her. Nothing was missed by his sharp brown eyes. Not the fiery mane of tousled hair streaming down to her tiny waist, not the flush of embarrassment heating her cheeks, not her near nakedness, and least of all not her sudden, breathless gasp. Nothing.

"He isn't!" she insisted forcefully. "No, certainly not. Please, I have better taste than that."

"If you say so, ma'am."

"I *do* say so. You bet your little—" Her loud tone made Mitch stir. The two by the fire tensed, their breaths held as their anxious gazes drifted in unison to see if he'd awakened.

Mitch grumbled in his sleep and shifted onto his side. He was facing them now, his cheek atop crushed bluestem, his arms crossed over the bedroll that molded concealingly over the lower half of his body. His bare feet poked out from the hem, attesting to either the blanket's shortness or to the man's rugged tallness.

"I could kill him for you if you want," Kit said quietly, turning back to her. His gaze locked hard with searching amber.

"He's dead drunk. He wouldn't know. He wouldn't even feel it."

Chelsea's heart skipped a beat. Her palms broke out in an anxious sweat and her breathing shallowed. The reaction was as instinctive as it was uncontrollable. She thought better of asking herself what it meant. "You're joking, right?" she asked, her voice strained and high. Her fingers had curled into the hem of Mitch's shirt. She didn't notice how tightly until she felt the sharp bite of her fingernails against her thigh. "You *are* joking, Kit. Tell me you're not serious."

"Well now, Chels—" He hesitated.

"Go ahead. You'll call me it anyway."

He nodded, continuing smoothly, "I'm dead serious."

To prove it, Kit rolled onto one lean hip and reached behind him. He pulled a small gun from where he'd shoved it beneath the frayed rope that served as his belt.

Chelsea didn't need a blinding midday sun to know a pistol when she saw one. She blinked hard, wishing desperately that she wasn't seeing one now. But she was. The moonlight glinted off the snubby barrel as the boy turned it over in his long, lean palm.

Damn it! she thought and swallowed hard, her gaze sealed on the pistol. A small portion of her mind acknowledged it was getting easier for her to form that curse in her mind and on her tongue—proof that she'd spent too much time in Mitch Bryant's corruptive company, no doubt. A larger part of her mind lodged on the pistol and on Kit's offer.

Her gaze widened, lifted, locked hard with determined brown. Fear twisted like a knot in her stomach. "Why?" she asked, her voice tiny and high. "Why would you do such a thing?"

He smiled. It was a soft turning of his lips, not meant to charm. "I'd do it for you, Miss Hog—Chels. Because you don't belong with a lowlife like him." His thumb jerked over his shoulder. "Because . . . well," he shrugged, for the first time hesitant. "I can take care of you, ma'am. If you'd let me. It's the least I can do to repay you."

Chelsea was shaking. She could feel the vibrations down

189

to her toes. To counter them, she rose to her feet and, crossing her arms over her chest, paced nervously around the extinguished fire. She stopped on the other side, the bed of ashes and rock a small barrier between herself and the boy who was willing to kill for her. What had she done to inspire such loyalty? Nothing that she could see.

"Kit," she said suddenly, firmly, "Mitch Bryant may be a thief and a liar, but I don't want him dead. Even if I did, I wouldn't ask a child to do the job. I'd do it myself."

The young chest puffed with indignation. His chin lifted. Moonlight shimmered below the brim of his hat, and in the pale silver glow Chelsea saw a flash of resentment spark in his eyes.

"I'm not a child," he argued. "I may be only fourteen, but I've seen and done things that would make the two of you cringe."

He wasn't lying. Chelsea's heart tightened with the knowledge. Dear God, he looked so young, so innocent! But he wasn't, she thought, and her tone softened. "I'm not saying you haven't. What I *am* saying is that you won't be doing one of those things tonight. Not for me."

"But—"

"No!" She stalked past the campfire, stopping beside him. Her fingers curled tightly into the flannel sleeve as she glared angrily down at the top of his concealing hat. "I said no, Kit, and I mean it. If I want Mitch dead, I'll kill him myself. Lord knows he deserves it after what he did to me today."

A rustle of grass and cloth sounded from behind in the tight, thick silence. It wasn't loud, but it was strong enough to snatch Chelsea's attention.

"Well, lady? Don't keep me in suspense. Do you want me dead or don't you? I'd like to know if I should be waiting to feel one of your bullets in my back."

Very slowly, Chelsea pulled Mitch Bryant into focus. She immediately regretted having done so. The bedroll had slipped, puddling around his taut, sun-bronzed waist in soft red folds. The furry wedge of his chest was exposed to enticing silver moonlight. His black hair was rumpled around his

190

face, belying the alertness shimmering in his narrow blue glare.

She returned his gaze levelly, though she was never sure how she managed it. Her knees felt watery, threatening to buckle beneath her. Her heart throbbed in her chest and she was afraid to draw in a breath lest she gasp.

"Well?" he repeated smoothly. "Do you want me dead?"

With effort, Chelsea gathered her wits about her. She gave a quick toss of her head and forcibly tore her gaze away.

"Should I?" she countered. A question for a question. It seemed only fair, since the answer to one hinged on the answer to the other. Her gaze swept over Mitch, blazing hot amber fire as she waited for him to confess what he'd done at the land office. For God's sake, when was he going to own up to stealing her land?

He shrugged, apparently indifferent to the snub-nosed pistol Kit had just leveled dead center at his chest. The *clink* of chambers shifting into place as the hammer was eased back was deafening in the ensuing silence.

Chelsea fully expected Mitch to lunge for the holster that was never far from his side. She braced herself, dreading the blast of twin gunshots that she knew she couldn't stop. Any minute now. Any second.

The night was silent and tense as Mitch tossed off the bedroll and rose to his feet. He was naked. He didn't seem to mind. His bare feet padded over the crushed grass, carrying him within a few inches of Chelsea's rigid form. His palms rose, cupping her shoulders as though trying to absorb her through his warm, calloused hands. He felt the nervous tremors she was trying so hard to hide.

"Lady, I made a promise to myself years ago that if I was going to die by a bullet, I'd damn well go out doing something worth dying for." His voice was calm and even, his gaze hypnotic as his head lowered with tantalizing precision.

His hot breath blasted over her face. She could feel the heat of his mouth flaring over hers even though he stopped before making the final, sizzling contact.

Chelsea froze, rooted to the spot, afraid. Oddly enough,

she wasn't afraid *of* Mitch as much as she was afraid *for* him. She was terrified that if she did as her mind dictated—run like hell!—the sudden movement would make Kit's finger slam back the trigger of the pistol. It was pointed at Mitch's head now. Gut instinct told her the boy would not miss.

"Kiss me, preacher's daughter," Mitch rasped huskily. His vibrant blue gaze held her captive. She couldn't have looked away if she tried, and trying wasn't a consideration. "God help me, but your kisses are one of the few things in this life that I'd die for. Kiss me now."

And she did. Heaven help her, she did!

Neither of them heard Kit's muffled curse or saw the glare he shot Mitch when the man scooped the tiny redhead close and molded her soft, pliant body to his hot, naked flesh. Nor were they aware of when the boy eased the hammer into place and returned the derringer to his waistband.

Chapter Fourteen

Though not one word passed between Chelsea and Mitch the next morning, their gazes met and held often. The contact was electric. His blue eyes smoldered, and every time he looked at her, Chelsea was reminded of their abruptly severed kiss . . . of the way his hands had dropped from her shoulders . . . of the way he'd spun on his heel and stalked away from her. His abhorrent grunt still echoed in her ears. Even now she was no closer to knowing who he'd directed it at — her, or himself.

After a swift breakfast of jerky and stale biscuits, they set out for "home." Mitch Bryant's home, she was quick to remind herself. His *stolen* home.

Through unspoken agreement, Kit rode with her. Mitch rode ahead, a small speck of rugged back and pitch-black horseflesh in the distance.

Chelsea passed the time talking with Kit, and as the day wore on, a vague disconcertion settled over her. It wasn't what he said, it was how he said it. When asked about his family, his tone had grown guarded, reluctant. "They left me at the Kansas border," he'd admitted, but only after much prodding. "Ten is too many mouths to feed when you haven't got much to start with. Us older kids were put out. Told to fend for ourselves."

"Oh, Kit," she'd sighed, patting the long-fingered hands entwined about her waist. "I'm sorry. I didn't know."

"Sorry? Why should *you* be sorry?" She felt him shrug

193

against her back. His voice cracked, but only slightly. "I mean . . . God, Chels, it's not like it was *your* fault."

No, it wasn't, she remembered thinking at the time. But she'd felt as though it were. There was something elusive about the boy that brought her protective instincts to the fore. Instincts that were no doubt honed from being the daughter of a Baptist preacher. The longer she talked to him, the stronger those feelings became.

As they neared Northwest Quarter Section number 30, Chelsea found herself relieved she'd insisted the boy accompany them. Kit had been reluctant but was easily swayed when he saw that the tall, bearded man he hated so much had no intention of leaving them behind. His vow to protect Chelsea stood firm, an unwavering commitment shimmering in his youthful brown eyes.

Mitch had been less than thrilled. In keeping with his brooding, closedmouth attitude, he hadn't said a word. He didn't have to. The stormy glare he shot Kit as the boy scrambled onto the paint pony behind Chelsea said it for him.

Mitch didn't like Kit. Chances were, he never would. In a way that was his alone, Kit made it clear the feeling was wholeheartedly mutual. Wisely, Chelsea kept out of it.

In the four days they'd been gone, the prairie had undergone a minor transformation. The stallion and paint pony clomped past more than one newly erected sod-house on recently staked claims. The air itself was thick with the scent of charred bluestem as families burned away the grass surrounding their claims. It was a crude but controlled fire preventative. The breeze gusted frequently into winds, making the danger of a fire sweeping across the summer-dry prairie a very real possibility. It was a risk none were willing to take.

The center of all Northwest Quarter Sections had been marked for a townsite. Even situated in the middle of rolling prairie, the place thrived as well as any small prairie town was apt to. A sloop-backed prairie schooner, reminiscent of days gone by, had been unhitched seemingly in the middle of nowhere. Half a dozen sod-houses and two skeletal shacks were in mid-construction around it. Lying on the ground behind the wagon were two rectangular walls that, when hinged with two more and a roof, would become a general store. At the moment, the shop itself was being run from the wagon.

People milled about in small, friendly groups. Some worked, though it was clear from the tone of their distant chatter and rumbling laughter that most had come to socialize with their new neighbors. Children raced through the swaying grass, the thick tips of which almost covered their heads. High-pitched screeches rang sharp and clear as their cutthroat game of tag raged on.

A hand-carved wooden sign was staked beside a rut in the grass that was quickly wearing down into a well-trodden path. It proclaimed in shaky, uncertain letters: Two River Crossing.

Chelsea grinned. Whoever had carved it, she thought his sense of humor sharp. Only one river cut through this part of the District—the Sweetwater—and its winding depths churned at least eight miles to the south.

"Kit," she said over her shoulder as she reined in her horse, "how much money do you have left?"

"Well now, Chels, that's a vague question. Do you want to know how much of *your* money I have left or how much money I have?"

"Is there a difference?" she asked tightly.

He chuckled. "What do you think?"

Chelsea didn't ask. She didn't want to know—not since it was blatantly apparent where any money the boy possessed had come from. Her gaze dropped to the tattered boots she'd first seen him wearing. The leather was worn and cracked, ripped in several places. The boots were worthless. Her nose crinkled. "I think it's about time, don't you?"

"Time for what?" His gaze followed hers. "Oh, no. You want me to part with *these* boots?" She felt his youthful body stiffen against her back, and she smiled despite herself. His horrified tone was oddly endearing. "Surely you jest! I mean, I've just softened the leather. Besides, these are the best boots

I've ever owned. We've been together through thick and thin. Through mud, water, and more than a little horse sh—"

"We had a deal, Kit," she cut him off, her tone light. "A warm meal, a new hat, new boots, new clothes. You have the hat. I presume you bought the meal. Now it's time for the rest."

"Aw, Chels," he grumbled. At her determined stare, Kit sighed melodramatically. "All right," he grumbled under his breath. "But I want you to know, you drive a hard bargain."

"So I've been told." Chelsea's grin broadened when she spurred the horse on. Her gaze swept the area, but she found no sign of Mitch. She wasn't surprised. She also wasn't pleased.

Five minutes later she was weaving the horses through the small tangle of people. Compared to the crowds in Guthrie, this amount was like a family picnic.

A vague feeling of discomfort settled over Chelsea when she glanced down at the few women around. Most were dressed in faded calicoes or threadbare cotton frocks. All were wearing skirts of one sort or another, in varying stages of disrepair. Mitch Bryant's baggy flannel shirt and her own loose-fitting trousers stuck out like a sore thumb. She cringed in the saddle, her self-consciousness growing with each curious stare that came her way. And there were far too many.

Chelsea's assessment that she looked peculiar hit the mark, but not for the reasons she thought. Harsh sun had weathered most of the women's faces, making them look old and haggard even when their lips split with a grin. Child-bearing had left their bodies soft and pliant. Chelsea Hogan displayed none of that. Her hair, freshly washed that morning in a churning creek, glistened like molten copper in the sunshine. Her skin was creamy, unweathered, and unmarked. Her body sat atop the saddle with comfortable ease. The trousers and shirt, though baggy, left no doubt of the firm, shapely figure beneath.

By the men, this difference was noticed with an appreciative eye. By the women, it was acknowledged with a touch of disdain.

Chelsea guided the horse toward the wagon. The hoof-beats clumped rhythmically in her ears, the sound overridden by the beat of her heart and the echo of speculative voices.

"Do you see that?" Kit asked, attracting her wandering attention by tugging on the fringed end of her braid.

"See what?" she asked, distracted. She was too busy trying not to return the women's skeptical glares — or the men's more suggestive ones — to pay the boy much attention.

"That woman." She felt him gesture but was unsure of where he'd pointed. "The one in the green dress standing next to your man. Over by the store frame. She's staring at you."

"He's not *my* man!" Chelsea snapped, even as her attention shifted to a spot past the wagon and the few people who milled about it. Her jaw clenched hard. Her fingers tightened on the reins. The thudding of her heart had reached a raucous crescendo.

"Do you know her?"

"No," Chelsea snapped, and tugged sharply on the reins. She *wasn't* lying, she told herself. She really didn't *know* the woman. She'd barely spoken to her that night on the prairie. But it had been enough. What she remembered most about the woman who was staring at her so intensely from over Mitch's shoulder was glossy blond hair, shimmering honey-gold in the moonlight, and the way the feline creature had gazed lustfully into Mitch Bryant's handsome face as he stroked her cheek.

With a flick of her wrist, Chelsea yanked the pony to an abrupt halt and slid from the saddle. Kit was quick to join her.

"Does *he* know her?" Kit asked, his voice hardening the way it always did when the subject of Mitch Bryant was broached.

"How the hell should I know?" she grumbled, then groaned. Sweet heavens, she was cussing again! Her feet stomped over the grass as she headed for the wagon.

Three men stood at the open rear bed. A black apron stretched across the middle of the shortest one, the dull leather straining to hold in the paunchy waist beneath. The owner, obviously. Her gaze strayed to the other two and froze. Her breath caught.

The aura of danger they exuded was tangible; the air reeked of it. She couldn't see their faces beneath the matching felt hats. Nor did she need to. In the years she'd spent with her father, she'd seen their type often. She knew the scenario, and if she didn't, the twin gunbelts each wore strapped low on tight, lean, faded denim hips would have told her.

They were criminals. Everything from the arrogant snugness of their trousers to the concealing brims of their dusty hats and the ragged hair peeking from beneath screamed it. No one went to that much trouble concealing his face with a low-slung hat and shadowy stubble unless it was a face that could be identified easily. Unless it was a face he didn't *want* to have identified.

The air was charged with tension. Even the plump proprietor felt it as he looked up from the spurs he held out for the men's inspection. Spotting Chelsea, he sent her a nervous smile and nod. His voice rose a pitch as he addressed the two men.

They no longer looked interested in the spurs. Their gazes had turned on Chelsea the second they'd heard her crunching footsteps approach. She didn't need to see their eyes beneath the murky brims, she could feel their gazes burning into her.

The proprietor rambled on about the quality of the spur nestled in his meaty palm. It was doubtful either man heard what he said. Or that they cared. This was confirmed when their heads—one blond, one dark—leaned together. The dark-haired one whispered something, and judging by the obscene laughter it evoked from his friend, the comment had been lewd.

Chelsea felt her cheeks color, knowing instinctively the comment had been aimed at her. And that it wasn't complimentary. The blond man's eyes sparkled a penetrating green from beneath the brim of his hat, telling her she was right.

"Forget the boots, Chels," Kit said, and slipped into place beside her. "I've lived without them this long."

From the corner of her eye she saw Kit's hand stray to the back of his cinched waistband. Her gut knotted. He was reaching for the tiny gun that, to her, didn't look like it could stop a fly, let alone men of these two's crude, menacing caliber. But when the two outlaws stepped away from the wagon and their confident strides carried them in her direction, Chelsea thanked God that Kit had the pistol. And that he knew how to use it.

"Well, well, well. Will you look'ee here, Jase?" the dark one drawled in one of the thickest southern accents Chelsea had ever heard. His grin was suggestive, his gaze lecherous. But that wasn't the worst of it. The worst was that his voice was familiar. Wretchedly familiar.

Jase stopped in front of Chelsea and grinned. A chill coursed up her spine, since the gesture looked more like a sneer. His palm stroked his bristled jaw as his gaze raked her from head to toe. His grin broadened, and there was no mistaking his pleasure at having found her again. Too bad she couldn't say the same.

"Howdy, sugar, I'd just about given up hope of ever seeing you again," Jase drawled.

"She don't look too happy to see ya, brother," the other man said, his chest puffed boastfully as he stepped to Jase's side. "Why don't ya let me talk to her. As I recall, she liked me."

He was wrong, Chelsea thought. She didn't like either of them. Not at all. And with good reason. She'd known the first time she'd seen these two men that they were ruthless. But now, with the harsh light of day shining on their faces . . . well, she'd forgotten how very dangerous they were. *Outlaws*. She shivered, thinking that even her father would not have tried salvaging these two men's souls — if they had any souls left to salvage, that is, which she doubted.

Lifting her chin, Chelsea kept her mouth firmly shut. Every nerve ending in her body tightened, protesting the tall, strong, sweaty frame standing much too close to her.

"You got a name?" the dark-haired one asked, and flashed her a yellowed, crooked, gap-toothed grin.

She took an instinctive step back but kept her silence.

"Come on, honey, tell us yer name. That's all we're askin'," he pressed, his tone light but cajoling.

"Yeah," Jase added, hooking his thumbs in his belt loops and rolling back on his stacked boot heels, "that's all we want . . . for now. Later"—his green eyes sparkled—"yeah, maybe later we can take up where we left off, sugar."

"Don't touch me," Chelsea hissed, breaking her vow of silence when Jase's hand reached up to finger the copper curls tossing over her brow. She recoiled from the contact, but the heat of his hand on her face was unavoidable. It was also repulsive, when mixed with his sweaty smell.

Jase chuckled. Chelsea felt the coldness of his laugh ice down her spine. "Why not? You might like me touching you. Ever think of that?" His eyes darkened to probing emerald slits. His voice lowered to a soft, deadly purr as his coarse finger traced her cheek. His eyes dared her to slap his hand away. When she didn't, he drawled, "Yup, might like it a lot. Sure know I would. I've been looking forward to it."

The dark-haired one, whose name she didn't want to remember, eased near Kit. The boy took a counter-step back, his hand still fumbling behind him as he tried and failed to grasp the handle of the gun that had slipped inside his trousers as he rode.

Jase's hand opened, caressing Chelsea's jaw. His scratchy fingertips fondled her earlobe. Biting down on the fleshy inside of her cheek, she willed herself to neither scream nor cringe—as she so desperately wanted to do!

His face lowered until their noses almost touched. The stubble coating his jaw and chin looked like a prickly layer of dirt close up. His teeth, as he bared them in a mocking grin, were only slightly yellowed and crooked.

Chelsea drew in a sharp breath and held it.

"What do you say, sugar? Wanna go somewhere"—his bushy blond brows rose and fell in lewd invitation—"private and . . . er . . . *talk* about it? Just the two of us."

"I don't want to go anywhere with you. I think I made that clear the last time we met." Her chin lifted, breaking the contact between her flesh and his repulsive hand. But the respite was much too brief. The calloused fingers came back in force, sliding like sandpaper over her skin, hooking around the back of her neck. Lightning quick, he coiled the thick braid of copper around his powerful fist.

His lips pulled back in a sneer. "Pity. Guess I'll just have to set about showing you that coming with me would be in your best interest. Now, let's see. Exactly how would I go about doing that?" His gaze narrowed, sparkling with evil intent. "Hmmm . . . I wonder. Any suggestions?"

Chelsea gulped and prayed that either Kit would find his gun—soon!—or Mitch would take notice of what was happening here and offer her some much-needed help. Of course, he would have to tear his attention away from the voluptuous blonde first. And there was no guarantee that, even if he did notice, he would help. Why would he bother? She meant nothing to him now that he had her land. And he didn't even like Kit.

No, she thought, hoping for Mitch to intercede would be worse than useless—and a horrible waste of time. He wouldn't help. The realization made her even more determined to get away from these two outlaws under her own steam.

A gasp left her as, with a flick of his wrist, Jase yanked her head back, at the same time pulling her hard against him. The collision was enough for the breath to leave her lungs in a whoosh. Her hands, closed into tight fists, were pillowed atop his lean, firm chest. She pushed and twisted, but to no avail. The only reward she got for her struggles was a searing pain as the copper braid was nearly torn from her scalp.

Her chin snapped up with the pressure of his yank. Her gaze locked hard with his. There wasn't a sliver of mercy to be seen in the swirling emerald depths.

"Change your mind yet?" he drawled. His free hand slipped around her waist. The flannel of her shirt scratched against his calloused palm. She shivered, feeling the toughened flesh biting through the material, chafing her tender skin. It was not a pleasant sensation.

Effortlessly, he held her struggling form against him.

Forcing the last of her courage, Chelsea plastered a tight smile on her lips and batted her lashes. With mock sweetness he said, "Go with you? Why, now that you mention it, *sugar*, . . . I think I'd rather die."

His expression clouded, his gaze grew stormy, his cheeks reddened with anger. The arm encircling her waist tightened to an iron shackle, forcing the breath from her lungs and refusing to loosen enough to let her draw in more. Apparently; Jase wasn't used to rejection.

"Sugar, you don't know who the hell you're talking to, do you?" he fairly shouted in her face.

Chelsea swallowed hard, trying not to gag on the hot, stale breath washing over her. Mutely, she shook her head, his booming voice still ringing in her ears. "Not only don't I know," she snapped, "but I don't *care* who the hell you are. What I do care about is that you're touching me . . . and that I don't like it!"

His grin was quick and merciless. The hand around her waist slithered up her body, joining the other until he was clamping her jaw cruelly between a gritty thumb and the curl of an equally rough index finger. "Is that a fact? Well, maybe I should just give you a taste of what you're missing, *sugar,*"he snarled. "Then we'll see how much you don't like my touch."

"Hey, mister . . ." the proprietor finally snarled. The dark-haired one must have made a threatening gesture, for the man's footsteps shuffling backward sounded loud and cowardly.

Jase paid no mind to the interruption as his lips crashed down on Chelsea's for a hard, bruising kiss. A strangled cry left her as she tried to twist away, but his fingers dug into her tender flesh, holding her steady.

His lips were warm and far too moist. They were also, she was shocked to learn, every bit as skillful and demanding as

202

Mitch's. Unlike Mitch's, however, the feel of this mouth moving hungrily over hers evoked nothing but disgust. A surge of bile rose in the back of her throat as she beat on the man's chest and shoulders with her fists. Her foot kicked at his shin. She missed more times than not, but at least she had the satisfaction of knowing she'd tried to resist.

"Let her go!" Kit shrieked. "Did you hear me? I—Ugh!"

More shuffling was heard. Chelsea squirmed in Jase's arms enough to see Kit fall face first into the dirt. Her anguished whimper was swallowed by Jase's demanding mouth.

Her eyes widened, and her hands stilled atop Jase's chest as a wave of shock crashed over her. Was Kit dead? Had the dark-haired one killed him to stop the boy from interfering with Jase's kiss? Dear Lord, he's just a boy!

At the front of the wagon she saw a figure step into the muted sunlight. At this angle she could barely make him out, but she knew by the color of his hair and the familiar grey shirt that it was Mitch. He didn't move forward, as she was mentally screaming for him to do, but stood there watching . . . waiting. As she'd feared, he made no move to help. A surge of disappointment stabbed through Chelsea, and even knowing that his reaction was no more or less than she'd expected didn't dispel it. With rigid determination, she squelched her frustration and commanded herself to do something. But what?

Jase had used her shock to his advantage. He deepened the intimacy of his kiss—if it could truly be called that. His hot, moist tongue was now probing the layer of teeth she'd clamped together hard, forbidding him entry. The taste of his mouth sent currents of repulsion rippling down her spine . . . and more than a little anger. It goaded her to act.

Her leg bent, lifting for a resounding blow at the same time her teeth bit down hard on his plundering tongue. The taste of his blood was sharp on her tongue. She had no time to notice as her knee collided with the firm bulge nestled between his denim-clad thighs.

His breath was hot and harsh as it slapped her face in a

strangled yelp. His hand fell away from her jaw. With a grunt, he doubled at the waist, his cheeks ashen, his hands clutching at his damaged parts as a string of vicious curses cut the air.

Chelsea wasted no time. Knowing his friend stood only a few feet away and would quickly intervene, she lunged for Kit. It took her only a second to discover he was still alive— *thank you, God!* One more second and she had the tiny pistol in her hand.

Her fingers were trembling as, still crouching beside Kit, she pivoted, leveling the squat barrel at the chest of the dark-haired man who was charging her.

"So help me God," she panted, her voice high and as shaky as the rest of her, "you so much as lay your rancid breath on me and I'll kill you. Damned if I won't!"

The dark-haired one stopped so fast a cloud of gritty dust spouted up from beneath his suddenly-still heels. His muddy eyes shimmered with uncertainty beneath the brim of his hat. "Ya gonna take on the two of us, gal?" he snarled, nodding to his bent-over, furious but impotent brother. "Ya better hope ya can, 'cause when Jase gets over what ya done to him, he ain't gonna be too easy to reason with."

Chelsea's gaze was narrow—hot and defiant—as she returned his glare. "Guess I'll have to shoot you both, *then* try talking reason."

The dark-haired one grinned from ear to ear. The sight was ominous. "If'n ya think ya can."

"Oh, I can all right," she snapped. "Make no mistake about it. I can, and I *will*."

Chelsea's fingers quivered on the gun. It was the only sign of nervousness she allowed herself. How many years had it been since she'd felt a pistol in her palms? Too many to count. But the feel for it, she was relieved to discover, flowed back quickly enough. Slowly, skillfully, her thumb eased back the hammer. The metallic click of chambers rolling into place sounded loud against the pulse racing in her ears. A trickle of nervous perspiration ribboned down her temple. She swiped it away, her narrowed gaze cautiously alternating between outlaws.

"You're gonna regret what you just did, sugar," Jase grunted, and straightened as far as his aching manhood would allow. His gaze was cold, filled with furious humiliation at having been bested in front of others by a mere woman. His tone was harsh and biting, frightening as it echoed in Chelsea's ears. "And I'll surely enjoy teaching you the lesson."

"I'll tell you the same thing I told your brother, mister. You so much as—"

Before she knew what he was doing, Jase had the straps to his holster undone. His movements were sure, precise, too fast to follow with the eye. Chelsea had time to draw in a quick breath before she found herself looking down the twin barrels of his pistols. Each circle looked large and round and shadowy, like twin tunnels leading straight to certain death.

"Looks like we got ourselves a little Mexican standoff," Jase drawled, his emerald eyes sparkling with amusement as he watched the color drain from her cheeks. "Now, just which one of us do *you* suppose'll get off the first shot? Better yet"—his grin broadened, and the sight made Chelsea's stomach roll—"who do you think's gonna *miss?* Already know who I'd bet on."

His animalistic laughter said Jase's money wasn't on her. For that matter, neither was Chelsea's. She was a good shot, yes. But she wasn't *that* good. And even if she did shoot Jase, what about his brother? She couldn't kill them both. That would be too much to hope for.

"Drop yer gun, gal," the dark-haired one said. "Jase is a crack shot . . . and I'd sure as hell hate for him to ruin all that nice, ripe skin a' yers before I get a chance to—"

"Shut up!" Chelsea shouted. "Just shut up!" Her control snapped. She could no longer suppress her trembling. She was shaking from the inside out, and she didn't even try to hide it. Why bother? They all knew. The beat of her heart was a frantic pounding in her ears as her gaze fixed on the barrels of Jase's pistols, both aimed at a spot dead center of her clammy forehead.

She'd never get off a dependable shot in her frightened condition. Everyone knew it. Unless, of course, she slammed back the trigger when they weren't expecting it . . .

Chelsea thought of Kit, now lying unconscious by her feet. She thought of Jase's kiss, which still tasted hot and sour on her tongue. She thought of the small crowd that had curiously gathered around them, and of how none of them were brave enough to offer assistance. Last, she thought of Mitch Bryant, standing somewhere behind her, so unconcerned for her safety he didn't offer a scrap of help. Of them all, it was the last thought that stung the most.

Swallowing hard, she decided that her only chance against these men and the sordid crimes they'd planned for her lay in acting quickly, in taking them by surprise. Even then, she knew she didn't stand much of a chance — but it was *something*.

Slowly, so as not to draw too much attention, she switched the aim of her pistol from the dark-haired one to Jase — the greater of the two threats. She aimed the snubby barrel at his heart and hesitated. If she jerked the trigger back now she would kill a man, two if she was lucky, and herself if she didn't kill them quickly enough. She also knew that if she didn't do it and do it soon, her punishment at the hands of these outlaws would be far worse than a quick bullet through the heart.

Her finger twitched against the hard, cold trigger as she mentally bolstered herself for the shocking blast. Whether a bullet would rip through her, Jase, or both, she didn't know . . . but she was prepared to find out.

"Drop it," a raw, husky voice demanded from close behind.

A shiver of disbelief surged through Chelsea when she recognized the familiar voice as Mitch's. It was all she could do not to cry with relief. Finally, he'd come to her aid! It was a belated gesture, true, but one that was appreciated all the same. Down to her shivering core, she appreciated it.

"I said drop it. *Now!*"

Chelsea's grip on the pistol slackened as her victorious

gaze met Jase's. Her breathing slowed as she waited for him to drop his gun. He didn't. Instead, she felt the cold barrel of a pistol nudging her temple, and she heard Mitch Bryant's soft, cold voice so close to her ear it stirred the wisps of hair there. Her blood ran cold.

"I won't tell you again. Drop it, preacher's daughter, or your life ends here. And wouldn't that be a goddamn shame?"

Chelsea winced. A stab of betrayal knifed through her, white-hot and sharp. Her eyes widened as, barely moving her head, she met Mitch's gaze. His eyes, she was disturbed to find, were cold and dead serious. She had no doubt he'd kill her if she didn't obey him. The realization chilled her, splashing through her veins like ice water.

"Last chance, lady," he growled.

The dark-haired man's laughter cut through her as, one by trembling one, she uncurled her fingers from the pistol and let it plop onto her lap. Beside her, Kit stirred but didn't awaken.

"Good girl," Mitch commended flatly as he reached over and plucked the derringer from her lap.

His fingers wrapped around the handle, hesitating for only a second longer than was necessary. His touch burned through the coarse pants, searing the flesh beneath, but Chelsea's thoughts were in too much turmoil to notice, much less care. Humiliating tears stung her eyes, but she refused to shed them. She *would not* let this bastard see her cry. Never!

Her jaw clamped hard as she fixed her gaze on the outlaws. But her words were for Mitch. "Friends of yours, Mr. Bryant?" she asked, her tone dripping sarcasm.

Mitch tucked the derringer into his trouser pocket, his gaze never leaving her. His thoughts flashed over the six years he'd spent tracking Dobbs. He could have ended the whole affair a minute ago . . . had he not been afraid to catch *this* woman in the cross fire. "Yeah, you could say that."

"I *did* say it," Chelsea sneered. Her gaze shimmered hot amber fire as it locked onto his profile. He was looking at the

207

outlaws as if he knew them with more than a passing familiarity. For all appearances, she'd been dismissed from his mind.

The no-good, two-timing, rotten skunk! The bastard!

The urge to reach out and punch his arrogant, bearded jaw was countered only by the Colt he still held so masterfully. In a split second he could turn the weapon back on her, shooting her where she knelt in the dirt. Her fear returned when she realized there was still a very real chance he would do exactly that. She wouldn't have thought the Mitch she'd known the night before was capable of such a cold-blooded act, but *this* Mitch . . . well, this Mitch she didn't know at all. Nor did she *want* to know him.

"I don't mind tellin' ya, Mitch, there was a second there when I thought ya was gonna let the gal shoot one a' us," the dark-haired one said. His grin fairly beamed from his face as he took a step toward Mitch.

"From what I could see, you didn't do anything that deserved dying for, Whip," Mitch said with a shrug. His gaze turned on Jase, who reluctantly followed a few steps behind his brother. He hadn't put his gun away. Then again, neither had Mitch. Both weapons had been lowered, though.

"I didn't need your help," Jase growled at Mitch. "The lady and I were getting along just fine on our own."

Chelsea thought the outlaw's voice was unnecessarily gruff and unthankful—since Mitch had jumped to *their* rescue! Looking closely at Jase, she saw that his green eyes shimmered with a mistrust she had a feeling wasn't new. His bristled jaw was clamped in a hard, resentful line. Just how well did Mitch know these men? More importantly, *how* did he know them?

Chelsea had a sinking feeling she already knew the answers. Deep down, hadn't she always known?

In a flash she remembered the expert way Mitch handled his Colt, and she remembered, too, the deadly glint in his eyes when he'd trained that pistol on her. She remembered the obstinate way he'd refused to lower his gun the morning after the thunderstorm. All of it made sense now, even if it was a difficult — make that damned impossible — realization to accept.

Dear Lord, the man is an outlaw! A criminal! Chelsea damned herself as all kinds of fool for not seeing the truth sooner. For not *wanting* to see it. All the signs were there, if one dug for them, but she just hadn't pieced them together . . . until now.

She sent Mitch one last, recriminating glare, then turned her attention to Kit. Lifting the boy's head, she cradled it on her lap. His hat had been knocked free in the scuffle. Soothing her fingertips over the unruly mop of hair, she found a large swelling beneath his hairline. She winced. Damn it, Kit had been trying to save *her* life! He shouldn't be the one lying unconscious in the dirt, *she* should be. Better yet, *Mitch Bryant* should be. The rotten traitor deserved no better!

Chelsea glanced up, her gaze fixing hard on Mitch's rugged back. He was in the middle of a conversation with Jase. So what? She didn't care if he was having a personal audience with the Pope! "The boy needs a doctor," she barked.

"He'll be fine," Mitch growled, then resumed his talk with Jase, whose hooded gaze had yet to leave Chelsea.

She stiffened, her hot glare searing the broad wedge of Mitch's back. "I said he needs a doctor, Mr. Bryant. *Now.*"

The conversation between Mitch and Jase came to a quick, tense end. Chelsea saw Mitch's back stiffen, and she felt the heat of his glare as only his head turned toward her. His eyes blazed a warning that Chelsea refused to acknowledge she saw.

"And I said he'd be fine," Mitch replied, his voice low, husky, and impatient. "Give him time. He'll come around."

Chelsea knew better than to force an issue she had no hope of winning. Truly she did. But she couldn't help herself. She lowered Kit's head to the ground, then pushed to her feet. Her knees trembled beneath the coarse trousers, but not in fear. Fury and betrayal were riding her hard, and they funneled into the only available outlet: defying Mitch Bryant.

Her fingers were closed into fists so tight they hurt. She planted them firmly on her hips. With a toss of her head, she returned Mitch's glare with a fury that surprised her. "You miserable bastard! It's *your* fault the boy's lying there, bleeding and unconscious. If you'd stepped in sooner, none of this would have happened."

"Watch it, Che—"

"No, I damn well *won't* watch it! You're a no-good criminal, Mitch Bryant. One who can't see beyond helping two friends escape the evil clutches of an hysterical woman. You'd rather let this boy die than waste your time helping him."

The silence stretched taut; it was thick enough to cut with a knife. The air filled with the sound of Chelsea's angry footsteps approaching Mitch. She stopped close enough for their toes to touch . . . close enough for her to feel the dangerous heat of him . . . close enough to be engulfed by his sharp, spicy scent. She noticed none of it.

Her temples throbbed with indignation as she thrust her chin up and met his gaze. His was hot, but hers was warmed with a fury she'd felt only once before in her life.

The air cracked with the stinging slap of her palm crashing into his cheek. The blow was hard enough to snap his head back on his neck. Hard enough to leave the angry imprint of her hand a bright red contrast to the sun-kissed skin above his beard.

Very slowly, Mitch's head came back around. His eyes were a dark, searing blue, unreadable of any emotion but raw, hard fury. His hand lifted, grazing the spot where his cheek stung. His eyes seared the same spot on hers.

He might as well have slapped her back, the result was the same. Chelsea flinched.

Mitch grinned—coldly, maliciously. His hands dropped to his sides, the fingers curling into fists. It took great effort not to gift her with a reciprocal blow, one that would have knocked her onto her tempting little rump. Damned if he knew why he didn't let his fist fly. God knows, she deserved a good smack!

"Are you done?" he asked, the fury in his tone tightly leashed.

A bell of warning pealed in the back of Chelsea's mind. She didn't find it too difficult to ignore. "Are you going to find Kit a doctor?" she countered, just as coldly.

"No."

"Then no, Mr. Bryant, I'm not done." Her palm rose for another stinging blow that never made contact. His hand snaked out, his fingers wrapped around her wrist in a grip that was both tight enough to make her wince and painful enough to threaten snapping her fragile bones in two.

His head lowered until she could feel the brim of his hat gouging her brow. Her breath caught when his hot breath washed over her. She arched backward, but the instinctive reaction was next to useless. He only followed her, putting her at a distinct disadvantage by making her stance precariously.

"Don't ever do that again," he snarled. Anger darkened the cheeks above his beard a bright red. Her handprint stood out in pale white. "Next time, lady, I slap back. With my fist."

"Better listen, sugar," Jase interrupted, his tone saying he was pleased one of them had shown her her place. "Mitch ain't never had much patience with women. You ain't no different."

"When it comes to the likes of this piece of scum," Chelsea snapped, her gaze locking hard with Mitch's, *different* is exactly what I want to be. Let go of me, you bastard!"

Mitch's eyes narrowed, hooding the brilliant blue depths beneath. "Watch it, preacher's daughter. Didn't your daddy ever tell you that swearing like that will send you straight to hell?"

Her chin lifted proudly, though she didn't break eye contact with him as she sneered, "It's a little late for that, don't you think, Mr. Bryant? Last night determined exactly where I'll end up when I die. I just pray to God we don't share the same fire when we get there."

His attention dropped to her lips. His gaze smoldered hungrily over the pouty, moist, shell-pink flesh. "We already do, preacher's daughter," he replied, his voice hoarse and low. "Don't you know that? Don't you *feel* it?"

Yes. She *did* feel the fire that was Mitch Bryant. Too much so. With an angry grunt, she wrenched her arm free. Spinning on her heel, she retreated to where Kit lay, then scanned the crowd that was starting to thin now that the fun was over.

Chelsea's gaze snagged on mint-green silk and honey-colored hair. The voluptuous blonde was now standing at the front of the wagon. Their gazes met. The woman's blue cat-shaped eyes held a glint of superiority in them when she tilted her chin and glared haughtily down her nose. Then, with a burst of high, airy laughter and a swish of her billowing skirt, the blonde sauntered toward Mitch.

He barely glanced down as the woman affixed herself to his arm, clinging like a vine to all that raw muscle. The look the feline creature cast up at him made Chelsea's stomach churn.

Tearing her gaze away, she shifted her attention to the meaty proprietor, who stepped forward when she beckoned to him. Behind her, she heard the conversation between the three outlaws resume as though she'd never interrupted it. It was joined by a melodious, feminine fourth.

"I ain't no doctor, lady, but my wife's pretty good with the kids' cuts and scrapes. Want her to take a look?" the large man asked as he lifted Kit's limp body in his meaty arms.

The sound of his voice, nasal and high, made Chelsea focus on him. He grinned at her, the gesture obviously an apology for not stepping in to defend her earlier. His eyes pleaded for understanding, and Chelsea's forced smile gave it to him.

"Do you think she'll mind?" she asked as she fell into step beside him.

He answered her, but Chelsea never heard what he said. At that moment, Mitch's laughter snaked out from behind. The sound was deep and husky, curling warmly up her spine and reminding her of things she'd do best to forget.

Her footsteps faltered as she glanced back. Mitch was watching her from over his broad, broad shoulder. The feel of his eyes boring into her back was tangible . . . and disturbing in that, even now, she had a base, wanton reaction to it.

"Damn it," she muttered what was becoming a horribly familiar curse under her breath, running her suddenly-moist palms down the thighs of her trousers. She was trembling. She could feel the instinctive quivers through both sides of the material. The vibrations cut her to the quick, not because they were there, but because of what they represented. And what — no, *who* — had caused them.

Mitch Bryant was a no-good outlaw. He'd saved the lives of his friends by threatening to take hers. But, even so, she couldn't honestly say she was immune to him. Not by a long shot.

Nor was he immune to her. Even now his gaze was hot and devouring. And his eyes promised her that things between them were far from settled.

Swallowing hard, Chelsea tore her gaze away and rushed to catch up with the proprietor as he turned the corner of the wagon. Mitch's gaze tracked her. She felt the burn of his eyes long after she'd disappeared from sight.

Chapter Fifteen

Mitch tossed and turned atop the hard-packed earth of Northwest Quarter Section number 30. Sometime during the last hour, he'd come to the conclusion there wasn't a snowball's chance in hell he was going to get any sleep tonight.

Pity. He was tired as hell and his throat hurt. It didn't matter. Even exhausted to the bone, with minor aches and pains, the image of his sexy-as-all-hell preacher's daughter refused to be wiped from his mind. Not that he hadn't tried! He had. But her image wouldn't go. Like a silk-threaded spiderweb clinging to a dusty corner, the sight of huge whiskey-amber eyes shimmering with hurt and betrayal wrapped around his heart and squeezed tight. The memory ate at him.

Goddamn it!

With a grunt of self-disgust, Mitch turned onto his side. His throat hurt, and his temple, already throbbing from gritting his teeth for the past hour, grazed a rock. Pain sliced through his head. He cursed out loud. What the hell? There wasn't anyone around to hear. Ch—Chelsea Hogan hadn't come back to her campsite. He doubted she would tonight. Knowing her, she was out nursing that abhorrent little thief somewhere in Two River Crossing. Mitch wouldn't be surprised if she never returned.

Nor would he like it.

That thought—quick and alarmingly sure—made him push himself up to a sit. The ground was hard beneath him, but not nearly as hard as his thoughts. Bending his knees, he rested his forearms atop them. Linking his fingers tightly together, he let them sway between his knees as he stared out over the meandering river—and the spot he remembered Chelsea's camp to be. The land stretching out on that side of the river was unwelcomingly dark.

What if she didn't come back? What if she'd somehow found out she had no land to come back to? What if she left Oklahoma and never returned? What if he never saw her again?

Yeah, Mitch, what then? The tightening in his gut answered the questions for him. He wasn't pleased with his response.

His throat closed tight, his stomach slimmed, and not for the first time did he damn himself for doing what he had that afternoon. God, the pain he'd seen in her hot, angry glare had sliced him to the quick. Damn, it still did!

His spirits didn't lighten when he told himself Chelsea really hadn't given him a choice. If he hadn't put his gun to her head and threatened to kill her, the hotheaded little wildcat might have tried to shoot Jason Dobbs—one of this country's most notorious outlaws. Even if she'd been lucky enough to kill him, there was a good chance Dobbs would have gotten off at least one clean shot before he died. And that bullet would have found Ch—Chelsea Hogan's passionate little heart.

Mitch had witnessed Dobbs's uncanny skill with a Colt enough times in the past to know the man was good—clean, precise, and quick. Probably better than Mitch himself. Dobbs's bullet would not have missed.

So, in his own peculiar fashion, Mitch had saved Chelsea's life, ruined six years' worth of work, and earned a resounding slap across the face—not to mention Chelsea Hogan's eternal hatred. People had hated him in the past. Hell, a lot of people still did. It had never bothered Mitch before; he was used to it. Until now . . .

The snap of a branch from the cottonwoods behind him jerked Mitch's attention to the present. He tensed. His gunbelt was a dark leather circle on the grass by his hip. It was relieved of its Colt lightning quick.

In an instant, he'd traced the sound to the midway point amidst the line of cottonwoods. Whoever the intruder was, he hadn't reached the edge but would soon. Mitch knew he hadn't been spotted . . . yet. Nor would he give his unexpected company the chance to find him. Years of hard-taught skill and honed caution had taught him to never, *never* be caught sitting out in the open with his back to an intruder.

Without a sound, he pushed to his feet and crept toward the trees, a good distance from where he suspected the intruder to be. The grass whispered around his booted ankles, but the sound was swallowed up by night noises — crickets chirping, the croak of a frog, the whisper of the constant Oklahoma breeze.

Anther *snap-crunch* reached his ears at the same time he flattened his back against a solid tree trunk. The cottonwood's bark was cool as it bit into his flesh through the shirt. His gun was pointed upward, held close to the front of his shoulder, as his narrowed gaze swept the moonlit shadows. He saw nothing unusual. He hadn't expected to. Experience told him the hair prickling at his nape was enough reason for caution.

He watched as a dark shadow disengaged itself from a nearby tree trunk. The intruder's steps were short and quick, the person obviously making little attempt to hide his presence.

Mitch didn't think, didn't assess, he just reacted. He hunched into a charging position and waited until the shadow was within striking distance. When it was, he lunged.

A grunt tore from his chest when his shoulder slammed into the intruder's midsection. The momentum of his thrust sent them both tumbling onto the ground.

Mitch knew instantly who he'd captured. Her distinctive smell and feel were as good as fingerprints. Unfortunately, he was going too fast to stop. He landed atop a cushion of soft female flesh, pinning the woman's writhing body beneath him.

216

Her breath was hot and ragged as it rushed over his face in a strangled gasp. His was equally as harsh as the collision of his body into hers pushed the air from his lungs in a whoosh.

It took them both a few minutes to catch their breaths.

"Christ, Mitch, a simple 'Howdy-do' would've sufficed!"

"Look who's talking," he growled. "Why the hell didn't you say it was you? And why in God's name were you creeping up on me like that? I could've shot you as easily as I tackled you."

"Creeping?" she cried, shaking her head in disgust. "I made enough noise to alert the next townstead I was here. *You*, of *all* people, should have heard me."

Mitch levered his weight on his elbows. Lifting himself above his captive, he looked down into the woman's delicate heart-shaped face. The black cap she'd been wearing had tumbled off when he'd charged her. Her long blond hair now scattered the ground around them like a blanket of spun silk.

"Sweetheart, if you didn't feel so good right where you are, I'd toss you over my lap like a sack of wormy flour and spank the tar out of you," he grumbled, his tone less than threatening now. His gaze shimmered as it met wide, teasing eyes that were a shade somewhere between blue and grey. "Let that be a lesson to you, Mennard."

"Humph!" Brenda snorted, and planted her balled fists on his chest. Eyes narrowing, she gave a hearty shove. She was tall, her body well-kept and athletically firm. Her shove managed to topple him to the side.

He landed with a thump and a hearty chuckle. Brenda had wiggled away and pushed to her feet the second he'd collided with the ground. Squinting, Mitch let his gaze travel up her length — of which there was quiet a bit, all of it perfectly shaped. The effect was dazzling.

She stood towering above him, her delicate face set firm. Her legs were encased in pitch-black trousers, her feet separated and planted unfemininely apart. Balled fists straddled her hips. A toss of her head sent the mane of wheat-gold hair tumbling around her face and shoulders.

Mitch recognized the gesture as something she only did when perturbed — the only word that adequately described her pinched expression. Yup, she was sure as hell perturbed. He wondered why but didn't ask. She'd tell him eventually. She always did.

"You know, Mitch," Brenda said, her eyes narrowing, "in all the time I've known you, this is the first time I've been able to sneak up on you that far. Mind telling me why?"

Pillowing one palm on her thigh, she extended a hand to help him up. Her palm felt warm and familiar in his own as his fingers closed around it.

"Where have you been?" he asked as he pushed to his feet and dusted off his grass-stained trousers. "You were supposed to be here hours ago."

"Hmmm, and you were patiently waiting for me, I see." She moved to where his fire had died hours before, extending her hands to it as though warming them on the cool, rustling breeze. Glancing over her shoulder, she caught him staring at her. His look was thoughtful. She grinned. "Don't tell me, let me guess. I haven't been far from your thoughts all night."

Actually, Mitch hadn't thought about her at all—except to wonder where she'd gone when the hour after their arranged meeting had slipped by and she hadn't shown up. That was the only time he'd thought about her. The rest of the time had been devoted to his favorite newly acquired pastime: contemplation of a certain sexy little redhead.

The realization made Mitch aware of just how much time Ch—Chelsea Hogan had spent in his thoughts lately. Compared to the amount of time he *hadn't* spent thinking about her—and dreaming about her and fantasizing about her—the total was staggering.

Not a good sign, he thought. His sour mood took a turn for the worse. It was reflected in his tone as he stepped to Brenda's side and asked, "Well? Did you see her?"

"Her?" she asked, her grin coy. It didn't fit her face, which had an honest quality about it that Mitch had always found attractive. "Her who? Could you be a little more specific?"

"This isn't funny, Brenda," he snapped, and jammed the pistol beneath his belt with enough force to make the belt loops strain. The temptation to reach out and grab the woman, maybe shake the words out of her, was strong. He didn't do it, of course. It would make him look like too much of a fool.

"You're right, it isn't. And no," she shrugged, plopping down to sit on the grass, "I didn't see her."

"You didn't? . . . Then where the hell have you—!"

Brenda grinned up at him, her face beaming proudly in the slivers of moonlight filtering down through the shiny leaves above. "I had a meeting."

"I don't care if you had a—" His jaw clamped shut, his gaze narrowing. "A meeting?" His tone tightened with speculation as he ran a palm down his bearded jaw. "With Dobbs?"

"No, Mitch, with President Harrison," she snapped. "Who the hell else would I be seeing?" She huffed and looked away. "Or did you forget I'm a happily married woman?"

"There isn't a thing about you I *could* forget, Brenda," Mitch replied absently, joining her on the ground. "Tell me what happened. Did he say anything? Did he tell you where—?"

Brenda held up a hand, stopping short the barrage of questions. "Whoa! Slow down a minute. I saw him for ten minutes, Mitch. That's all. Your plan worked. I have a feeling the only reason Dobbs saw me in the first place is because he thinks I'm yours. He won't tell me anything for a while yet. But"—a charming, confident half-grin turned her lips—"he *will* tell me."

For the first time since Dobbs's name had been mentioned, Mitch's anxious expression softened. He reached out, entwining Brenda's warm, soft fingers with his own. His gaze dropped to her breasts, straining against the black cotton shirt. "Jesus, you're a cocky piece of baggage. Are you sure there's a woman in there? Maybe I should check."

"You go right ahead, sweetheart. Just remember, Clancy will have your head for it." Her gaze met his. Her blue eyes were sharp, but the warning there was dulled with a teasing glint. "And didn't we have this discussion years ago?"

They had. It was one of the few conversations Mitch had

had with a woman that he could remember verbatim — mostly because they had both been naked at the time. Usually when he had a woman naked the last thing either of them did was talk. But he and Brenda had talked, which made the occasion memorable.

The conversation had been short and sweet, punctuated by the sound of drunken laughter and bad piano music drifting up through the floor slats from the saloon beneath their room.

"Do you want me?" he'd asked her.

"Yes. You?"

"Oh, yeah." At the time he had wanted her. More than anything in the world. But . . .

"We've got to work together, Bryant. It could make things hard."

"Things are already hard, Mennard. Physically speaking."

She'd chuckled huskily at that. Then, after a brief but poignant pause, she'd asked, "Do you love me?"

It wasn't a question Mitch was comfortable answering. The few times he'd been forced to, he'd always spoken the truth. Even with Brenda he wouldn't make exceptions. It wouldn't be fair to either of them if he did. "No," he'd said finally, running the tip of his finger down her long, smooth spine. "You?"

"Hell no!"

From anyone else, Mitch would have taken offense at such a quick, blunt, vehement response. But this was Brenda. This was different.

"I have more sense than that," she'd added. Hesitating, she'd frowned and asked, "So, what happens next?"

"I don't know." He'd turned then, burying his nose in her cotton-soft hair and inhaling her flowery scent just one more time before he let her go. "I expect we'll get dressed and go downstairs. Maybe split a bottle of whiskey between us and forget tonight ever happened."

They had. And from that night on, both were careful to never be put in a position where temptation reared its ugly head again.

220

Sighing, Mitch turned his head, only to find Brenda sitting close enough so he was able to catch her flowery fragrance. Three years had not abolished the potency of it. She smelled fresh and clean, soft and sweet. Oddly enough, he didn't find the scent as tempting as it had once been. He exhaled a long, slow hiss between his teeth. Somewhere along the line, he'd acquired a taste for a more earthy aroma — the spicy kind that clung to Baptist preacher's daughters.

That realization hit him like a punch in the gut.

"Why didn't you go see her?" Mitch asked suddenly. He'd put off the question that was burning a hole in his mind long enough. He wanted — needed — an answer.

"Why do you think?" Brenda asked. Shaking her head, she plucked a handful of long, thick bluestem and ran it though her fingers. "Think, Mitch. The last time the woman saw me I was glaring at her with that he's-mine-and-you'd-better-keep-your-paws-off-of-him look. Call me stupid, but I don't think she'd be very happy to see me again. Do you?"

"I don't really give a damn *what* the lady's receptive to, Brenda. I want to know how the hell she's doing!"

Brenda tilted her head to the side and glanced at Mitch shrewdly, one brow cocked. "Why?"

Mitch opened his mouth, but the words withered on his tongue and he snapped it closed again. He plowed his fingers through his hair and shook his head. He said the first thing that popped into his head, anything to get that contemplative look out of Brenda's eyes. "Dobbs. He seemed pretty taken with her this afternoon. God knows what he'll do if he gets the chance."

"Not that you care, of course," she said, her tone oozing insincerity. "And I take it you've finally decided she isn't in with Dobbs?"

"Yeah," Mitch grumbled, and glared into her widened, laughing eyes. Actually, he'd known for a while that Chelsea had nothing to do with the outlaw he'd spent the better part of six years trying to find. Only now, though, did he give himself permission to acknowledge that fact.

"I was wondering how long it would take you to admit it,"

she said. "Of course, it was nice when you thought she knew Dobbs. Gave you a real good reason to stay so close to her."

Mitch grinned, though the gesture didn't reach his eyes. "Jealous, sweetheart?"

When Brenda's chuckles subsided, she said, "Thought you might want to know. I found out where she's staying."

Mitch's sudden interest was so quick and so intense that it made her hesitate. It didn't take too much effort for Brenda to see the look on his face and read it for what it was. If she didn't tell Mitch what he wanted to know, he was going to reach down her throat and pull out the words. A slow grin curled over her lips, but she kept her mouth shut.

"Spit it out, Mennard," Mitch growled, his voice thick and gravelly. She just smiled. "This isn't funny. I want to know where she is, and I want to know now!"

"Why? So you can charge over there? I don't think she wants to see you any more than she wants to see me, Bryant."

Even in the flickering moonlight, his blue eyes burned. His hands clenched into fists that he had to concentrate hard to uncurl. "I don't give a damn what she *wants*. Any woman who's fool enough to pull a gun on a man like Jason Dobbs doesn't have the brains God gave an ant. She certainly isn't smart enough to stay away from any traps the guy might have set out for her."

"Would you care if she did?" Brenda's question was soft and to the point. It demanded an answer Mitch didn't want to give—even to himself. "Walk into one of Dobbs's traps, that is."

"Yeah, I'd care. Hell, the woman and I share a claim—one that will be coming under dispute in the not-too-distant future. If she turns up missing or dead, who do you think they'll blame?" His index finger jabbed at his chest. "Me, that's who. You know I can't afford to have my name talked about like that. Not right now. We're too close."

"And that's the only reason?"

Mitch glared at her. "Yeah, it is. What other reason could there be?"

"Damned if I know." Brenda shrugged, and hid a smile behind her hand. She knew Mitch too well. Knew when he was lying. And he was lying through his teeth right now. She had a feeling she knew why . . . and the knowledge delighted her. It was past time Mitch Bryant found a woman who turned his world upside down, the way he did to so many others.

"Speaking of your claim," she said, "what happens to the land once the Dobbs Gang is out of the way? You said your name's the one on the deed, didn't you? Are you planning to keep it?"

"I . . . don't know."

"Come on, Bryant! That's all you've talked about for the last year. Settling down, growing roots, trying your hand at all that domestic stuff you tease me and Clancy about. Well?" She gestured to the moonlit land around them "Don't tell me you'd let a place this beautiful slip through your fingers."

Mitch sighed. "It's not the land, Brenda, as you damn well know."

"Do I?"

He sharpened a glare on her. "You do," he growled. "And isn't this conversation just a bit premature? We have to find the Dobbs Gang first. I'll worry about the claim and . . . all the rest of it when that's over."

"Christ, Mitch," she huffed, "it was just a question. No need to get so touchy."

"I get touchy whenever I think of Jason Dobbs."

"Seems to me you get touchy when you think of a lot of people lately. Hey, where the hell are you going now? Mitch? Mitch!"

Mitch didn't answer. He'd already pushed to his feet and was strolling away.

Chapter Sixteen

The lamp Chelsea had left burning when she'd left the wagon had been extinguished. The wagon itself was now a black silhouette against the moonswept night. The canvas top shimmered like a billowing sail over a sea of swaying bluestem.

The air was still scented with the charred odor of the day's burning grass fires. Occasionally, a whiff of wildflowers would intrude, but it was rare. Somewhere a coyote bayed at the three-quarter moon. The sound was too distant to be alarming.

Chelsea stopped beside the wagon and listened. No sound except the crunching of footsteps could be heard. Oh, and the sound of her heart beating furiously in her breasts. That, she heard quite loudly. It reminded her of the visit she'd just paid to Sam Henderson, Two River Crossing's new deputy. What a fruitless visit that had been!

Her gaze fixed on the wagon. The Ralstons had left at dusk for Guthrie, generously giving Kit and Chelsea use of their wagon in the interim. They wouldn't be back for at least four days. It was all the time Chelsea had to find another place to live or to get her land back from that no-good rattlesnake Mitch Bryant.

Spinning on her heel, she leaned back against the hard side of the wagon. Squinting, she focused on the clear, moonswept sky and its smattering of tiny stars. As peaceful as the sight was, it did nothing to calm her.

It had taken her five hours to screw up her courage and pay Sam Henderson a visit. And for what? The man was a coward and a fool. He wouldn't help her. He wouldn't arrest Mitch. Sweet heavens, just the outlaw's name was enough to send the young deputy into a tailspin.

What on earth had Mitch done to deserve such fear? *Men who carry guns carry them with the intent to use them.* Oh, she knew he was an outlaw; his actions this afternoon proved it. As did his choice of friends. But what was he wanted *for?* And why hadn't she asked the cowardly deputy when she'd had the chance?

Because I don't want to know.

It was true. She didn't want to know what Mitch had done, if only because she'd foolishly allowed herself to be intimate with him. If she were to find out now that he was a cold-blooded murderer . . .

Wrapping her arms about her waist, she stifled a shiver. The gesture had nothing to do with the cool night breeze. It had everything to do with Mitch Bryant's hands. How well she remembered the calloused feel of them skimming her flesh. A warm, prickly sensation washed through her just thinking about it. But had the hands that had brought her such pleasure ever ended a person's life?

This is the West, girl, her father had once said. *It's a wild, untamed place. People out here kill each other every day. 'Course, that don't make it right. Now, it's up to you and me to show these folks the error of their ways. Lead them back on the road to redemption. Only way to save their poor damned souls.*

Chelsea snorted in reproach. Saving souls. Mitch Bryant had teased her about that several times. She'd always taken the ridicule in stride, biting her tongue against it. Little did he know she didn't want to save anyone's soul—his least of all. She never had. That had been Papa's call in life, not hers.

Still, she had a feeling even Papa would draw the line at trying to redeem a man like Mitch Bryant. There were cases where a glimmer of hope could be seen in a man, and cases where there wasn't a trace no matter how hard you looked. Mitch fell into the latter category. And yet . . .

Chelsea would be lying if she didn't admit she *had* looked for the good in him. Many times. She hadn't found much. No matter how deeply she looked, there was little merit to be had in his actions or his words. That proved one of two things: Either he didn't have an ounce of old-fashioned decency in him, or he was an expert at masking it. She wondered which it was.

After this afternoon, she'd have to suppose it was the former. No decent man would put a gun to another person's head—a *woman's* head—and threaten to pull the trigger. No one.

She leaned her head back, pillowing it against the pliant canvas. She tried to wash her thoughts clean of lingering traces of Mitch, but traitor that her mind was, his image kept flooding back. She couldn't rid herself of it.

A distraction. That was what she needed. Her gaze swept the area, resting on the sacks of flour, sugar, beans, and other assorted dry goods that had been stacked outside earlier to make room in the wagon for Kit. She'd promised the Ralstons the sacks would be put away in the smaller supply wagon before they returned from Guthrie or before it rained, whichever came first.

There wasn't a cloud in sight, but Chelsea needed to do something with her churning fury besides clench her fists and pout and think. Putting away the sacks was as good as anything.

The supply wagon was parked behind the skeletal shell of the store. It was already loaded with tools and covered by a floppy canvas cloth. The muscles in her arms screamed a protest as she dragged the first heavy sack over to it. By the time the fifth was propped against the wheel, the muscles in her legs were burning. Only one more sack to go, and the chore would be done.

Trudging back to the prairie schooner, she hunched over and grabbed the tied-off ends of the last sack. She yanked. The sound of rending cloth tore through the air. The weight of the sack evaporated. Suddenly, she was tugging on air.

She landed on her bottom, hard. Her hands still fisted the

floppy ears of the sack. The very *empty* sack. Apparently, the cloth had a hole in it. Her pulling had enlarged the hole until a goodly portion of the sugar inside had pillared onto the ground . . . and herself, as the sudden lack of weight caused her to stumble backward. When she'd fallen, the half-empty sack had landed on top of her.

"Damn it! Damn it all to hell and back!" The curse felt good, very satisfying as it curled around her tongue. What didn't sound nearly as good was the dry chuckle that shot out from somewhere near the end of the wagon. Chelsea's spine went rigid as the pleasant, husky sound lapped over her.

Her attention jerked in that direction. A chill trembled in her bones. Her narrowed gaze settled on the tall, well-muscled form vividly outlined against a backdrop of silvery moonlight.

He was leaning a shoulder against the tail end of the wagon bed. No hat graced his head, leaving the breeze to toss his dark hair recklessly over his cheeks and brow. His thumbs were hooked in the belt loops of snug denims that both the pale light and the cocky angle of his hips outlined to perfection. The moonlight glinted off the blue-cast metal of his Colt. It was, as always, strapped low on his hip.

His blue eyes burned out of the shadows, straight into Chelsea. The amusement swimming in his eyes caused a splash of hot color to warm her cheeks — especially when she realized she was dusted from head to toe in sweet, grainy sugar.

"For a preacher's daughter, you look pretty good like that," Mitch said. His voice was light, and as airy as the cool breeze that lifted the sticky copper curls back from her brow.

"How long have you been standing there?" she demanded. Her stomach rolled — with tension, or excitement? Tension, she decided. Of course it was. What else could it be? Mitch Bryant was the last person she wanted to see right now — unless, of course, he was standing at the end of a lawman's rifle.

"Here?" His shrug was negligent. "Not long. Outside Sam Henderson's sod-house" — he paused succulently, making

227

her surprised gasp sound louder than it actually was—"a good deal longer. What took you so long to hunt him down, sweetheart? I'd have thought you'd do it a long time ago."

"A long time ago I didn't know you were a criminal," she spat. She'd been leaning up on her elbows, her neck craned to make eye contact with him. She now pushed herself to a sit and felt grains of sugar wiggle beneath her clothes, gritting against her flesh. It was a strange feeling.

"And now you do?"

"Yes." The *s* was pushed through tightly clenched teeth; it hissed through the brisk night air.

His lips were hidden beneath the curl of pitch-black mustache. She didn't have to see them to know he was grinning. The knowledge washed down her spine like a chunk of melting ice.

"Yeah, well, I guess that changes things then," he said. Pushing away from the wagon, he took an ominous step toward her. When she wiggled back, he stopped. "Or does it?"

"Go away, Mr. Bryant. I have chores to do, and I—I don't want to see you."

"I didn't ask what you wanted, preacher's daughter."

He took another step. Another. He was close enough for Chelsea to feel the heat of his body melting through her—*his!*—shirt and trousers. His scent, spicy and sharp, mingled with the smell of sugar. The two scents combined to confuse her already-flustered senses. Her reaction worked against her anger, taking the biting edge off the fury she'd nursed for the better part of the day . . . the fury she had clung to the way an autumn leaf clings to the branch, to its root of life.

Mitch took another step, stopping once he was towering over her. He was within touching distance, though his thumbs stayed hooked through his belt loops. But for how long?

Chelsea thought about pushing herself to a stand—if her watery knees could manage it—and running to seek the shelter of the wagon. Though the path was clear, she refused to do it. It would be a sign of weakness, of fright, of defeat. True, she felt weak. And she was frightened to the quivering core—but more from the flagrant, carnal power this man held over her than from any threat of danger. But, damn it, she was *not* defeated!

"Help you up?" he asked, his eyes dancing in the moonlight as he extended a calloused hand.

Chelsea regarded that hand with all the warmth she'd show a pit viper. Make that less. Shaking her head, she refused his assistance. His hand dropped to his side, and she couldn't help but notice the enticing sound of his palm slapping against a solid thigh that no longer held any mystery for her.

"Why are you here?" she asked, her voice a soft croak.

Mitch's eyes darkened to glistening turquoise as he looked steadily down at her. "Why do you think?"

"I don't know." But she did. They both knew it. Closing her eyes from the potent sight of his, lest she drown in their dark blue depths, Chelsea sucked in a sharp breath and said, "Why do you do that, Mr. Bryant? It's annoying as hell."

He grinned. Because he was annoying her, or because she was getting so good at cussing? she wondered, but wasn't sure.

"Do what?"

"Keep answering my questions with questions?"

"Do I? I hadn't noticed."

And he hadn't. In fact, he hadn't noticed anything beyond the way her hair clung like strands of twisting copper to her cheeks, or the way the moonlight ignited fiery highlights in each satiny strand. The pale glow danced over her cheeks, heightening the color to an endearing pink. And her eyes . . .

Mitch sucked in a quick breath through his teeth. Her eyes were large and expressive, sparkling a rich shade of honey in the flickering moonlight. Her gaze burned with betrayal, but the sharpness was dulled by an emotion that was hard to mask. It was desire, pure and physical. Mitch would have bet his horse she had no idea how easily her feelings could be read in her eyes.

The sight was potent, intoxicating, hypnotic. It threatened to pull him into the large irises and drown him. For that reason alone, he tore his gaze away and fixed his rigid attention on the spot where the horizon molded into the velvet-black sky. "I take it Henderson wasn't agreeable?"

"Would I be here if he was?"

"Probably not."

"Definitely not."

He glanced down and was awarded with an unobstructed view of her profile. The moonlight softened it, bathing her creamy skin in soft silver shadows, turning the color of her hair to hot, molten copper. He saw sparkles of sugar clinging to her cheek. His mouth watered, and his tongue curled when he fantasized about what it would feel like, taste like, to lick her clean.

He looked quickly away. "What did you ask him to do?"

She shifted restlessly and shrugged. "Arrest you."

His laughter was harsh and cold, mildly derisive. So were his words. "No wonder he refused. Do you have any idea what you were asking him to do? *Who* you were asking him to go after? Jesus, lady, I'm surprised he didn't pack up his family and run for the hills the second you left his house."

"I was asking him to go after *you,* Mr. Bryant."

Mitch hunkered down. His hand snaked out, clamping her jaw between the knuckle of his index finger and his thumb. He yanked her gaze around. His voice was gritty and thick with reproach. "My point exactly. You asked him to go after *me.* Mitch Bryant. Outlaw. A man with a price on his head steep enough so only idiots try bringing him in. It didn't matter that it wasn't true, that it was all just a story Thiels had concocted to get him close to Dobbs. *She* believed it. And I stress the word *try.* There isn't a lawman alive I can't outrun or outshoot. Or didn't your daddy ever tell you. . . . A man doesn't earn his reputation by words, he earns it by actions. My actions speak loud enough to warn away all the Sam Hendersons you could ever dig up."

Chelsea's gaze flashed as she wrenched away from his touch. No, she realized, it wasn't the touch she pulled back from, it was the sensations his warm, calloused palm caused to shoot like lightning down her spine. Confusion raced through her blood, stemming from nothing more simple than mere physical contact—as searing as that contact was.

"And what, exactly, are those actions, Mr. Bryant?" she asked in a shaky rush of breath. The question had been tickling the tip of her tongue ever since her encounter with Sam Henderson. Her curiosity forbade her from dropping the subject until she had an answer—as much as she dreaded hearing it.

"You really want to know?"

"Would I have asked if I didn't?"

"I don't know. You tell me."

Her chin lifted. She returned his gaze with a probing stare, trying to ignore the feel of sugar melting against her escalating body heat. "Yes. I want to know."

His bearded chin lowered, his hungry gaze feasting on her lips, softly parted and pouty. Moist and inviting. The pink flesh was dusted with sparkling grains of sugar. His gut churned, his voice lowering two husky pitches. "Do you? Well, I'll tell you something, preacher's daughter. I want something else entirely. Wanna guess what it is . . . and whether or not I'll get it?"

His hand was back, the palm open, scraping the quivering line of her jaw. A shiver raced down her spine before she could hide it. His gaze darkened. He'd seen the weakness and read it for exactly what it was: excitement, desire, dread.

With the last of her resolve, Chelsea batted his hand away. Surprisingly, he let it drop to his side. But not before his blue eyes pierced her with a flash of regret.

With an impatient sigh, Mitch rolled his weight back on his heels. His legs were bent, knees apart. The angle made the coarse denim encasing his thighs tighten, drawing attention to the hard bands of muscle beneath. He was close. His knee brushed her shoulder. The touch was both stimulating and disturbing at the same time. Tipping his head back, he cast his gaze heavenward and asked, "All right, lady, what do you want to know?"

"Why the hell you stole my land!" Her amber gaze widened, her throat working up and down in a swallow that refused to form. The question had just popped out. It wasn't the one she'd meant to ask. Mitch didn't seem surprised, she noted, although she could feel the tension building in him, radiating from him. It bolted through her like a flash of hot summer lightning.

He pulled the makings of a cigarette out of his breast pocket. With deft fingers, he rolled it, clamped it between his teeth, and lit it. The tip glowed orange, illuminating his harshly sculpted features when he drew on it. He hissed out a long, slow stream of smoke, and only then did he look at her. "How'd you find out?" he asked finally and amazingly smoothly.

Briefly, in clipped words and short sentences, she explained how she had arrived at the land claim office and what had happened in the few minutes she'd been there. She ended by demanding, "Why? Why did you file *my* claim?!"

"I had my reasons." The corners of his mouth quirked down.

Chelsea turned her head and glared up at him. "Then explain them to me. Please, Mitch. I need to understand."

"Always the preacher's daughter, aren't you? Always looking for a way to see inside a man's soul, sniffing around for the good." His chuckle was bitter and cold. So were his eyes. "Don't waste too much of your time on me, lady. In case you haven't figured it out yet, I don't have a soul."

"Everyone has a soul," she snapped. "Some just don't have one that's worth saving." To keep her hands busy, she began to brush off the sugar. When she saw the way his eyes followed the flicking motions she made over her breasts, she stopped.

Chelsea jerked her arms over her heaving breasts. A toss of her head sent the thick copper braid slapping at the small of her back. "I'm going to dispute the claim," she stated firmly. "I'll take you to court, and I'll win. I was on the land first. We both know it. There isn't a court in the world that would toss out my claim and give it to you."

"Maybe." He shrugged, that casual rise and fall of his

shoulders that looked so practiced and so damn callous. The movement brought shoulder and knee back into contact — but the touch was blessedly brief. With a flick of his fingers, he sent the barely smoked cigarette flying, a hot orange streak arching through the night.

"Why the hell do you want the land so badly?" he asked suddenly. "There are still a few tracts not claimed yet. Wouldn't one of those do for you?"

"No." Chelsea's voice was strong and firm as she met his gaze. "And if you know so damn much about what land is and isn't available, why don't you do something useful for once and go stake one of those unclaimed tracts for yourself!"

Thinking that was the best exit line she was likely to get with this man, she pushed to her feet and drew herself up with as much dignity as a woman with flakes of sugar raining from her body could. She made to step around him and heard him shift a split second before she felt his fingers close like steel bands around her wrist, stopping her short.

She glared down at his biting grasp, hoping the power of her furious gaze would melt the shackle away. It didn't.

Slowly, he rose to his feet. Still imprisoning her wrist, he leaned toward her. Their noses were mere inches apart. His expression was hard, unreadable, his eyes chips of cold blue ice that froze her to the spot. "Uh-uh, lady. You aren't going anywhere. I want to know why *you* won't go after one of those free tracts."

His breath rushed hotly over her cheeks and neck. The feel of it sent a tingle of shock rushing through her blood. Her heart slammed against her ribs. She stifled a tremor and tried to summon her fury back to the fore. It wouldn't come. Anger was overridden by the onslaught of Mitch Bryant's feel and scent — and her own crazy reaction to it.

"Because I want the land I worked for," she said finally, her voice still shaky but firmer. "The land I made the Run for. The land I earned. I want *my* land, Mr. Bryant."

"Uh-uh. *My* land," he corrected tightly. "You don't have any anymore. Or did you forget whose name's on the deed?"

"Why, you — !"

Lightning quick, Mitch grabbed the claw she sent flying at his cheek. It took very little effort to twist her arm behind her back. A flick of his wrist drew her struggling body up hard against his chest. His back came up just as hard against the wagon. Her hips slipped between his thighs, the feel warm, inviting, and achingly familiar. His knees closed around her wiggling hips, clamping her against him with intimate firmness.

"Didn't I warn you about slapping me?" he growled.

"Let me go!" Chelsea struggled. His hold on her was crushing, but the sting of it was nothing compared to the erotic feelings that tingled in her breasts when she grazed his rock-solid, enticingly warm chest.

Mitch felt it too. His eyes darkened with hunger when his gaze dropped to the spot where their bodies blended.

Chelsea arched her back, trying to sever the contact. But the forearm around her waist and the hand that manacled her wrist stopped her feeble struggle with a pinning grip. The position only made her press against him more closely, more intimately.

Mitch glared down into large, fearful amber eyes and tried to remember the reason he'd come to Oklahoma in the first place. A reason that had been six long years in the making. A reason that, right this second, was at war with the gut-wrenching feel of soft, soft breasts crushed against his chest. The feel of her hips wiggling against the heat of him was a bittersweet torture that drove him both hard and crazy at the same time.

"I want you, woman," he murmured huskily. "Here. Now." His gaze locked with wide whiskey-amber. Sparks of sugar tipped her lashes and glistened on her skin. Mitch bit back a groan.

Chelsea was no more immune to the heat of their embrace than Mitch was. His words caused a delicious thrill to trickle down her spine. A surge of desire warmed her blood. Ignoring it was the hardest thing she'd ever done, and she didn't do it well.

"You want me?" she echoed flatly. Her gaze narrowed on

234

him, shimmering with the sour memory of his betrayal. "How much, Mr. Bryant? Do you want me badly enough to put a gun to my head and demand I surrender to you?"

Slowly, dangerously, Mitch's eyelids lowered, then raised. The emotion glinting the dark blue depths was not the same when his lashes swept up . . . as though the lazy blink had bought him time to absorb and deflect the bitterness of her words.

When he said nothing, just stared at her, she added, "It's the only way you'll have me again, you know. Even then, I swear to God I'll fight you with everything I've got."

One corner of his mouth quirked up in a cynical grin. "It's 'everything you've got' that's making me so damn hot for you, lady. I wouldn't advise you to threaten me with it. Not if you're trying to convince me of why I *shouldn't* throw you down on the grass right now and take what I damn well know we both want."

The fingers shackling her wrist loosened, then fell away. His hand didn't drop back to his side. Instead, his open palm covered the small of her back, then gradually lowered.

"Mitch?" Chelsea whimpered oh, so softly. She tried to get her voice to sound plaintive, beseeching. She failed miserably.

His head lowered. His beard scraped her cheek as his lips, hot and moist, grazed the sensitive hollow in front of her earlobe. He tasted the sugar clinging to her skin, tasted the way it mixed with the salty, sexy taste of her. Her shiver vibrated through his chest like a clap of thunder. "How long do you think you can fight me, preacher's daughter? How long do you think you can fight yourself?"

"As long as I have to," she answered. Her voice was too high and too weak. It was not the voice of resistance.

"Liar."

He was right. For the first time in her life, Chelsea was lying. She had no choice. She couldn't tell him her defiance melted away at the feel of his hard, spicy maleness pressing against her. If he didn't think she'd fight, Lord knew what would happen between them. Something she didn't want to have happen again; a shared intimacy that wouldn't bear repeating.

His hands cupped the firm curve of her backside. The gentle swell filled his palms. The fit was perfect. Mitch groaned. His fingers curled inward, tunneling through the coarse cloth of her trousers as he dragged her hard between his thighs. He lifted her up on tiptoe, and when he eased her back down, he'd positioned himself between the soft, warm cleft.

"Do you feel that, preacher's daughter?" he rasped while nuzzling her neck. More sugar. More sweetness. Oh, God.

Her answer was a breathless, defeated little sigh.

His tongue darted out, tasting the shell of her ear. His teeth nibbled the delicious flesh before he sucked it into his mouth, swirling it beneath his tongue. Sweet. So damn sweet.

"No, Mitch, don't," she breathed. Her arms lifted and wrapped around the thick cord of his neck. She hadn't given them permission to do that. Then again, she hadn't given her body permission to arch into him, either, and she was doing that, too.

"Why not?"

"Because it's"—she paused long enough to suck in a ragged breath—"wrong. It's a sin. We'll burn in hell for it."

"Too late for me, baby. My soul was damned years ago," he sighed. His hot breath puffed against her ear as his fingers massaged her sensitive bottom. "It's *your* pious little soul that needs a good, healthy dose of sinnin'. . . . of nice, hot fire . . . of the kind of corruption that burns you up inside."

Sweet heavens, she felt like she was already burning up! An inferno boiled in her blood, fanning through her body alarmingly fast. The feeling seared away fury, resistance, and any of the normally good sense that should have been begging her to stop this madness before it was too late . . . but didn't.

And as for sin . . . well, nothing in her life had ever felt as deliciously sinful as her breasts being crushed against Mitch Bryant's chest. Or so wonderful. His fingers were roughly kneading her bottom. She felt like a glob of pliant clay aching to be molded to his hard male contours.

His lips found her neck. He licked and teased. His breath washed in hot, ragged waves against her flesh. Her sticky-sweet flesh. Mitch tasted the sharpness of her on his tongue. Nothing in his life had ever tasted this good. He yanked her so close he half expected her to melt right into him.

He knew the exact moment she dissolved in his arms, knew the exact second she surrendered the fight and gave herself over to some good, healthy sinnin'. She liquefied against him, and Mitch thought he would die when her head turned to the side and her lips grazed his neck.

He absorbed a shiver, but he wasn't sure if it was his or hers. Nor did he care. Right now, he could feel some grainy sugar scraping against his neck, between his flesh and her moist little tongue. The feeling was enough to break him.

The last time he'd taken her, he'd given her the chance to refuse. Only a fool would offer twice. Mitch Bryant was many things, but a fool wasn't one of them.

Holding her tight, he lowered them both to the ground, under the wagon. He didn't realize he'd placed them on a pile of sugar until he felt the stuff dusting through his fingers and gritting beneath his knees. He grinned. Oh boy, did he grin.

"Open your eyes, preacher's daughter."

The words, a reflection of last night's, heated through Chelsea's blood. Her lashes flickered up, her eyelids hooding the swirled amber depths beneath. Her arms, she noted, were wrapped tightly around his neck. When had she done that? Then she felt his hair tickling her palms and wrist, and found she didn't care *when* she'd done it, just that she had.

"I should hate you," she said, her gaze fixing hungrily on his lips and on the dark whiskers that curled over them.

"You will. Tomorrow. I promise you that."

She shook her head, and his hands came up to sandwich her cheeks and jaw. "No, Mitch. I should hate you now. Tonight."

"Do you? Do you hate me enough to make me stop?" He didn't know how bad he needed to hear the answer until he

237

asked the question.

A self-deprecatory grin curved her lips. She shivered when she felt his thumb stroke her trembling lower lip. She tasted the sugar clinging to him. The tobacco. The manly tastes. It was her turn to groan. "No," she answered on a ragged sigh. "I don't hate you. And, sin or no sin, I never want you to stop."

His eyes slitted, but not from anger. The heavy-lidded stare was passion, pure and simple, carnal and raw. His finger trailed over her jaw, tickled her earlobe, traced the line of her neck. "Good. Because I couldn't stop now if you begged me."

"And if I begged you to love me? What then?"

It was a double-edged question. Mitch knew it even as he answered. For once, he didn't lie to her. "Do you think I could do anything else?"

It wasn't the answer she wanted, not the one she needed to hear. Then his lips claimed hers and she found a different answer, and the fulfillment of a separate but entwined need.

"Kiss me, preacher's daughter," he rasped against her sugar-sweet lips. "Kiss me like you mean it."

She did. And she meant it. Every hard, demanding second of it, she meant . . . with her life. She knew her submission meant more than mere physical surrender. To both of them. A lot more.

It must have been the sugar clinging to her skin, slipping beneath his tongue, that drove him crazy and impatient. The taste was sharp and sweet in his mouth. It clawed at his gut, snapping his restraint in two.

Mitch stripped off both their clothes fast. He didn't acknowledge the way his hands shook — really *shook!* — when he let them roam hot and fast over her body. She felt small, soft, grainy beneath his palms. She felt good. The way she molded against him was heaven. The way she arched beneath him, grinding her hips against his, was pure hell. It was a bearable hell, though. Especially when he knew hot release was in sight.

Last night he'd taken things slow and easy, afraid he'd

238

scare her away. But tonight . . . ah, tonight he didn't think he could scare her away if he tried. She was ready for him. His fingers tickled down her taut belly, dipping low to find out just how ready she was.

The breath she sucked in released and rushed in his ears. To Mitch, it was the sweetest kind of music. But it wasn't nearly as beautiful as her husky, plaintive, "Now, Mitch. Please."

He didn't need to be asked twice. Things were going fast, perhaps too fast, but he was beyond caring. All he cared about was the feel of her, the smell and taste. The need to possess her was driving him hard. He had to bury himself inside of her, had to feel her tight, moist warmth closing around him. Now.

He levered himself atop her, glorying in the feel of her soft curves straining beneath him. His gaze fixed hungrily on her sugar-dusted face, boring into her tightly closed eyes, mentally willing them open. He'd told her last night what he liked. He wouldn't ask again.

Her lashes swept up at the same time she hooked her legs around his hips and arched beneath him. His hard, scorching heat was a much-too-gentle intrusion. She wanted, needed, more.

Brilliant blue locked hard with whiskey-amber and held as he plunged into her.

She gasped. So did he. They released simultaneous sighs of pleasures. Their breaths mingled, entwined, became one.

His strokes were smooth and deep. He rocked against her, into her. Greedily, she arched her back, tightening the hold of her legs, straining to meet each demanding thrust.

His eyes darkened, holding hers as he increased the rhythm to a frantic tempo. She matched it and quickened the pace.

Too quickly she felt the sparks start low in her belly. It fired in her thighs, heating her blood until it pumped through her veins in tingling, simmering waves. It was too soon. Much too soon. She didn't want this pleasure to end so fast, but she was as powerless to stop the spasms from slamming through her body as she was to stop Mitch from climbing to that highest of peaks with her.

Her nails dug into his back. Her head twisted, her lashes started to swoop down. His gaze alone had the power to pry them back up again.

Mitch chanted her name, over and over, sweet and long as he felt his own blinding surge of release.

Chapter Seventeen

If this was the Fire of Hell, Chelsea wanted to be damned. Eternally.

She snuggled against the warm chest cushioning her cheek, nestling into the spicy-smelling shirt Mitch had tossed over them. The collar scraped her chin. She sighed, remembering the way his calloused fingers had done much the same thing only a little while ago. And sugar. She recalled the gritty feel of sugar the second time he'd taken her. His tongue had flicked over her skin, licking the sweet-tasting particles from places she was embarrassed just thinking about. But not too embarrassed.

The hair pelting his chest tickled the tip of her nose. She smiled. It was a delicious sort of tickle, the kind that started slow and mellow. The kind that quickly built to a sensuous burn.

The ground beneath them was hard-packed and chilly. But Chelsea felt none of its rigid stiffness. How could she? From the knees up, she was cradled against hot male strength. Beneath her palm was the beat of Mitch's heart. The rhythm was steady and soothing.

His bearded jaw snuggled against the top of her head. The ragged whiskers made her scalp tingle as they prickled through her tousled hair. One heavy arm was wrapped around her waist, the palm branding her back beneath the shirt as he pinned her atop him, gently but securely. His other hand was coiled around her upper arm. His grip was light but firm, as though he was afraid she would realize what they'd done, what they'd shared, and would quickly clamber from her natural space atop him.

Her fingertip traced tiny playful circles around the pink disk buried in a sea of twisting black hair pelting his chest. She felt as well as heard him suck in an uneven breath. Her grin broadened. No, the very last thing Chelsea wanted to do right now was to clamber . . . *anywhere*. Not unless it meant clambering after Mitch Bryant. That she would do. Pride be damned.

"Mitch?" she sighed. Her eyes darkened to honey as she watched her breath stir the curls tickling her lips.

"Hmmm?"

"Mitch, is it always this . . . good?" She ducked her head shyly when she felt his chuckle rumble beneath her cheek. It was a deep, husky, pleasant sound. One that struck an immediate chord in her.

"Chelsea?" he countered lazily, stifling a yawn.

"Hmmm?" She shifted to look up at him. Could he see the blush heating her cheeks? After the passion they'd just shared, did it matter if he did?

"Are you always so direct?"

"Only when I want to know something."

His eyes slitted open, capturing her. "Well then, I guess I'll have to tell you the truth. No, it's not always this good."

The palm covering the small of her back tightened, the calloused fingers curling possessively into her satin-soft flesh. So warm . . . so smooth . . . so goddamn sexy! His voice thickened as he planted a kiss on the top of her head. "It's never been this good before, sweetheart. Never."

Mitch stiffened, the words he *hadn't* said ricocheting through his mind with all the force of a gunshot. *And it'll never be this good again, Chelsea. Never!*

"Never?" she asked skeptically. Again, she buried her face against his chest, reveling in the feel of flesh and muscle beneath her even as her mind began to churn. "Now, why don't I believe that?"

"You should. It's the truth."

"Oh, Mitch, please," she groaned, trying to keep her voice light. She didn't want him to know how much this conversa-

242

tion meant to her. She would rather die than have him guess how her entire life — everything she was, everything she ever would be — hinged on the questions she asked him now . . . and his answers.

Squirming against his side, she took a pinch of silky black chest hair and gave a playful tug. "You know, I may be a Baptist preacher's daughter, but I'm not stupid. Flattery has never turned my head."

"Uh-oh. I think my integrity is coming under fire," Mitch grumbled under his breath. The fingers wrapped around her arm peeled away, only to slide over her shoulder and cup her cheek. His hand turned inward, his roughened fingertip tracing the moist, pouty line of a mouth that had kept him awake more than one night just thinking . . . and wondering . . . and fantasizing about the sugary taste it promised.

"What makes you think I'm trying to flatter you?" he asked finally. His tone turned raspy when she began to nibble on the tip of his finger. If she sucked it into her mouth, he was going to shake. Mitch knew it, and he hardened himself against the weakness . . . because that was exactly what she did.

Chelsea ran the tip of her tongue down the long, calloused line. A surge of victory coursed through her when she felt the tiny quivers beneath his skin. He tasted slightly salty, slightly sugary, and all male. She liked that.

Turning her head, she planted fleeting kisses on the backs of his knuckles. "Isn't that what all you men say afterwards?" she asked, her breath a hot gust of air on his skin.

Chuckling softly, he dragged the moistened tip of his finger across her lips, wetting them. It was Chelsea's turn to shiver.

"Christ, you've got a lot to learn," he rasped, and felt himself tighten when he thought about how much fun it would be to teach her all of it. "Sweetheart, we men don't have to say a thing *afterwards*. It's what we say *before* that counts."

"To get a woman into bed," she stated matter-of-factly.

"No, not *always*. Believe it or not, we manly creatures do occasionally hand out compliments to you womenfolk for reasons other than to get you beneath us."

"Really?" Curious, she lifted her head and peered at him.

243

"Like what?"

His grin was a soft lifting of one corner of his mustache. The sight was heart-stopping. "Oh, I don't know. To see a woman smile, I expect. Maybe bring the hint of a blush to her cheeks. And, of course" — he shrugged beneath her — "to get her into bed."

"Ah-ha!" This time when she pinched a clump of chest hair, she gave a hard yank. He yelped and batted her hand away.

"Ah-ha nothing." Mitch's arm drifted to a waist that was so incredibly small and tight it jarred him. Hugging her was like hugging a ragdoll; both were about as big. But ragdolls didn't have breasts that seared a man's chest, or thighs so white and creamy and inviting. And they sure as hell didn't taste so goddamn . . .

Nipping *those* thoughts in the bud, he wrapped her in a tight embrace and flipped her onto her back. His fingers linked behind her head, protecting her from the collision as he spread himself atop her.

The shirt covering her fell away. Neither of them noticed.

The sight of her fiery red hair scattered around them, and the feel of the silky strands in his palms was distracting as hell. What had they been talking about? Jesus, who cared!

"Something's changed," Chelsea whispered, her voice hushed. Blinking hard, she looked at him. It was the same handsome face, the same ragged beard and incredible blue eyes as always. But . . . Turning her head, she gazed, unfocused, over his shoulder. "You feel it, too, don't you? Don't you?" she insisted when he remained silent.

"Yeah, I feel it," he grumbled, and added to himself, *I shouldn't — never, never with this woman — but I do*.

His gaze sharpened, raking her face. Her lips were full and pink from his lusty kisses, her cheeks flushed from the heat of passion that had yet to be entirely doused. Even her tousled hair looked like it had been sexily corrupted. Damn it! she looked . . . edible. Catching a glimpse of his reflection in her whiskey-dark eyes didn't help matters. She looked edible all right, and he looked downright famished!

"Why, Mitch?" she asked, her voice thick and confused.

244

"Why did things change? What happened to *make* them change?"

One raven brow cocked high in his sun-kissed forehead. "You don't know?"

She shook her head. Her hands had wrapped around his neck when he'd tossed her onto her back. Her fingers now twisted nervously in the ragged fringe of his hair. "No," she whispered hoarsely. "I don't think I do. But I want to."

His hands slipped from behind her head until he had her face wedged firmly in his palms. His gaze was dark and patient. "We made love, Ch—Chelsea Hogan. That changes things between a man and a woman. How could it not?"

"No." She shook her head . . . well, as much as she could within his firm grip. A scowl furrowed her brow. "No, it's more than that. I can feel it. We . . . you know . . . did that before, but nothing changed between us. Why now? Why this time?"

Because last time I made love to you with my body. This time I made love to you with my heart. And you, smart little preacher's daughter that you are, sensed the difference.

"I don't know, Chelsea," he lied, his gaze piercing the moon-lit shadows beside her head. "Does it matter?"

"Yes. No. Oh, I don't know! It isn't *that* things changed, it's *why* they changed. Do you understand?"

His lashes swooped down. Thickened lids hooded the deep penetration of his gaze. "What I understand, lady, is how damn good you feel when I'm inside you. You feel tight, warm, and soft and . . . right. And no, I can't even begin to understand why."

Nodding, she closed her eyes and surrendered briefly to the hard, naked feel of him pinning her to the ground. He felt firm, powerful, yet oddly gentle. His touch was magic, her reaction to it sinful. She wanted to feel that touch again, but first . . .

"Mitch?" she said, her voice soft, high, uncertain. "About my land . . ."

His head dipped, his lips nuzzling the sensitive spot between tapered neck and oh, so slender shoulder. Her skin still tasted sweet. Her flesh quivered beneath his mouth. "What land?"

"Northwest Quarter Section number 30," she answered breathlessly. Her body was starting to burn again. She yearned for another taste of the fire that was Mitch Bryant. Of the sin.

"Never heard of it."

"Mitch!"

Sighing in resignation, he sealed the contact with a kiss, then lifted his head. His hands smoothed the hair from her brow, his fingers tunneling through the soft, soft strands beside her temples as he returned her gaze with level intensity.

"I can't," he said hoarsely, his expression inscrutable. Good thing, too. If she knew how much the soft sadness glinting her eyes sliced through him, he'd never be whole again. It was bad enough a part of him had already been carved out for her. It would be twice as bad if she knew just how big a chunk of him she had. "Don't, Chelsea. Don't even ask it."

Her fingers tightened in his hair. She felt torn, half of her wanting to obey him and not ask, the other half demanding that, even if it meant shattering the moment, she ask. The latter, unfortunately, won out. "I have to. Will you —?" Her tongue darted out, wetting suddenly dry lips. The taste of him was still there, clinging to her flesh, sharp and tangy. "Will you give me my land back without a fight? Please?"

Mitch's eyes rolled back, his lashes sweeping down. Hell, he'd give her the moon, the stars, the sun . . . *anything* she wanted if it was within his power to give it. But it wasn't. And neither was Northwest Quarter Section number 30. Son of a bitch!

He opened his mouth to reply. Before he could, she slashed a trembling finger over his lips and said, "Wait. Before you answer, let me tell you why I want it so badly."

"Don't," he growled against her finger. "It won't make a difference. It can't."

"But it might."

Sighing, and hating himself one hell of a lot, he nodded and rolled to the side. He landed hard, scooping her up and fitting her against his side as he went. She felt small and warm, soft

246

and vulnerable when she pressed against him like that. She felt perfect . . . and so goddamn right! "Tell me."

She nestled her cheek atop his chest and sucked in a deep breath, as though her explanation would be long and she wanted to start it in a quick rush of words. On its release, she said, "Freedom."

Mitch waited for her to continue. When she didn't, he grew curious despite his resolve not to. "That's it?"

She nodded against his chest, and he felt her slender body stiffen. "I shouldn't have said anything," she muttered. "I knew you wouldn't understand."

"Try me. I might surprise you."

She shrugged and thought, Why not? What else did she have to lose? "All right. My father used to call your type 'windy-wild'. A man whose life blows in whatever direction he wants it to go in. A man who molds life to suit him, consequences be damned. A person like you — who's always had freedom — can't imagine what it's like for a person like me — who never had it, but always wanted it."

"And this land is your freedom?" he asked softly.

"Not all of it. But it's a good place to start, don't you think?" She shifted, glancing up at him, only to find his eyes pinched closed. "Are you going to steal this chance from me, Mitch? It might be the only one I'll ever get." Softer, she added, "And I may never be able to forgive you if you do."

"There are other ways to get freedom, Chelsea," he answered noncommittally. His words felt parched as they worked around the guilty lump in his throat, in his heart.

"Not the kind of freedom I want. Not the kind I need."

"And what, exactly, do you need?" He knew the answer he wanted her to say — *me. Say you need me!* — and he felt oddly cold and bereft when it wasn't the same one that passed her lips. Ah, God, he was in deeper than he thought.

"To prove myself," she said, her tone firm and hard, as though she were trying to sway him, as though she had to. "I want to stand on my own two feet and either proverbially sink or proverbially swim." She paused, then plunged on, "I need to crawl out from under my father's shadow. *That's* what I need most. I'm a preacher's daughter — I can't deny that — but I'm no angel. Please, stop measuring me by those standards. I'm not as fragile and as sweet and as nice as you seem to think I am."

To Mitch's way of thinking, that wasn't exactly true. He'd never met a woman like Ch — Chelsea Hogan. And no woman had ever before inspired these protective, possessive instincts in him. She *was* an angel, he thought. *His* angel. He'd just knocked her halo a bit crooked, maybe tarnished it a little . . . but he couldn't regret that. He'd had a hell of a good time corrupting her. And he knew, given the chance, he'd do it again.

"So, will you give me my land back?" she asked, then held her breath, waiting, praying for his response to be the one she needed desperately to hear.

"I . . . can't."

"Why not?"

He squirmed, trying to think of a way to steer this conversation onto another, safer track. Nothing came to mind. Odd, since he was usually good at leading conversations in the direction *he* wanted them to take. "You don't want to know, lady. Believe me, you don't."

Her head dropped back to his chest. Her heart tightened with a defeat she refused to acknowledge. "Mitch?"

He stiffened, bolstering himself for whatever she was about to say next. He dreaded the sound of her voice and the feel of her hot breath searing across his chest almost as much as he dreaded leaving her. One would come sooner than the other, but both would inevitably come.

"Hmmm?" he murmured finally, reluctantly.

"It's changed again, hasn't it?"

"Yeah." Damned if it hadn't! And damned if there was anything he could do to stop it or change it back.

A few throbbing heartbeats passed.

"Mitch?"

"What?" he asked, his voice gritty. He swallowed hard and noticed that his throat was starting to burn again. Then her breasts pressed against him, and he was incapable of noticing anything beyond that.

"Make love to me again. Please."

Mitch closed his eyes, knowing he should refuse and also knowing he wouldn't. "Ah, preacher's daughter, that's the first reasonable request you've made all night."

Wiggling seductively up his hot, firm body, she stopped when their lips were only a few sizzling inches apart. Their gazes met and clashed. Both were dark with newly awakened desire and the memory of hot satisfaction burning in their eyes.

Reaching up, she brushed a raven curl from his brow and whispered, "Feel free to grant it . . . outlaw."

Mitch sighed dramatically, the bitter tension between them seductively severed. "Gee, lady, I don't know if I can. At least, not without a gun pointed at my head."

She caught his meaning. Her grin was enough to make his heart stop beating. His gaze grew curious when he saw her wink. Her hand came away from its padding of his chest. Her bottom three fingers curled in until her thumb and index finger formed a wide L. He blinked hard. Dear God, she was teasing him!

Chelsea pressed the tip of her "gun" against the place in his temple where his pulse throbbed. "Then consider me armed . . . and very, very dangerous."

Her melodious giggle pierced the brisk night air, warming him to the marrow. She was dangerous, all right. More than she knew, he thought as he again tossed her onto her back and pressed her straining body onto the ground beneath the hard length of his own. She was dangerous to his heart, to his sanity, and most of all, she was a very real danger to life as he knew it.

She was also soft, sweet, and sexy as hell. Well worth the risk, he decided as he set about showing her how much he'd chance to hold her in his arms, in his heart, just this one more time.

Chapter Eighteen

Damn it! This was a hell of a time to be getting sick — yet sick was exactly how Mitch felt. He burrowed deeper beneath the bedroll, but it didn't help. His head hurt, his throat felt burning and raw, and God, was he cold! Groaning, he tried to focus on something besides the chills icing through his body and the herd of buffalo thundering in his head.

Think, Bryant. Think! Where the hell are you?

Shortly before dawn he'd deposited his sexy preacher's daughter in the borrowed wagon she shared with Kit, then returned to Northwest Quarter Section number 30 for some much-needed rest.

The furrow creasing his brow smoothed. He was on the claim. Good, good, that was a start. He remembered collapsing on the ground for some much-needed sleep. The tightness in his body, caused by the uncomfortably hard ground told him the nap had been a long one . . . much deeper than would be considered safe for a man in his profession. But the rest had been well earned. Ch—Chelsea Hogan's greedy passion had drained him dry.

He tossed onto his back, his aching body aware of the lumpy ground beneath him. Foggily, he became aware of something else. Something cold and hard. Something that pressed into his throbbing temple. If he didn't know better, he'd swear . . .

The gun barrel gouged his flesh as he absorbed the cold

metal feel of it. A dazed corner of his mind remembered the "finger" gun Chelsea had held on him during the long, passionate night. He would have laughed at the image *that* thought evoked had he thought his head could stand it.

Chelsea Hogan. That's who was holding the gun to his head. Apparently, his sexy little preacher's daughter wasn't feeling as drained as he was.

Slowly, he peeled through the cloying layers of a dream. He was only vaguely aware that this was no ordinary sleep; it was too deep, too murky. Pushing away an unfamiliar feeling of unease, he wondered how Chelsea had managed to get ahold of his gun without waking him. Then he toyed with countless ways he could disarm her. Each variation ended the same . . . in waves of mutual pleasure. Such delicious contemplation worked wonders on his headache and sore throat!

It wasn't until he felt the barrel jerk slightly and heard the metallic click of chambers rolling into place that Mitch started to get concerned. How much did his sexy preacher's daughter know about guns, anyway? Enough to leave the tent that morning on the way to Guthrie without one, yet enough to hold one on Jason Dobbs. He only prayed she knew enough not to shoot him by accident.

His Colt was always loaded. That was the first thought to pierce his clearing brain. And this *was* his gun; that was his second thought. A small chip in the barrel scraped his tender skin, making the pistol distinct. He felt the cold metal shiver, which meant the fingers clutching it were trembling. Any outlaw worth his salt would tell you that trembling fingers and loaded guns did not make for a healthy way to start the day. And his day had already gotten off to a lousy start.

Any good humor Mitch might have felt soured. His headache came back in throbbing force. This wasn't funny anymore.

"All right, sweetheart," he grumbled. His voice sounded loud as it echoed, magnified, in his ears. The noise made him wince as he continued, softer, "Enough. If you want to use my body again" — his heavy sigh was appropriately martyred — "all you have to do is ask. And if you're a good little preacher's daughter, when my head feels better we can . . ."

His eyes slit open, only to be pierced by blinding sunlight. He hissed in a breath and squeezed his eyelids shut again. That hurt almost as much as the barrel digging into his flesh. Waiting until the waves of pain subsided, he snapped, "Just put the damn gun away, lady. Before one of us gets hurt."

"Oh, one of us will get hurt all right. You! And this gun won't get put anywhere until I've had the pleasure of splattering the ground with your blood, you yellow-bellied son of a bitch!"

"What the — ?"

In the split second it took for the voice to strike a chord of familiarity, Mitch reacted. His arm felt weighted as it came up fast, slamming into the one that trained the gun on him. The blow of bone hitting bone was stinging to them both.

A yelp of pain rushed in a hot blast in Mitch's ear. It was followed by a crunch that sounded like his gun falling onto the crushed bluestem.

Pain sliced through Mitch's head. He ignored it as, with an agility born of years of practice, he lurched to the side and rolled into a squat. The world swayed. He blinked hard, his eyes burning from the bright light, the throbbing in his head, and the struggle to focus his vision on something other than the foggy yellow haze stabbing through his eyes.

His survival instinct had been honed to a fine pitch years ago. It took over where sight left off, dulling his pain and sharpening his sense of hearing and smell. The intruder — Kit? — was to his left, near his feet. The crunch of dirt and grass was loud as the boy lurched for the gun.

Mitch wasted no time. He lunged. His head felt as though it had split wide open when he crashed into a slender body, sending them both flying. They hit the ground hard.

Mitch's vision cleared enough to make out gaunt cheeks

and light brown hair pillowed atop the hard-packed ground. It was Kit's lean body he was straddling, sure enough. The familiarity of the boy's hateful features was far from soothing. The kid looked angry as holy hell, his glare youthfully hot and savage.

"Get off me, you rotten bastard!" Kit cried, his voice reverberating through Mitch's pounding skull like a runaway locomotive. "I can't kill you with you crushing me this way!"

"Then damned if I'll be letting you up any time soon." His angry outburst cost him. Mitch didn't need a mirror to know his cheeks drained ashy white; he could feel it. The pounding in his head was almost unbearable. He felt his shirt, cold and wet, pasted to his body. He was sweating, and had been for some time by the feel of it. Goddamn it!

Kit didn't reply. Instead, he used his energy to arch off the ground, trying to buck the raw muscle and strength that rode him. His slender hands balled into fists, lashing at whatever part of the outlaw he could reach. His knuckles smarted, as though he'd just pummeled a brick wall. He had. The brick wall was Mitch Bryant's chest.

Kit doubted his blows hurt Mitch as much as they hurt him. But he was wrong. Every muscle in Mitch's body was screaming, the ache intensified by the boy's struggles. He felt as though the brat's fists were weighted with stones.

Mitch, his vision clearer but still blurred, made a grab for Kit's wrists. Youthful agility kept them annoyingly out of reach. "What the hell is wrong with you?"

Kit paused in his struggles long enough to glare up at Mitch. His eyes narrowed, the irises a dark, hellish black. "You," he spat. "It's *your* fault. All of it."

"*What's* my fault?" Mitch demanded, just as a lean fist connected with his jaw. For all its size, the punch packed ead. His vision exploded in white sparks and his head snapped back, though his fogged gaze came back quickly to Kit. He was just in time to see, and feel, the kid twist to the side, his arm outstretched. His long fingers wiggled, trying o reach the gun.

"Like hell!" Mitch roared, and instantly regretted it. The

253

kid might be young, lithe, and a hell of a lot healthier at the moment, but Mitch had size on his side. It wasn't difficult to reach out over the smaller, thinner arm and pluck the Colt from its cold bed of grass.

The jaw beneath the beard tightened as he shoved the gun under Kit's nose, lowering the hammer back into place with his thumb. "I hope like hell you know how to use this thing."

The young chin lifted indignantly. "Would I have pointed it at you if I didn't?"

"Hmph!" Mitch's gaze blazed hot blue fire. He'd never liked Kit. Right this second he despised him. And not because of the boy's obvious devotion to Chelsea or the easy companionship the two shared . . . something Mitch had been oddly envious of. No, right now he hated this boy, this goddamn *kid,* because he'd managed to sneak up and catch him unawares. Nobody did that, not even Brenda, who'd been trained to do it and still couldn't.

The brat needed to be taught a lesson, Mitch decided as he gazed down into unrepentant brown eyes. Unfortunately, he wasn't sure he was up to teaching him anything. His stomach was churning, and a knot of bitter-tasting bile rose in the back of his throat. If he'd had any doubts before, they were gone now. He was sick as a dog, and with no mere head cold, either.

Without warning, he grabbed a fistful of the kid's tattered collar. He climbed off Kit with clumsy movements, dragging the boy with him as he went. His knees were shaky, liquidy.

Kit's hands wrapped around forearms that felt like they were made of steel. He hung by his collar, his feet dangling a few feet off the ground. The feet were put to good use kicking the daylights out of Mitch's aching thighs and shins.

"Enough!" Mitch roared, wincing at the pain that ripped through his head. His grip on the shirt tightened, his booming voice causing the annoying lashes of the brat's booted feet to come to an abrupt halt.

Mitch's strides were angry and long, fueled by an iron-hard resolve to get to the bottom of why the kid was acting this way . . . quickly, while he could still think reasonably straight.

He slammed Kit against the bark of the first tree trunk he came to. Not hard enough to hurt the boy, but hard enough to send the breath rushing from Kit's suddenly pale lips. Leaning forward, Mitch placed his angry face mere inches from Kit's and growled, "I could kill you right now, kid. And after the way you just woke me up, I can't think of a soul who'd blame me for it."

Kit's expression remained adamant and a good deal less than contrite. "No? I can think of one." Chin high, he glared down his nose at the outlaw. "Chelsea Hogan," he sneered, as though the name clearly were too good for Mitch's tainted ears. "She'd never forgive you for hurting me."

"I said kill, not hurt." Mitch was breathing hard now, his lungs burning with each gasp of air he sucked into them. And shivering. He only now noticed just how badly he was shivering. God, he was cold . . . to the bone! "Believe me, kid, right now I'm more than willing to take that chance."

Kit gulped, his cheeks reddened with doubt. No, if Bryant were going to kill him, he'd have done it by now. Outlaws felt no remorse about such things; they had no conscience.

Marginally relieved, Kit let his gaze rake Mitch. Slowly, he noticed subtle changes in the outlaw's appearance. The man's skin, normally a swarthy shade of tan, was as white as a fresh-bought sheet. His dark beard pronounced the sickly pallor above and below. The blue eyes were slightly glazed, the skin around them a hollow circle of dark smudges that made it look as though the man hadn't slept in weeks. But it was almost midday, and Kit had just woken him up!

There was more. Kit watched a bead of sweat trickle down Mitch's too-moist temple. The drop wound down his ashen cheek, jaw, and neck before soaking into the shirt plastered to the broad chest and shoulders. The man was

255

breathing hard, and the powerful hand twisting the shirt collar was trembling and as hot as a burning coal. The heat of Mitch's body seared through the coarse flannel of Kit's shirt, scorching the young skin beneath.

"You're sick," Kit blurted out, his brow furrowing.

"Yeah. Tell me something I don't already know, brat."

Kit shook his head. A trace of concern he'd rather not have felt lit his eyes. "No, I mean you're *sick*. Real sick."

Mitch blinked, and Kit thought it took an unnaturally long time for the dark lashes to sweep up again. Even that small motion brought a wince of pain to the outlaw's eyes. The fingers clutching his collar slackened enough for Kit to slip away.

Mitch leaned heavily against the tree trunk. He didn't go after Kit. He couldn't. He knew his legs wouldn't support him, and he'd be damned if he'd humiliate himself by collapsing to his knees in front of a goddamn kid. "What do you want?" he asked tiredly. Mitch knew what *he* wanted. Sleep. A lot of it. *Years* of it. He nodded his aching head to the dented spot of bluestem where Kit had found him. "And what the hell was all that about?"

Kit bristled with the memory of what had brought him there in the first place. His cheeks paled, the brown eyes widening in alarm as he shouted, "Christ, Mitch, you can't be sick. Not now! *She needs you!*"

The boy's voice shot like an arrow through Mitch's skull. His head throbbed. The words filtered through his mind, incoherent and distorted by the heartbeat hammering in his ears.

Sighing, Mitch plowed his fingers through his hair. The strands were wet. Sweat formed heavy, salty droplets on the tips. He felt more moisture bead his brow, drenching his scalp.

"Kit, please," he groaned, leaning his head against the rough bark. His breath came in shallow gasps that broke up his words at erratic intervals. "If you came here to kill me, either do it and get it over with, or wait. This fever just might do the job for you."

"No!" Kit reached Mitch in two enviously firm strides. Small fists worked at his sides. His dark eyes were savage and bright. "You aren't going to die on me, you son of a bitch. Not until you get her back. It's your fault they took her!"

"Yeah, right." Sooty lashes swooped down. Mitch had no intention of making them go back up again . . . until Kit's words sank in. His eyelids snapped up with a vengeance . . . pain be damned. "What did you say?"

"I said it's all your fault."

"No, what did you say about her? About . . . Chelsea?"

Kit sent him a look of utter disgust. "I said they've got her, you goddamn fool. They came to the wagon at dawn, tied me up, and took her with them. Since it's *your* fault they took her, it's *your* responsibility to get her back."

Mitch's gut knotted. He felt like a leaden fist had just landed a blow to his midsection. Breathing was almost impossible. *The fever,* he thought desperately. *I'm not hearing the brat right. Either that, or this isn't happening; I'm dreaming it all up. Having a nightmare. Good God, I don't care which it is; just let it be one of them. Let Chelsea be safe!*

"How do I know you're telling the truth?" Mitch asked, his voice a husky, whispered promise of what he'd do to the boy if he ever found out the little thief was lying.

"How . . . what?" Kit countered imperiously. "Christ, Bryant, that fever's really addled your brain if you can't figure this one out. Some outlaw you've turned out to be!" When Mitch didn't reply, he elaborated, "Those guys made damn sure I knew who took her and why. Why do you think they didn't drag me out with her? I was there. They could've. But they didn't because they needed someone to get word back to you."

Mitch sucked in a burning lungful of air, shivered as a cool breeze washed over him, and tried to focus on thinking straight. Hell, just *thinking* felt like a monumental chore at this point. But he didn't have a choice. If what Kit said was true, then Jason Dobbs had Chelsea, and . . .

I'll kill the rotten bastard. If he so much as looks at her sideways,

I'll kill him! And if he touches her . . .

"Aren't you going to ask me who took her?" Kit taunted. He watched the outlaw's expression melt from veiled pain to raw fury. The flesh covering Mitch's angular cheeks drew tight, the pale skin flooded crimson. The dark beard split to reveal clean white teeth as his lips pulled back in a feral sneer.

The swaying carpet of bluestem rustled as Kit took a quick step back, suddenly afraid all that anger was directed at him. His long fingers came up, fluttering over the tender lump beneath his hairline. He gulped. The bruise was a lover's peck compared to what this man was capable of doing—sick or not.

"Get my horse," Mitch barked. "I said get it!" he ordered when Kit hesitated.

The blue fire sparkling in the outlaw's eyes prompted Kit's feet to move. He turned on his heel, bolting toward the river. He had no idea where the horse was tethered, but he'd find it . . . somehow. He didn't dare ask where to look.

Mitch waited until the boy's tromping footsteps receded before crossing unsteadily to his saddlebag. The jostling movements ricocheted through his screaming muscles with each step. The world swam, righted itself, them swam again.

He crashed to the ground beside his saddle, landing on his knees, panting and trying to catch his breath. His fingers shook as he wiped the sweat from his eyes. They were still shaking when he peeled back the leather flap of the saddlebag. He rummaged around inside it, using only his hands to guide him. He couldn't see right now; the white sparks dancing in front of his burning eyes wouldn't ease up, and he couldn't look past them.

He located the box of ammunition with no trouble. Enough shells were extracted to fill the spare loops in his holster strap. The Colt was taken from where he'd jammed it into his belt, the load checked and replenished before the gun was secured inside the holster. His fingers felt clumsy and thick as he kneeled in the grass and buckled the gunbelt around his hips, clumsily tying the straps of the holster boot around his thigh as best he could.

I'm coming, Chelsea. I'm coming. Just hold out a little longer, baby. He chanted the words over and over in his mind. It gave him something to concentrate on besides pain.

Fighting a wave of dizziness, he settled back on his haunches and waited for Kit to come back with his horse. His stomach closed into a tight, grinding fist as he fought back a surge of nausea. The feeling might have been bearable had it been caused by the sickness fevering his body. But it wasn't. It was born of a sudden, too-clear image of Chelsea Hogan, his sweet, sexy little preacher's daughter, in the hands of one of the meanest men Mitch had ever known.

Damn it, Bryant! he thought angrily. *Dobbs doesn't want her, he wants you. You! She's just a means to an end. An end whose tempting little tail you'd damned well better save if you want to be able to look at yourself in the mirror tomorrow.*

If ever there was a time when Mitch needed a rational head, it was now. And he didn't have it. He could barely think, barely function. Christ, how was he supposed to save Chelsea, and himself, and Kit when he felt like he was clawing his way through hell?

"I'll do it," he seethed under his breath. "I don't care how, but I *will* do it. And if Dobbs hurts her . . ."

There wasn't time to finish the sentence as Kit came back with the stallion. But Mitch finished the thought. It was the only thing that got him onto the back of that horse, the only thing that kept him straddling the saddle when a weaker man would have fallen off and given up.

The blow she'd taken to the jaw was a beaut. It must have been; it had knocked her out cold for the better part of the day.

When Chelsea finally pried her eyes open, it was to be blinded by a scalding midday sun. The hot rays beat down on the prairie, pounding on her head almost as fiercely as the pain that throbbed in the lower left portion of her face. Squeezing her eyes closed, she winced and leaned heavily against the hard, jostling form behind her.

Jostling? Sweet heavens, she was on a horse. She placed the feel of hard saddle beneath her, together with the sound of hoofbeats clomping unhurriedly over the prairie. Yes, she was definitely on a horse. But it wasn't just any horse, she realized suddenly, her memory of that morning flooding back in a surge of despair. She was on Jason Dobbs's horse. Which meant . . .

She sat bolt upright, straining to keep as much space as the confining saddle would allow between herself and the man who rode behind her. The solid form she'd been leaning against, as well the warm air washing over her head in sour waves, belonged to Jason Dobbs. The same disreputable outlaw who'd accosted her twice now had his arm slung around her waist, his thick fingers splaying her side. The lowlife who'd landed her with a solid, demeaning kiss, not to mention a nasty right hook, had his thigh brushing against her own . . . too often, and much too intimately.

I'm doomed, Chelsea thought as a shiver iced down her spine.

"It's about time you woke up, sugar," a husky voice gritted close enough to her ear to stir the copper wisps there. Chelsea shivered in revulsion as his grip around her waist tightened and he yanked her back. "I was starting to get worried. You slept a long time for such a tiny bruise."

"Tiny? *Tiny!*" she yelled, her jaw aching from the effort. "Is that what you call it?"

"Sure do. That's what it is."

The swelling she gingerly explored with her fingertips was not as minor as this man would have her believe. Her jaw was swollen. It felt as though someone had stuck a turnip under her skin. The flesh was tender enough to bring tears to her eyes when she tested the severity of it by opening and closing her mouth a few times. Goddamn, that hurt!

"You planning to catch flies with that thing, sugar? Or'd

you have something a little more . . . male in mind to use those lips on?"

His hot gaze seared her lips. Pain or no pain, Chelsea slammed her mouth shut. Again, she straightened. Again, she was yanked back. She would have turned to glare at him, but she didn't trust herself to look at that bristled face without surrendering to the urge to slap it soundly. Not a smart idea. Not, at least, when his partner in crime rode only a few short yards away.

With the sun at his front, Chelsea could barely make out the figure on horseback riding silently ahead. What she could see were the twin holsters, the loops stuffed with ammunition, riding low on the man's hips. Those she saw all too well. The ominous sight convinced her that angering her captors this early in the game wouldn't be in her best interest.

What would be in her best interest was to find out what sort of game they were playing with her. Whatever it was, she sensed the danger involved and knew it was very, very real.

"Are we going to stop soon?" she asked, forcing her voice to sound pleasant, even though pleasant was the last thing she felt.

His rumbling chuckle vibrated straight up her spine, telling her Jase knew exactly what she was feeling . . . and trying so hard not to convey. "What's the matter, sugar? Tired?"

His tone, she noted, lacked concern. Now, why wasn't she surprised? "A bit," she admitted, and thought she'd just made the understatement of the year. She feigned a non-committal shrug and repeated tightly, "Will we be stopping soon?"

"Nope." The hand around her waist shifted. His index finger drew small, invisible circles against her stomach. The feel of calloused fingerpads catching on the dusty flannel of her shirt was grating to her already-raw nerves. "That is, not unless you can think of a way to sweet-talk me into making an extra stop. Just for you. Gee, sugar, I wonder

261

what it would take to convince me you need a rest?"

"Rest" was the very last thing his words implied. Chelsea's stomach knotted. The pain in her jaw receded to indignation as she snapped, "I'll never be *that* tired."

Again, he laughed, except this time his cackle seemed to say it was only a matter of time before he changed her mind.

When hell freezes over, buster! she thought, then almost laughed at the one time she'd heard the same saying spouted from her father's pious lips. He hadn't said the phrase in this context! And he would have been mortified to know she'd just thought the words that way. Mortified and furious.

The hand around her waist lowered, caressing her abdomen. One by one, his index finger circled the buttons trailing up the flannel. He paused when he reached the swell of her breasts.

That's it! she thought. *I'm going to be sick.* It was a real possibility. The feel of his hands burning through the shirt went beyond disgusting; it was downright repulsive. The threat of him taking even greater liberties made a bitter lump clog in her throat. If he tried to . . . to . . .

No! He wouldn't. She wouldn't allow it, even if it meant he killed her. She'd rather die than let a no-good piece of scum like this one steal away something that should be given only by consent. And she would never, *never* consent to an intimacy like cleaning this man's boots, let alone . . . no *never!*

The man in front — Whick? Walt? — drew back on the reins, slowing his mount until his brother caught up. When they were side by side, he sent Jase a worried frown. "Well? Where is he? Ya said he'd be here by now. Hot on our tails." His muddy gaze fixed hard on Chelsea. "Or hers."

"Hold your horses, Whip. He'll come." The fumbling hand made a bold ascent. Jase laughed when she slapped his arm and shoved it away. The laughter wasn't caused by what she'd done so much as the way she'd almost fallen off the horse doing it.

"Bastard! Touch me again and I'll kill you," she hissed. She made a grab at the pommel to keep from slipping off the saddle and being crushed by the horse's mighty hooves.

"Bastard?" the one called Whip echoed with a chuckle. His eyes met his brother's in silent question. "Just how much'd ya tell her, Jase?"

"She's just guessing," Jase said, and his hand stole back around her waist.

Chelsea let the hand stay, but only because she had no choice. With a toss of her head, she sent Whip a poignant glare. "It wasn't an educated guess, pal. No parents worth their salt would admit to having born the likes of you two."

The arm around her waist hardened into a steel band, crushing her against a chest that felt whipcord-lean and hard. The air rushed from Chelsea's lungs in a whoosh as her fingers tightened around the pommel.

"That weren't too nice, sugar," a low, threatening growl hissed in her ear. His arm jerked, the pressure increased, and for a split second Chelsea thought she was going to faint. Any second now her ribs were going to snap. "Now, what say you give Whip and me the apology we both deserve?"

The sunlight turned blinding yellow as she struggled to draw in a breath. The haze soon tinged a velvet-black around the edges. Chelsea gritted her teeth, trying to fight the swirling, sinking sensation, knowing she couldn't. She was going to faint if the man didn't loosen his hold and let her breathe soon.

"I'm waiting," Jase prodded.

Chelsea pinched her eyes shut and rolled her lips inward to swallow back an apology that was temptingly close to the surface. Let him rob her of air, she thought, let him torture and abuse her, but . . . no, damn it, she would *not* apologize!

"Lordy, but you're a stubborn one."

Jase's arm loosened. Though his grip was still crushing, Chelsea could now draw in air. And she did . . . big gulps of it. Her lungs burned from deprivation, her lips felt dry and cracked. She didn't care. The blackness was beginning to fade, the world had stopped spinning, and her head no longer felt so light.

Jase gave a disgruntled huff.

Whip laughed. "She's a handful, ain't she? Maybe we shoulda' took the kid instead. Not so much trouble."

Chelsea couldn't see it, but she felt the glare Jase sent his brother. She *did* feel the body behind her stiffen.

"Now wouldn't that have been a bright idea?" Jase sneered. "Take the damned kid, who Bryant cares nothing about, and leave this pretty little thing behind. Brilliant, Whip. Just brilliant. Don't know why I didn't think of it myself. We'd have had Bryant eating out of our hands in no time."

With a quick side glance, she saw Whip's leathery cheeks go ruddy. His muddy eyes snapped with anger. "Well, it'd be better than *her.*" He jerked his bristled chin at a stiffening Chelsea. "She's gonna be trouble with a capital *T*, brother. Ya mark my words."

"Maybe, but it'll be sweet trouble," Jase said, and his hand strayed down. Greedily, he filled his palm with the curve of womanly hips. "Sweetest trouble I'll ever have."

"*Last* trouble, more like." Flicking the reins, Whip gave a sharp kick to his horse's flanks and thundered out in front of them. The dust the hooves kicked up made Chelsea's still-aching lungs burn. She didn't need to see Whip through the cloud of dirt to know he didn't look back.

"Hope you're happy, sugar," Jase grumbled close to her ear. "Now you've got the two of us fighting. And Whip and I don't never fight. Not since we was in shortpants, leastwise."

"Everyone fights," she snapped, then wondered why she'd bothered. Because she wanted to talk, that's why — though not necessarily to Jase. Anyone would do. Any conversation that could keep her mind off other topics . . . like why they thought Mitch Bryant would bother coming to her rescue.

He wouldn't. She knew it, and oddly enough, she under

stood it. She'd learned a lot about outlaws and their "code of ethics"—warped as they were—during her time with Papa. No matter what the fancy Eastern papers said, wanted men had a bond . . . helping each other's hide, providing alibis for each other's crimes. They shared a mutual respect born from knowing each minute could well be their last.

Mitch Bryant, while not your usual criminal by any standard, *was* an outlaw. And he was also a friend to these two. He wouldn't risk his relationship with the Dobbses by coming after a woman he cared nothing about. Why bother?

Chelsea felt Jase's hand shift, and she breathed a sigh of relief when it was no longer fingering her upper thigh. The sigh was stifled when he lifted a stray copper wisp from her cheek.

Fingering the silky strand and gazing at it thoughtfully, he said, "Yesterday Bryant called you a preacher's daughter."

Chelsea stiffened warily but said nothing.

He continued, "Is it true? Your daddy really a preacher?"

"Was. My daddy is dead."

"Well, ain't that a damned shame."

The words echoed in her head, blending with others from yesterday. It wasn't a fond memory. "So much for compassion," she snapped.

"Should I feel bad?"

"No."

A tense moment of silence passed. But Jase wasn't ready to give up the subject of her upbringing yet. "What kind of preacher was your daddy?"

"Baptist."

He whistled low through his teeth. "The worst. Was he all fire and brimstone? Damn the bad folks, down with injustice and violence, all that fun stuff?"

It went against her grain to be speaking of her father with a criminal, but she dared not aggravate him further. Her ribs still ached from the last time. "Yes," she said. "Why?"

"I don't know. You just seem awful feisty is all."

Chelsea almost chuckled. Almost. There was really nothing to laugh about. "I take it a preacher's daughter is supposed to be meek and mild, just by right of birth?"

"Hell no, sugar. By right of *upbringing*. Living with all those sermons should've made you mild tempered and sweet. Like a woman's supposed to be. I mean, stands to reason, don't it? A kid ain't got no choice but to grow up to be like his parents — or so I'm told."

Chelsea sent a curious gaze over her shoulder despite her resolve not to. If she'd thought to find he was teasing her she was mistaken. His stubbled jaw was set hard, his dark green eyes flashing with curiosity. Turning back in her saddle, she said, "Is that what you're all about, Jason Dobbs? Are you just like your daddy?"

Salvaging souls. Mitch had accused her of doing just that at the same time he'd warned her against salvaging his. Was he right? Was she more like her father than she'd thought? Is that why she'd let this conversation with Jase-The-Outlaw-Dobbs go on as long as it had? She could have stopped him with a few clipped words. But she hadn't.

He didn't say anything for so long that Chelsea began to wonder if he'd terminated their peculiar conversation. Just when she decided he had, he spoke. His voice was husky and soft, oddly different than it had been before.

"I don't know if I'm like my daddy or not, sugar," he grumbled, his fingers dropping the wisp of hair. His palm slipped down to cradle her shoulder. The touch wasn't gentle, but neither was it rough. "I never met the bastard, and never want to. I'm like to kill him if I do. He ran out on Ma and me when she was heavy with Whip, and I was still cradling. No money, no food, no land . . . no nothin'. Just left his name — and that's something we've been trying to out run ever since." He shook his head. "Sure like to think I ain't like him. Yup, that's what I'd like to think."

Don't do it, girl, a tiny voice in her head screamed. *Don't feel sympathy for this man. Don't feel anything for this man. It's too dangerous. He'd just as soon shoot you as look at you.*

266

It didn't matter. The words tumbled out before Chelsea could stop them. "My sister, Emilee, went a little crazy after Papa died," she confided, her voice high and confused. The image of Emilee's golden hair and perfect face flashed in her mind. "She was always wild, but something inside her . . . I don't know, *snapped* the day we buried Papa. She started taking up with men . . . a lot of them, often. She ran off a few times, and I had to track her down and drag her back home. The one time I got fed up and let her go, she came back by herself."

Sighing, she pushed the image of Emmy from her mind. She hadn't thought of her sister in days—thanks to Mitch. And he was right. It was past time Emmy learned to take charge of her own life. Chelsea couldn't be there for the girl forever.

"Now, why'd she wanna do a thing like that?" Jase's drawl brought her back to the present.

"She said she couldn't stand any more piousness. That it was all a bunch of lies—everything Papa said and stood for. She said she'd had it up to here with fire and brimstone, and that if she had to pay for her pleasures by burning in hell, that was just fine with her. But at least she'd have *lived*."

Jase chuckled. "Don't sound like any preacher's daughter I ever heard of."

"Emmy isn't your average preacher's daughter." Chelsea shifted, uncomfortable with everything she'd just said, as well as who she'd said it to. But it was too late to stop talking now. She had a point to make, and in a way that would have made her father proud, she set about driving her point home.

"What I'm trying to tell you is that Emmy's wildness was her way of rebelling against everything Papa taught us. If he said it was no good, Emmy did it. She didn't want to be pious, and she'd be the first to tell you she's no saint. Don't you see? What she did and what you're doing now are the same thing. Except your rebellion is leading you right down the path your father took, *not* in the opposite direction."

The body behind her tensed. Chelsea could feel the lean

muscles ripple against her. She stiffened and pulled away. He didn't yank her back again, and for that she was grateful.

"Well, don't that beat all?" he said finally, his tone thick with laughter. "You sure convinced me, sugar. Nobody but a bona fide preacher's daughter would speak like that. Wouldn't've believed it if I hadn't heard it myself."

Chelsea's spine, already stiff, went rigid. Her jaw tightened around firmly clamped teeth. "Well, now you know."

"Yeah, sure do. And just so's *you* know"—he leaned forward, his breath hot and sour in her ear—"I'm gonna have one hell of a time sinnin' with you, sugar. Looking forward to it. Maybe you could teach me some of the tricks Bryant taught you? I hear tell he had a whore back in Houston who knew a bunch of the kinkiest—"

"Shut up!" Chelsea shouted, her heart drumming so loudly in her ears she could barely hear her own voice. "Just shut up!"

"Sure thing, sugar. Just so's we know where we stand with each other."

Oh, Chelsea knew exactly where she stood with this repulsive creature. The knowledge terrified her, making her mind scream one word over and over in time to the throbbing hooves thundering beneath her: *Mitch!*

"Mitch? Christ, Mitch, what the hell—?"

Brenda had barely enough time to clear the distance between her small sod-house and the horse Mitch Bryant was in the process of clumsily sliding off. She reached him in time to wrap a lean arm around his waist and take on the portion of his weight that he seemed unable to manage. Grunting under the strain, she started to guide him toward the sod-house, unmindful of the youth sitting atop the dappled grey until he spoke.

"Are you a . . . *friend* of his, ma'am?"

"The best," Brenda snapped, panting as she took on more of Mitch's weight. Her legs threatened to buckle from the pressure, but she refused to stop. "And if you were a friend, too, you'd get off that damned horse and over here and help me with him."

The boy merely chuckled and shrugged. "I'd rather not waste my energy, thank you all the same. Once he realizes where you're taking him, he'll just want to get back in the saddle again."

Brenda looked at the man she was supporting with a critical eye. His face was too flushed, the color too splotchy. His brow was beaded with a sweat that had already dampened his hair to his scalp and plastered his shirt to his body. His face was wet with it. His lips were lined blue, his eyelids scrunched closed.

Good God, what happened to him? Had he been . . . ? No! Please, not Mitch! But it was a possibility. One Brenda had long since prepared for. After all, she was in a business where being pumped full of lead was a constant threat. Only a fool wouldn't know what to do.

Her attention jerked back to the boy. "He's in no condition to be going anywhere except bed. And from the looks of it, he'll be there for weeks. What happened to him?"

The boy shrugged, easing the black hat back on his crown. "Do I look like a doctor, ma'am? Do I have a degree? No. I don't know what's wrong with him, but whatever it is, he's been like this since he woke up."

The woman frowned, scanning the front of Mitch's shirt for the crimson stain she prayed not to see. There was none. "You mean he hasn't been . . . he's *sick*?" The boy glanced at her as though it was about time she noticed.

"Sick," she muttered under her breath. Shaking her head, she hoisted his heavy, limp arm higher around her neck, forcing him to lean into her side. He was hot; his body felt like it was on fire. *Mitch Bryant is sick,* she thought again. Didn't that beat all? "It doesn't matter. He still needs to be in bed."

"No." The voice was Mitch's, thick and gritty as it passed a throat so raw it burned just to swallow. "No bed."

"Of course you're going to bed," Brenda insisted sharply.

She started toward the sod-house again, but Mitch planted his feet on the ground, refusing to budge another inch. He might be sick, but she was no match for him. Heaving a sigh that was as much disgust as exertion, she glanced up. "Don't be a fool, Bryant. You look like hell, and I'll bet you feel like it, too. If you don't get some rest . . . *Nothing* is worth dying over."

"Maybe" was all he said. He disentangled his arm from around her neck and stumbled toward his horse. Twice he almost landed on his knees from the jarring pain each footstep made in his head. But he righted himself and trudged on.

"Mitch . . ." Brenda started.

"I said no." He reached the horse, though he was never sure how he'd managed it. Pulling a deep breath into his burning lungs, he leaned his forehead against the cool, cool saddle and willed the throbbing in his temples to fade. It didn't respond, but just kept hammering away. "I came here for help, Brenda," he said, his voice raspy and sharp. "If you won't give it to me, fine. I'll go after Dobbs myself."

He lifted a foot with the intent to place it in the stirrup and heave himself up into the saddle. His toe missed by a good three inches, his clumsiness a product of vision that refused to clear. Cursing savagely, he tried again. This time, he was successful. The world spun as he settled himself atop the stallion, but he'd already discovered that if he didn't move too fast too soon, the spinning faded quick enough.

He glanced down at Brenda, who was now standing beside the horse. He had to squint to draw her into focus, and even then she stayed blurred around the pretty blond edges. Goddamn it! "Well? Are you going to help me?"

"To do what?" she snapped. Her voice softened when she saw a reflective wince crease his sweat-dampened brow. " can't help if you don't tell me what you want me to do."

An hour later, Brenda maneuvered her mount to ride parallel with Mitch's stallion. Kit rode ahead, on the lookout for any ambushes Dobbs might have set. So far, there were none.

Brenda scowled. In the harsh light of day, Mitch looked ready to collapse. A lesser man would already have done so. How he'd managed to stay in the saddle this long was beyond her. At any time she was ready to scoop him up from the dirt, tie him to his horse, then lead him back to her sodhouse to recover from the fever that raged through his body.

He surprised her. When she'd agreed to help, she'd thought she would have already brought him back to her claim by now, unconscious and near death. She'd forgotten about the streak of Bryant stubbornness he'd always taken so much stupid pride in.

"Jase wants you, Mitch. Not her," Brenda said. With a flick of her wrist, she slowed the brown mustang, timing its gait to match the stallion's. The horses were used to each other, and they didn't complain at the nearness.

"I know." His voice was so harsh and raspy it hurt Brenda just to hear it.

"And you're in no condition to go charging in there."

"I know that, too."

"Then what the hell are you—?" She stopped short. Arguing with this man had never worked; in fact, it only fueled his unreasonable determination all the more. Perhaps if she *reasoned* with him? "Mitch, think about what you're doing. Look at you! You can barely sit that damned wild horse of yours. You're sick, and you aren't going to get any better by staying out underneath this beating sun, sweating buckets, and exhausting yourself. You need rest. You need to be in bed."

"Yeah, that's what I need all right," he grumbled. But it wasn't what he needed at all. Mitch made no attempt to either stop the stallion or to turn it around. Instead, his blue eyes focused forward, his gaze intent. The passing prairie couldn't pass soon enough to suit him. If his head could have stood the pounding, he would have picked up their pace miles back.

"But you're not going to stop," Brenda muttered flatly.

Mitch glanced to the side, his gaze shadowed by his hat.

271

A trace of his former self could be had in the quick smile he flashed his pretty companion. "Nope."

"Mind telling me *why?* You know, Bryant, if you're *that* worried about the girl, I could take you back and go after her myself. You know I could do it."

"No."

"Why not?"

Mitch sucked in a sharp breath as her angry voice cut through his head. His fingers tightened on the reins until his knuckles were white. He didn't answer her. He couldn't. He didn't know what to say. His reasons for going after Ch — Chelsea Hogan weren't that clear to himself.

"I know, you have to do it for yourself," Brenda answered for him. Her gaze strayed to the cloud-strewn sky as she shook her head in disgust and muttered, "God save me from conceited male peacocks! Heaven forbid a woman tries to do the job *this* man sets his sights on doing *himself.*"

Her blue eyes sparkled in the afternoon sunlight, her gaze sharpening on the stubborn man who rode stoically beside her. "I wish I knew what the hell was wrong with you, Mitch, but I don't. And while I may not know what kind of sickness you've got, I do know it's bad. I'm not exaggerating any when I say this trip could kill you. Now, are you still so all-fired set on not letting me go after her alone?"

Mitch's fingers were shaking when he reached up and tugged the brim of his hat low. It scraped against the bright red bandanna he'd tied around his forehead to soak up the sweat of his fever. The bandanna was now dripping wet. His gaze was fixed ahead again, his jaw set hard beneath the beard. "Yup."

Brenda launched into every unfavorable term she'd ever heard for members of the opposite sex; she had a storehouse of them, none of which even a deaf mule would consider complimentary.

Mitch barely heard her. Between the thundering of hooves in his ears and the hammering in his skull, he could hear nothing beyond his own thoughts. And every one of them centered around his sexy preacher's daughter.

Her face, soft and sweet, gave him the determination to push on when he would have given up. The sound of her voice, rushing like a spring breeze in his ear, gave him the strength to make sketchy plans of what he'd do once the Dobbses camp was reached — providing they hadn't lied to Kit about where they were located.

All of these images combined to fuel his determination to a degree that outburned his fever. But it was the memory of Ch—Chelsea Hogan's soft, cool flesh gliding beneath his palm, the feel of her pouty lips moving hungrily beneath him, that really haunted Mitch. And tormented the hell out of him.

Chapter Nineteen

The sky was melting from blue to fire-orange dusk when Kit dropped back to join the other two. The ride had been long, with one quick stop for water at a creek bed and none for lunch. The strain showed on the boyish face peeking beneath his brand-new hat, but the brown eyes were still bright with a determination to find Chelsea Hogan and save her from even worse outlaws than the one he was now riding with.

"Over that hill," Kit said, pointing to an upgrade barely a mile ahead. "That's where Dobbs said he'd set up camp. Do we go in now, or do we wait?"

The ground was shadowy, clay-red in the dimming light. To Mitch's exhausted eyes, the hill looked like it would take days to reach, a lifetime to crest.

"We wait," Brenda said, drawing her horse up short. She reached over and snatched Mitch's reins from his slackened grasp, pulling the stallion in. He didn't protest. She doubted he had the strength left. Kit looked as though he was about to complain, but her sharp glare melted the words on his tongue.

"There's a stream about a quarter mile east of here," the boy said, jerking his thumb over his gaunt shoulder. "Maybe we should . . ." His voice trailed off, mostly because there was no one to hear the rest of his words. Brenda was already guiding Mitch's horse in that direction. Mitch himself was cushioning the upper part of his body atop the horse's neck. Kit thought the man looked like he'd passed out miles ago.

Nothing is worth dying over. Brenda's words, thick with concern, echoed through Mitch's barely lucid mind as he relaxed his aching body atop the stallion's back. The thought was followed by his own voice. *Kiss me, Chelsea. Your kisses are one of the few things in this life I'd die for.* Those words had never rung more true for him than they did at that moment. God help him, Mitch knew at that instant that he *would* die for that woman. In fact, he thought he might be doing exactly that.

The jostling beneath him stopped, yanking him from his memories. The pommel ground into his stomach. He didn't mind. He didn't have the energy to mind. He became aware of the sweet gurgle of water, and his burning, parched throat convulsed.

"Come on, Bryant. Off that horse and into the water. If we're going to bring that fever down, we'll have to do it quick."

Mitch grinned weakly. Brenda's voice was as sharp and as commanding as ever. Hefting his right leg up — goddamn it, his pants felt like they were encased in lead! — he slid indelicately out of the saddle. He gasped, his face losing what little color it had when pain sliced through his stiff knees . . . knees that felt as though they had the consistency of the stream that churned temptingly nearby.

A slender form was there, catching him before he embarrassed himself by collapsing in a heap. It wouldn't be an embarrassment for long, Mitch thought in disgust. He knew he'd be out cold before his face hit the dirt. Brenda's arm snaked around his waist. His left arm coiled around her neck. Leaning on her for support, Mitch let himself be guided to the streambed.

"We're not going to bother undressing you," she said matter-of-factly. "Your clothes could use a good soak almost as much as the body they're covering."

Mitch's eyes snapped open the second he realized the voice had not come from beside him, as it should have,

275

but from behind. His dazed blue eyes struggled to focus on his helper, illuminated by the flickering orange light of dusk.

Kit? The boy glanced up, and Mitch realized he'd spoken out loud. He scowled. "What the hell are you doing, brat?"

"Damned if I know," Kit muttered as they reached the stream. "The ground slopes here. Better hold on or we're both going in."

He held on. They slid more than they walked down the gently sloping bank. Mitch didn't ask the boy his reasons for helping him, though the question did burn on the tip of his tongue. Right now, he was too anxious to immerse himself in the promise of cool, sweet water.

With Kit's help, he wiggled his sore feet out of the boots. They made twin thumps when Kit tossed them to the ground. Then, hoisting Mitch to a stand, the youth helped him into the water.

The groan that left Mitch's lips was part shock, part relief, as the cold, lapping water closed over his hot, tired body. The frigid temperature was welcome, invigorating. He sank down into the water gratefully.

"I don't want to see your ugly mug for at least an hour, pal," Brenda grumbled from where she was rubbing down the horses. While her words were light, her meaning was not. Mitch didn't doubt she'd lead him back to the stream at gunpoint if he tried to get out of the water before the allotted hour was up.

Closing his eyes, he sighed, rolling on his spine until his head was cradled atop the sandy bank. The rest of him relaxed in the water's healing depths. It wasn't until he heard Kit start to move away that he looked up. "Wait a minute, kid."

Kit glanced hesitantly over his shoulder, but he didn't turn around. His eyes sparkled in what little daylight was left, and if Mitch weren't so tired he would have put a name to the emotion he saw shimmering in those large brown depths.

"What?" Kit prodded when Mitch said nothing, just continued to stare at him.

His gaze narrowed thoughtfully, raking the boy from head to toe. Slowly, Mitch shook his head, his hand raising from the water and waving the boy away with a splash. "Thanks," he muttered, then closed his eyes again.

"Don't thank me. I was ready to kill you this morning."

"I know. But you didn't pull the trigger."

"Because I needed you to help me get Chels back. Because—"

"Does it really matter why?" Mitch grumbled tiredly.

"Yeah," the kid muttered, his young voice gritty with self-reproach. He spun on his heel and stalked away, but not before Mitch caught his faint parting words. "It does to me. It matters a hell of a lot to me."

"Ah, another soul, newly salvaged," Mitch muttered under his breath, his first real grin of the day curling over his lips. "Now, why aren't I surprised?" His thoughts, while still on the boy, strayed down his favorite path of contemplation: Ch—Chelsea Hogan, his fiery, sexy-as-all-hell preacher's daughter. "I'm coming, sweetheart. Hold on a little longer. I'm coming for you. Damned if I'm not!"

"You're going to starve if you don't eat, sugar."

Chelsea gritted her teeth. If this man called her "sugar" one more time, she was going to scream. Her jaw hurt from the bruise Jase had given her, as well as from gritting her teeth, biting back agitated replies that she knew would win her nothing but another slap. Of course, it didn't help that every time she heard "sugar," she thought of gritty flakes of the stuff sticking to her skin . . . and remembered the way Mitch Bryant's tongue had felt—hot, wet, delicious—when he'd licked it off her. No, that didn't help at all.

"I'm not hungry," she said, barely glancing at Jase when he plopped down on the grass beside her. The leaves of the tree she leaned back against rustled as they were tossed on a soft breeze.

"Why not? Whip makes the best hardtack I ever tasted."

A copper brow rose as Chelsea glanced down at the plate cushioned atop the grass. She'd placed it as far away from her as her outstretched arm could get it. It still wasn't far enough. Her nose wrinkled in disgust. The sight was bad, but at least that could be looked away from. The smell couldn't be avoided, and the sickening sweetness of the beans, combined with the charred odor of the meat, made her stomach roll.

"Thanks, but no," she grumbled, drawing her legs up to her chest. Wrapping her arms around her shins, she hugged her knees close and shivered.

They were only an hour into the darkness now, and already it was getting cold. It was one of the things she disliked about Oklahoma the most—warm days, cold nights, no consistency. It was also one of the things she loved the most—the unpredictability. The land reminded her of Mitch, and the way her feelings for the outlaw kept batting around inside of her head and heart.

"You sure?" Jase asked, even as he reached over her to scoop up her plate. He must have noticed the way she recoiled, trying to melt her body into the biting tree bark. He chuckled coldly, easing himself back to a sit. "Might be a good idea to keep your strength up for Bryant's rescue. You don't wanna go into a swoon just as he's scooping you up onto that big, frisky stallion of his, do you?"

"Somehow, I don't think that's a concern." Resting her chin atop the shelf of her updrawn knees, she focused her gaze on Whip. He was lying beside the fire, wrapped in a bedroll that looked thin but enviably warm. He was also fast asleep—something else Chelsea found enviable. If she weren't so anxious about being alone with Jason Dobbs— *I'm gonna have one hell of a time sinnin' with you, sugar*—she'd probably be sleeping herself.

Right now, however, sleep wasn't even a remote possibility. She'd be a fool to risk turning her back on this criminal, even if it meant rolling over to find a more comfortable position. Not after the way he'd baited her this afternoon.

Feeling Jase's stare, she turned to look at him. His face was sharpened by the flickering glow of the fire. The dancing light made the blond whiskers stubbling his jaw and upper lip look more like smudges of dirt that wouldn't scrub clean. His eyes were narrowed, the green depths sparkling with a hint of cruelty that she could never understand. The stringy hair hanging around his face only enhanced the demonic illusion.

"You really don't think he'll come, do you?"

Chelsea shook her head. Hadn't she already said as much? "Why should he?"

Jase shoveled a spoonful of beans past his grinning lips. "What's the matter, preacher's daughter?" he asked around chewing vigorously. "Are you too pious 'tween the sheets for Bryant to wanna keep you?"

"That's none of your goddamn business," she hissed, lips pinched. His light brows shot up, but that was his only sign of surprise. Chelsea looked away. "And don't call me that again."

"Why not, sugar? It's what you are."

It's what Mitch calls me. Preacher's daughter. Someone who is in the business of salvaging souls. A warm flush splashed over her cheeks — a flush that had nothing to do with the heat of the crackling campfire. Mitch's voice — oh, so husky and sweet — whispered in her ears and tingled down her spine until her toes curled inside her boots.

Well, look good and hard, but don't waste too much of your time on me. In case you haven't figured it out yet, I don't have a soul. But he did. He just masked it behind elusive pangs of conscience — and any morals he kept locked deep inside of him. Then there were those rare, memorable times when the mask slipped . . . when she caught a peek of the real Mitch Bryant. It was a fleeting glimpse but an enticing one. Because behind the outlaw's mask, Chelsea found a soul that she liked. A lot.

279

How long do you think you can fight me, preacher's daughter? How long can you fight yourself? She hadn't fought him. Hadn't wanted to. Then again, she hadn't seen him making any Herculean efforts to stay away from her, either. Did that mean? . . .

Chelsea lowered her head to her hands and groaned. Sweet heavens, it was all so confusing! Her life had been so simple before Mitch Bryant had entered it. His presence had turned her nice, tidy world inside out. Now everything, even a simple feeling, was complicated, her every emotion contradictory to what she'd been taught from the cradle.

She huffed bitterly. Emotions these days were linked to Mitch Bryant's hot embrace — and his even hotter kisses and caresses. Lord, the depths to which she had sunk! She was glad her father hadn't lived to see it all.

Chelsea picked her head up, a thought striking her from nowhere. Her brow creased with concern. "What if he does come?" Breathlessly, she waited for Jase to chew and swallow a bite of the stringy meat before answering. It felt like a lifetime.

"What do you think?"

"I don't know."

His upraised brows, combined with the way the spoon paused midway to his grinning lips, said she damned well *did* know.

Chelsea's heart slammed against her ribs when she suddenly remembered witnessing her father's death. Joseph Hogan had walked into the middle of a dusty California street, stepping between two outlaws who were about to settle their differences with their guns. Bible in hand, spouting religious platitudes, he'd confidently stepped between two loaded pistols. His sanctimonious bluster had gotten him killed.

A shiver iced down her spine. She saw it all as though it were yesterday. But the fear she'd felt then was *nothing* compared to the white-hot terror coursing through her now.

"You really are mistaken, Mr. Dobbs," she said, her voice betraying her only a little. "He won't come for me if it means having your bullets in his back."

Jase laughed. "Mister? Ain't that a hoot? Don't remember anybody *ever* calling me . . . *His back?!*"

The humor was gone from his eyes. They sparkled murderously as Jase threw the half-empty plate to the ground. He was on his feet, glowering down at her, before the tin dish could clink to the ground, spilling most of its contents onto the grass.

"Lady, do I look like the type of guy who'd shoot a man in the back?" he sneered, and yanked the pistol that was ever-ready at his side from the holster. He tossed the gun back and forth between his hands, each catch and retrieve perfectly timed as the carved wooden handle slapped rhythmically in his palms. "I ain't got the need. Even face to face, there ain't many who could beat me. *Your* man included."

"He is *not* my —" The words she'd uttered so many times to Kit died on her lips. Half of the reason was that she thought it might be best if Dobbs *did* think Mitch would come for her. It would buy her time to think of a way to escape. The other half of the reason she didn't dare contemplate.

"I don't give a good goddamn what the bastard is to you, lady. By this time tomorrow, he's gonna be a corpse. Buzzard meat." Jase's eyes narrowed, and he glared down at her. "Let Thiel's chew on *that* awhile! Show those sniveling law-abiders what happens when they send a man sniffing after Jason Dobbs. Way I see it, enough of their damn agents come back packed in pine, they'll think twice about sending more."

Chelsea's mind whirled, skipping over all but the choicest bits of crudely formed phrases. Corpse and — she shivered icily — buzzards . . . Thiel's . . . law-abiders . . . agents. *Agents?* Her gaze shot up. What on earth was he talking about? What agent? Who? Certainly not! . . .

Jase stared at her for a very long minute, then tipped

his stringy blond head back and laughed. It was a blaring, harsh, grating sound.

"Christ, you don't know nothing about that, do you?" he muttered between gritty chuckles. The gun barrel wagged in the air as he dragged his forearm over his eyes and fixed her with a pitying glance. "Don't Bryant tell you nothing, sugar?"

"Apparently not," Chelsea answered flatly, her mind numb. Stretching her legs, she entwined her fingers and let her hands fall limply to her lap. She couldn't think, couldn't move, couldn't begin to understand all of what this outlaw was saying.

"This is gonna be a real learning experience for you then, ain't it, sugar? Never heard of Thiel's, I take it?"

"Never."

"Pinkerton?"

Her chin snapped up. "Them, I've heard of. Don't tell me Mitch—?"

"Nah, Pinkerton wouldn't have him, so he went to Thiel's. John Farley snapped him up right quick. Bryant turned out to be the best agent they've ever had, too. I should know . . . he's been hot on my ass for the last six years." Jase's chest puffed, obviously proud this Thiel's— whoever or whatever it was—had sent only their best after a criminal the likes of Jason Dobbs.

"Thiel's," Chelsea repeated dumbly.

"It's a detective service out of Denver. The boys and I had a little . . . er . . . accident around those parts a while back. He's been after the gang ever since. 'Course, not much of a gang left for him no more—'cept Whip and me."

"Denver," she muttered, her mind still phrases behind him.

"Yeah, sugar, Denver. You got a problem with that?" Jase's mood was degrees lighter when he settled on the grass beside her again, close enough for his thigh to brush hers.

Chelsea was stunned enough not to give the contact a

bit of notice. *A problem with that?* her mind echoed. *Yes, I have a problem with that!* Oh, not with the Denver part—she didn't give a fig where this *service* was based—her problem was with the *detective* part. More specifically, in the *Mitch Bryant* detective part.

How could he do this to her? How could he let her believe he was an outlaw when he really worked for the government? Well, if not the government, then at least for a private firm whose specialty was upholding the law. She shook her head, trying to clear it of the numbness that went hand in hand with shock.

Mitch Bryant, a detective. She couldn't believe it. She *wouldn't* believe it . . . not until she heard it from his own traitorous lips. An image of those lips, teasingly outlined under the curl of his pitch black mustache, sprang hotly to mind. Chelsea groaned and buried her face in her hands.

"You don't look like you're taking all this well, sugar," Jase said, his voice edged with renewed laughter.

She picked her head up and sent him a scathing glare. Not taking it well? She wasn't taking "it" at all!

"I like that," he said, shoving his gun back in the holster. The second he'd snapped the strap over the butt, his palm was on her shoulder. His fingers, long and thick, sloppily caressed the tension-bunched muscles beneath the flannel. "I like the way your eyes turn all fire-bright when you're riled. Like a cat's."

I'm gonna have one hell of a time sinnin' with you, sugar.

Let him try, Chelsea thought, her entire body tensing. Just let him try. He'll find out soon enough that this cat has claws. She batted his hand away. "Don't touch me," she hissed. "Don't you ever touch me again."

His eyes narrowed, shimmering dangerously. "Oh, I'll touch you all right, sugar. All over. You can count on it." The sudden curl of his lips, she thought, was supposed to be a grin. It looked more like a lecherous sneer, the sight of which chilled her to the bone. "And you know what else? You're gonna like my touch just fine. Count on that, too."

283

"Really? And do you want to know what *I'm* counting on, Mr. Dobbs?" One copper brow rose in icy challenge as she met his gaze with a level, daring one of her own. *"I'm counting on killing you before the night's over if you so much as breathe on me. You can count on that!"*

His grin was cocky and arrogant, born from being held at the killing end of a pistol and walking away intact one too many times. "Ah, sugar, I do like a gal with spunk. Not too much now, y' hear? But a little. Just enough to make it interesting."

"I'll give you interesting, you son of a—" Her hand came up, her nails bared to slice ribbons down his cheeks. She came close to doing just that, but not close enough. He caught her wrist in a bone-crushing grip before any damage could be done.

"Now that," he growled, all trace of humor gone, "I don't like a'tall." He leaned toward her, his face harsh and menacing. "Say you're sorry, sugar."

"No."

His hand squeezed harder. Her fingers curled limply toward her palm. Feeling faded with the circulation his grip cut off.

"I said, say you're sorry. Now!"

Chelsea winced at the pain slicing through her arm and the cold numbness that settled like a tingling pool in her hand. Still, her chin lifted defiantly. "And I said *no*."

"You just went past the point of being interesting."

Before Chelsea could stop him, he shoved her down on the bed of grass. The ground was hard and cold against her back, but not for long. She didn't intend to stay there for long.

Kicking and hitting anything she could reach, Chelsea managed to fight her way up . . . only to feel the heels of his fists plant firmly against her upper chest. He shoved her down again. The back of her head met the ground in a collision that stunned her for just a second. It was enough time for Jase to make his move.

He wasn't about to risk her trying to escape. The second her head hit the ground he was on her, his lean body crushing hers into the grass. His legs wrapped around hers, stilling her feet from their bruising kicks.

Chelsea tried to twist away, but his fingers coiled like steel bands around her wrists, pinning them on either side of her head. She arched, trying to buck him off. But she may as well have been trapped beneath a boulder; he didn't budge.

Jase waited until she was panting and limp beneath him — it took a full ten minutes — before lifting himself up, his face looming above her. His green eyes were dark with the lust her struggles had aroused. Chelsea cringed at the sight of it and renewed her feeble, weakening struggles.

His fingers clamped her jaw. He ignored the free hand she curled into a fist, beating and pushing at his chest. His grin was cold, merciless. "Ready to say you're sorry yet, sugar?"

Chelsea spit in his face. But it wasn't until she felt his hand close cruelly over her breast that she freed the scream of terror bubbling in her throat.

Chapter Twenty

"Feel better?" Brenda asked Mitch as he settled on the grass beside her. His stumbling, she noticed, was less pronounced. The color in his cheeks was high but almost natural.

Mitch grumbled beneath his breath and leaned back against the sturdy trunk of a cottonwood. The leaves rustled above, and the cool breeze felt good as it wafted over his clean, dry body.

Brenda sent him a sideways glance and continued munching on her stick of jerky. The meat was stringy and salty, but filling nonetheless. "Aren't you glad I convinced you to wait to go in for her?"

No, Mitch thought. He wasn't glad. Now that he was feeling better, now that the thumping in his head had receded to a dull roar, he was feeling restless, tense, and worried. He wouldn't feel good again until he had Chelsea away from Dobbs and his weasely brother. Not until he'd seen for himself that she was all right, unhurt, intact.

"Okay, Bryant," Brenda said, her voice cutting his thoughts like a knife. "About time we started planning, wouldn't you say?"

"I already told you my plan," Mitch grumbled impatiently.

"And I told you why it won't work. Look, we can't ride in there, guns drawn, and just demand her back. You know that. We've been after Dobbs too long for him to fall for it

286

"He doesn't know that." He cast her a quick glance.

"No? Well, I for one think he does. I think he saw through our cover a long time ago. How else could he slip through our fingers so easily every time we got close?"

"Because he's a lucky son of a bitch, that's how."

Brenda shook her head, sending the long blond braid bobbing at her waist. "Uh-uh. Not lucky. If anything, I think he's a hell of a lot smarter than we've given him credit for."

Mitch's glare was hot and piercing. "He took Chelsea. The man isn't brilliant."

Brenda turned her head, sending him an appraising glance. "Maybe, but it worked, didn't it? Taking her got you this far. Don't tell me Dobbs doesn't have some intelligence inside that greasy head of his. This proves he does. He watched you with her, saw how much interest you showed in her, and took her to use as bait. That shows more than just passing smarts on his part."

Mitch plowed his fingers through his still-wet hair and shook his head. The action brought a trace of throbbing back to his temples, but it faded quick enough. "No, Brenda," he argued, "what it shows is that the man is every bit as stupid as I always said he was. He took Chelsea, yeah, and if he has a brain in his head, he'll know I aim to kill him for it." His eyes narrowed to dangerous blue slits. "Real slow if he's hurt her."

The statement was uttered husky-low, his voice edged with so much fury that Brenda stopped chewing to stare at him.

Mitch caught her look. The grass beneath him crunched as he shifted uncomfortably. "What?"

"What? Didn't you hear a word you just said? If I wasn't looking straight at you, I wouldn't believe I'm sitting here talking to Mitch Bryant. Jesus, Mitch, you're acting like some lovesick—"

She had no time to finish the sentence as a scream pierced the air, echoing off the flat, bare prairie before it receded.

The sound chilled Mitch to the bone. He was on his feet in an instant, even though the scream was too distant to be a threat to himself or to Brenda. "Where's Kit?" he demanded, his voice gruff and breathless as he imagined Chelsea's sweet, pouty lips making that bone-chilling sound.

She nodded to the line of trees. "He went . . . you know."

Brenda couldn't remember a time Mitch had looked as scared or as fearsome as when he spun around to face her. His blue eyes caught the moonlight, and even in the silvery shadows, the gaze that shone from his face with burning intensity went right through her.

"Find him!" Not waiting for a response, he spun about and stalked toward the trees.

They met back at the campfire a few minutes later. Both were breathless. Both were without Kit.

"You don't think he —"

Mitch's angry glare stopped the words short. "Let's just hope we get there before he does."

Brenda kicked dirt over the campfire.

Mitch cleared the distance between himself and the horse in four strides. His head was throbbing again, his fever escalating. But the symptoms were not caused by his sickness. No, the churning in his gut and the ache that came with the blood rushing in his ears stemmed from the second scream that ripped through the night . . . the one that ripped just as surely up his spine and knifed its way through his heart.

Chelsea!

Mitch was in his saddle, gun drawn, leaning low over the stallion's neck and charging toward the scream before it had completely rolled away. Brenda had yet to reach her horse.

The only consistent thought to slice through his panic was that if he was to rescue Chelsea — if he was lucky enough to find her alive and well — he was going to strangle Brenda with his bare hands for making him wait this long to go in for her.

Dear God, he never should have done that. Never! No

when Chelsea needed him. He'd never forgive Brenda for a delay that might cost his precious preacher's daughter her life. What was worse — God help him, God help *Chelsea!* — Mitch knew he'd never forgive himself.

The lips that silenced her scream were grinding, hot and moist. The feel of Jase Dobbs's mouth on hers was revolting.

Chelsea tried to turn her head to the side, but his grip was too strong. His hand came up, his fingers bracketing her jaw. Pain exploded in her head when he squeezed the still-fresh bruise there. He held her steady, his tongue bulldozing its way past her lips. Wet and sour-tasting, he pillaged her mouth.

His body squirmed on top of her. The air rushed from her mouth into his as she was forced to take on all of his weight. The hand painfully clamping her jaw fell away. Where it fell to made her shiver in abhorrence, especially when he squeezed her as though he were testing the ripeness of a melon.

Her struggles increased. They were ineffectual. He laughed at her pathetic attempts. The feel of his hot breath washing over her face, the taste of it bitter in her mouth, made a surge of nausea rise in her throat. Chelsea gagged on the stench, but even the threat of her being sick didn't stop him.

He lifted his mouth only far enough to speak. His hand never stopped its bruising torture. "Come on, sugar, I'm waiting for that apology."

"I don't care if you beg for it, you bastard!" she spat, and clamped her teeth hard on his grinding lower lip.

His blood was hot and tangy on her tongue. His yelp of surprise, laced liberally with pain, rang sharply in her ears.

"Why, you little — !"

The upper part of his body rose, making the lower part grind into her stomach and hips. His hand pulled back, his intent gleaming hot in his eyes.

Chelsea scrunched her eyes closed and prepared herself for the blow. She prayed only that he would slap the other side of her face this time. If he hit her in the bruise that still ached on her jaw, she knew she'd lose consciousness. Sweet heavens, it didn't bear contemplating what this man would do to her if she passed out, unable to fight . . . or to stop him.

"Shut up!" Jase barked, his green eyes glaring down at her.

Chelsea's lashes snapped up. She scowled. Shut up? But she hadn't been saying . . . Oh yes, she thought warily, she had. Unconsciously, she'd been chanting the prayer her father had made her repeat every night before bed. She hadn't said it in years . . . not since Papa had died. She was saying it now, though. Loudly, precisely. Chanting the words, every one fresh as it screamed through her mind and tumbled off her tongue.

"I said shut up, preacher's daughter, or I swear I'll—"

"Do it and die!" a third voice shouted from behind.

Chelsea's gaze widened, sweeping over Dobbs's shoulder, fixing hard on the shadows behind him. The figure was small and lean. The knife he wielded in his long-fingered fist glinted in a downward arch in the firelight.

Kit! Chelsea's mind screamed at the same time Jase, realizing they weren't alone, turned. A crunch of grass to the right told her the commotion had woken Whip. He was fumbling beneath the bedroll, trying to draw his gun and throw off the blanket at the same time. Her gaze swept back to Jase in time to see his hand lunging for his pistol.

Chelsea didn't waste time thinking. She thrust herself to a sit just as the barrel of Jase's gun cleared the holster. Using the momentum, she rammed the heel of her palms into the outlaw's shoulder blades and shoved. Hard.

The force sent Jase forward. The second Chelsea felt his weight lift, she scooted her legs out from under him.

Kit's blade sliced into Jase's shoulder as he lurched forward. He landed on his knees with a grunt, but the sound was severed by the blast of a gunshot.

290

Chelsea stifled a scream with her hand, her gaze flying to Kit. The bullet missed him — thank God! He lunged to the side, rolled, and came up in a squat. The knife made wild, impotent slashes in front of him.

"Stupid little brat," Jase muttered. Pushing to his feet, he towered over Kit. His left hand came up, pressing into the wound on his shoulder as he tried to stem the blood pumping sticky red wetness onto his shirt. He took care not to get close enough for the sweeping blade to touch him again.

"Want me to finish him off?" Whip asked as he strolled up behind the boy. His gun was drawn, but for the most part, he looked oddly bored by the entire situation.

"No," Jase snapped, glaring down at Kit. "The pleasure's all mine. The little bastard's gonna pay for drawing my blood. Nice and slow, he's gonna pay!"

The threat spurred Chelsea into motion. Her gaze scanned the area, settling on a nice fat branch only a few feet away. If she could just reach it before . . .

Keeping her movements slow, and careful to use Jase's back to shield what she was doing from Whip's prying eye, she inched toward the branch. Jase said something she couldn't hear over the pounding of her heart in her ears. The branch was close. So damned close! She extended her arm, her breath catching when she felt her fingers close around the rough bark. The branch was heavy but not unwieldy.

She came close to dropping the weapon when she heard the click of Jase's gun being cocked.

"Time to get rid of you once and for all, kid," Jase growled. "Past time. Now, let's see . . . what part should I blow off first? An arm? Maybe a leg? Better yet, since I'm gonna kill you anyway, you'll never be old enough to need —"

Chelsea's grip tightened. The bark sliced into her palms as, staying behind Jase, she lifted the branch. Taking a deep breath and praying for forgiveness, she brought it down on the back of the outlaw's head with more strength than she would have given herself credit for having. The *thunk* the wood made when it smashed against Jase's skull was loud.

The vibrations of the blow ricocheted up Chelsea's arms. The tremors of Jase Dobbs's body slamming face first onto the ground rippled underfoot and matched the quaking in her legs.

She was shaking uncontrollably now, inside out, but the danger wasn't over. There was still Whip to deal with. Her eyes snapped up to the second outlaw just as that man's shocked attention came away from his brother's unconscious form. Their gazes locked in white-hot challenge.

"I'll kill ya for that, gal," he growled, his leathery hand lifting the gun and aiming it dead center of her forehead. A spiteful grin curled over his lips. "But not b'fore ya give my brother the apology he was workin' so hard to get."

Chelsea gulped and looked down the long, shadowy barrel of his pistol. It was the second time in twenty-four hours that she faced death. Her cheeks drained white, her gaze dropping in silent thanks to Kit. If she were going to die—and there seemed no doubt at this point—then she would leave this world with Kit knowing how much she appreciated all he'd risked for her.

But Kit wasn't there. Her gaze shifted back to Whip, but he didn't seem to notice the boy's absence. Apparently, the outlaw had discounted the kid and his puny knife as too unimportant to be watched as closely as the woman.

In a split second, Chelsea's attention swept the area. She didn't see Kit, but she saw where Jase's pistol had landed. It was near her feet. She didn't stop to question how it had gotten there; she was too busy trying to think of a way to get her hands on it before Whip killed her.

"Say it, gal. Ya tell Jase yer ever so sorry, and when he wakes up I promise I'll pass on yer message. It'll tickle him somethin' fierce to know yer last words were for him."

"Y—yes," Chelsea murmured, forcing her voice as well as her lower lip to tremble. It wasn't difficult. After all, the rest of her was already shivering uncontrollably. "Yes, you tell M—Mr. Dobbs that I truly am—" With a sigh she knew was too heavy, too melodramatic to be believed, she rolled her eyes back and let her knees buckle beneath her. The grass crackled as she collapsed limply atop it, her body curled around the gun.

In the not-too-far distance she heard Whip's disgusted "Goddanged women! Always swoonin' just when yer about to —"

His words faded to the sound of blood pumping in her ears. Chelsea's quaking fingers closed over the pistol. A surge of adrenaline shot through her like an electrically charged current. Now, if she could just convince Whip she really had fainted, if she could wait until he came to check, she might be able to . . .

Through a veil of lashes, she watched the toe of a leather boot, caked with dried mud, come into view. Her hand tightened on the gun that was quickly warming to the heat of her palms.

It seemed to take forever before the perfect time to make her move came. Tensing, she was just about to leap and fire — hopefully at the same time — when she spotted another boot. This one was tattered and cracked, and just as dirty as the first. It was also horrifyingly familiar. Kit was easing up on the man's back! And, sweet heavens, he had only a knife to defend himself. Whip had a gun — and the sure knowledge of how to use it.

Chelsea couldn't wait any longer. She felt the heat of Whip's body, smelled the sweaty stench of him as he leaned over her, trying to decide if this was a feminine ploy or if she really had fainted. The tattered boot moved closer to his back.

The foul smell of breath rushing over her face was all the incentive Chelsea needed. She snapped her eyes open and, with a well-placed kick, sent his pistol flying. Bringing up her own gun, she pressed the barrel hard into the bulbous tip of Whip's nose. His muddy eyes widened, first in surprise . . . then rage . . . then, finally, in shocked disbelief.

Chelsea couldn't remember ever seeing anything so terrifying as the gleam in the outlaw's eyes when he met and held her gaze. She gave the gun a shove, making his weathered nose wrinkle from the pressure. Unfortunately, the gesture didn't frighten him the way she'd hoped it would.

"Go ahead, gal," he hissed, his lips curling up in a feral sneer. "If ya think ya got the guts, pull that trigger. But if ya don't . . ."

Her fingertip trembled against cold metal. All she had to do was ease it back, and she would end a man's life. A portion of her mind—the part that wasn't numb with fear—was aware that the Chelsea Hogan of two weeks ago wouldn't have had the stomach to do such a thing. That same part of her was excruciatingly aware that the Chelsea Hogan of here and now *did* have the guts to slam the trigger home if it meant saving her life and Kit's.

Most men who carry guns carry them with the intent to use them. Chelsea intended to use hers. Her mouth turned up at the corners in a tight, cold, merciless grin. Hot amber fire met and held unconvinced brown. "About that apology, Whip—"

"Chelsea!" Mitch's anguished cry tore through the night an instant before the stallion tore into the ring of campfire.

It was only a split second distraction. But it was enough.

Through the haze of his rising fever and the thicker haze of rising fear, Mitch spotted Chelsea. Her eyes were wide, her face strained and flushed. And he saw a gun. *Whose* hands the gun was in registered in his crazed mind a second too late. His gun was already drawn and pointed. The bullet spit from the barrel with a deafening blast.

Chelsea screamed as the force of the shot made Whip's body lunge forward. She fell back, her head coming up hard against the ground. The outlaw's forehead slammed into her hand and knocked the gun from her fingers. She heard it bounce to the grass. Instinctively, she tracked it. The handle was dark, catching the moonlight in a dull glint. She reached out and, for the second time that night, snatched the weapon up.

"Jesus, Chels, are you all right?" Kit asked, his voice high and frantic as he stepped to her side and squatted beside her. "I mean, I saw the look on that guy's face and thought for sure he was going to—"

"I'm fine," she said, her voice too calm and too steady. Her free hand tightened into a fist and she shoved against Whip's heavy, pinning chest. Trying to writhe out from under him was next to useless. "Help roll him off me, will you, Kit?"

The boy scowled, his look an odd mix of relief and confusion as he leaned forward to help. Between the two of them, Whip's body was shoved aside. It rolled limply to the ground, thumping onto the grass. Neither mentioned the last time they'd done something like this. Chelsea didn't even want to think about it!

"Chels, are you sure you're—?"

"I said I'm fine," she repeated tersely. "At least I will be soon. You go check the other one, then tie them both up. I'd like a . . . er . . . word with Mr. Bryant."

She shoved herself to her feet, only to find her knees were shaking more than before. The fear had left her now that the two outlaws were no longer a threat. But the repercussions of that fear were staggering. What she wanted to do was plop down on the grass and have a good long cry. But she didn't. Maybe later. Right now there was still one "outlaw" she'd yet to deal with.

Her gaze strayed to where Mitch slumped in his saddle. His features were strained, flushed, but his blue eyes were sharp, reflecting the glow of the campfire. He was staring at her intently, but she didn't detect as much as a trace of concern etched in his handsome, bearded features.

She knew the second he became aware of the gun in her hands, though his expression remained guarded, indifferent. With a toss of her head, she demanded, "What happened, Mr. Bryant? Was your aim off this time?"

"My aim's as good as always . . . *Miss Hogan.*" Out of respect for his throbbing head, Mitch kept his scowl at a minimum. It didn't help. His skull still felt like it was being cracked in two by a sledgehammer.

"The hell you say!" Chelsea raged, the fervor in her tone

surprising them both. From the corner of her eye she saw Kit's head come up from where he leaned over Jase, but she kept her sights trained on Mitch. "Next thing I know you'll be telling me the bullet you fired was *meant* for Whip."

"Christ, lady, if I'd known you were going to be so damn ungrateful, I would have stayed at home."

"Well, maybe you should have! As you can see" — her free hand pointed out the two outlaws, just in case he'd missed them — "I can take care of myself."

Mitch's eyes narrowed to angry blue slits. The jaw beneath his beard bunched. "Women who can take care of themselves don't get in the position you were in, preacher's daughter. Proper women cook, clean, and don't tangle with outlaws with guns."

"*Speaking* of outlaws, Mr. Bryant . . ." The gun she had held at her waist now rose. Using two hands to steady her aim, the way her father had taught her, she leveled the barrel on the hat riding the crown of Mitch's damp head. "I'll take an explanation from you now. I suggest you make it good and make it quick. You've got exactly two minutes."

It was the fever, Mitch thought as he saw the blue-cast barrel glint with a pale sliver moonbeam. Yes, it had to be the fever blurring his vision. That was what made it look as if his sexy preacher's daughter actually *knew* how to use the weapon she cradled in her palms. "Better be careful with that thing, sweetheart," he mumbled, nodding to the pistol. "Someone could get hurt if it goes off."

She smiled coldly, furiously. "Don't I know it! One minute, forty seconds left, Mr. Bryant. Better talk fast."

Mitch, with an expression that was annoyingly patronizing, sat back in his saddle and sighed. His gaze strayed to Kit, just to make sure the kid wouldn't try anything foolish, then back to Chelsea. "All right, *Miss Hogan,* what do you want to know?"

"Why the hell you lied to me!"

His grin was quick and lecherous. "Which time?"

Which time? Sweet heavens, had he lied to her more than once? *It's never been this good before, baby. Never.* Had he lied about that? She didn't think she could stand it if he had. Anything else, but not *that*.

"Forty seconds," she snapped, her voice trembling almost as much as her knees.

"Christ, Chelsea, how the hell am I supposed to know what you want to hear?"

"Are you telling me you don't?"

"Would I ask if I did?"

"You're doing it again. Twenty seconds."

"Doing wh—? Never mind." Irritated, Mitch shifted his aching body in the saddle. He dragged the tip of his tongue over his hot, dry lips. Blind habit made him keep his gun drawn, though he knew he'd never use it. Not on his sexy little preacher's daughter. Never.

"Four . . . three . . . two . . . one." The click of the hammer being yanked beneath her thumb was loud. The sound of a bullet exploding from the barrel was deafening.

For one horrified second, Mitch thought the slicing pain in his head came from a bullet embedding itself in his skull. His breathing stopped. So did his heart. It wasn't until he noticed the hat had flown from his head that he realized the shot had missed him by inches. Damned *few* inches!

His glowering gaze fixed hard on determined whiskey-amber. Slowly, his attention flickered from her eyes down to the pistol that was now taking aim at the gun in his hand.

"Shall we try again, Mr. Bryant?" she asked, her voice dripping sweetness. "This time I'll give you one minute to tell me why the *hell* you lied to me!"

"Because I *had* to," Mitch growled. He was taking a chance here—a damn big one—by hoping his comment was generic enough to answer whatever question she was asking. He didn't know what Chelsea was talking about, but he could guess between several of the lies he'd told her. The land he'd stolen and his status as an outlaw were the two that popped immediately to mind—only the first of which she could possibly know about.

"Be more specific, Mr. Bryant. You've got thirty seconds."

"Chelsea . . ." he began, his voice gritty and rough as he lifted a leg and slipped awkwardly from the saddle. The impact of his feet hitting solid ground made him grit his teeth, but it didn't stop him from stepping toward her. Mitch hoped he could stay on his feet long enough to disarm her, but it was doubtful. He was losing ground fast. The invigoration he'd felt after his dousing in the stream was slipping quickly. Still, he couldn't risk her getting off another shot as lucky as her first.

"Ten seconds . . . nine . . . eight . . ."

"You'd better hope you stop counting before I reach you, preacher's daughter, or there's going to be hell to pay."

"Three . . . two . . . one."

Mitch didn't have the chance to lunge before another bullet exploded from her gun. He grunted as it hit his own weapon, tearing the pistol from his stinging hand.

"That does it!"

Chelsea gasped as the gun was knocked from her hands with a sharp blow. The pistol sailed through the air, then thumped to the ground not far away. She didn't track it this time. She didn't dare. Mitch looked angrier than a lion with a thorn stuck in its paw. It wouldn't be safe to take her eyes off him.

"Care to tell me what the hell this is all about?" he roared, then winced at the pain his booming voice brought to his aching head. "You could have killed me."

"I told you once I'd kill you myself if I wanted you dead." Her chin lifted, and she met his chilly blue gaze unflinchingly. "Apparently, I don't want you dead, Mr. Bryant. You *are* still here, aren't you?"

The arrogant way she spoke, combined with the memory of how confidently she'd held the pistol, finally registered in Mitch's fevered mind. The revelation was less than welcome. "I thought you didn't know how to shoot."

"I never said that."

"No, but you *implied* it."

She shook her head. "No, I didn't. In fact, I believe my exact words were 'I'd never touch one of those things.' " She

298

smiled sweetly, glancing at the place where his hat had rested atop his damp raven head — until she'd blown it off. She wrinkled her pert little nose. "Hmmm. I must have learned how to lie from *you*, Mr. Bryant. Let's just say I prefer to settle my differences unarmed."

"And you have differences to settle with me?"

"Oh, yes. Quite a few."

"Such as — ?"

Kit, all too aware of the tense undercurrents crackling in the air like the threat of a vicious summer thunderstorm, stepped between the two adults. "Okay, Chels, I did what you asked. They're all set. You didn't say to, but I gagged them. Guess that means we can leave . . . if you're all done taking target practice on Mitch here, that is."

Chelsea's gaze widened. Her copper brows shot high as she glared down at Kit. " 'Mitch,' is it? When did you stop calling him 'that no-good piece of scum'?"

Kit's cheeks colored, but he didn't take the statement back. His easy acceptance of the "outlaw" was a recent change — as was the glint of admiration she saw flash in the boy's eyes when he sent Mitch a quick glance over his slender shoulder.

Kit ducked his head, slipping from between them. "I . . . er . . . if you don't need me for anything else, I . . . er . . . I think I'll go over and wait with Brenda." Ramming his fists in his trouser pockets, he hurried to where the blond woman stood beside her chestnut-brown mustang.

Chelsea hadn't noticed the woman standing there. She noticed now, though. With a vengeance. The familiar blue eyes were dancing with laughter as her gaze flittered between Chelsea and Mitch.

Gritting her teeth, Chelsea's gaze sharpened on Mitch. "Why is *she* here?"

" 'She' happens to be a friend of mine."

"I'll just bet!"

Mitch continued as though she hadn't spoken. "And 'she' is here because 'she' was trying to help me save your sexy little ass, lady. Keep that in mind . . . and try to sound grateful when you thank her for it."

Jealousy—white-hot and quick—pumped through Chelsea's blood. It boiled. Her gaze flashed fire as she spat, "The only thing I'm likely to thank her for is leaving. And I'll thank you to do the same thing, you lying son of a—"

Mitch reached out and grabbed her upper arm, spinning her back to face him when she made to turn away. With a flick of his wrist, he brought her up hard against his chest. The collision of their bodies cost him, but it was a price he was willing to pay to feel her warm, unharmed softness molding into him.

His arm came up, circling her waist, holding her tighter than he had ever held a woman before. Each ragged breath she took made her breasts swell into him. It was the sweetest torture Mitch had ever known, for during the few short minutes—that felt like a dozen lifetimes!—it had taken him to get to her after her second scream, he'd been afraid he'd never hold this woman in his arms again.

Mitch had never been so scared in his life. He'd been sure she was dead, especially after the first gunshot had cut the air. The thought of never seeing, never holding, never touching his sexy preacher's daughter again had been a shattering blow, one he knew if he lived to be a hundred he'd never get over.

But she wasn't dead. *She wasn't dead!*

He hugged her tightly, as though he were trying to melt her body through clothes and skin and somehow absorb her into himself. Closing his eyes, he reveled in a final, blinding surge of relief. He lowered his head until his cheek was pillowed atop her soft, soft hair. She smelled good and felt so damned right nestled in his arms this way. Her curves filled out the hard valleys and plains of his body, like two halves of a whole melding together, joining as one. Perfection.

Drawing in a shaky breath, he knew in that instant that he'd never let her go again. Damned if he would! Damned if he'd let her convince him to!

"Tell me, preacher's daughter," he rasped oh, so softly against her hair. "Tell me what you think I lied to you about."

Chelsea tried to hold on to her anger, really she did. But some things were beyond a mortal woman's abilities. How could she fight the fire that raged through her whenever this man touched her? Held her? And why would she want to?

The instant Mitch had scooped her close, the second she'd heard his heart drumming against her ear, her anger had faded. In seconds, the flames of fury had been exchanged for the blinding heat of desire. It was frightening the way anger had swiftly channeled into something much stronger than physical attraction. Something that scared her to death. The emotion was so powerful, so overwhelming and intense, it stole her breath. Her heart clenched like a fist in her chest.

"Everything, Mitch. You lied to me about everything," she whispered finally, her voice soft and shaky from the magnitude of emotions rushing through her. "You lied about the land, though I'm not exactly sure why. You lied about what you do for a living. And . . ." *No, please, God, don't let him have lied about that!* "You lied to me about everything." She swallowed hard, her voice catching. "I trusted you, Mitch. Even though I knew better, goddamn it, *I trusted you!*"

Mitch eased back and cupped her cheeks in his hands. He looked down into her eyes and, his voice husky and thick, said, "No, Chelsea, not everything. I never lied about the way I wanted you. I never lied about how good it was when we were together. Damned if I did."

"Mitch," Chelsea breathed. The conviction in his voice washed over her like a hot, bittersweet caress. Condemning herself as all kinds of a fool, Chelsea knew she believed him. She *had* to believe him. To think he was lying to her yet again meant she would wither up and die on the spot. Closing her eyes, she rushed on before she could change her mind. "Sweet heavens, Mitch, you . . . that is, I . . ."

"Chelsea, don't say it," he muttered raggedly, his body swaying into her. "Save it for when I can hear you. For when I can remember every word. But right now I think I'm going to—"

The grass crunched with the force of Mitch's knees smashing onto it. He crumbled to the ground, his grip on Chelsea too tight to avoid taking her with him. His last memory—before the blessed, unfeeling blackness—was that of rolling to his side to avoid crushing her beneath him.

Then there was nothing except Ch—Chelsea Hogan's heartfelt cry as she screamed his name . . . and even that faded quickly.

Chapter Twenty-one

Mitch groaned. Didn't he? It was hard to tell. The dry, croaking sound that scratched past his parched throat and echoed softly in his ears didn't sound like much of anything.

Slowly — very, very slowly — he pried open his eyes. They felt gritty and burned as he absorbed the sights around him. Everything was a blur; all fuzzy, flickering orange light. No shapes, no sounds. He forced himself to blink, forced himself to bring one particular piece of orange fuzz into focus.

The corners of his lips turned up in a weak grin when the distorted blur manifested into a shape. Oh, not just any shape. Nope. It was a very pretty, very petite, very red-headed shape.

Ch — Chelsea Hogan, his sexy little preacher's daughter, was sitting with her legs curled beneath her in a rocker that looked as old as Methuselah. Clutched in the hand pillowed atop her lap was the black scarf he'd tied around her arm what felt like a lifetime ago. The cloth was wrinkled and ragged. The sight of it made his heart constrict. Not only had she kept his scarf, but from the looks of it, she'd slept with it nightly. Nothing could have pleased Mitch more — or made him feel better.

Slowly, his gaze rose. Her head was tipped to the side, pillowed in back by the rocker's chipped headboard, at the cheek by a deliciously slender shoulder. And everywhere — sweet Jesus, *everywhere!* — was a wild scattering of unruly, copper-red hair.

Mitch's fingers, limp atop the coarse blanket covering his stomach, twitched when he imagined burying them in all that fluffy softness. He sucked in a breath, as though inhaling her sweet, sweet scent. The smell of her hair would be flower-fresh, he thought, her skin soapy-clean and tangy. She would smell like heaven. And the feel of her . . . Christor, the *feel!*

Perfection, Mitch decided. No other word described what it felt like to run his palms over her warm, creamy flesh. No other word described how he felt when he touched her . . . or when she touched him. Perfection. Yup, it was that, all right. Damned if it wasn't!

She stirred in her sleep, her head tossing back to expose the elegant taper of her neck. The curl of copper lashes against her cheek was like the delicate batting of a butterfly's wing. Her lips parted, oh, so invitingly.

Mitch's jaw bunched. His fingers fisted the scratchy blanket. His tongue, already dry, felt like the Sahara in mid-July. His heart was beating a mile a minute, slamming against his ribs. His breathing had gone from slow and even to rapid and hard in a matter of seconds. So had other, more integral parts of him, now that he thought about it.

She must have sensed his gaze, for the lashes kissing her cheeks swept up. Before Mitch could prepare for it, his lusty gaze locked hard with sleepy whiskey-amber. The scarf slipped from her slackened fingers and floated unnoticed to the floor.

"Mitch?" Chelsea whispered. The rocker creaked as she sat up straight, blinking the grains of sleep from her eyes. Her gaze was cautious but excited. Was this a dream? she wondered tiredly. Or was Mitch truly — *finally* — awake? Scowling, she repeated hoarsely, "Mitch?"

One corner of his mouth turned up in what had to be the most charming grin he'd ever flashed her. Chelsea's heart stuttered in her chest, trapping the air in her lungs.

"I thought you said you were no angel, lady?" he rasped, his gaze raking her boldly. His eyes sparkled, telling her more clearly than words that he wished it were his hands doing the stroking, not merely his eyes. His grin broadened at the confused flush staining her cheeks.

"I . . . What?" For four days she'd wondered what his first words would be when he awoke. Those weren't even close.

He shrugged, just the barest lift and fall of his shoulders beneath the blanket, not at all the practiced, arrogant gesture she was used to from him. "You told me once you were no angel. Well, sweetheart, as much as I hate to argue, if I'm where I think I am, then the quality of heaven's sure as hell improved since the last time I read the Good Book."

"As if you ever read it!" One copper brow shot high. The gaze that pierced him was now wide awake. Only the barest trace of a grin tugged at the corners of her lips. "As much as I hate to argue with you, Mr. Bryant, I think if you were truly dead, angels would be the *last* thing you'd be seeing right now."

He cushioned a palm on his chest in mock offense. "Is that so? And what, pray tell, would I be seeing . . . *Miss Hogan?*"

Her grin blossomed. "Oh, little red rascals, I imagine. You know, the guys with long tails and pointy ears. You'd recognize them, Mitch. Really you would. Unless my father was mistaken, they have horns on top of their little red heads and carry pitchforks. Sound familiar yet?"

"Hmmm, now that you mention it . . ." His gaze fixed on her tangle of fiery red hair. "Did you say red? Kind of coppery and long? Yeah, I think I might've seen one of them. But just to be sure, sweetheart, why don't you part your hair and let me have a look? See if you have anything sprouting up there."

Chelsea giggled. She couldn't help it. Her relief to have him awake — and joking — was so great she thought she might burst from it. Sending him a glance of feigned indignation, she clasped her hands in her lap and shook her head. "I will not. You'll just have to take my word for it. I have no horns."

His lips pursed, his eyes sparkling a devilish shade of blue as his gaze dipped. His attention settled on the curve of her hip, his grin turning positively sinful! "What about the tail part? Do I get to check for one of those instead?"

Chelsea's eyes widened. Her cheeks felt as though they were on fire. "Certainly not! My tail, or lack of thereof, is none of your business."

"Like hell it isn't," he argued, a chuckle softening his words. "Lady, what do you think got me into this mess in the first place? If you didn't have such a delectable little tail, I wouldn't have been out there risking my life saving it tonight."

"Last week," she corrected absently. His compliment, crass though it was, washed over her in pleasant, tingly waves. So he liked her tail, did he? Now, why did that thought please her ever so much?

Mitch blinked hard. "What?"

"I said last week. You've been —"

"For a week?"

"Well, no. Only four days. Mitch, are you all right?" Chelsea perched on the edge of the chair, ready to catch him as he pushed up on his elbows. He looked as if he was about to throw himself off the bed, but she doubted he had the strength to do it yet. She was right. The sculpted cheeks above his beard drained ashy-white, and the mattress crunched as he just as quickly collapsed back on top of it.

"Damn it!" he grumbled, but the word was very, very weak. He reached up and plowed a shaky hand through his damp raven hair. The sweat moistening his scalp was fresh, caused by even that small burst of energy. "I feel as weak as a kitten."

She chuckled dryly. "Believe me, Mitch, you weigh a hell of a lot more than one. You nearly killed Brenda, Kit, and myself when we tried to lift you onto the saddle. I still don't know how we managed it."

What baffled her even more was where she'd found the strength to climb onto the saddle behind him and not only balance *his* weight atop the stallion, but keep her own supporting body there as well. Her arms still ached! Somehow, she'd gotten him back to Brenda's sod-house, yet even now she had no idea where the strength to do it had come from. Fear, most likely — fear for his safety, fear for his *life*.

Her eyes darkened with concern. "How are you feeling? Do you hurt anywhere? Do you want me to get you anything?"

"A drink of water would be nice."

She flipped off the blanket and shot to her feet. Her attention snagged on something lying beside the chair's chipped, dented rocker. Mitch's scarf.

Chelsea's first instinct was to reach down and retrieve it. Her second was to leave it where it was. Of them both, the second urge was stronger. She didn't want Mitch to know she'd kept his scarf. If he found out, he might guess how many times she'd held that hopelessly wrinkled scrap of cloth close to her heart. Just held it. And thought of him. It was information about her that Mitch Bryant didn't need to know.

Averting her gaze, she padded barefoot across the floor and was back at his side in less than a minute, a dipper filled with water from the bucket of freshly drawn river water in her hand.

Squatting down beside the bed, she slipped a hand under his shoulders and levered him up, placing the cold metal rim of the dipper against his mouth. "Drink slow," she warned as he gulped down three quick mouthfuls. "I said *slow*, Mitch. Keep gobbling it up like that and you'll make yourself sick again."

Mitch's gaze lifted, locking onto hers. His blue eyes were dark and probing. "Would you care if I did?"

She shrugged, easing his head back to the pillow. Her fingers lingered a bit too long on the silky curls at his nape and the tight cord of his neck, but she didn't think he noticed. "I might," she mumbled flippantly, then straightened. "Who do you think's been taking care of you for the last four days? Believe me, buster, I want nothing more than for you to get well. The sooner the better. I could use

307

the rest."

Turning her back on him, she padded back across the packed dirt floor and replaced the dipper in the bucket with a splash. It wasn't an act of neatness that prompted her movements as much as the need to hide the flush warming her cheeks . . . the one that proclaimed her statement a bald-faced lie.

She cared. In the four very long days and nights she'd nursed him, Chelsea had come to realize *that* if nothing else. Sweet heavens, she cared about him so much it hurt inside! But she couldn't tell him that. There were too many things haunting her, too many lies and deceptions heaped up like a brick wall to make a confession of that magnitude . . . yet.

Mitch's gaze settled on the sway of her hips beneath the coarse beige skirt. His eyes darkened to a lusty shade of blue when he remembered the curve of that luscious bottom beneath clinging trousers. Better yet, *without* the trousers, or any other barrier of cloth. Ah, how he remembered the creamy feel of her oh, so soft bottom filling his searching palms! The memory was a torture unto itself. Rolling his lips inward, he closed his eyes tightly and groaned.

The sound echoed off the sod-house walls and brought Chelsea spinning on her heel. A worried scowl furrowed her brow. The skirt rustled around her ankles as she rushed back to the bed. Crouching down, she ran a palm over his cool, dry brow and asked, "Are you all right?"

His hand came up. The calloused fingers wrapped around her hand, tugging it down. He forced her fingers open when she instinctively curled them inward. He pillowed her palm atop his chest, feeling the frantic pounding of his heart beneath her hand. His gaze searched out the pulse in her throat and, to his satisfaction, found it was beating just as hard. Just as erratic.

"No," Mitch muttered huskily. "I don't think I am." The fingers on his chest trembled. His grip tightened. "Jesus, woman, you're shaking like a leaf."

"A—am I? I hadn't noticed."

308

"Well, I sure as hell did. Come here." Mitch swatted her hand off of him, then flipped a corner of the blanket up. It wasn't until he felt the cool morning air wafting over his skin that he realized he was stark naked beneath. He didn't drop the blanket, though his gaze did take on a devilish glint as he beckoned her inside. "Come on, climb under here where it's warm." He winked slyly, clicking his tongue twice. "I think you're catching my fever."

Chelsea thought he might be right. Her cheeks felt hot. In fact, her whole body felt as if it were burning up. She wasn't sick, though. Oh no, far from it. The fire came from the inside, starting in a place just below her stomach and fanning through the rest of her body until her blood boiled in her veins. The fire — her light-headedness, her inability to breathe, her pounding heart — was the result of where her gaze had shifted.

Amber eyes widened in shock. Mitch Bryant might be sick, but there were parts of him that were undeniably well. She tore her gaze away from those parts, her cheeks flaming scarlet.

"Boy, I'll bet you're hungry!" she said, her voice hard and forced. Pushing to her feet, she stumbled across the room, toward the fire that crackled in the hearth. "After a few days of watery broth, I'll bet you'd like —"

"Chelsea."

"— something hearty to eat. How about a nice bowl of rabbit stew? I made it fresh a few hours ago."

"Chelsea!"

"No? Well, then, I suppose I could make you a few biscuits to go with it. They taste so good when you let them —"

"Woman, if you don't get that sweet little fanny of yours over here by the time I count to five, I'm coming after you."

"— soak in the broth." Pretending she hadn't heard him, she knelt before the fire and picked up the spoon she'd propped against the large black kettle. Her fingers were shaking hard enough to make some of the broth slop over the side, sizzling as the juicy drops hit the licking flames.

"One."

309

"Of course you can't eat too much too fast. You'll just make yourself—"

"Two."

"—sick again." She gulped when the last part of her sentence came out high and squeaky.

"Three."

She heard the swish of blankets, then the twin thumps of his feet hitting the floor. *He isn't strong enough,* she told herself, but she didn't believe it. Mitch Bryant was strong enough to do anything he set his mind to.

"Mitch," she muttered breathlessly, not daring to look over her shoulder and see his naked body. "Please don't. If you fall on your face, I'll never be able to lift you onto that bed again. Not by myself."

"Four."

The mattress crunched as his weight shifted. Chelsea shot to her feet fast enough to make her head spin. She did not turn around. "All right! I'll come over there, but only if you promise to get underneath that damned blanket again."

Mitch muttered a quick agreement, then snuggled back on the bed. As he smoothed the blanket over himself, he wondered who was happier about it—Chelsea, or himself. Truthfully, he'd found it too damn cold to swing his naked legs over the side of the bed. And tiring as hell. He doubted he had the strength to chase her down. Damned if he wouldn't have given it his best shot, though. But as luck would have it, he wouldn't have to.

"Are you decent?" she asked over her shoulder, her gaze politely turned away.

His chuckle was low and deep. It ripped straight up her spine. "Oh, sweetheart, don't you know me better than that yet? We outlaws are *never* decent."

Chelsea tensed. She wondered if his reference to that night at the Dobbses camp had been made intentionally. Was he testing her, slyly trying to get at what she'd been referring to the last time they'd talked? Or had the allusion been coincidental? It didn't matter. Whatever his reason, her reaction to his words was very real, and very quick.

The skirt whipped around her ankles when she spun on her heel and stomped to the side of the bed. Lacing her arms tightly over her chest, she glared down at him. "What do you want?"

"You." With more quickness than she would have given a sick man credit for having, his hand snaked out. His fingers looped around her wrist. "Come here."

"No," she cried, her heart pounding. She gave a sharp tug on her arm, knowing that getting any closer to him would be a fatal mistake. His grip didn't budge. She wasn't surprised, though she did tug again. "Mitch, let go of me. I have to—"

"It can wait."

"It can't. I didn't work so hard making that stew only to have it burn."

"And what about me, preacher's daughter?" he asked, his voice a husky-sweet caress. "I'm burning, too. Or doesn't that matter as much as your stew?"

Chelsea gasped as his other hand, warm and rough, closed over her forearm. Very, very slowly, he reeled her in until she was bent at the waist, leaning over him. Her hair slipped past her shoulders, trailing like strands of molten copper over the blanket and over the firm, sun-bronzed chest exposed above it, then over his cheek.

"Where's Brenda?" he asked, his gaze shooting to the curtain that served as a temporary door.

"She went home." Her voice was breathless and low. "She waited until the fever broke last night. Once she knew you were going to be all right, she said she had to get back to Clancy. She left yesterday."

"And Kit?"

"He took her into Guthrie."

A slow grin curled the lips enticingly hidden beneath the pitch-black curl of mustache. "Good. We're all alone then."

Chelsea moistened her own suddenly parched lips. It was a mistake. The second the tip of her tongue darted out, his gaze latched onto it hungrily. "Well, actually, S—Sam Henderson said he'd stop by after the guys from Denver came by to pick up the Dobbs brothers. He should be here soon. A—any minute now."

"What guys?"

Her cheeks colored, and she looked quickly away. Her shrug was too quick, too measured to be believed. "How should I know?"

"Liar."

"I'm not lying! Sam said he'd come by. He . . . er . . . wanted to check on you."

His eyes narrowed to penetrating blue slits. The intensity of that gaze seared her profile. He remembered coming to once and talking to Brenda. She'd told him Jase and Whip were all that were left of the Dobbs Gang, and that they'd been taken into custody. He hadn't had time to ask how much Chelsea knew about everything. He'd been afraid to. It would explain too much, and in the condition he'd been in, explanations were the last thing he'd wanted. He wanted them now, though.

How much *did* she know? And if she knew everything, how much did she hate him?

"You're not talking about Sam Henderson, woman," he growled suddenly. "And I damn well know it!"

"Do you?" Her head came around slowly. Mitch's gaze wasn't the only one that shot fire. "If you know so much, then why don't you tell me what I *am* talking about?"

"The guys are from Thiel's, aren't they, Chelsea? *Aren't they?!*" His grip tightened as he warred with the urge to shake the words out of her or to hug her close. Both urges were equally strong. Since he couldn't decide which one to give in to, he did neither. "You know, don't you? That's what all that talk about me being a lying son of a bitch was about, wasn't it?"

"You *are* a lying son of a bitch, Mr. Bryant. No question about it." She lifted her chin as haughtily as a woman in her awkward position could and snapped, "Now, if you'd kindly let go of me, I'll see what can be done about fixing us some supper."

"Like hell you will!" Mitch stormed. "We're going to talk.

Right here. Right now. It's past time you knew the truth."

"I'm not sure I'm still interested in hearing it, Mr. Bryant," she sniffed haughtily. But she *was* interested. They both knew it.

At that moment, Chelsea wanted nothing more than for Mitch to take her into his arms and explain why he'd lied to her. Why he hadn't trusted her when she'd put so much of her trust in him. The need to know his reasons was strong, and at war with an equally strong desire *not* to know. What if his reasons were selfish? What if he told her he'd only used her to get to Dobbs? An explanation like that would cut to the soul. It would tear her heart in two. It would . . .

"Five!"

Chelsea had barely enough time to suck in a shaky gasp before his fingers tightened. He yanked, and she landed hard enough atop the sinewy cushion of his chest to make the breath from both their lungs rush out with twin whooshes.

By the time she'd managed to draw in air again, his arms had wrapped around her waist in steely bands. His fingers laced, locking at the small of her back. His grip was tight, but not painfully so. It was also firm. Uncompromising. Possessive. She didn't doubt he meant to keep her pinned atop him until she'd heard everything he had to say. There was only one problem with that: Her heart was pounding so loudly in her ears she could barely hear herself think!

"Let go of me, Mitch," she snapped. She twisted, trying to slide from his grasp, to slide off the bed. But the stubborn male arms coiled about her more tightly, refusing to let her go. "Damn it, Bryant! Let go of me before I—"

Mitch heard the telltale crack in her voice. He pounced. "Before you what? Tell me, Damn you! Before you what?"

Before I forget how angry I am and start enjoying the feel of you, her mind finished the sentence for her. But she refused to let the words slip out. Wasn't it bad enough her breasts burned with the feel of them being crushed against his chest? Wasn't it bad enough she was already much too aware of another hardness, lower, that felt as though it were burning

313

into her? No, she wouldn't tell him. Her pride wouldn't let her.

Gritting her teeth, she kicked her feet again, still trying to gain her freedom. Mitch shifted. Chelsea felt a surge of victory when she thought she'd won. She was wrong. She hadn't won anything but the feel of his calloused hands smoldering over her spine a split second before he tossed her onto the mattress.

Startled, she could do nothing but lie there, her head cushioned by the thin, soft pillow, her front a cushion for something much, much harder. Where a second ago she'd been gazing at the firm wedge of Mitch's furry chest, her gaze now fixed on the squared-off layers of a sod ceiling. This sight, she had to admit, wasn't as appealing as the first one had been.

The thought was erased when another, more enticing sight came into view. It was Mitch's sharply chiseled face looming above her. All at once she became aware of his rugged body pressing her down on the mattress. Of the corded bands of muscles in the calves that easily captured her legs between his knees. Of the way his pelvis ground — *accidentally? She thought not!* — into her own.

"F—force is the devil's own tactics, Mr. Bryant," she panted. Their gazes clashed. Her heart raced when she saw his reckless grin.

"Another of Daddy's little proverbs?" he asked, and chuckled dryly when she nodded. "Jesus, that man had a ton of them, didn't he? What a wit."

"Stop it, Mitch," she spat, suddenly furious. "Don't you dare poke fun at my father. He was a good man. Better than you could *dream* of being." Her gaze darkened, her eyes piercing him to the core. "At least *he* never lied to me."

"Ah, back to that again, are we?" Mitch grumbled, his expression guarded. His gaze dropped, caressing the pouty line of her lips, the long taper of her throat. He raised up on his elbows, his attention lingering on the swell of her breasts and the way they heaved erratically beneath him. His palm itched to reach out and cup one, but he didn't. Instead, he

314

captured a wispy red tendril, rubbing it between his thumb and index finger.

"Well?" she prodded. Her fury weakened as she watched him play, fascinated, with her hair. "Aren't you going to deny it?"

"No." His gaze latched onto the silky red strand and the way it curled around his calloused fingertip. His gut tightened. The realization that something as minor as the texture of her hair could have such a powerful impact was staggering. He'd known he loved this woman for weeks, but the reality of that love, its *strength,* was never as acute as it was at this moment.

"No?" she echoed softly, surprised. "Aren't going to say you didn't mean to her Aren't you going to tell me you really trusted me the whole time? That it was all just a misunderstanding?"

"No." His gaze shifted, locking hard with brilliant amber. Like the first time he'd ever seen them, he was again reminded of smooth, expensive whiskey. And, again, he felt himself drowning in the large, shimmering pools of her eyes.

"Well, why on earth not?!" A haze of tears stung Chelsea's eyes, but she blinked them back. Sweet heavens, the pain that tore through her chest was almost unbearable! Why wouldn't he say the words she wanted to hear? *Why?!*

"If I did, I'd be adding on still another lie," he answered simply. Sincerely. "And I don't want to do that. I don't ever want to lie to you again."

"You lied to me before," she whispered hoarsely. "It didn't bother you then."

"You know that? For a fact?"

She shrugged uncomfortably. "Well, no. But it didn't *seem* to bother you."

"Like hell," he growled. "It bothered me more than you'll ever know. But I didn't have a choice."

"Because of your job?"

He glanced down sharply. He'd forgotten for a second that she knew about that. "Yeah, because of my damn job.

Thiel's did a good job plastering wanted posters with my face on them all over the country. I would have been a fool to risk my cover by telling you who I really was. Chelsea, it wasn't that I didn't trust you. Everything in me wanted to. I *couldn't*. It was too big a risk. Brenda and I have hunted Dobbs for six years. I couldn't throw all that work away . . . for both our sakes."

"What about my land? You stole my claim," she added, feeling somewhat soothed to know he'd *wanted* to trust her at least. Unconsciously, her hands strayed up, cradling his back. Was there ever a feeling as wonderful as this man's flesh gliding beneath her palms? Of the tight bands of muscle rippling beneath her fingertips? Chelsea didn't think so.

Mitch cleared his throat. Though the temptation to look away from her was great, he didn't. "Yeah," he grumbled, "I stole your land. By that time, Brenda was pretty sure Dobbs was on to us. I still had my doubts. Either way, I couldn't risk riding in here and not staking a Quarter Section when everyone else on God's green earth was going after one. It would have looked damned suspicious — and it would have tipped Dobbs and his men off before we were ready to nab them."

Her gaze dropped to his lips, almost but not quite hidden by the downward curl of his mustache. The blood heated in her veins. Her lids thickened with a desire that was as consuming as it was undeniable. "You made me think there was something between you and Brenda."

"Yeah . . . well, Dobbs was the one who was supposed to think that. Brenda figured that if he thought she was my woman, he'd go after her. And when he did, we'd finally have the lot of them. In a way, I suppose you could say it worked."

"But it was all for nothing, Mitch. Dobbs said he and Whip were all that was left of his gang. And now they're —"

"I know. Brenda told me." He hesitated, a thoughtful scowl puckering his brow. His arm tightened around her. "But I'm not sure I agree about the 'all for nothing' part."

It was a cryptic response, the meaning of which Chelsea

316

didn't dare wonder about. She took a deep breath and brought up the subject that was most important of all. The one that had been eating at her for the better part of a week. "And you m—made love to me."

Mitch closed his eyes tightly. His throat worked beneath the stubble of his beard, as though he was fighting to hide an emotion he was afraid to let her see. He scowled. The gesture deepened the suntanned creases shooting out from his eyes.

"Yeah, I did," he answered finally, his voice thick and gritty. "And before you ask, I'll tell you up front that I had no choice about that, either. I . . . Damn it, preacher's daughter, I *had* to have you. Right or wrong, I had to know what it felt like to have you beneath me, around me. I wanted to know how it felt to be inside of you. The hell of it was, once I knew, I wanted to feel it all again . . . and again . . . and again."

Her fingers slipped lightly down his spine, over his taut waist, lower. She filled her palms with his leans hips and felt his instinctive arch inward. She met it with a grinding arch of her own. "How did it feel Mitch?" she asked, her voice small and more timid-sounding than it had been in weeks. "Please, tell me how it felt. I need to know."

"Oh, God," Mitch groaned. He rolled his weight atop her, burying his face in the satiny cloud of her hair. The fiery strands were soft, tickling his cheek and neck. They smelled as good as he remembered . . . as good as they had in every fevered dream he'd had of her—and he'd had a thousand or more. Flowery and fresh. Tangy-sweet. Wonderful.

"Heaven, sweetheart," he rasped. Swallowing hard, he turned his head, his lips grazing the side of her throat. His breath was hot against her quivering skin, and she melted under the scorching feel of it. "Absolute heaven."

Chelsea's lashes flickered shut. She breathed out a heavy sigh of relief as he put to rest her last—her worst—fear. "Oh, God," she groaned, her fingers uncurling from where he'd dug deep grooves in his waist. Her palms opened, sweeping urgently up his sinewy back, hooking over his wonderfully broad shoulders. When her body arched up into his rigid firmness, she didn't try to stop it. "Sweet heavens, I wish you weren't so sick."

Mitch levered himself up on the elbows flanking her rib cage. His eyes came open slowly, gradually revealing the incredible blue hidden beneath . . . eyes that were lusty and dark with desire. "I'm not *that* sick, baby. I'll *never* be that sick."

A teasing grin tugged at her lips. "Mitch, you just woke up after four days of a raging fever. I don't think—"

"Exactly." His mouth lowered by teasing, sensuous degrees. "Don't think. *Feel*."

"But—"

His mouth was so close she could feel his lips brushing hers as he said, "I have to, Chelsea. I can't stop myself now any more than I could that first time. I don't *want* to stop myself." He sucked in a weak, shaky breath and said, "Jesus, woman, haven't you figured it out yet? I love you."

Chelsea's heart stammered in her chest. Her eyes widened in disbelief, but for the life of her she couldn't find a hint of insincerity in his expression. Cautiously, she felt her spirits soar. "Y—you do?" she whispered, unable to believe it . . . *afraid* to believe it. "You love me?"

The ragged ends of his hair scraped her cheek and nose as he shook his head. "Do you think I'd ride hell-bent for leather after a woman I *didn't* love?"

"You were sick," she reminded him. "You didn't know what you were doing."

"Like hell I didn't. I had a fever, yeah, and a headache and sore throat that would kill most barnyard animals, but I knew damned well what I was doing." His gaze pierced her to the quivering core. It was hot and branding. "I was getting back what's mine. My woman. *My* sexy little preacher's daughter."

Chelsea's brows arched. *Sexy little preacher's daughter?* her mind echoed. She'd never been called that before. Still, it had a nice ring to it — especially when her "outlaw" said it so huskily, so sensuously.

"Now that I've bared my soul, lady, I have a question for you." His hand came up, his index finger hooking beneath her chin and tilting it up until she was forced to meet his gaze. It was hot and probing, his voice strained and oh, so shaky. "Do you think you could ever love me, Ch—Chelsea Hogan?"

Chelsea's eyelids flickered closed for just a second. When her lashes swept up, it was to reveal large amber eyes that shimmered with all the emotion she felt welling in her heart. "Yes, Mr. Bryant, I think I could be persuaded to. In fact, I think I already do." Her hand cupped his cheek, and he felt the familiar scratch of beard against her palm. She shivered, her gaze dark as it met his. "I think I love you very much."

"You do?" he asked. Neither of them was more surprised than Mitch to hear his voice crack. Ducking his head, he cleared his throat, swallowed hard, then, his voice stronger, said, "You do."

His head came up, and his lips curled in a rakish, charming, heart-stopping smile that made Chelsea melt. If the room had been pitch-black, that smile would have lit it up.

"Good," he said as, without warning, he flipped onto his side, dragging her with him. He cradled her close, but his hands were never still. "Now that we've got that straightened out, there's something I've always wanted you to do for me."

Chelsea's lips rolled inward, her mind immediately flooding with all sorts of illicit images. "Oh?" she asked, her voice breathless and high. "And what's that?"

"Weeell," he sighed, his hand coming up slowly until it molded over one firm, creamy breast, "ever since that night I stole your supper—you forgot to mention *that* one—I've had this hankering for having my soul salvaged." His cheek pillowed the top of her head. His calloused fingertips scratched down the cloth covering her stomach, then drifted lower. "Think you're up to it, preacher's daughter?"

"I don't know, Mr. Bryant," she said very, very slowly as

her hand began a sensuous investigation of its own. She grinned when her fingers curled around him, and she felt him almost jump off the bed in shock. "You see, salvaging souls is a very long, very hard process. I mean, a man can't be saved in one night, you know. It takes time."

"I think I'm up to it." Mitch almost choked when he felt her sweet, sweet fingers begin to stroke him. Dear God, she was driving him crazy! "How much time?" he croaked.

"A lifetime . . . at least."

"A lifetime, eh?" His fingers tangled in the fiery copper nest between her thighs . . . searching, finding, exploring. "Lady, make it two and you've got yourself a deal." He nuzzled her ear, his tongue dipping, tasting, stroking. "Come on, preacher's daughter, salvage me."

"My pleasure, Mitch," she sighed, her voice throaty and light as her own strokes grew hotter, bolder, more demanding. "My pleasure indeed."